# Enslaved by a Viking

D1255345

# Enslaved by a Viking

*Delilah Devlin*

HEAT | NEW YORK

**THE BERKLEY PUBLISHING GROUP**
**Published by the Penguin Group**
**Penguin Group (USA) Inc.**
**375 Hudson Street, New York, New York 10014, USA**
Penguin Group (Canada), 90 Eglinton Avenue East, Suite 700, Toronto, Ontario M4P 2Y3, Canada
(a division of Pearson Penguin Canada Inc.)
Penguin Books Ltd., 80 Strand, London WC2R 0RL, England
Penguin Group Ireland, 25 St. Stephen's Green, Dublin 2, Ireland (a division of Penguin Books Ltd.)
Penguin Group (Australia), 250 Camberwell Road, Camberwell, Victoria 3124, Australia
(a division of Pearson Australia Group Pty. Ltd.)
Penguin Books India Pvt. Ltd., 11 Community Centre, Panchsheel Park, New Delhi—110 017, India
Penguin Group (NZ), 67 Apollo Drive, Rosedale, Auckland 0632, New Zealand
(a division of Pearson New Zealand Ltd.)
Penguin Books (South Africa) (Pty.) Ltd., 24 Sturdee Avenue, Rosebank, Johannesburg 2196,
South Africa

Penguin Books Ltd., Registered Offices: 80 Strand, London WC2R 0RL, England

This book is an original publication of The Berkley Publishing Group.

This is a work of fiction. Names, characters, places, and incidents either are the product of the author's imagination or are used fictitiously, and any resemblance to actual persons, living or dead, business establishments, events, or locales is entirely coincidental. The publisher does not have any control over and does not assume any responsibility for author or third-party websites or their content.

PRINTING HISTORY
Heat trade paperback edition / October 2011

Library of Congress Cataloging-in-Publication Data

Devlin, Delilah.
Enslaved by a Viking / Delilah Devlin.—Heat trade pbk. ed.
   p. cm.
ISBN 978-0-425-24317-6
1. Vikings—Fiction.  I. Title.
PS3604.E88645E57 2011
813'.6—dc22
                                            2010054384

PRINTED IN THE UNITED STATES OF AMERICA

10  9  8  7  6  5  4  3  2  1

# Prologue

Eirik tried not to breathe too deeply. The rotten, sour smells of his dark, dank prison already made his skin stink. He didn't want the awful stench inside his lungs or belly.

He hadn't seen the other prisoners, not after they'd been herded like cattle through a chute once the hatch had been opened at the side of the ship and his keepers applied prods to their backsides to move them out in single file.

With only brief impressions of his new home, of searing heat and blinding, harsh sunlight, he'd shielded his arm over his eyes and stumbled down the gangway, through the iron-barred alley that disallowed any thoughts of escape.

He'd been led to this cell, deep inside an enormous stone building. A brief glimpse of an open arena, and then he'd been shoved down two flights of narrow stone steps.

Once they'd slammed the solid door and slid the eye-level window closed, he'd been left alone, no sounds penetrating his prison other than the hum of the light above him, and the sounds his own body made.

His thoughts drowned it all out, screaming inside him. He'd wanted to beat his fists against the door, rail at his captors, but he didn't know if anyone watched him, and wouldn't give them the satisfaction of knowing how close to abject despair he was coming.

Hel, he'd even suffer Fatin's derision, her cold, calculating touch, just to feel or hear another human being.

He didn't know how long he'd been here, there being no window and no way for him to know how the natural passage of time was counted on this planet, but he knew it was long enough that he'd stopped believing anyone would come to his rescue.

*They must think me dead,* he thought. *Like Father, lost on the ice.* One day waving as he skimmed away across the frozen blue water, never to return. Only Eirik wasn't lost. He wasn't dead.

A key grated in the lock at his door, pulling his glance. The heavy door swung open, and two sweet-smelling women strode inside, dressed in short white skirts. Their breasts were bare. Leather sandals with straps laced up to their ankles. Both were dark-haired and ombré-skinned. Like the witch Fatin. They carried linens and an urn of water.

He pressed a hand against the wall of his cell and pushed up from the floor.

"There's a guard outside the door," the one nearest him said. Her dark sloe eyes glittered as they raked his body. "We're here to bathe and dress you."

Pushing past them would earn him nothing. He clenched his fists at his sides and held himself still as they brought their clean, sweetly fragrant bodies close enough to strip away his clothing and bathe him like a mother might a child. Only their hands lingered over his sex, and although he might have wished otherwise, his cock unfurled, coaxed by their hands and then their lips to deliver his body's nectar. Or so they called it.

Dressed now, and more relaxed, he allowed another woman just outside his cell to lead him through a winding warren of corridors until they climbed a final set of steps and she pushed open the door, letting sunlight drench them.

Eirik closed his eyes, lifting his face to the light. But he wasn't allowed to savor the sensation. A prod behind him reminded him not to dally. He stepped out onto a platform in the center of the arena. A stage surrounded by thousands of men and women dressed in long robes and jewels.

A blended roar of voices greeted him. Women's excited chatter, men's laughter. He emptied his mind of the indignity, of standing in the center of the stage, hands rising, voices shouting. Then one voice separated from the throng, for it was nearer and familiar. His head swiveled toward the sound, caught the triumph glittering in Fatin's eyes as she met his gaze for a moment, then turned back to the crowd, accepting rapidly escalating bids.

A woman near the front of the stage shouted something that sent the crowd into gales of laughter.

Fatin turned toward him, warning him to behave with her cold, black gaze. When she was within arm's reach, she pulled at the tie on his hip and unlaced it, letting the short, skirtlike garment the women had dressed him in fall away.

He stood nude, his body exposed to the air and the rapacious gazes of the crowd. His head cleared of the numbing despair, all focus on Fatin's slender frame. No matter the outcome of today's shameful events, he vowed to have his revenge. One day, Fatin would be the slave; one day she would know the shame he felt.

Something of what he thought must have transmitted. Fatin's look of triumph faded, and her eyes became dark mirrors of doubt.

Slowly, his body warmed; his cock expanded. The things he would do to her, the many ways he would take her, filled his mind. No woman would ever know the depths of depravity he would visit on her body.

Frozen, her gaze locked with his. Eirik let the smile tugging at his mouth expand.

*Be frightened, sweet Fatin. Be waiting for me.*

# *One*

It was a long-standing joke among *Ulfhednar* warriors that when they perished on a battlefield, they would tell the Valkyries who came to deliver them to Odin's hall that they'd prefer the fiery underworld of Muspellheim. For Icelanders had lived so long on their frozen world that searing heat seemed a more fitting paradise.

However, Eirik *Ulfhednar* knew the truth. The realm of fire wasn't a mythical land. Due to one fateful error, he'd landed there, and the sultry heat of this godless place wasn't anything to be envied.

Despite the fans circling high above the garishly appointed salon, the temperature of the room where he stood was sweltering, the air stifling and thick in his lungs. Sweat gathered on his forehead and glazed his bare chest.

For the first time, he was thankful for the inadequate and embarrassing clothing he'd been given. The linen garment draping his hips allowed air to cool his nether regions.

However, the fabric was so thin he might as well have stood naked before those gathered to examine the new arrivals—or "offerings," as the whore-mistress called them. A term that somehow made him and the men standing in a straight rank behind him seem less human, more like a feast spread out on a banquet table to be devoured. A feast of twenty rugged Icelanders—all with their long hair slicked back in queues behind their heads, their muscular bodies oiled and perfumed like women, and wearing the same transparent swath of fabric about their hips and silver cuffs around their wrists that proclaimed them the lowest order of slaves—*sex-thralls*.

Every trace of their proud heritage had been erased except for their large, rugged builds—the very qualities that had precipitated their capture and enslavement.

"I count only two guards inside this room," Hakon murmured beside him, lifting his chin to point toward the tall wooden doors at the entrance to the salon.

Called Hakon the Bold on their former world, Eirik's new comrade was just another of the captives being paraded to satisfy the lusty appetites of the Heliopolite elite. All female, thank the stars.

Eirik gave an equally subtle nod toward the windows overlooking the landscaped grounds. Lush green grass, oases of tall flowers and leafy trees, couldn't hide the armed guards patrolling openly around the facility's perimeter. "I've counted six soldiers so far. Armed with stunners. We haven't shields to protect us should we try to make a break. They could take us all."

Hakon grunted. "But we have hostages. Or are you too squeamish to harm women?"

Eirik gave him a narrowed glare. "I wouldn't hesitate, not for a second, to do what I must to secure our freedom."

His companion's casual shrug belied his sharp scrutiny. "I thought I should ask, given how eagerly your body reacts to the vicious bitch that brought us here."

Not accustomed to having his motives questioned, Eirik bristled. "If I grow hard in Fatin's presence," he bit out, "it's because I envision all the ways I will make her suffer."

Hakon chuckled. Suspicion cleared from his face. "Good to know you will not shed a tear over her death."

However, as furious as Eirik was with the woman they discussed, the thought of standing over her lifeless body gave him a moment's pause. His chest tightened uncomfortably.

Perhaps he felt a connection to her because of the way they'd met. She'd been a gift from the men operating his family mine, a companion to warm his bed while he visited. Due to the hesitant way she'd mounted his body, he'd thought her young and untried. That first impression had been obliterated by what had happened next. He'd felt the prick of the needle she'd used to subdue him, experienced his body disintegrating into molecules as he'd been transported to a ship orbiting his planet. When he'd next awoken, he found himself caged inside the hold of a cargo ship bound for Helios, the Outlanders' home planet.

Even enduring the humiliating auction had done little to blunt his desire for the woman. He just wanted to punish her, he told himself. To visit untold demeaning acts upon her supple body. Only then would his thirst for revenge be quenched. His hesitation to end her life existed only because he didn't want her suffering to end too quickly.

"I think I could take the first thirty or so," Hakon murmured dryly beside him, eyeing the throng entering the room.

"But will you fuck them or beat them to death?" Eirik muttered, watching the scores of wide-eyed, feverishly animated women streaming inside like water breaking through a dam. The doors had just been opened, admitting the first customers.

Hakon snorted, his chin jutting upward. "I've never struck a female, but I am sorely tempted now," he said, his tone filled with disgust. "I'm a *Berserkir*, not a sex-thrall."

Not for the first time, Eirik reflected on the fact that he'd grown close in a very short time to the cousin of the enemy king. They'd raised swords against each other in "friendly" skirmishes back on their home world. Neighbors, *Berserkir* and *Ulfhednar* had warred for centuries, but now they were bound by their shared plight. And although Eirik was the only *Ulfhednar* in their midst, all the assembled Icelanders turned to him for leadership. He was, after all, a Wolfskin prince, the fiercest clan among the Icelanders and brother to the legendary Black Wolf.

Too restless to stand still, Hakon rubbed his chest and grimaced. "Do you think it is true?"

"What?" Eirik ground out, only part of his attention on the conversation as he studied the curvaceous crowd filling the large room, wondering how many he would be expected to pleasure.

"Do you think our hair will never grow back? I'm as smooth as a woman."

Eirik grunted. He'd been every bit as dismayed as Hakon to awaken and discover his current smooth-skinned state. "My friend, I think that's the least of the indignities we will suffer."

The Norsemen were lined up in the center of the salon. Because they were close in stature and musculature, Hakon and he had been placed just in front of the line of new offerings. The most valuable prizes among the men who'd been procured for this event.

"Hymir's bollocks!" Hakon whispered furiously.

Eirik glanced down to where Hakon stared and noted that his

companion's cock tented the linen, a fact that had the women strolling by to examine them tittering.

Hakon shrugged, a blush staining his cheeks. "I can't help it. I haven't enjoyed a release since that white-coated witch Miriam milked me like a dairy cow aboard the frigate before we arrived on this frigging planet. After she finished, I thought my manhood would remain shriveled forever."

The scientist hadn't come near Eirik, but only because another cold bitch had seen to stealing his semen to test its potency. Eirik searched the throng of robed women, wondering if the heartless bounty hunter would dare show herself today.

Still, as furious as he was with Fatin, Eirik's own man-staff thickened at the memory of her mouth tugging at his sex to coax him into spilling his precious seed.

The last time he'd seen her had been two days ago when she'd stood beside him on the stage erected in the arena and whipped away his clothing to display his attributes to the bidders gathered there.

Dark eyes flashing with triumph, she'd been beautiful.

He'd been furious, blood pounding at his temples and racing south to harden his cock. He'd glared daggers her way, promising her silently that one day she would know the same humiliation. That one day she would be at his mercy, and he'd show just as much of that tender emotion as she'd spared him.

"Do you think they did more than remove our hair?" Hakon whispered.

Rage made Eirik tremble anew at the thought of how he'd awoken that morning, feeling sluggish from the remnants of the drug that had been slipped into his food, his entire body denuded of its manly fur, his arse sore. He'd wondered if he'd been taken in his sleep, raped by some unknown person, and for those first waking moments, he'd felt a searing despair.

Everything else he possessed had been stolen—his clothing, his rank, his standing among his people. Had they also taken his pride?

But he'd been assured by the female technician who'd loosened the bindings around his wrists and feet securing him to a gurney that he'd only been examined to assure his health. Had the pink-cheeked woman read his dismay? He was accustomed to hiding his emotions. The shame of her recognizing his weakness had hardened his resolve.

He was Eirik, heir to the Wolfskin kingdom of Thorshavn, and he'd not remain a slave for long.

"We could take them," Hakon repeated in a whisper. "There are only the two guards, and we could use the women as a shield when we rush the gates. You only have to say the word and the men will follow your lead."

Eirik nodded, his gaze sweeping the room again, looking for clues as to how their Helio captors intended to keep the Vikings subdued. The room was large and airy with rich red and brown upholstered sofas and thick carpets strewn on top of smooth gold marble floors. The large windows were unbarred and opened to display the grassy lawn surrounding the facility. Cool air spilled from vents in the ceiling and was pushed downward by the whirring blades of the fans.

Cool enough to suit the Heliopolites who were accustomed to the heat of their planet. Not for the Vikings who were fresh from New Iceland, a cold, ice-bound world.

Hakon was right. There were only two armed guards. How did they intend to force the Norsemen to do their will? "We wait," he whispered. "Something isn't right."

Hakon growled beside him, but nodded. "Do we cooperate? Do we let them command us like thralls?"

"For now. Use them as they intend to use us. Find your pleasure, but keep your eyes and ears open. We must discover how they intend to keep us confined."

"Yes, milord," Hakon gritted out, clearly unhappy at having to wait.

Eirik gave him a sharp glare. "I've said it before. Don't call me that. And don't use my name. I do not want them discovering too soon who I am."

"Do you think they would kill you rather than letting anyone know they kidnapped a noble?"

"I don't know, but it's possible. The offense *is* punishable by death among the Consortium worlds. To be safe, for now, simply call me Wolf."

Hakon chuckled. "A slur the men will have no trouble remembering."

"Ugly Bearshirt," Eirik rumbled, suppressing a grin. He panned the room again, and then caught a fleeting glimpse of a familiar slender figure. His entire body tensed. His fists curled at his sides.

That his cock stirred right along with the rest of him reflected only his zeal to exact revenge.

The crowd of painted and perfumed women swelled, drawing closer, and then parted. Now he saw her clearly.

Fatin, the bounty hunter. Fatin, the procurer. An enigma he hoped was more than the sum of her beautiful parts. He wanted a worthy adversary upon which to concentrate his anger.

She stood out from the others, not by physical appearance, but by her dress. Her long black hair, worn in a braid down her back, and her dusky skin weren't all that different from the other Heliopolite women. But she wasn't dressed in silken robes that draped in soft folds from one shoulder, skimming a slender body.

She dressed as he'd last seen her, in figure-hugging olive-colored trousers tucked into shiny black boots. Gone was the brown, fur-collared jacket, and in its place was a sleeveless black shirt that melded to the contours of her small, uptilted, unbound breasts.

Unbidden, his cock filled.

Again, Hakon chuckled beside him. "At least I'm not the only one finding them hard to resist. The smell of them . . ." He breathed deeply and groaned. "'Tisn't fair."

Perfume, floral musk for the most part, filled Eirik's nostrils, but he knew Fatin's scent wasn't the same. Her skin smelled of spicy nutmeg. He'd been close enough the first time they'd met, with her woman's channel swallowing him whole, that he'd licked her, tasted her, smelled her—losing his mind and his defenses as she'd skillfully distracted him until that last moment when his body splintered away.

That had been two weeks ago, or so he'd been informed by the other Vikings who'd witnessed his arrival. The longest days of his life. His current circumstance was so foreign to anything he'd known, but so familiar now, that he sometimes wondered whether, if he stayed here long enough, New Iceland would seem like a dream.

His fists tightened as he glared, following her progress across the room. She had yet to meet his gaze. Did she think that if she never looked his way, she would be protected from his wrath?

"Be careful, Viking," came a soft voice at his side. The whore-mistress, Aliyah, touched his hand, a silent warning to smooth the anger from his face and stance. Her lips formed a pretty pout. "A grim scowl might arouse them from afar, but you wouldn't want our clients so afraid they won't venture closer."

Eirik suppressed the growl rising up his throat and schooled his face into an impassive mask. He didn't give a frig about their *clients*, but he also didn't want her knowing how eager he was to escape.

"Much better," she said, lifting her hand to trail her tapered nails along his jaw. "Harsh and proud. You shall earn me a fortune."

His head swiveled toward her, and he glared down his nose.

Her eyes widened for just a second, and then she chuckled and withdrew her hand. "Perhaps too proud. Heed my warning."

*Or what?* He ground his teeth in frustration at her vague threat. But something in her smug expression said she had a secret. Something she was eager to reveal. Although he wanted more than anything to simply explode into action, act like the proud Viking he was, that hint of excitement simmering in her brown-black eyes held him in check. For once, he'd proceed with caution, learn all he could about his new circumstance and his new prison before he acted rashly.

After all, following a wild impulse had landed him in this unbearable mess.

Slowing his breaths to calm his temper, he eyed the slender woman beside him who held his slave's papers. Did she have no fear at all? She stood next to a phalanx of battle-tested *Vikingar*. Eirik leveled a killing glance on her, but her expression never wavered. She had courage to accompany her careful beauty.

Although tall for a Helio, the top of Aliyah's head reached only the edge of his shoulder. Her crow black hair was swept into a knot high on her head. Her eyes were rimmed with kohl and her lips darkened with a berry gloss. A white, whisper-soft gown clung to slender curves. A large, diamond-encrusted amulet lay nestled in her cleavage. Diamond earrings in the shape of delicate chandeliers dripped from her ears. She was beautiful, and had she been any other woman, he might have been tempted to give her a toss.

However, now she was their captor. The highest bidder at the auction, where he and the rest of the Vikings had been sold like cattle, her deep pockets supplied by a government contract that funded her newest enterprise. And although the men had been offered at auction, the outcome of the sale had never been in question. The sale had been staged as a way to whet Helio appetites for the new manly fare the brothel would offer, to highlight the recently procured, exceptionally breed-worthy specimens.

Norsemen plucked from New Iceland would supply sperm to birth a new, physically stronger generation of Helios. While not being milked for their sperm in the adjoining research facility, the men would be available for pleasure.

Two days earlier, minutes after they'd arrived at their new prison, Aliyah had calmly explained why the Vikings had been taken.

Eirik had grown hot and cold, rage and a hideous horror rolling through him in waves. She'd been smart enough to deliver the news while the men were still caged in the docking area beneath the facility after they'd been transported by rail-tram from the arena where the auction had taken place.

Aliyah had given them a day to digest everything she'd said, and then appeared again yesterday in their common area, surrounded by a contingent of armed guards. The brothel had been inundated with requests, and she saw no reason to postpone their unveiling.

She'd then schooled them in how they must appear—their hygiene, their manners. She'd given graphic instructions about how they had to please and entice the women who would purchase their services.

Lessons that had left each and every Viking bristling with outrage, as though they were mannerless savages and didn't already know how to fully pleasure a woman.

Eirik had wanted to rail at her, to tell the whore-mistress that his favors were his to give, not for sale. But something Fatin had told him before he'd left her ship made him hesitate.

*As long as you live, Viking, you have a chance to earn your freedom.*

He had no intention of earning his freedom through giving these Helio whores sexual release, but he did have to bide his time. Acting now would only ensure that the guards they placed on their quarters and around this salon would remain alert and perhaps double in number.

Yes, he would wait and plan. And one day soon, he'd turn the table on his captors and force the coldhearted Fatin into the life she'd pressed on him. Silently, he added Aliyah to the growing list of those who would suffer his wrath.

Aliyah lifted a finger, and a servant appeared at her elbow with a tray of drinks. "Take one. Each of you should relax. If you must, *pretend* to enjoy the attention." She gave a wry smile. "Where is the harm in partaking of the pleasures that await you?"

Eirik firmed his lips to hold back his retort. The harm was to his pride. A man without choice was no man at all. He took a beaker of amber liquid, arched a brow, and drank. The alcohol, although not a sweet honey-mead, a Viking preference, was tasty if a little tart. He took another swallow and ignored her widening smile. Did she hope that a little intoxication would cool his anger and set fire to his loins?

Nodding to the other Vikings to do the same, he forced himself to relax and let his gaze sweep the room again.

The twenty *Vikingar* warriors held the rapt attention of more than a hundred eager women. He shook his head in disgust. This wouldn't end well, or at least not with his men's dignity spared.

Aliyah shot him a final warning glance and mingled again with the women moving ever closer, their curiosity overcoming any fear of the tall savage creatures who'd been captured and tamed for their pleasures.

Again, Eirik searched for Fatin, wanting to keep her whereabouts fixed in his mind before the debauchery began. If he was given even a sliver of a chance to sidle up beside her, he'd make her suffer.

"There, by the doorway," Hakon murmured, then made a face as he took another sip of his drink. "She looks ready to bolt."

Eirik didn't bother asking who "she" was. The focus of every man here was tuned to the one responsible for their current plight. "If she strays nearer . . ."

"One of us will delay her."

"Save her for me."

"Why should you have all the joy of killing her?" At Eirik's swift glare, Hakon grunted. "Have her first, then hand her to me if you haven't the stomach to snap her neck."

Eirik didn't answer. The image of her body wilting beneath Hakon's deadly grip stirred a toxic blend of emotion. He recalled something else she'd said to him aboard her ship. Something that had made him squirm inside.

*You never questioned how Fatin the sex-thrall came to be in the miners' camp. Did you care? Give it even a moment's thought?*

Thor help him, he hadn't cared. From the moment he first saw her kneeling naked beside the fire pit awaiting his pleasure, he hadn't thought at all—only reacted—with lust for her dark beauty and sweet, slender curves. With long silken legs, a narrow waist his fingers could enclose, small, apple-shaped breasts—she was perfectly formed, if a little too small for his taste. Her long black hair, bronze skin, and pretty features had been too enticing, too exotic, for him to proceed with any caution.

He'd sat on the edge of the mattress, dragged her over his lap, and impaled her. When he'd heard her gasp, he'd felt a momentary remorse and forced himself to gentle his assault, despite the knowledge she was a thrall and accustomed to giving herself to rough men.

Fatin had tossed back her hair, her eyelids lazily drifting

down—she'd enjoyed his actions. He knew it by the ripples that had caressed his shaft. He'd promised her reward, wondered briefly how he could keep her for a while, but then she'd betrayed him.

And he still wanted her. Not just for revenge, but to slake his appetite and rid himself of his unwise obsession for such a lowly creature. Eirik Wolfskin was destined to rule Thorshavn, the Wolf-skins' kingdom, and no lowborn procurer would ever find a place inside his keep.

And yet, he did wonder at the shadows he'd detected in that first moment of attraction that haunted her almond-shaped eyes and made her seem vulnerable even when her chin jutted in challenge.

There was more to Fatin than what she projected—something that had made her what she was. By the time he was through with her, he'd know her secrets; he'd own her heart.

And only then would he exact the cruelest revenge.

# Two

Fatin Sahin mingled among the crowd, wishing she'd dressed less conspicuously so that she would blend in with the beautiful, pampered women who filled Aliyah's salon. But she hadn't expected to be invited to stay for the unveiling. Such invitations were coveted, limited to only the wealthiest patrons. Fatin clearly didn't fit that description.

She'd hoped to gather her payment from the whore-mistress, inquire about her sister, perhaps even attain a private meeting with her sibling, and then slip away before the festivities began. However, this was an invitation she couldn't refuse.

Everything she'd done, every dirty trick she'd played, had been to get inside the most exclusive salon within the brothel. And she was close. Closer than she'd been in four years. The building that housed the captured Vikings sat next to the women's *saray*.

That her sister was sequestered there, offered to only the wealthiest patrons, sickened her. Most days, the thought of her sister, sweet Zarah with her delicate, ethereal beauty and tender soul, forced into prostitution, was more than she could bear.

Fatin was so close, and still she'd never catch even a glimpse to assure herself that Zarah was safe, not unless Aliyah granted her that audience. Which seemed unlikely. Tall walls enclosed the *saray*, hiding away the living treasures housed there—the most beautiful creatures, the "exotics" of Aliyah's collection.

The whore-mistress liked to play games. Liked to string her along with vague promises. To bring her here among the slaves she'd captured and to taunt her with proximity to her only living relative . . .

Fatin sighed. She should have expected Aliyah to twist the knife. The woman had never been a good loser. Surrendering Fatin's papers all those years ago still stuck in her craw, and having Fatin at her beck and call again had to be satisfying.

Without any other recourse, Fatin had entered into a devil's bargain to provide suitable breeding material and entertainment for those who could afford entrance into the private brothel compound within Pandora's Garden.

Most would kill for the privilege she'd been given. And yet, the last place she wanted to be was here. Too many painful, shame-filled memories clamored inside her. The smell of the room—cloying perfumes, garlands of fresh-cut flowers, and the potent scent of arousal—made her feel slightly nauseous.

But she couldn't really blame the smells for the sick feeling in the pit of her stomach. As much as she'd tried to steel herself against feeling anything at all about her part in this "triumph," guilt roiled inside her belly.

Firsthand, she'd experienced the humiliations that would be visited upon the captives. And yet, she'd eagerly entered into the venture with her former mistress. The gold had been tempting enough to make her consider, but sly Aliyah had sweetened the pot, offering her something she couldn't walk away from. Something she'd thought completely beyond her reach.

Laughter interrupted her thoughts. The women milling in the room pressed closer to the front, eager for a clearer view of the nearly naked captives.

"Have you ever seen men such as these?" came a tremulous voice behind her.

"Only in the lists," her companion whispered. "They each possess a gladiator's build."

Sighs sounded. "I wonder how deep I will have to dig into my husband's pockets for a first taste."

Fatin smirked. Faithless bitches all. Every bit as depraved as their husbands. But she could understand the allure of the temptations housed within the walls of the Garden. She too felt the sensual thrill that wafted like an airborne aphrodisiac.

Unbidden, she grew warm from simply a glimpse of the men all lined up in a row. A familiar tableau. Bodies washed. Oil rubbed into muscle to emphasize the bulges and hollows of their hard flesh. Every one of the offerings was handsome—she'd personally seen to that—and so virile the testosterone could be licked from the air.

From blond to red to black hair, lean to burly in build—something to please even the most discerning palate. She hesitated over that one dark head and sinfully brawny set of shoulders she saw above the crowd and moved on, her heart skipping a beat. She didn't think he'd seen her yet. She didn't intend to get close enough for him to know she'd come.

She wasn't here to gloat. Or to receive praise for her feat. One lone woman had conquered them all. Aliyah said she'd be a legend. But for what? Luring men into a life she herself had hated and escaped?

Most of the men had followed the crook of her finger into a dark corner, and before their hands could strip away her clothing, she'd hit the button on her communicator to let her crew know when she was ready to transport. As soon as she'd dropped them with a prick of the sleep-drug, they were stripped of their weapons and clothing, and then caged. Readied for the start of their journey.

Men never thought too hard about how a beautiful woman came into their midst. Not with their brains. They'd followed their baser instincts, ready to take her at her first flirtatious glance. Each time, she'd told herself they deserved their fate for the casual way they treated the women who served them.

But the acid boiling in her gut said she'd lied. She'd been where they stood now. Standing in a line, nearly nude, while strange men walked by and combed their fingers through her hair, cupped her breasts, her ass, and even fingered her pussy to test the fit. Every indignity imaginable—she'd suffered through it. But here she was delivering a fresh batch of unbroken slaves to the whore-mistress.

The Vikings' appearance, so tall and strong, caused an upswell of excitement in the crowd around her. No one pretended a jaded nonchalance. The fabric draping the warriors' loins did little to hide their attributes. Accustomed to men of their own race, the women couldn't deny the attraction. The Vikings' larger bodies and matching cocks were lethally seductive.

Not that Aliyah had left anything to chance. The drinks pouring from burbling fountains were spiked with sexual enhancers. Familiar with the effects, Fatin knew the women would grow warm, their pussies swollen. Damp heat would begin to slip down their thighs. Their bodies readied for sex, they'd be eager to part with their gold and credit for a chance to feel the thrust of a barbarian's thick cock.

Only their relief would be brief. The drug's powerful effects were slow to abate. The orgy would likely last throughout the night until all were exhausted and happily sated. They'd leave with a reluctance that would have them parting with more of their wealth for future appointments with their favorite stud.

But first, there would be a demonstration, proof of how well controlled the barbarians were. Of how they would perform on command for the women's pleasure. However, that would happen only after each woman had examined the men.

Once Aliyah gave the nod, women would pass along the line and bid for the privilege of the "first taste."

The crowd shifted, and she drew farther to the back to avoid detection, her nose twitching at the mix of perfumes surrounding her. She wore none. Only the scent of her soap. She hadn't bothered with cosmetics because she'd have felt foolish if one particular man noticed that she'd primped. She wasn't here to *taste* the offerings. Wasn't looking to excite them into sexual frenzy and feel the thrust of their exaggerated penises.

She'd already experienced that with one of them. Her body remembered his touch and the memory still haunted. Fatin fought the butterflies in her belly, the nervousness she felt every time she came within spitting distance of the Wolfskin prince. Aye, she knew who he was.

Aliyah had invited her to the unveiling because she was the one responsible for the capture of so many wondrous specimens. She'd pleaded and wheedled when Fatin balked, saying that Fatin would be feted, praised, her name remembered for her courage and cleverness.

Not that Fatin wanted the praise or the glory. She'd accepted the contract to procure Norsemen for the breeding facility for only one reason. If Aliyah believed her complicit, even eager to do her bidding, Fatin would stand a better chance of being invited here again and of having free rein to visit the other salons within the compound.

Somewhere, deep inside the most cloistered salon, was her sister. She didn't know for certain whether Zarah still lived except for the occasional rumor of an exotic, so treasured and pampered that only the wealthiest among the Helio elite could afford her company. Zarah had to be inside the women's *saray*.

Fatin slipped among the crowd, listening to the excited whispers of the women, and wondered what their husbands thought, and whether they knew at all where their wives spent their money. Or if this was one of those acceptable lies, so long as the wife was pleasured and bore fruit from her privileged womb.

Declining fertility, weakening genetic material among the men of this world, had seemed like reason enough to steal the Vikings from their home. She'd been a bounty hunter, retrieving criminals who'd jumped planet to stand trial. She had the experience and the beauty necessary for this dangerous mission.

Just weeks ago, she'd listened to Aliyah's pitch, nodded her agreement, and brushed aside any niggling doubts that what she did was right. The men would be milked of their seed, and that seed used to breed stronger Helios. The scientists assured them that superior Helio intellect would be bred into the next generation.

Why did no one remember the promises made the last time the experiments began or the awful results?

But that wasn't her problem, and she didn't have the luxury of worrying over the Vikings' fates or even the stain left on her own soul. These human men weren't doomed to a lifetime of servitude, not if they played the game. Each could be wealthy beyond their dreams. Each stood the chance to earn his freedom.

Just as she had.

She would stay focused on the deal she'd made with Aliyah. The blocks of ore and the fat sack of gold coins she'd earned for this first delivery were a nice down payment. She had enough worries on her plate after stealing the cargo from her partner in this venture. The pirate Roxana wouldn't rest until she had her head.

"Have you ever seen the like, Calliope?"

The awe-filled tone of the woman beside her made Fatin pause.

"I must have the dark one. Did you see him at the auction? His cock is twice the size of my husband's."

The women giggled and moved away, seeking a word with Aliyah while they pointed toward the dark one, Eirik.

Fatin didn't want to care that the man they bargained to have had been the one she'd been most reluctant to steal.

From the first moment she'd heard his name spoken by the mining camp supervisor on New Iceland, she'd fixed her sights on the *Ulfhednar* heir, even knowing that kidnapping one of the ruling class was a capital offense. The temptation had been too great. A chance to exploit his plight and the unsavory practice of sexual slavery was more than she'd hoped for.

Why had he kept his identity a secret for so long? Did he fear he'd be killed the moment he did expose the crime? The excuse was plausible. Still, she didn't think much frightened the man who'd surprised and enthralled her at every turn. Perhaps he hoped to escape and avoid the humiliation of having been bested by a woman, a situation made all the worse by his gentle treatment of her.

She'd posed as a contracted sex-thrall at the remote mining camp. As soon as he'd entered the small, curtained sleep chamber she'd been assigned to await his pleasure, he'd been eager to take her. Moments after yanking closed the curtain, he'd slid away the blanket she'd used to hide her naked form. As any man presented with a whore for his use, he'd begun without any thought except for his own pleasure.

However, once he'd plunged inside her, and she'd gasped, shocked by the fierceness of his invasion and the size of his sex, he'd gentled his assault, taking the time and care to pull her into an arousal so strong, she'd felt a moment's regret about causing him harm.

"What is your name?" he'd murmured against her lips as she'd straddled him while he sat at the edge of his sleeping bench.

"Fatin," she'd whispered, meeting his gaze, liking the heat banked in his blue eyes.

His chest had expanded, pressing against her swollen nipples. "You please me," he'd said, in his deep, rumbling baritone.

She'd felt a twinge of conscience, knowing what she would do.

Then he'd said, "I'll see you're well compensated."

She'd bitten her lower lip to still her disappointment. For just a moment, she'd thought he'd seen her as more than just a whore. Her glance fell away to hide the anger welling up inside her.

With a callused finger, he'd nudged up her face. She'd tilted it, meeting his kiss, her eyes never closing.

He'd gently suckled her lower lip, seducing rather than forcing her cooperation.

So many thoughts had swirled inside her head. Regrets that she hadn't met him under other circumstances because she would have liked to know whether he would have treated her any differently. Fear, because he was brawnier than any of the others she'd captured and could easily overcome her if she didn't catch him unawares. *And gods, how he filled her.*

With her channel stretching to accommodate his girth, her breath had seeped into his mouth. She'd loosed a sigh and then a delicate moan that seemed to increase the tension in his body.

He'd pushed back her hair, cupped her head in one large palm, and tipped her face higher still to deepen the kiss.

As she rose and sank on his cock, she'd panted and shivered.

Eirik had growled deep inside his chest, sounding every inch the barbarian he was. She'd given him a little half smile while her womb quickened, then shook back her hair.

He'd gripped her hips hard, urging her to rise and fall faster.

Her orgasm had caught her by surprise, flaring outward from her pussy, causing her belly to tremble, her hips to buck. Ripples had slid along her channel to caress his thick length.

"How you please me, darkling," he'd whispered.

She'd been impaled on his cock, a powerful orgasm unlike anything she'd ever experienced before rippling through her, when she'd plunged the needle into his neck and activated the locator for her men to find and transport her from the planet's surface to the ship's hold.

How embarrassing that had been—their molecules reassembling on the cargo floor, their groins still intimately connected. His cock had slid from inside her, and she'd had to force steel into a body gone liquid and pliant. In that moment, she'd hated him for making her doubt herself, for making her feel as though she'd committed a great sin.

He was just a man. Led by his bollocks. Like all the other captives she'd ensnared.

And yet, she'd visited his cage often to ensure he'd survived and to ogle and admire his large frame. His fury with her hadn't lessened her interest even a little bit.

Only to herself, and reluctantly, would she admit that she was obsessed with the fierce giant, although he was likely angry enough to kill her if she came within reach. Even now, she sought glimpses of him through the crowd, her gaze eating up every inch of his tall, muscled physique.

"There you are," came a soft, drawling voice.

Fatin jerked toward Aliyah, who watched her with her avid black gaze.

A dark brow rose. "The women already clamor for first rights. But I think you've earned your choice. Would you like to start the games?"

Heat filling her cheeks, Fatin shook her head. The last thing she wanted was to be the center of the spectacle soon to occur.

"Come," Aliyah said, her long-fingered hand wrapping around Fatin's wrist to pull her through the crowd. "You don't have to pay. Consider this a bonus for your hard work."

"You've already been very generous, mistress," Fatin gritted out between her teeth, dragging her feet.

"I saw the way you looked at that dark-haired barbarian. Your eyes ate him up. And the way he looked at you during the auction—" Aliyah broke off and laughed, fanning herself with her free hand. "His 'attention' was all for you, my dear."

The crowd parted, making a path that led straight to the Vikings lined up at the front of the room. Every hard, male gaze homed in on her approach.

Panic surging through her body, Fatin dug in her heels and tried to break free of Aliyah's grip, but the whore-mistress was surprisingly strong. Fatin was unwilling to use any fighting moves she'd learned to harm the woman. Too much rode on Aliyah's continued goodwill.

"Really, mistress," Fatin said breathlessly as they neared the edge of the crowd, "I'm very happy to stand back and let another have the first taste."

"I wouldn't hear of it." Aliyah drew back her arm and flung Fatin forward.

Fatin spun toward the Vikings. The one standing next to Eirik opened his arms, and she landed against his naked chest.

Laughter surrounded them—high-pitched gales from the women, low, edgy chuckles from the men—but not a hint of humor softened the tall blond Viking's taut features. His hazel eyes narrowed, and those tree-trunk arms of his banded around her ribs to give her a crushing embrace.

She remembered how Hakon had insisted that she strip in a cold, narrow passage inside the *Berserkirs'* keep, shortly after she'd "accidently" bumped into him. His gaze had hungrily raked her frame, his features growing frighteningly intense as she'd peeled away the layers of her clothing.

Again, as before, she shivered at the way his features sharpened with deadly intent.

Unable to catch her breath, she felt her face heat, her lungs burn. Pressed so close, his hardening ridge digging into her belly, she wondered if he'd simply keep squeezing until he snapped her back or smothered her. Was the thought of killing her really so arousing? "Bastard!"

"Hakon . . ." Eirik's voice cut through the tension with a note of warning.

The tall barbarian grunted, and then abruptly opened his arms.

She stumbled backward, catching herself before she fell in a heap at his feet.

Eirik's hand snaked out and grabbed her wrist, tightening like a manacle. The crowd around them grew silent. Perhaps they'd already heard the tale of the men's capture and knew she was the one responsible. Like the ruthless, bloody games they enjoyed watching in the arena, did they hope to see her pulled apart?

The moment stretched. Fatin swallowed hard; her gaze locked with Eirik's icy stare.

His grip didn't tighten, but it didn't ease either. With his fierce, glittering stare drilling into hers, he dragged down his arm, forcing her closer.

And even though she resisted, stiffening her body in rejection and scuffing her boots on the marble, he pulled her inexorably closer.

When her breasts touched his chest, his strong arms clamped

around her. Again, she fought for breath, but this time her inability
to draw air into her lungs wasn't entirely due to how hard his arms
constricted.

Eirik's cold blue gaze swept her face. A tight, cruel smile curved
his lips. "Fatin," he growled, "at last . . ."

She tossed back her hair. "At last? You sound so satisfied," she
whispered harshly, pretending she wasn't nearly fainting from lack
of oxygen and because he was the one holding her so tightly. "You
seem so eager to hold me close. I thought you would have felt well
rid of me. Yet here we are."

"You underestimate my desire," he said, his voice grinding as
deliciously as his cock did against her belly.

His head bent over hers, forcing hers back. To anyone watching,
theirs would appear to be a lover's eager embrace.

"You may have him, Fatin," Aliyah said, her lilting voice sounding distant. "A demonstration of your acquisition's prowess is in
order."

*A demonstration.* Her throat closed as burning panic burbled up.
Something of her fear must have entered her expression.

The corners of his lips curled higher. "You may have me," he
whispered. "Here? Now? Do you tremble because they will see or
because I am the one who will thunder inside you?"

He couldn't have used coarser words and made her feel any more
uneasy. The picture he painted in her mind, of a storm unleashed,
made her knees weaken.

The arm banding her back caught her before she slid downward.
His eyelids drifted down to narrowed slits while his gaze remained
locked with hers. "We have unfinished business, sweet Fatin."

# *Three*

Fatin's dusky cheeks filled with furious color, and Eirik adjusted his arms to pull her flush with his body. Which only heightened the tension in his own. Every muscle, even his wayward cock, flexed and expanded with his excitement.

His hands adjusted, fingers digging into the long indent at the center of her back. It would be so easy . . .

She was slender—fragile in comparison to the women of his own race. And yet he hesitated. He told himself the timing wasn't right. That he shouldn't sacrifice his own life for a momentary satisfaction. His hesitation could have nothing to do with how her body felt cradled against his.

Aliyah drifted around them, her cloying perfume and low chuckles reminding him there was more afoot here—that she pulled his strings for her own benefit. *Think!* Why had she placed Fatin's fate in his hands?

"Let me go," Fatin said, her voice pitched low but harsh. She wriggled in his arms like an eel.

He tightened his grip, knowing he would leave bruises on her tender skin. "I've been given a rare gift," he drawled. "Do you think I would be so ungracious as to throw it back?"

She struggled inside his embrace, her head ducked, but he wanted to see her expression, see fear fill her dark, lying eyes. Just before he snapped her spine.

*Gods*, he had trouble even telling himself that he could do that.

Disturbed and angry, he bent his neck and licked the side of her cheek.

Laughter sputtered from the women crowding closer.

"Do you think he will eat her?"

"A lick followed by a bite? I should die so happy."

Eirik growled like the beast they considered him and slid his hands down her back to cup Fatin's nicely rounded ass. Her firm flesh filled his palms. His caress sent a shiver through her frame. *Interesting...*

"If you harm me," Fatin hissed, "they will put you down like a rabid dog."

Eirik teethed the edge of her jaw, nipping none too gently, and then he nuzzled her throat, drawing in her spicy scent. Unprepared for the potency of her allure, his arms grew rigid. His body tightened in rejection. He wouldn't be aroused by her. Never her.

He felt the frantic flutter of her pulse, noted the sharp intake of her breath. "Are you afraid of me, *elskling*?"

Small hands braced against his chest. Her dark eyes sparked with anger. "No! But are you willing to shed your regal blood over one such as me?"

His gaze studied her face, and he wondered if she knew that panic lingered in her widening eyes. The last time they'd been this close, after she'd stolen his semen as he stood with his hands locked in stocks, he'd leaned down and kissed her. Fury had heated his body—and yet his kiss hadn't been cruel. Confusion, mixed with desire, had swirled inside him, gentling his anger.

However, after the indignities he'd suffered over the past couple of days, he was ready to give her only a calculated coldness. Despite her small frame and widening doe eyes, he knew better. She was a hard, avaricious bitch. He'd not waste another moment of compassion on her.

"You have a point," he said, his voice even. "You aren't worth dying for." With a jerk, he released her and stepped back.

The men behind him grumbled. He knew any one of them would be willing to shed his blood for the chance to kill the woman responsible for their enslavement. But he didn't owe them any explanation for why he passed up the chance to exact revenge. *Let them think what they like; I'll not kill a woman.*

Fatin eyed him warily, then shook back her hair, straightened her shoulders, and glared.

Again, he caught a hint of vulnerability in her glance, something that gave him pause. He'd been fooled by that look once before. Still, he took another step back and hardened his expression, rejecting her.

"No, no, no . . ." The whore-mistress stepped forward, tsking. "Do you think you have the choice of partners, Viking?" Her eyes glittered with satisfaction—as though she'd waited for his reaction and was pleased. Her hand closed around her amulet as her gaze sliced through him.

For a moment, nothing happened, but then a sensation, unlike anything he'd ever felt—a sharp, clenching cramp just beneath his balls—made him double over. He bent low, gasping for breath as pain seared through his body.

The edge of Aliyah's white gown entered his view. "Did you

think we wouldn't take precautions?" she asked, a nasty edge to her voice. "While you slept, we implanted a device, nestled against your prostate. We can send you into instant agony or paroxysms of lust." Her hand petted his head as though he were a dog. "I think you must serve as the example, my dark Viking."

The cramping abruptly disappeared, but in its stead, another sensation caught him off guard. Although still aching, he straightened and aimed a deadly glare at the whore-mistress.

However, he couldn't hold her glance for long. The heat of embarrassment filled his cheeks. His cock filled steadily, rising against his belly, thickening even though he fought an internal battle to quell the urge. His linen garment tented obscenely.

Comprehending at last the vile and devious weapon she meant to use against them, he gave a deep-throated groan. "Bitch! What have you done?"

Aliyah moved closer, two bright spots of color on her cheeks, eyes flashing angrily. "Do not fight my will. You will fuck when I tell you to fuck, *whom* I tell you to fuck. And right now, I say that you will take Fatin. Only then will you know relief."

Tempted to grip her shoulders and give her a hard shake, instead, he cupped his erection, determined to steal his orgasm for himself. Dignity already in shreds, he pumped his fist twice down his length through the thin linen, but the cramping agony started again. His cock wilted.

Glaring daggers, he bent and braced his hands on his knees while he ground his teeth against the sudden flaring pain. "Enough!" he roared.

"Truly? Will you surrender so easily? I'm disappointed."

He glanced up. Fatin was backing away, a hint of wild fear in her eyes now, but the whore-mistress caught her, digging her claws into her arm.

Fatin shook her head, pleading silently with the other woman.

"Do you refuse my gift?" Aliyah asked, sly humor in her tone.

Fatin's mouth opened, but she clamped it shut again and shook her head. "No, Aliyah. I'm not ungrateful for everything you've done for me."

"That's better, dear. He's yours." She released Fatin and clapped her hands. Two burly men strode forward, carrying a long chaise, which they placed between Fatin and him.

The cruel pinch of the device inside him relented, and he breathed in deep, ragged breaths to still the trembling in his body.

Behind him, he heard the rumbling murmurs of the other men, the nervous slide of their bare feet as they restlessly stirred. Because he was their leader, he steeled himself against the dull ache still throbbing inside his body and straightened again, forcing his face into a neutral mask.

"I will let your natural paths follow now," Aliyah said, her tone gentler, even slightly regretful.

It was an act. He could read the satisfaction in her tight smile.

"Now that you understand the consequence of defiance. Do not deny us the enjoyment of watching a Viking make love."

"Make love?" Eirik muttered. He spared a glance behind him at the rest of the men. Their expressions were set—jaws straining, gazes furious and hot.

Hakon, his jaw squared and tense, nodded at Eirik to let him know he understood he would do what he must to survive to fight another day.

Another snippet of Fatin's advice, given to him days ago aboard her ship, lingered in his mind. *If not love, show them the savage . . .*

Drawing in more deep breaths to slow his heartbeats, Eirik fisted his hands on his hips. "One of us wears too many clothes," he said loudly.

Fatin's eyes narrowed, and she turned sideways as though readying to flee.

Fury at the woman who had forced this moment, at his helplessness to halt what was inevitable, had his heart pounding. His fists tightened and he widened his stance.

"Don't be shy," Aliyah said, issuing a challenge with her hard black gaze. "Show us how you would take a captive, Viking—if the situation was reversed."

In an instant, he lunged for Fatin, ignoring her shocked gasp. He grabbed her arms and pulled them behind her, then lifted a foot to press against the back of a knee and force her to the floor.

She landed hard on the marble, crying out in her distress, but he couldn't let himself feel remorse. She'd stolen so much. He'd take his ease of her whether she wanted him or not.

Then he was on her, straddling her thighs and rucking up her shirt. He raised the hem, bit into it to cause a tear, then grasped it between his hands and ripped it open, baring her chest.

Fatin wriggled beneath him, freeing her arms and reaching to claw at his face, but he was faster, flipping her to her belly, then slipping his hands under her to work at her belt and the slide at her waist, which he scraped open. Then he came to his knees again and dragged down her trousers, exposing her round, firm ass.

She braced herself on her hands and bucked beneath him, trying to lift him from where he sat on the backs of her thighs, but he was too heavy. She gave an angry, growling groan and collapsed, her back jerking with her harsh gasps.

Eirik stilled, sucking in his own jagged breaths. His cock was thick, charged with furious heat. But he'd never taken a woman against her will. And even though she deserved every bit of his enmity, he couldn't allow himself to complete the act. He levered himself off her knees.

She scrambled to her own, pulling up her pants to cover herself, and then rolled to face him, drawing up her knees and covering her breasts with an arm.

The whore-mistress stepped between them, her face red and her eyes glittering. "Finish it." She dug a finger under his chin to lift his glance. "You really don't have a choice."

Shaking now with fury, he ground out, "I am not an animal."

"Don't pretend you're anything but what you are. A barbarian. The women you will serve want nothing less than every bit of your strength."

"Do they wish to be raped?"

She gave a feminine snort. "It's not rape. They want to be over-come. To be forced, yes. But they surrender to your mastery of their own free will. Do not disappoint us. There are far worse things that can befall you if you're stubborn."

Her gaze whipped to Fatin. "You wish an agreement. I won't even consider it unless you prove the men you brought me are every bit as feral and savage as you promised."

Fatin's gaze held his for a long, tense moment before falling away. With slow moves, she opened the buckle of the belt at her waist, then peeled down the slide to loosen her trousers again.

Standing, she toed off her boots, pushed down her trousers, and slid her socks off until her lower half was nude. Then she slowly eased down the torn shirt still hanging from her shoulders, baring the rest of her body.

Arousal crept across his skin. She was every bit as lovely as the day she'd knelt beside the fire pit in the mining camp. Bronze skin. Large brown nipples on her small, rounded breasts. Her nude pussy shone with dampness.

And this time, Eirik didn't need a burst of electrical current to cause his cock to swell.

Fatin took a seat on the chaise and turned, lying lengthwise on the wide, benchlike bed.

The loin skirt loosened at his side, and he glanced down at a plump Helio woman who gave him a shy grin and swept away the linen garment.

"Let me serve you, Viking."

He grunted, bemused at the woman's eagerness to assist a slave, but he shook himself and dropped a knee onto the bench, flattened his hands on the mattress on either side of Fatin's shoulders, and climbed over her.

The crowd shuffled, whispers sliding around them, but all his attention remained on the woman trapped beneath him.

He thrust a knee between her legs, and she resisted for a moment, clamping them together tightly, her chin beginning to wobble.

When her eyes filled, he wondered if she cried from embarrassment or regret. He hoped she regretted every moment and every action that had brought her to this. She deserved to never feel a moment's peace for her crimes.

And yet, when he lowered his body over hers, the softness of her skin and her feminine frame eased some of the anger flowing through him. Again, he found himself wanting to go gently. He lowered his face toward hers, focusing on her mouth.

Fatin's dark eyes held his gaze. "You can pretend," she whispered. "Let them think you will woo them. You will earn their adoration."

"I don't want your adoration. I don't want theirs."

"Think, Viking." With shaking fingers, she loosened the band that held his hair and spread it over his shoulders. Low murmurs of appreciation echoed in the chamber. "I know you want your freedom. Do whatever you must to earn it."

He didn't want to hear her advice, didn't want to think about the way her voice thickened as he gave her more of his weight, the way her soft body yielded. "What acts would interest them?" he asked, pretending to play along while he tried to master the desire raging through him.

"A man who finds pleasure in tasting every corner of a woman's body will be coveted above all."

Eirik slid his lips over her cheek, inhaling her spicy scent, and then roamed lower, gliding over the delicate collarbone to the tops of her small breasts. "Like this?" he asked, pretense quickly becoming true desire as his tongue stroked her warm skin.

Her fingers dug into his scalp, and she tried to center his mouth over one straining breast.

But he nipped the tender underside and nuzzled into the fragrant crease.

Her nipples were erect, the tips quivering with her ragged breaths. "Don't be too gentle or tease too long."

"Do you want the savage again? Is that what will fire your blood?"

She yanked his hair and pulled his head closer. As she locked her gaze with his, her eyes narrowed to furious slits. "I did what I had to do," she whispered harshly. "You don't understand."

He felt her hands soften in his hair, her fingers tunnel through the strands. "Soon you will tell me what drove you to this. But, sweet Fatin, for now, you will serve my pleasure." He grabbed her hand and forced it between their bodies, pushing it down toward his cock. "I want your mouth on me, working me like a whore."

He jerked back and knelt in the center of the chaise, then grabbed her braid and wound it around his fist.

Her face tightened, her lips lifting in a snarl, but there was no one willing to rush to her aid as he forced her down. "Use your teeth on me, and I will beat you."

Knowing the scene he must create, he pushed her face against his cock, pinched her chin to open her mouth, then shoved the tip between her lips.

Her body quivered; her teeth clamped around him.

At the sensation, he held his breath, cupped her jaw, and feathered a thumb along her lower lip.

She was tempted to deliver a bite—he could read her intent in the flare of anger in her dark eyes. Instead, her tongue touched him, then swept over the plush cap. A thin moan vibrated around him.

He slowly stroked forward, testing her, ready to pull free if she tried to harm him, but her lips wrapped around the sharp edges of her teeth and began to suction, her eyes closing as she pulled and sucked.

Eirik's head fell back, his eyes wide open and trained on the ceiling above them. On the gilt-covered plaster, on the whirling wooden blades of the fan.

She was skilled, the suctioning strong and rhythmic, tugging his arousal into a blazing heat that had him thrusting into her mouth, past her wicked tongue, to butt against the back of her throat.

Again, he looked down to watch her mouth consume him.

Her eyes opened, glancing up. Something sparkled, a hint of challenge, and she swallowed around him, the deep, intimate kiss massaging the crown; then her throat eased open for him to slide even deeper.

*A whore's trick.* He'd do well to remember Fatin had secrets. If she pleasured him, the act was to fulfill her own agenda. Nothing more, he reminded himself.

Watching the billow and hollow of her cheeks as she worked him, his focus narrowed on the sensations, on the tension building in his balls.

Her teeth strafed him, and he pulled her hair, pushing her off his cock.

Eyes flashing, she straightened, wiping the back of her hand across her swollen mouth.

Eirik breathed slowly, taking in the restlessness of the crowd around them, the breathless silence of the women. From the corner of his eye, he saw the faces of the men—hard, savagely tense. They wanted him to punish her.

And punish her he would, but not in any way that would leave him feeling empty at the end. He grabbed her forearm and pulled her toward him, over his lap.

"Viking!"

With one arm anchoring her over his knees, he raised his hand and slapped her bare bottom, the sound loud and shocking in the quiet.

A giggle erupted, followed by murmurs rising, blending. The sounds of deeper rumbles from the men, hard chuckles at his manner of domination, fueled his anger. He spanked her soft, rounded bottom until his palm burned and her bronze skin grew pink. Realizing how aroused he was becoming as he spanked her, disgust twisted inside and he shoved her off his lap.

Tumbling onto her knees, she looked upward, glaring, her chest quivering on choked gasps.

Yet when he reached for her again, she melted against him. He took her down to the chaise, climbing over her, and slid his legs between hers, angling his cock to thrust against her wet folds.

He slid as smooth as a knife through butter into her body, lost in the wet heat, in the womanly warmth that surrounded him. Wet lips trailed along his cheek, and he turned to rub his mouth against hers, forcing his tongue inside for a deeper taste.

But she welcomed him there, stroking her tongue over his, then sucking it as she began to undulate beneath him, encouraging him to drive deeper into her body.

Pushing off the sofa, he braced his weight on his arms and gave her long strokes that exposed the length of his cock to the watchers. Again and again he drove deep, his movements languid but strong. Her channel warmed around him, melting, moisture easing his way through the tight confines.

Her vagina was a perfect glove. Hot, moist, rippling along his shaft.

He shifted, bringing in his knees. He thrust a hand beneath her and lifted her as he sat back on his haunches and kept her impaled there, their bodies facing each other.

Her expression was questioning, her eyes wide and searching. Eirik didn't know what she saw, but her chin firmed; her fingers dug into his shoulders. She lifted herself, then slammed down his cock, the shock of her violence spurring his own as he pounded upward to meet her rough strokes.

The crowd around them grew silent, seemed to breathe as one, but Eirik pushed aside the thought of them watching, judging. He didn't care anymore, couldn't think beyond the moment of enjoying her sweet body.

Fucking Fatin with an audience wasn't any different from the hundreds of other public sessions he'd reveled in at home. All that was missing was the sound of familiar voices calling out lewd suggestions, spurring him on by inciting his competitive nature to be the best, the strongest, last the longest, drive the hardest. Sex was often just another sport, another way for men to prove their prowess.

He thrust and burrowed, screwed in circles, then thrust hard toward her core again, gauging by her breaths and the convulsions rippling up and down her channel just how far along she was.

In this circumstance, he shouldn't care whether she came, but he was hardwired to succeed. Always standing in the shadow of his brother, he'd had a tough standard to meet—in warfare, in governance, and in lovemaking.

He slammed upward, forcing a hiss from Fatin, which pulled him back to the present.

Angry color flooded her cheeks. "Just finish it," she whispered.

At her words, he remembered how she'd finished him, taking his sperm into her mouth, then spitting it into a vial. Stealing his semen to prove his worth to his captors.

His and the other captives' sperm could breed a legion of warriors to storm his world. One day, his brother, Dagr, might raise a sword against his own nephew. The thought pierced Eirik with a blinding pain, and he shoved her off his cock, flipped her, and forced her to bend low. He pushed his tip against her small, furled hole, and without benefit of lubrication or care for the pain he might cause, he drove deep into her arse.

Her strangled cry drew a roar of approval from the Vikings, who then fell silent again. The crowd around them murmured, stirring as they shifted on their feet, trading whispers.

Let them whisper about his savagery. Let them tremble at the thought of him turning his unleashed wrath loose upon their bodies. They should be warned that crossing a Northman didn't come without consequences.

Fatin mewled, her fingers gripping the upholstery so hard, her knuckles whitened.

Something inside him cringed at his violence. No matter how deserved, he'd never been so careless with a woman. He thrust back his head and closed his eyes to shut out the sight of her trembling body, and thought only of losing himself again, forgetting where he was. The tightness of the ring clamped around his cock built a burning friction. His fingers dug into her buttocks, forcing her forward and back. His groin slapped her ass with each deep, hard thrust, the sounds accompanied by her helpless gasps and his own breathless grunts.

Orgasm slammed through him, sucking away his breath. His whole body tightened, his balls near to bursting as cum jetted through his cock in rapid spurts, emptying his balls, emptying his anger . . .

When at last he stopped, he glanced down. Sweat dripped from his chin, landing on her dusky skin to slide away like a tear.

Fatin's bottom quivered against his groin; her back shook with the force of her rasping breaths.

Sickened again, and angry with himself, with her, with the Helborn whore-mistress who'd orchestrated this "demonstration," he pulled slowly from Fatin's body.

Attendants rushed forward to bathe Fatin with cloths and ointment.

Another group approached him, but hung back, wide-eyed when he speared them with a warning glare.

He steeled his expression and stood beside the chaise, glancing over the heads of those who'd come to be entertained to meet the gazes of the warriors who were his brothers in this test.

Each of their expressions seemed carved in granite; their eyes glittered with triumph.

He strode toward them, not glancing back at Fatin or Aliyah, but focused on his men, his contingent when the time came to battle for their freedom.

When he was near enough, the crowd fell away between them. He dropped his glance to the linen shrouding Hakon's loins.

When he raised his head, Hakon's lips curved in a wicked smile. Sparing only a short look over his shoulder, his second-in-command gripped the fabric. Every other man did the same.

At the downward tilt of Hakon's chin, they ripped away their short slaves' skirts.

*Let the games begin.*

# *Four*

Birget, daughter of King Sigmund of the *Berserkir* clan, rubbed the black amulet hanging on a cord around her neck. Her thumb smoothed over the runes carved into the cold stone. A gift from the *Ulfhednar* king, Dagr, when he'd given her command of the mission to free his brother—her betrothed, a man she'd never met.

She stood behind Cyrus Tahir, the Outlander who'd piloted the first ship they'd taken when Dagr and his wolves had left New Iceland to begin their quest. Cyrus had transferred, along with her and the contingent of Wolfskins she now led, to the *Daedalus*, the pirate ship they'd commandeered when Dagr came up with his bold plan to let the Consortium retake their original ship to give the Vikings fulfilling the mission a chance to escape.

Thus far, their mission had gone off without a hitch. No Consortium warships followed in their wake as they made their way to the Helios's world.

"Have you heard anything on the comm channels?" she asked, hating to repeat her question a second time in the span of an hour. *Does the man enjoy forcing me to betray my bout of nerves?*

Cyrus glanced over his shoulder. "Only that the *Proteus* has been captured."

His address was so casual that she ground her teeth in irritation. Did he have no respect for her rank?

"The official channel's been silent ever since," Cyrus continued. "Strange, really, how quiet it's been."

His expression remained neutral, unnatural behavior for the Consortium traitor. He'd been close to the Wolfskin king and hadn't been happy to leave him and the other volunteers to their fate. That Cyrus resented her role in this mission was impossible to mistake.

"Dagr's a strong man," she said, meeting his gaze with the same stoic resolve. "And a resolute warrior. I can't imagine them holding him for long. If not for the fact he's a Wolf, I'd admire him."

Cyrus gave her a stiff smile. "You'll be a Wolf soon yourself, Princess."

Birget grunted. Dagr had already accepted her as a sister, but the thought of taking her place among the Wolfskins still felt foreign. She was proud of her own *Berserkir* heritage.

She glanced up to lock gazes with her Outlander lover. Other than a fleeting glint of humor in his black eyes, Baraq Ata's expression was every bit as remote as Cyrus's, but for very different reasons.

Did he regret taking her virginity? Yes, she'd goaded him into it, but he hadn't seemed to mind so much after the initial shock. When it became apparent Dagr wasn't going to seek retribution, they'd entered into a discreet arrangement that continued even after they'd left the *Proteus*.

Outside of the berth they'd claimed aboard this ship, they treated each other as though they'd never lain with their limbs tangled, with their bodies locked in passionate embrace. The memory of all the wicked things they'd done caused a flare of heat to curl deep in her woman's core.

She wondered how quickly she could convince Baraq to make another round of systems checks.

"We'll make port in a few hours, Princess," Cyrus said. "Do you have a plan yet for how you'll find your betrothed?"

Her lusty thoughts interrupted, Birget studied Cyrus, wondering not for the first time where the Helio traitor's true allegiance lay. Lord Dagr might have full confidence in the man, but she didn't like his arrogance. Didn't like how he eyed her as though she was a very poor substitute for his beloved Viking king.

So maybe she had acted the brat, sneaking aboard the Consortium transport ship *Proteus*, defying Dagr to the point he'd threatened her with a woman's punishment. However, in the end, Dagr seemed to see her inner strength and resolve. He'd finally realized she was stubborn and willful enough to follow through on her mission to free Eirik and exact appropriate revenge against his abductors.

The golden breastplate she wore embossed with the figure of Freya standing in her feline-drawn chariot was more than just a symbol. Like the warrior-goddess she emulated, Birget would allow no man other than Odin himself to stand in the way of victory.

Firming her jaw, she gave Cyrus a glare. "Since there are so many contingencies to consider, I will wait until we can reconnoiter on the ground. Just get us there."

Cyrus lifted his chin, pointing toward the viewing screen at the front of their borrowed pirate ship's bridge. "We've passed the outer planets. Helios is straight ahead."

"Thanks for the warning," she said, her tone dry.

Behind her a throat cleared. She glanced over her shoulder to find that Baraq had moved and was standing at a respectful distance, his black gaze shuttered.

"Cyrus, get us into the port. You will not be a part of the raiding party, seeing as how you are a convicted criminal and might be recognized." She leaned closer to issue a warning for his ears only. "Don't underestimate me or question my authority in front of others. Dagr may have given you free rein to speak your mind, but I am much less impressed with you."

Cyrus's face flushed an angry red, but he gave her a curt nod. "My apologies, milady."

Birget left the bridge with Baraq on her heels as she climbed the stairs to the gangway that traversed the length of the *Daedalus*. With tighter quarters than even the *Proteus*, the ship they'd bartered for with a fortune in Viking "pure light" ore made her claustrophobic. She couldn't wait to debark, even if onto a Hel-lish planet.

"Hold up, Princess," Baraq said, laying a hand on her shoulder.

They were alone, and thus she didn't mind the intimacy of his gesture. She turned, let him slide his arm around her back and pull her against his torso.

Birget sighed and returned the embrace. "I wish there were more time . . ."

His smooth cheek rubbed against hers. "This might be our last opportunity to be together."

She loved the way he talked. His deep voice with its lilting Helio accent soothed her rough edges. And Odin knew she had many of those. "I'm glad you were my first," she whispered.

His arms tightened around her back.

Tall and ruggedly built for an *Utlending*, her people's term for

Otherworlders, she enjoyed the comfort he offered. He was her first lover, chosen precisely because he was such an inappropriate partner. A childish revenge goaded by her unhappiness at being pushed into a political marriage she didn't want and her anger with Dagr, who'd done his best to exclude her from this adventure. But she'd grown fond of the dark-skinned former Consortium officer despite his unfortunate birth.

Only with Baraq was she free to voice her doubts. "Baraq, do you think we can do this? Is it possible we will prevail?"

"The plan's so outlandish, infiltrating the Helio capital, that it just might work. Who would imagine that a band of barbarians would have the intellect to accomplish such a feat?"

She pinched his sides. "Do you think me lacking in intelligence?"

"Taste, perhaps," he said, his voice laced with humor. "You did choose me, milady, a lowly soldier, to breach your maidenhead. Arrogant, yes. Courageous, of a certainty. Who else could have stood toe-to-toe with the leader of the Wolfskins and shouted him down?"

She pulled back to stare into his face. A wide grin curved her lips. He'd known exactly what to say to bolster her confidence. "Yes, who else would have dared? But I would dare so much more." Almost his height, she liked that she didn't have to tilt her head much to meet his lips. "You say such pretty things to me."

Baraq's laughter rumbled through his chest. "What woman would want those qualities extolled above her beauty?"

She cocked her head to give him one of those flirting gazes she'd been practicing. "Do you think I'm pretty?"

His grunt was fully masculine and reflected the amusement gleaming in his eyes. "I think that's a pale, tepid word for what you are, Princess."

She smoothed her hand down the front of his deep-space suit and cupped his sex, which was stirring, filling with heat—for her. "We have a little time before we dock . . ."

He gave her a wicked grin. "Shall I add 'insatiable' to this list of your many admirable qualities?"

She kissed him, full on the lips—an openmouthed caress given to a man who was every bit her match in strength and fighting capability. A worthy partner for any *Valkyrja*—but only if she wasn't of royal lineage.

Baraq's hand closed around her long braid and pulled. She arched her back, pressing her chest against his and growling because she wore too many layers of cloth, fur, and breastplate to feel his hard muscles press her nipples. "Find a cabin," she whispered against his mouth. "Quickly."

A wicked, devilish brow arched. "We won't have time to do more than open our clothing."

"It will be enough. I burn, *Utlending*."

"The pretty names you call me."

"Should I call you *elskling*? Would you move faster if I did?"

"Call me nothing if you don't mean it."

Caught by the sudden somberness of his expression, she paused. Had he come to care for her as more than just a sexual partner? However thrilling the thought, part of her was dismayed. They had no future. Nothing beyond this last encounter. Her destiny was to rule a kingdom. He was far, far beneath the handsome warrior-prince her father had bargained for.

"Don't look so dismayed, Birget," he said, his tone cooling. "I'm not in love with you. Most of the time, I don't even like you."

His words stung, but she understood his intent. "Then we are in accord. I want this." She ran her palm up and down his length.

"Anything her highness commands . . ."

They didn't wait to find that cabin.

Baraq thrust his hands beneath her clothing, found the draw-string to her trousers, unlaced it, and pushed the wool fabric down her thighs to bunch at the tops of leather boots, which she toed off with zeal.

With even more efficiency, his suit was opened, his thick, straight manhood exposed. Then he lifted her and stepped forward to trap her against the ship's metal bulkhead.

Birget reveled in his roughness. He'd been gentle after discover-ing her inexperience, but he gradually accepted that she didn't need a light touch, didn't fear a little savagery from a lover. Not that she'd ever dreamed she could be this way with a man.

Her only disappointment was the fact she'd never found her peak while he moved inside her. Always, he found his first, and then patiently, with tongue and fingers, coaxed her toward climax.

Baraq lifted her higher, and then turned and slammed her against the opposite bulkhead. "You think too much."

"And you try my patience, *Utlending*."

His grunt this time sounded closer to a laugh, and she smiled over his shoulder as he nudged his cock between her legs. When he rubbed her folds, she felt the thrill of arousal, the dampening he coaxed as he circled inside her entrance. She turned her head and bit his neck. "Enough teasing."

"You should let me take my time. I'm not usually this ham-fisted with other women, and they seem to enjoy what I do."

"I am not other women," she ground out, not liking that he thought of other lovers when he held her in his arms. "Fuck me, Baraq. I do find pleasure in this act, and you will be diligent afterward."

He groaned and his hands slid down to cup her bared buttocks. With a rough squeeze, he pushed her down on his cock. As he forced himself into her tender opening, he asked, "Am I hurting you?"

"I've felt no pain since our first joining. And even then, I only screamed loudly because I was surprised."

Again, he grunted, but his breathing quickened, and she knew he would soon be past arguing. Her thighs clutched him tighter. "Fuck me hard, *Utlending*."

"Baraq. My name is Baraq." He dipped his knees, pulled most of the way out, and then powered upward again, thrusting deep.

Air hissed between her teeth. No longer raw, but still so new to lovemaking that every nerve inside her fired, exciting tension in her womb, she rewrapped her legs around his hips and clutched his shoulders, matching his movements. They banged against the bulkhead, their faces heating, their movements growing more frenzied.

Tension coiled inside her womb. She bit her lip, hoping it would wind tighter and tighter, but he was already rutting wildly, his thrusts sharper, shorter, and less rhythmic toward the end. She stifled a sigh as he groaned and shuddered, semen spurting in scalding jets inside her channel.

His arms enclosed her, and he hugged her close. Then he moved away from the wall, carrying her with his hands clutching her rump. At the first oval door, he gestured with his chin.

She reached to the side and opened the latch.

He stepped through the door, headed straight to the shelflike bed against the far wall, and lowered her.

When his cock slid from inside her, she moaned in protest.

He knelt between her legs, lowering his head toward her sex. She opened her legs.

The sight was one she'd never get used to. A man bending in intimate supplication as he selflessly pleasured her. His large hands caressed her buttocks and thighs as his lips smoothed over her folds. His tongue lapped to steal the moisture coating them.

At the first tug of his lips on her clitoris, her hips bucked.

He glanced up into her eyes. "Too much?"

She was still so sensitive, the sensations all so new she hadn't developed any defense to hide how overwhelmed she felt. Her lips trembled. "More, Baraq," she whispered.

"So sweet," he said, tonguing the slick knot. "So pretty."

She came up on her elbows. "Cunts aren't pretty," she ground out, fighting the urge to moan and writhe as he suckled harder.

"You aren't a man. Look at me."

She cracked open her eyes, not realizing she'd been squeezing them shut since he'd begun his seductive offensive.

His features were tight, the skin pulled over his sharp-bladed cheekbones and powerful jaw. His gaze narrowed in challenge, and he stuck out his tongue to flutter it over her hooded clit.

Her lips parted as she watched, enraptured by his darkening expression.

"You are beautiful." His fingers swirled around her entrance.

All she saw was a blond ruff, swollen lips, and a reddened nub that was slick with his saliva. "Why does it matter what I think?"

"Because I want to pleasure you, and I want you to understand what I feel when I fuck you."

Even his breath as he talked caused trembling sensations. "And you think flattery will help?"

"It isn't flattery. But I would have you watch and learn. Maybe if you see yourself through my eyes, you'll relax and know that everything about you is feminine and attractive. That letting yourself go with me won't leave you vulnerable or any less a princess."

"It isn't your fault that I haven't come with you inside me," she said, her voice thick with emotion.

"I shouldn't have been so rough that first time," he said softly.

"Do you think I'm afraid?" No one had to go easy on her. "That your cock was so big you wounded me forever? Don't flatter yourself."

"Now you're just being nasty because you're embarrassed."

"You don't know me. I'm only getting angry because you're talking when my legs are splayed. How attractive do I feel now when you'd rather argue than make me come?"

His gaze sharpened. "I won't be goaded into finishing you so quickly."

She flopped back on the mattress and groaned. "Why didn't I seduce Cyrus? He wouldn't have given a damn about why I have difficulty coming. He'd have happily rutted away—"

His thumb and forefinger pinched her turgid knot.

A strangled scream escaped, and she jerked her head up to give him a glare. "What was that for?"

"For mentioning another man when I'm the one with my face between your legs."

Could he be jealous? The thought appealed. Since she'd never allowed men of her own clan to approach her, they'd learned never to tease her as a woman, or they'd find their teeth shattered on the stone floors of the keep. Baraq didn't fear her reputation, nor was he impressed by the fact she was a noble.

Arousal seeped from inside her.

His gaze darted down to the fingers stroking her labia. He tunneled one long digit inside. "Sweetheart, you're wet."

She rolled her eyes. "Of course I am. I'm filled with your seed."

"This is you. It's warm, thin." He bent and licked between her folds. "Delicious."

She snorted. "Again, you take flattery too far."

"But I'm thirsty for your essence." One eyebrow arched, and he gave her a wicked smile. "Parched." His fingers parted her and his mouth rubbed over her slippery inner folds. His tongue darted out to lap lazily, then paused to sink inside.

Her thighs tightened around his head, and he chuckled, the sound muffled by her slick flesh.

He thrust two fingers inside her, and began to pump them in and out. His mouth smoothed upward, then rubbed over and over the distended nub that seemed to grow more sensitive with each caress.

A ripple of pleasure slid sinuously down her channel. Her belly trembled. "Baraq!"

"Yes, Princess?"

"Oh, gods!" Her head thrashed side to side as the onset of an orgasm tightened her core.

"Are you close?"

"Yes!"

He halted, heaved upward, and gripped his shaft.

Birget's face crumpled. "Please, I was so close."

"Trust me." With his hand stroking his hardening erection, he sought her clit again with the other and rubbed his thumb over and over it. "Press your knees higher, toward your chest. Now spread them wider."

Eager, desperate for release, she did as he asked, grabbing her knees and pulling them high, then opening them lewdly wide.

Her entrance stretched, she could feel cool air against flesh that had never felt a draft before.

Never slowing the lazy scrape of his thumb, he bent over her and placed his cock at her entrance.

"Lovely, so fucking beautiful . . . See how I fit there? See how well we fit together?" he said, as he slowly pushed inside.

She watched as the tapered head sank inside her. Groaned as the thick shaft disappeared, pushing deeply through her narrow channel. Her walls were thick, pressing around him, forcing him to tunnel. Each pulsing shove crammed deliciously until he was seated; then he pulled back two finger widths and began the back-and-forth motions that matched the heavy thud of her heart.

"Squeeze your inner muscles around me. Now release. Do it again."

She squeezed harder and felt the ripples working up and down inside her, felt how her body clutched around him, urging him deeper. But he moved too slowly to suit her. "Please, Baraq," she whimpered.

"Need more?"

"Yes, oh, yes!"

He thrust deeper, gliding easily in a fresh gush of fluid that was so copious it trickled down between her buttocks. The nasty feel of it, and the way he watched her pussy so avidly, as though the lewd picture she made fascinated him, loosened something inside her.

A wave of pleasure caught her off guard and her back arched off the mattress. She gave a groan, then arched again as he began to move faster and faster, his strokes deepening, strengthening.

When he lifted his thumb, she found she didn't need it anymore. His groin crashed against hers, each jolt slapping her clit.

And the movement was enough.

She gave a strangled scream as her orgasm swept over her in a hot tide. Her skin tingled. Her belly quivered. Light exploded behind her eyelids, the pressure in her head stealing away all thought except the exquisite feel of him moving inside her.

Slowly, she came back to herself to find him studying her. Masculine pride showed in the curve of his firm mouth. She'd allow him a moment to gloat.

He'd proved she was made like other women, after all.

*  *  *

Birget strapped herself into a seat in front of the viewing screen as the *Daedalus* rattled through its approach. Cyrus had ceded control of the ship to ground control moments ago. Remote guidance would land the vessel in its assigned slip on the ground.

Everyone aboard the starship crowded onto the command deck, watching the approach. Judging by the stern cast of the faces of the Vikings planted on every available seat or stair, she wasn't the only one feeling a little nervous about what lay ahead.

She shot Baraq a glance and found his gaze was on her, not the screen. Although not smiling, his eyes gleamed. She hoped she didn't look as well satisfied, not that everyone aboard didn't know about their intimate relationship. Still, she had a reputation to maintain. No one needed to know that inside her Valkyrie's body, she purred like a pussycat.

Baraq gave her a wink.

She turned sharply away, heat rising on her cheeks. She hid a smile and turned her attention again to the front of the deck.

The view as they burned through Helios's atmosphere took her breath away. A large green and brown continent grew before her eyes. Green along the edges of a dark blue ocean and in the deep valleys surrounding wide rivers. A dusty brown everywhere in between except for a long, rugged ridge of white-capped mountains to the northwest. Those whitecaps were the only similarities in the landscape this world shared with hers.

As they drew closer to the ground, her focus homed in on the largest river and the city that sprawled at its wide mouth and then tapered southward along its banks.

"The Blue Nile. The lifeblood of the continent. Fed by runoff from the Olympian mountain range," Cyrus said behind her.

"'Tis Heliopolis?"

"Yes. The capital. A Greek name for an Egyptian city from the old world."

Without taking her gaze from the screen, she murmured, "We think of you Helios as a single people."

"We've become that, but we still have those who take pride in their ancestry, whether it is Greek, Roman, Persian, or Egyptian. Our culture is a blend. As is our language."

"It's our language too," she said, her tone bitter, "since you tried so hard to eradicate our Norse tongue and culture."

"I see how well that worked for us," he drawled.

Nerves must have made her smile. "You live in the open, without walls around your city?"

"We live in peace and are ruled by a single entity, an elected council. No need for curtain walls or castles for defense."

"There are roads and buildings in the center of the river."

"We built up the islands in the estuary. The river is controlled by a series of dams. We no longer worry about flooding, so the islands are now considered prime real estate."

She looked back, troubled by how insurmountable her goal seemed at this moment. "The city's so large. How will we ever find them?"

Cyrus sighed. "If what Dagr suspected is true, that the men were abducted for breeding purposes, then that narrows our search." Despite the shaking of the ship, he pushed up from his chair and walked to the screen. "Computer, zoom in." He touched the screen at a place to the west of the river. As though they fell toward the ground faster, the view tunneled down before opening again over a long road with a series of paved lots lined up one after another. "We'll dock here." His finger trailed up the road, the screen switching quickly, turning to the west, through a densely constructed area. "We should move freely through this district and gather intel. But this—" He pointed toward a large collection of uniformly shaped white buildings surrounded by a waterway. "This is Pandora's Garden. My best guess is that the men will end up here."

Birget studied the map. "I'm assuming that we should infiltrate under the cover of darkness."

"Your pale faces and large builds will be pretty conspicuous in daylight."

She nodded, for once not wishing to argue with his every statement. She had more important things to worry about than their ongoing distrust. Before this day was through she'd be leading a contingent of Icelanders into an *Utlending* city. The first time her people had stepped onto another planet since crossing the Bifrost to New Iceland centuries ago.

What would Dagr or her father say to his men on this momentous occasion to stir their blood for the coming fight? She'd never given a rousing speech and hadn't a clue how to begin.

With a shove, she pushed up from her chair, ignoring the rumbling beneath her feet, and walked along the aisle. She eyed Grimvarr, Dagr's younger cousin. "You may stay aboard the ship," she said. "Even now, you may be the only *Ulfhednar* heir."

With reddish brown hair and a trimmed beard that skirted his mouth and chin, he was nearly as handsome and as largely made as Dagr. Shoulders squared, he gave a grunt. "I'm Wolfskin. I'll not sit back while others toil."

Not expecting any other response, she nodded. "Then I am glad you will be with us." To the group at large, she said, "When we debark, we will split into teams of two. The smaller groupings will make us less noticeable and give us a chance to cover more ground. We'll search at night, then return to share what we've learned before morning rise."

She aimed a glance around the deck, saw a few nods and some fierce smiles. The Wolves were as eager as she was to quit this ship.

"You must wonder why Dagr put me in charge of this mission and of you."

This time gazes narrowed and stances shifted.

"It's not our place to wonder," Grimvarr said, his tone soft.

An underlying firmness infused his words, hinting that she should stop. Raising her voice to be sure everyone heard, she said, "I'm a Bearshirt."

Grunts, nods, followed. She'd stated the obvious, but she had their attention.

"True, I'm betrothed to Eirik. But I've never met him. I have no affection for the man. I don't battle to save him. I do this for my own family's pride. Dagr understood this about me. My loyalty to the Wolfskins was sealed when he made me your leader." Her gaze skimmed over the assembled group. "You are mine to command. I'm bound to you as you are to me."

She strode toward Cyrus at the front. The ship shimmied and she clapped a hand on one of the Wolves' shoulders.

His eyebrows gave a waggle.

With the mood lightened, she smiled. "I'll not land in your lap."

Chuckles sounded, which she didn't mind. Humor before a fight strengthened a Viking. "Scour the ship for clothing that will be less conspicuous. If you must, steal it after we hit the ground. Our furs will mark us. We carry no weapons we cannot hide. So leave your daggers and swords in their scabbards aboard the ship.

"Do not lead anyone back to us. Keep to the shadows. Do not engage in conversation in crowds. Your accent will give you away. Seek no fights, only information. Cyrus will give each of you ore should you need it to loosen tongues." She paused, searching for the words she needed to strike a fire.

Grimvarr cleared his throat, drawing her attention. "We haven't shields to beat or Thor's sword to swear by, but you do wear the Black Wolf's totem."

Grateful for the suggestion, Birget lifted the black stone and pulled the cord from around her neck. She raised it high. "For the Wolves! For Icelandia!"

Every man there shot to his feet; fists hammered the air. She passed the stone to Grimvarr, who faced the men and raised his arm high. "For the Black Wolf!"

As man after man shook his fist and shouted his allegiance to the *Ulfhednar* king and thus this mission, Birget felt pride burst inside her chest. The backs of her eyes burned with tears she refused to cry.

She and every proud Viking here would see this through—that or die trying, happy to ascend to Valhalla in the arms of the Valkyries.

# Five

"She's an eel-skinner, that one!" Hakon said, his words slurring before he turned on his side and began to snore. He'd had a little too much of the tangy liquor the attendants served to the gathering as though it were water.

Eirik shook his head. His companion's skin was reddened from exertion, his naked body gleaming with sweat. And he reeked of sex.

Except that his mind was clear, Eirik was in little better condition.

After Fatin had fled the salon, he'd plowed his way through half a dozen of the women who'd bought his favors, looking at the sexual play like a warrior might a day in the lists, since he hadn't worked his body hard since his capture. The last of the women, a plump but attractive matron, whose hair was too pale a shade of honey to match her dark brown brows and the trimmed bush below, was still pressed against his side. She slept, a soft snore tickling his neck.

After the reckless abandon of the first hour when the Vikings had ripped away their clothing and chased squealing women around the salon before settling down to seek their pleasure—an unchoreographed moment that Aliyah had been quick to claim as her own idea—the debauchery resembled the mindless repetition of a mining crew's labors. Drill, toss a shovelful of minx, and then move on to the next shining vein to plunder.

Aliyah opened small chamber rooms just off the main salon to allow the women who could afford it the luxury of privacy. As the beds were large, the bleached blonde and her girlfriend decided to pair up and share a bed and men. Not an uncommon thing on his own world, but he was grateful not to be on display anymore. Although he suspected the large gilt mirror on the far side of the room was intended for private viewing.

*Let them watch*, he'd growled beneath his breath, and then he'd given them a show they'd not soon forget. Everything he'd learned while sampling the many women who'd swarmed him in his own keep prepared him well to pleasure and surprise these jaded women. He and Hakon took their turns with the girls, happily spanked and pounded away, competing to elicit the loudest moans and screams.

However, pleasure, when dictated, soon tarnished. And since he hadn't drunk as deeply of the aphrodisiac that kept everyone else's spirits and libidos running high, he'd grown bored.

Unable to nap while his patron dozed, he studied the room until he counted the tiles on the floor and every fold in the curtains that drifted in the warm night air, wafting through the open window.

A streak of orange fire ran across the wall opposite his bed. He jerked until he realized it was one of the small, double-headed creatures the Helios treated like pets. They fed on insects, long tongues whipping out of their mouths to wrap around a bug and pull it squirming into their bellies.

He shuddered. For his peace of mind, the small creatures were too reminiscent of his own planet's giant ice dragons that lurked in the ocean beneath the icy crust, save that their bodies were smooth, not scaled and spiked.

Wondering whether he could roust a man for a bit of hand-to-hand to relax, he edged from beneath the woman's cheek, which was plastered to his skin, and climbed off the sumptuous bed.

His back hurt, his pride felt dirtied, and he was grumpy as hell.

Walking back through the dimly lit salon, he didn't keep his footsteps quiet, slapping his feet noisily on the marble. But he needn't have bothered. Bodies lay in piles, women using male and female chests and bellies as pillows on the floor, the couches—any soft or hard surface—lying in unattractive sprawls.

Eirik cursed the fact he'd landed on this Hel-world with a pack of lazy bears. His brother and he held a much tighter rein over the behavior of their own warriors. But then he drew back, sighing, and realized that he'd never trained with these men. And they didn't have his measure either. When they assembled for the morning meal, he'd have to figure out a way to set an example so they would begin to look to him for how they should go on.

In the meantime, he would do what a leader must—learn his surroundings, test the limits of his prison.

Careful to hide his resolve behind a slackened expression, he slowed his steps and yawned, then rubbed a hand over his smooth chest and scratched. Damn, he missed the feel of hair on his chest. Anger flared again, but this time rather than letting it build until he stomped with a bearish tread, he kept up the facade of a man looking for refreshment.

On a nearby side table, he found a large bowl with ice melting in the bottom. The color was pale enough he didn't worry that he'd spike his blood again with the seductive poison. He picked up the huge silver dish and drank noisily, letting the cold liquid slide down his chin and onto his chest.

In truth, the chill sobered him instantly. Reminded him of home. Of the icy ocean just beyond his keep's curtain wall where he and his brother sometimes fished through ice holes for succulent black eel and feathered fish.

What did Dagr think had happened to him? An ache in the center of his chest had him tossing away the silver bowl to crash against the floor. The noise caused only a small stir.

One woman draped over the thigh of the red-haired *Berserkir*, Hagrid, lifted a lid, and gave him a tired half smile. She fluttered her fingers, and then turned her nose to nuzzle Hagrid's cock.

Before she fully woke and thought to follow him, Eirik quickly headed through the open entrance of the latrine just off the salon.

Gold troughs on tall stems stood against one wall. He grabbed the edge of one bowl and raised its height, pointed his cock toward the center, and let his stream flow. All the while, he searched his surroundings with a sharper eye. Besides the urinals and another, longer trough with gooseneck faucets for washing one's hands, the appointments were spare. There was only one closed stall in the room. And yet a large, lifelike statue of a creature with a man's upper body and a horse's lower, stood next to the entrance, its vacant gaze trained on the room.

Eirik shook himself, ignoring the automatic swirl of water, and studied the statue, finding it comprised entirely of fire-hardened clay, except for its concave glass eyes.

Here would be their captors' view into the room.

Knowing what to look for now, he traced his way back through the salon, found the other "eyes" in gold-painted fish and frogs, in peepholes hidden in the murals and jeweled fabric covering the walls.

Satisfied he'd found most of their watchers' devices, he re-entered the room where Hakon and the two women slept. Just as he lay back, the door to the chamber swung inward and the whore-mistress, Aliyah, swept inside, snapped a finger to brighten the lights, and cleared her throat.

Eirik stiffened but didn't bother to rise.

The woman beside him gave a sharp inhalation, grumbled, and then slowly opened her eyes. Glancing up, she blushed a deep red.

He gave her a scowl, which made her eyes widen. Perhaps full-blown arousal had lent her courage enough to approach him earlier. The chilly aftermath leeched every bit of strength from her. Her body trembled.

Feeling like a bastard, he softened his expression. "I don't bite," he said, growling the words.

Her wide brown eyes blinked; another flush swept over her cheeks. The hand lying on his abdomen twitched, then opened to glide across his skin.

"Leticia," Aliyah drawled. "Your transport has arrived. The driver's waiting for you at the hoverpad. You wanted me tell you."

"Oh!" The woman abruptly sat up. "I have to go home. Marcus will be rising soon. I shouldn't be late."

Marcus? A husband, perhaps? Or a child?

He shook his head, wondering what constituted a normal married life among these people. Despite the freedoms afforded men in his own culture, women, once wed, were expected to keep their wombs pure to ensure that only their husband's seed took root. That was, unless Eirik or his brother showed interest, and then a wife would be allowed the pleasure of their bed. A man was proud if his mate was singled out for such an honor.

As Leticia scurried off the bed, she dragged the top sheet with her, uncovering his body as well as Hakon's and his companion's.

The couple stirred. The sticky slurp of a cock leaving its mooring filled the air.

Eirik's lips twisted into a snarling smile. The effects of the drink had long dissipated. The stink inside the chamber, the stickiness of his own skin, disgusted him.

The room reeked, and yet Aliyah's nose didn't twitch. The bitch likely smelled only gold. Lots of it.

Her gaze went to the other woman, who stirred lazily beside Hakon.

Eirik reached across and swatted the woman's bare rump. A high-pitched giggle erupted, making him wince.

When she, too, hurried out of the room, Aliyah closed the door, and then turned to face the men, her posture regal, her expression set.

Hakon shot him a glance. Eirik shrugged. Perhaps she wanted to praise them for their performances or remind them once again that they were hers to command—just to keep them humbled.

Whichever, Eirik was grumpy enough not to care. He shoved a pillow behind his shoulders and spread his legs on the bed, making sure she understood that he didn't hold her in high regard.

The insult caused a slight pinkening of her cheeks, and her lips to thin, but otherwise she remained silent. She still wore the white gown, but her jewels had been removed, except for the diamond amulet and a broach holding together the dress at her shoulder. Her long, black hair was down around her shoulders.

Her gaze flicked from Eirik to Hakon, then darted down to Eirik's cock, which lay curled against his thigh.

Eirik felt his stomach tighten at the narrowing of her gaze. "We should bathe," he said, sitting up and sliding his legs over the side of the bed.

"Don't bother. I don't mind," she said, her tone even. "Your debut was a stunning success. I don't think we'll have trouble filling the salon every night."

Her continued perusal of their bodies sent warnings clamoring through his mind. "Since you watched over us, you must know we need rest," he said, keeping his own tone uninflected. "To be ready for tonight."

Her lips curved into a faint smile. "Have no fear; you'll be petted and pampered by my attendants, but not until after you've pleasured *me*."

Eirik glanced over at Hakon, who lay with an arm thrust beneath his head.

His expression was shuttered, but his cock was already hardening. Hakon shrugged, sliding a large hand up and down his shaft. "A chance to fuck our mistress?" he said, playing the barbarian to the hilt. "To bend her to our will?"

Eirik didn't miss the inflection on the word "bend." Nor the sparkle of sly amusement in his friend's eyes. Hakon had a murderous streak. Which was just one of the things Eirik liked about him.

Aliyah's chin rose. "So long as you understand that if you try to harm me, the implant will be activated."

Although he wasn't similarly inclined as his friend, anger at having every impulse leashed pulsed through him, pounding at his temples and his groin. He pushed off the bed and strode toward her. "What is it you wish from us?" he bit out. "Supplication? Do you want us to hold up our cocks for you to ride?"

Her gaze slid to the side, and yet her demeanor was no less composed. Not for the first time, he noted that her delicate features weren't in consonance with the crude, avaricious role she played here.

"You know what I want, Viking. What all the women wanted."

Hands fisted on his hips, he stopped in front of her. "Not all wanted savagery. Quite a few were content to be tongued and caressed into a gentler climax."

"Only because they knew the power you leashed for them."

He circled behind her, and then bent toward her ear. "Do you wish to be taken?" he asked softly. "Will you submit—so long as we cause no permanent harm?"

Her breath caught on a soft gasp. "I am not delicate."

He translated that to mean she liked a little pain. His interest piqued. Boredom slid away like an ice serpent sloughing skin.

With another glance at Hakon, who gave him a shrug to indicate he'd follow his lead, Eirik circled around to her front, eyeing her much the way she had him when he'd been oiled and polished for the unveiling. Assuring his worthiness.

Aliyah's back stiffened as he stepped closer, forcing her to raise her glance. Her eyes glittered. When he was close enough to smell her perfume and the musk of her arousal, he braced his legs apart to draw her attention down to his filling cock.

Her gaze swept down his body, then slowly back up.

Feeling like a potentate addressing a new concubine, he stroked his flesh within inches of her belly. "I know that you can force my arousal with the snap of your fingers," he said, keeping his voice low and seductive. "But I am not a thrall—despite the band I wear on my wrist and the device you implanted inside my body. However, you don't want the thrall, do you, madam?"

Her mouth opened; her chest expanded, but lowered again as she breathed slowly out. "No," she whispered. "Slaves I have aplenty."

Her answer pleased him on a level that didn't bear any scrutiny. For the first time, he felt as though she'd addressed him as a man. He released his shaft and bowed his head to acknowledge her unspoken concession. He would lead. She would submit.

Lifting his hand, he threaded fingers through her thick, wavy hair, bringing a handful of it to his nose to inhale the scent of roses. Her berry-glossed mouth parted. Her head swung toward him.

Without a smile or a softening of his expression, and keeping his eyes wide-open, he bent to take her lips. They trembled against his. His cock stirred, and he deepened the kiss, stepping closer to press his full body against hers. And even though he was dirty, his skin coated with salt from his sweat and smelling musky from the half dozen women he'd bedded, she melted against him, unmindful of her pristine dress.

He liked her lack of care. She might still be a bitch, and he could hate her outside this room, but for now, she was just a lusty, driven woman, begging for a stronger lover to dominate her. Here was a challenge to lift the enervating boredom.

Behind him, Hakon's feet slapped the floor. When he stepped into view behind Aliyah, both his eyebrows were raised, asking silently what was needed.

Eirik reflected with silent amusement that he didn't have to wait until the morning meal to begin instructing his men how he wished to be followed.

His fingers gently pinching her chin, Eirik broke the kiss and held her stare. "Undress her, Bearshirt."

With relish, Hakon tore away the broach at her shoulder and flung it to the floor, where it clattered.

Aliyah jerked but made no sound of protest. The soft white slip of gown dropped to the floor in a puddle at her feet, revealing her nude body.

Tall, slender as a sapling tree, her skin was a smooth, creamy tan. Her breasts were set high with small, rusty brown nipples at the centers. The tips were already engorged, and Eirik didn't resist the urge to touch them, rolling them between his thumbs and fore-fingers before plucking harder.

Gasping, she rose on her toes, swaying toward him, and then fell again when he let them go.

He lifted his chin to Hakon, and his second backed away while Eirik circled her now-trembling body again, his gaze sliding over her, noting the nude cunt, her lightly oiled skin, the roundness of her small bottom. And the way her short, shallow breaths made her breasts and belly quiver.

He stopped to unlatch the necklace at her neck, but she reached back a hand to stop him.

She didn't want him to touch it. One question was answered.

Hakon's lips thinned, and his gaze flicked to her nape.

He too had noted her action. Eirik gave a subtle shake of his head to warn Hakon to ignore it, then waited silently while she removed it and carefully laid it atop her ruined gown.

When she stood, he cupped her buttocks, lifting the globes to measure their weight and parting them to remind her of her vul-nerability. Then he gave her rump a soft pat. "Go to the bed and bend over the edge."

Her eyelids fluttered nervously, but she followed his instruction without hesitation, striding to the bed, then settling on her knees, her torso on the bed and her hands resting beside her shoulders.

He bent and picked up her gown, ignoring the way she stiffened as the amulet fell with a clink to the floor. He dipped again, and picked up the amulet, but walked to the windowsill and laid it gently on the masonry.

Pretending he didn't notice where her glance went or how she sighed her relief, he began ripping the soft fabric into strips.

Aliyah's glance darted to his hands, and she gave a soft groan.

"Expensive, was it?"

"A fortune." But she laughed, and he found himself smiling as well.

Hakon gave Eirik a heated glare as though to remind him that they stood in a chamber with their whore-mistress, but Eirik wasn't unmindful of the need to beware.

However, he thought he had her measure. That he understood her need. He'd played at domination with women before and knew some females had a deep-seated desire to be used and toyed with by a man, that they found relief from whatever stresses or troubles they had in their lives only through rough, humiliating play.

He wondered what issues weighed on her mind, and scoffed inside at the thought that she struggled with her conscience concerning the Vikings' plight. But he thought that, as a woman who held so much power in her hands, she might appreciate a momentary weakness of spirit. Perhaps her femininity would bloom beneath a firm hand. A strategic advantage might be gained here.

Striding slowly toward the bed, he dangled strips of fabric from his palms. When he stood behind her, he trailed the ends of the strips over her back and buttocks. "I will tie you."

Her head lifted, but she didn't look back. "Yes."

"And blindfold you."

She gasped and nodded quickly.

Hakon's scowl eased, and his stance widened as his cock lifted from his taut groin. When his gaze rose again to Eirik's, a small, self-satisfied smile tilted the edges of his firm mouth.

At last, he understood the opportunity they'd been afforded. If they played this right, if they curried her favor, they might find that breach they needed in their prison's defenses. They already possessed one key bit of information.

Both men shared a smile, then dropped their gazes to the woman whose buttocks quivered with ill-concealed anticipation.

* * *

Fatin stalked toward a dockside saloon, feeling edgy and angry, and ready to drink herself blind.

Aliyah had denied her request to see her sister.

To add insult to injury, the whore-mistress had made a spectacle of her, tempting her with an elusive promise of an audience with Zarah in order to manipulate that scene at the Viking's debut.

However, to be honest with herself, Fatin acknowledged that she hadn't dug in her heels hard enough to insist on limits or to bargain harder for an agreement. The sight of Eirik's large body and unyielding face had been all that was needed to drive her to her knees.

He was her Achilles' heel. But whether it was because she was falling beneath his spell or some scrap of conscience had made her weak, she didn't really want to know. Either was a luxury she could ill afford.

Her body and soul ached. Bruises on her wrists and buttocks reminded her of how vulnerable she'd been—and how close to disaster she'd been. If Eirik's need to slake his frustration and lust on her body had been any less, he might have sought the ultimate revenge she'd seen burning in his eyes those first few moments when their gazes connected.

He'd kill her if he got a second chance. Or his friend, the blond barbarian, would do it for him. That one's libido was much less tempted by her feminine distress. Without remorse, he'd have broken her spine had Eirik not intervened, and Aliyah, the bitch, might not have been moved to save her because then she could reclaim the small fortune she'd paid Fatin for her precious cargo.

Fatin shrugged off her disappointment, determined to wash the taste of the dark Viking from her mouth with as much liquor as she could hold before the *meyhane* closed.

In the morning, she'd seek out Adem Pantheras, and let him know that she was ready to join his cause. She'd play both ends against the middle and see which strategy won. Besides, she'd danced around him long enough and knew his patience was at an end. With fingers deep in the Heliopolite underworld, he could easily have her killed rather than risk her changing sides. He knew what she wanted. And he also knew that she'd do anything, even betray him and risk her life, to get it. That he was attracted to her wouldn't stop him, any more than Eirik's attraction would still the hands he'd wrap around her neck.

Music blared through the open doorway. The sickly sweet odor of opium wafted in the air. Light from runners tracing the edges of the street didn't begin to pierce the murky shadows as she stepped through the entrance of the seedy establishment.

Inside, darkness masked dancers gyrating to mechanized lutes and a tribal drumbeat. Small pots of pure light gleamed on table-tops, but did little to intrude into the upholstered cubbies where male patrons played with the prostitutes who crawled beneath tables to pleasure them, or where women straddled their man-whore companions for an illicit fuck.

This *meyhane* was small and dingy, and hadn't the advantage of privacy the more exclusive clubs offered. Not that she cared. She wasn't here to fuck. Only to forget.

The bartender, who was on Adem's payroll, glanced up, his expression growing wary as she approached. He ducked his head, poured her an ale, and slid it across the bar.

Sucking down the sour foam, she eyed him again. Something was making him nervous. Had he heard that she'd stolen a pirate's cargo? Did he think she was marked? Too dangerous to be around now? Well, fuck, she couldn't stay here long. Certainly not long enough to drink herself into a stupor, not with this one acting so cagey. She set down her drink and leaned over the bar. "Samson, have you seen Adem?"

He shrugged and swiped a towel on a nonexistent water spot. "Not tonight."

She slid her bottom off the stool. "When you do, tell him we have something to discuss."

"Sure. Gonna finish that?"

"Not really thirsty. But thanks."

His gaze roved past hers, then narrowed.

She glanced over her shoulder but saw nothing out of the ordinary. "You expecting trouble?"

"No. Just busy."

"Huh. Well, good night. Tell Adem I might stop at Suffrage House."

He gave her a vague nod, and turned his attention to the patron next to her.

She wandered away, the hairs on the back of her neck rising. Something was up. Best to move along.

She headed toward the lavatory at the back and entered the unisex room, first making sure no others were inside.

Water spilled automatically from the faucet, and she washed her face, her hands, and lifted her hair to scrub a wet hand across the back of her neck. The night air was humid, sticky. And she needed a bath in the worst way.

Her thoughts turned to Eirik and Zarah, and she tried not to think about what they must be doing at this moment. Eirik was a big boy. He'd figure something out. Zarah wasn't as worldly, and didn't have the Viking's strong will. And she had no one other than Fatin to care whether she ever gained her freedom.

Fatin stared at her reflection and grimaced. Her lips were swollen, her eyes large in her face. Dark half-moon shadows rimmed her lower lids. She needed sleep. In the morning, she'd find Adem herself.

She shoved away from the basin, wincing. Her wrists, with their matching bands of bruises, were complemented by the lovely reddish scrapes Aliyah's fingernails had dug into her forearm.

Her hand ran over her backside as she felt for the tender spots where Eirik's fingers had gripped her hard and where his slaps had left swollen welts. Those she couldn't regret. She'd loved every moment he'd held her. And also couldn't hate him for the spanking or even for that last demeaning act. She'd earned the punishment. So her ass would be sore for a week. Now she didn't have to feel so guilty about leaving him there to his fate. They were even.

Retying the knot between her breasts that kept her torn shirt closed, she let herself out of the room and strode past open stalls with deep bench seats. She headed toward the exit when a large hand gripped her wrist. For an instant, she froze.

Spinning, she ducked beneath the hand and aimed a balled fist between the legs of the man foolish enough to assault her.

But her blow was caught inside a strong fist, clenching hard enough to pop her knuckles.

An arm looped around her neck from behind, pulling her up and cutting off her air. "Don't fight. I have a blade poking your ribs."

The voice was husky, but feminine. And the prick of a blade drew blood from her side.

Fatin held still, eyes trying to see into the darkness, but she found only a tall, burly figure in front of her. Had Adem run out of patience and already put a bounty on her head? How ironic would that be?

"We're taking this outside," came another rasping whisper. "Call attention to us, and you'll be dead before anyone can rise to help you."

With her heart thumping hard against her chest wall, and her mind clouding from lack of air, Fatin let the pair lead her across the threshold and into the dark alley beside the bar. The arm around her neck loosened, and she was turned and slammed against the hard, mud-brick wall. The bruises Eirik inflicted would be nothing in comparison to the sharp edges of the bricks now digging into her back and shoulders.

"Who are you?" she asked, rubbing her neck and squinting into the darkness to make out two tall shapes.

Her mind clearing, she realized that the harsh inflection of the woman's voice had held traces of an Icelandic accent. This couldn't be good.

"The barman pointed you out to us," said the female. "For a price. You're Fatin, the bounty hunter. And we've been looking for you."

# Six

Hakon and Eirik left the whore-mistress tied to the bed, her arms and legs spread wide, her body bucking as she cursed them.

No one had rushed to her aid when they'd trussed her up, so they assumed she'd given explicit orders for no one to intrude. Eirik had seen the evil glint in Hakon's eyes, but Eirik didn't believe Aliyah would be so foolish as to leave herself completely vulnerable. He'd shaken his head, telling Hakon silently that no harm would come to the woman.

And while Hakon grimaced, he gave a brief nod.

Freed to play rough, they'd teased and petted, pinched and spanked—not nearly hard enough to please the wanton. A delightful discovery for both men.

But then they'd bound her, letting her think they were ready for things to take a darker turn, only to leave her as they ordered baths for themselves.

Short, hip-height bathtubs filled with steaming water were

rolled inside. Female attendants, keeping their gazes carefully averted from Aliyah's distress, silently delivered towels and soaps, and then quickly left.

Eirik stepped into one of the bathing tubs, and sighed as the hot water enfolded his hips. Flesh that had been rubbed nearly raw with use was instantly soothed. Who knew fucking could leave a man's rod this chafed?

Hakon stopped in front of a rolling cart and turned over the towel that hid the rest of what they'd requested be delivered. An array of dildos in assorted sizes lay spread on a white linen cloth. He picked up one and squeezed the base. Humming sounded, and Hakon's eyes widened. He tentatively closed his hand around the tip, then grunted in surprise. "It warms, like flesh."

A devious idea bloomed. Eirik chuckled and rose from his bath, unmindful of the trail of water he left behind him. Passing Hakon, he held out his hand for the phallus, snagged a beaker of warmed oil from the tray, and more strips of silk, and then strode toward the bed.

He crawled over the edge, right between Aliyah's legs, and tipped the beaker to dribble oil over her mound, letting it seep between her parted folds and into the bedding beneath her.

Her nude pussy was still reddened from where he'd suckled and gently teethed the lips. He smoothed his fingers in the oil, rubbing it into her abraded skin, soothing her and lubricating her entrance— and ignoring her pitiful moans. Then he reached for the phallus and squeezed it, turning it on, and slid it quickly up inside her.

Her body stiffened, and she would have shouted a curse, but he'd stuffed a balled strip of her gown into her mouth to muffle her cries.

He pressed the dildo deeper, using the flat of his hand to push against the base until it was fully seated. Then he lay down on his side beside her. With a finger under her chin, he turned her face toward his. He trailed his lips along her cheek. "I have to finish my bath," he murmured beside her ear. "But I'll leave this running so you won't grow bored. *You may not find your pleasure, madam.*"

Then, sliding strips between her legs, he tied them around her outer thighs, forming a small basket that held the base of the dildo firmly in place. He pinched a nipple, and she groaned against her gag. "If you come, I will know it, and we are done. Do you understand?"

Her eyebrows furrowed, but her body remained still except for the telltale moist sounds her pussy made clasping around the humming device he'd lodged deep inside her.

Hakon watched from his bath, lifting a tankard of ale in silent salute. The devilish grin indicated he was enjoying the sensual torture.

Hakon's mean streak didn't bother Eirik so much. He needed a constant reminder of just how delicate a line they walked between sensual torture and the uglier brand. Hakon's glee tempered his actions, kept him mindful of the fact a woman lay at their mercy.

In Thorshavn, his kingdom, women were pampered, their safety assured by their warriors' might. However, things in Hakon's Odin-land were very different. Their feminine counterparts, the *Valkyrja*, demanded no such cosseting.

Eirik shuddered at the thought of the Valkyrie Birget he'd marry upon his return. The match had been arranged between Dagr and Sigmund. Eirik had never felt the need to meet her, seeing as the impending event was a political match. He hadn't given the marriage much thought at all until the stories of his betrothed's exploits were carried by a traveling bard.

Birget led the *Valkyrja* squad responsible for the protection of the Bearshirts' king. She trained for battle with the men, winning many physical contests. She'd even saved her father from an assassin's knife with a somersaulting kick that deflected the thrust, and then fought the assailant with short blades until she'd pierced his neck.

Visions of a tall, manly woman, her fists curled around his cock, began to haunt him. His body tensed.

Dagr had laughed himself silly when Eirik confided his doubts about the match, assuring him Sigmund promised him a comely woman. But what father would admit his daughter was more of a prince than a princess?

The woman trussed up like a goose here and now was a far more attractive prospect to bed.

Eirik returned to the bath. As much as he wanted to linger, for her sake, he found himself too eager. He washed quickly, dried off, then went back to the cart.

From the tray, he selected a short flogger with bundled flanges made of soft suede and feathered the edges with his thumb. Then he approached the bed again and loosened the makeshift belt that held the dildo in place between Aliyah's thighs. The dildo slid easily from her passage, thin, whitish arousal coating its length.

She sighed with relief and flexed her legs and arms.

"Don't get too comfortable," he warned her.

Eirik made a low, growling rumble as he looked his fill of her beautiful body. She was perfect. Every tender curve balanced and womanly. Her skin was the color of a dark cream and even, as though she never walked in sunshine, which perhaps she did not. He'd noted how the women here seemed to prefer a lighter skin tone, which no doubt increased interest in the spectacle of twenty pale-faced Vikings.

Aliyah's breasts were round, but not overly large. She possessed a figure that would stand well against the test of age. Her belly was a concave hollow that tempted a man to scoop his hand inside. Her hips were lightly flared.

Her sex, however, was a rosy, slick delight.

When he trailed the flanges of the flogger along her thigh, she tightened again, knowing exactly what tickled its way up her body. Moisture oozed between her pink lips. When he lifted it from her skin, she cried out, anticipating the sting, even before he flicked her breast.

A deep, agonized groan gurgled against the gag.

He flicked it against the other nipple, then swirled the edges over the entire breast to soothe the ache he'd caused, watching as both tips beaded into round nubbins, perfect for plucking. He took his time watching her reactions to where he laid the next stinging flicks, and nodded to Hakon when he found how sensitive her lower belly and mound were.

With increasing vigor, he plied the flogger, leaving her tender skin pink and blotchy as he tapped a fresh spot each time. Working his way lower and lower, he then bypassed her pussy, which had her writhing in frustration against her bonds. He whipped her inner thighs, letting the flanges glance against her labia, but never fully connecting.

More of her arousal wet her sex, and he thrust two fingers inside her, gratified at how hot and swollen the tissues of her channel had become.

His cock swelled as his own urgency built.

Tossing aside the flogger, he knelt between her legs, roughed his palms over the well of her belly, and then swept them up her thighs until his thumbs touched her folds. He parted her and bent toward her fragrant sex to lick between the split, stroking her like a dog lapping at water, until her hips followed his motions and rocked up and down.

Her muffled moans came faster.

Two fingers pushed inside her again, and he latched his mouth around her woman's bud, sucking gently until he felt the faint, fluttering ripples working up and down her channel. "You may not come," he said, his tone hard.

Her legs stiffened, and she shouted against her gag, head thrashing on the pillow.

He grinned at the strength of her fury. A well-aimed swat against her pussy cut short her tirade. He liked the wet sound so much he did it again, his palm warming against her reddened lips.

Her cunt would be hot and quiver all around a man's staff. He'd not make her wait much longer, because he was just as eager. "Will you let us take you however we wish?" he asked, and he nuzzled her sex.

Her forehead wrinkled while she considered his softly spoken question. But then she nodded.

"If I loose your bonds, will you be pliant, submitting to our whims?"

Again she nodded, breathing harshly through her nose.

Hakon untied her feet and her hands, then stood ready to subdue her again.

But she lay still.

Eirik smoothed over her shoulders, rubbed her belly and down her thighs. Then he backed off the bed and indicated to Hakon that he should lie beside her.

Hakon stretched out on the bed, cupping his erection and then gliding a fist down his shaft as he awaited Eirik's next command.

Hakon's cock was his equal, thick and pulsing. Crude and huge compared to the exquisitely small and feminine opening it would intrude upon. But Aliyah wanted this. Craved it, if the sucking of her nether lips was any indication.

Satisfied with his preparation, Eirik walked around the bed and reached to pull off the blindfold.

Aliyah's dark eyes blinked, and then narrowed on Eirik's face.

He arched a brow. "You wanted this," he reminded her. He plucked the gag from between her teeth, half expecting her to scream.

She licked her mouth and swallowed hard, but otherwise made no sound.

Eirik bent and kissed her mouth, dragging his lips off hers, then whispering, "Climb over my friend and seat yourself on his cock."

Aliyah's breasts shook around her ragged inhalations, but she climbed jerkily over Hakon's hips, eyeing his cock greedily before fitting him between her folds and sliding slowly down his length. Her eyes closed and a long sigh escaped.

Eirik tapped her nose.

She blinked again and glared.

"Don't hide," he said, giving her a small half smile. "You will not pretend you aren't here with us." He bent to retrieve the beaker of oil and coated the fingers of one hand with the warm liquid, making sure she watched.

Her eyes widened, questioning.

"Bend over him."

She shook her head.

He ignored her hesitation and slid his fingers down the crevice bisecting her buttocks. He rubbed the tiny, furled hole, which caused her eyes to widen even farther.

"Has this entrance ever been tried?" he asked, deepening his voice while he continued to tease.

"Yes," she rasped, "but never with one as large as you."

"Will you deny me?" he asked, gently sliding a finger inside her.

Her back arched. "No, gods, no!"

He didn't care whether she meant he shouldn't. He climbed behind her, forced her lower over Hakon's body, and cupped her buttocks, parting them. Then, gazing down, he flexed his hips, placing his cock against her small hole.

Body tense, Aliyah whimpered, the sound pleasing in its distress. His thumbs eased her open, and he pushed. Her small tight ring gave as he pushed harder.

Her whimpers grew in tenor.

Hakon muttered, and then fisted his hand in her hair and pulled her down for a rough kiss while Eirik worked his way inside her.

Her back and buttocks shivered, but she held still for him.

When he breached the ring, he paused for a long moment, savoring the strong clasp of her muscles around his girth. Then he adjusted his knees, widening his stance, and bent over them both, beginning to slide in and out in shallow pulses.

Hakon growled deep in his throat. "Feel that, mistress? He rubs us both. *Frigg!*"

Aliyah's whole body shuddered, but began to rock, forward and back, meeting his tentative strokes.

Assured she would take him and not be harmed, he increased the fervor of his thrusts, tunneling deeper, reveling in this ultimate act of subjugation.

The triumph was momentary, he knew, but it strengthened his heart. After two weeks of helpless rage, he had a way to lose a little of his fury and fear for the future on one of his enemies. He slammed forward, fucking her in earnest.

Hakon's hands clamped around her hips and guided her into a rhythm that pleased them all.

With his body consumed by the heat surrounding his cock, Eirik's thoughts wandered back to Fatin, whom he'd treated with even less respect, less care. He wondered where she was, whether she thought of him, and if the marks he'd left on her skin pleased or horrified her. Whether he'd left her insides raw.

If she'd been the one to enter this chamber, would he have shared her as easily with Hakon? Or would he have kept her for his own pleasure? And when he was through, would he have wanted to save her from the wrath of his companion and his own deep-seated rage?

Buffeted between two large, virile men, Aliyah's body quaked. Her breaths grew increasingly jagged and her whimpers more desperate.

Eirik nodded to Hakon, and then bent toward her ear. "Mistress, you may come now."

Her cry was broken, agonized. She flung back her head and screamed, bouncing back against his groin, forcing him deeper, harder, inside her, until her movements finally slowed, and she shuddered to a halt. Breathing hard, her body soothed by the strokes of their hands, she slowly stiffened between them.

Taking his cue, Eirik pulled free and sat back on his haunches while Hakon lifted her from his cock.

She crawled sideways off the bed, her gaze never meeting theirs. With unsteady steps, she walked to the windowsill and picked up her amulet, then retrieved a long towel from the trolley and wrapped it around her body. At the door, she glanced over her shoulder.

"Posture like a king if you like," she said hoarsely. "For now. Just know that when you leave this room, you are still my thralls. Attendants will escort you to the baths. You'll have freedom to exercise on the grounds." Her gaze flicked toward the bed. "You've earned a respite. Enjoy your ease."

With her tattered dignity drawn tightly around her, she exited.

Eirik drew a deep breath, wondering if he'd placed himself and his men in even deeper peril with his rough handling of their keeper.

Hakon grunted and stroked his still-engorged cock with a mighty fist. "She's an eel-skinner, that one." His voice held a note of admiration.

Muscles relaxing a bit, Eirik shook his head. Dawn was breaking.

And they had another evening of frolic to endure. "We'd better find our breach soon."

The dirty gag loosened around her head, and Fatin spat it from her mouth. Her two captors walked around the chair they'd slammed her down into. For the first time, she got a good look at their faces in the greenish glow given off by the overhead lighting.

One was definitely a Norsewoman, though dressed in a Helio man's light trousers and tunic. By the deep indention showing through her clothing, her slender waist had forced her to cinch a belt tightly to keep her pants from sagging down her sturdy hips. However, her height and generous frame weren't the only clues that gave away her ethnicity. A waist-length blond braid fell over one shoulder, her skin was as pale as cow's milk, and her eyes were a brilliant green.

And for all her manly height, she was beautiful—a fair-haired Diana in the flesh. *Wouldn't Aliyah love to get her hands on this one?* Fatin schooled her expression.

No wonder Eirik was so furious to be stolen from his home world. Helio women could never compare. She tamped down the thought. What in Hades did it matter if her own stubby height and mud-colored skin fell short in his estimation?

The other, by his dark complexion and black eyes, was clearly Helio, although an unusually muscular specimen. They made an odd pair.

She glanced around the room they'd brought her to. A ship's canteen by the looks of the long tables and the stoves in the back. Fatin sat sullenly while the two eyed her up and down. Her own trousers and ragged shirt were covered in dirt from the struggle in the alleyway. Her dark braid was ratty, and she'd lost the band holding it together at the end.

They'd forced her at knifepoint to march all the way back to the end of the dock. Then the male had covered her body in a sack to hide her, and hoisted her over his shoulder to get past the guard shack, smacking her rump with a little too much enthusiasm whenever she gave him a kick.

The layered bruises on her bottom ached like fire, and now she was seated on a hard wood chair. Cursing all men in general, her anger flared. She lifted her chin and spat at the woman's boots.

The blonde raised an arm and backhanded her.

Fatin's head jerked. The coppery taste of blood seeped into her mouth. A quick push of her tongue against her teeth assured her none was loose.

The male stepped forward and snagged the woman's hand before she could strike Fatin again. "We want her awake. Question her first. Then make her clean your boots, Princess."

*Princess?* Fatin sincerely hoped it was just a term of affection. But something of the woman's pride, which she wore as easily as some women might wear silk, showed in the tilt of her chin. Her narrowed green eyes looked straight down her nose at Fatin.

Feeling like the grubby street urchin she'd been before being led into the Garden, Fatin hated the sick feeling building in her gut. This wouldn't end well.

The woman slipped a long, lethal blade from the sleeve of her shirt and held it up to catch the flickering light. "Your life balances on the edge of a very sharp blade, bounty hunter." She leaned toward Fatin, braced her hands on the arms of the chair, the blade of the dagger flattened against the wood, and glared into her eyes. "I want to know the location of the men you abducted from my world."

Hadn't she known all along what this was leading to? How the hell had they followed her? The Icelanders had long been denied space travel by the Consortium. Fatin crimped her lips together. Her answer would spell her death.

"You will deny it," the woman said, her voice soft and hard at the same time, "but we have the manifest bearing your name. A very helpful dockworker told us your cargo had already been off-loaded and sold. And the barman pointed you out. It's funny, really. He was only too eager to give you up. Tell me, do you have any friends?"

The woman's sneer rubbed salt into an already festering wound. She didn't. Not unless she counted Adem. But even he would slit her throat rather than let her stand in the way of his plans. "They're safe," she muttered. "Your Vikings. Healthy and fed." *And very well sated by now.*

"Was there one called Eirik among them?"

Fatin felt her cheeks turn clammy. The way the woman had said his name, rather husky and hesitant, as though he stirred deep emotions inside her, made Fatin's chest tight. "There might have been."

Green eyes sharpened. "He would be dark-haired. Unusual for my people."

Fatin realized denial was fruitless. The Viking woman would only find someone else to bribe to discover it for herself. "Yes. There was a dark-haired one." *With icy blue eyes that could look right through a woman.*

"We were told you sold him at auction, along with the other men, like a thrall."

Fatin's shame dried up. The way the woman spat the phrase, like a thrall was something low, something dirty, infuriated her. "Like a thrall?" Fatin drawled. "Well, it's what he is now. And a sex-thrall at that."

The woman's lips drew away from her teeth. She took a step closer and raised her arm again.

Fatin gritted her teeth, preparing for the blow.

The Helio man cleared his throat. "Who procured their papers?"

Fatin turned toward him. "The Garden."

His body stiffened, and he cursed under his breath.

The blonde shot a glance his way. "It's the place you mentioned. This is bad?"

"The worst. It will be like breaking a prisoner out of a Consortium gaol. Tricky. It's well funded by a very generous government subsidy and wealthy patronage. They have their own security force."

"What kind of place is it?"

"A research facility that specializes in reproduction and genetics. With a very exclusive brothel on its grounds."

"A brothel!" The blonde's voice rose; her head swung toward Fatin. "Do you even know who you took? Do you have any clue?"

Fatin knew all too well, but would never admit the fact. Not and hope to make it off the ship alive. "An Icelander. One of twenty." She shrugged. "They are what I contracted to procure."

"But you didn't procure; you abducted."

"I could find no Viking thralls to purchase," she said, lying because she hadn't been willing to part with an ounce of gold or ore to get what she needed. She'd set out from the beginning to kidnap the men.

"Eirik is the *Ulfhednar* heir," the woman roared. "A prince."

"Which would make you what?" She forced her lips into a downward curl. "*His* thrall?"

The woman drew back, eyed the male who held up his hands, smirking.

"Not stopping you now, Princess."

Fatin had time only to blink as a fist flew toward her face.

# Seven

The next day, Eirik kept careful note of the route he and Hakon took as they were escorted under armed guard from the brothel.

They'd been rousted from their beds in the thrall's barracks midmorning and taken to the common room, where some had been fed, while others were led away in pairs. It was his and Hakon's turn now.

Their prison was a compound, comprised of whitewashed, concrete buildings connected by flagstone walkways that all led to the tallest building at their center—the facility where he'd awoken the morning before—his body denuded of hair and the implant placed inside his body.

Dressed again in the short loin skirt, he felt the bright, blazing sunlight warm his shoulders and back. Around him, birds twittering in the lush pockets of forest artfully planted on the grounds were the only sounds he heard save for the thuds of marching feet.

The guards were dressed in gray, lightweight fabric trousers and short-sleeved knit shirts. Composite, lightweight armor covered their torsos. Helmets with black visors protected their heads and eyes. They sported stun guns in holsters strapped to their upper thighs and carried long, pronged spears that delivered a jolt of electricity every time they tapped a back or buttock. And they seemed to enjoy the jerk of their thralls' muscles and tightening jaws.

But why were they so heavily protected when all they escorted were two nearly naked, unarmed men? Did they really expect them to resist?

Yesterday's demonstration had made an impact. Eirik remembered all too vividly the pain that had doubled him over and left him clutching his knees to stay upright. None of the men doubted the intensity of the jolt the implant had delivered. And situated where it was, none wished to experience it.

No wall surrounded the larger compound. Only a water-filled moat that separated the lushly planted grounds from a sandy plain beyond the edge of the water. Recalling Aliyah's promise of freedom to roam the grounds, he suspected the landscape hid many more watchers' devices or perhaps heat-imaging equipment to track their movements.

Metal rails bisected the grounds and traversed a bridge over the moat where a tram rolled to a halt beside the main building. The same one that had transported the Vikings in a cargo car from the arena after the auction.

Discounting the device that emasculated with pain, how else did the facility keep out intruders or hold inside anyone who might seek escape?

A shove against his shoulders reminded him not to make his interest in his surroundings so apparent. Glass doors opened with a soft whoosh as they approached, and once again they entered the sterile environs of the heart of the compound.

This morning, he studied his surroundings with new purpose, looking beyond the artifice.

Pleasure was only an offshoot of the main trade that went on inside Pandora's Garden. The logo of the industrial entity, a locked and banded chest set at the foot of a heavily branched tree, was rendered in gold foil and wood on the wall above the wide desk that sat at the back of the tall, vaulted foyer of the building.

From the bathing attendants, he'd already heard the story of the first woman of earth, doomed by her feminine curiosity to open the casket and release evil into the world. A Greek myth that had been carried here with the first travelers the Consortium stole away from Midgard.

"Why call this place her garden?" Eirik had asked the woman bathing him. "She opened a bloody casket."

The woman had shrugged, but her hands never left his muscled torso as she scrubbed him. "She had to have someplace to play."

In the cool, dry air, Eirik's skin prickled into goose bumps. Not so much from the cold air, but from the fuzzy, disjointed memories he had of his first visit.

Men and women dressed in white lab coats, pricking his arms, lifting his cock to take measurements, sinking lubricated tubes down his penis to empty his bladder for their mysterious purposes—entering his ass to prod and examine him. Ensuring his health, so they'd said, but also his enslavement.

Bile burned the back of his throat. He knew why they'd been led here again, and that this would be a daily occurrence. His seed would be extracted, stored, mixed in a scientist's dish to mate his sperm to a Helio woman's egg. A child would form and be implanted in a ripe womb. A child he'd never know.

While he'd fucked his way through the women the evening before, he'd closed his mind to the true purpose of the gathering.

Drowning in perfume and pleasure, he sank his cock in mouths and pussies while he'd tried to forget the abomination practiced on him and every one of the Vikings held here.

Sperm donors were all the men were. And their seed wasn't prized for the people they'd breed—the Vikings' intellect wasn't valued. Only their muscle and taller, more powerful frames were wanted. The children born to contracted wombs wouldn't be loved or treasured. They'd be warehoused, trained in combat, and one day led in a great battle against their own kin.

The son of a Wolfskin prince might slay his uncle. And what of daughters? Would they be disposed of since they wouldn't be needed? Would that be the kindest fate? Or would they be sold as slaves, servants to the wealthy? Made whores at seedy brothels for Helio men to visit and lord themselves over their savage captives.

Even Hakon, who wasn't one to ponder things, looked somber. He met Eirik's gaze, hatred boiling in moist eyes.

They broke the glance, jaws grinding.

"Look. Listen," Eirik whispered, before being prodded with the business end of a spear again. He jerked away and aimed a glare over his shoulder.

"No talking," the guard said, a grim smile stretching beneath the edge of a dark visor, revealing two gold-capped teeth.

Hakon gave a rumbling growl, fisted his hands for a moment, but unwrapped them and held them up when another of the guards aimed the point toward his crotch.

A sadistic bunch of thugs, these soldiers.

They were led down a long gray corridor to the right of the foyer, through another set of hissing doors, and into an open room with overhead lighting that gave off a staticky hum. Here were long, white tables lined with beakers and cabinets, and workbenches pulled in front of viewing devices that peered into small dishes.

Above, a screen showed squiggles of sperm engulfing an egg, its outer membrane resisting the attack, until at last, one persistent and wriggling sperm pierced the shell. Was it a Viking child forming in the dish? Was it his?

He wasn't given time to worry. Inside the room, technicians wearing gloves and white coats over thin, dark uniforms hurried toward them.

They were parted, and Hakon was led farther down the long tables toward a set of stocks at the back.

Eirik was prodded into another. Since he'd been forced into just such a contraption aboard Fatin's ship while she'd milked him, he groaned inwardly, understanding the process.

Bindings were latched around his wrists over his head and around his ankles. Then the smirking guards moved away to chat up one particularly pretty female.

Another woman, her hair tied in a queue behind her head, approached him with something in her hands that looked like one of the milking machines dairymen used on cows back in Thorshavn.

His balls drew close to his groin; his cock twitched. His stomach knotted, the muscles of his abdomen clenching so tightly they quivered. When she was directly in front of him, he could no longer stand still. He rattled the stocks, screwing up his face into a wild grimace, trying to frighten her away. Eirik Wolfskin would not be milked like a frigging cow!

The woman hesitated in front of him, her lips thinning. She was young and attractive in an understated way, but smelled of antiseptic. Her gaze swept his face, and she gave him a look that surprised him. Compassion shone in her soft brown eyes. "I will use this if I must. But if you prefer, I'll manipulate your penis into surrendering your nectar."

*Manipulate.* He almost laughed, but he was afraid the bark

would sound too raw. These days, his whole existence centered around his cock and his precious seed, a concept he would never have imagined growing stale in his former life, but he hated how helpless he was now.

When he escaped this place, he swore silently that he'd never take another thrall for granted. "Your hands," he said, his voice grating. "I prefer your hands."

Her head bobbed in a single nod, and then, without a blush, she untied his linen garment and knelt. She gave a sideways glance to another tech who held a wide-mouthed beaker, then resettled on her knees in front of his flaccid cock.

Her gloved hands cupped him, kneading his balls gently and squeezing his cock until he felt his flesh warm and begin to stiffen with blood.

When there was enough firmness for her to work, she reached into her pocket and pulled out a tube. She squeezed gel into her hands, and then wrapped her fingers around him again. The gel warmed with contact, heated even more with the friction she worked with agile fingers as she tugged and stroked until his cock was hard and rising toward her.

Breaths deepening, he gave himself up to the pleasure, letting his mind wander and dream.

Another's face replaced the woman in the lab coat. Fatin's almond-shaped eyes peered up as she tossed back her dark hair, issuing him a silent challenge. Blood surged south, engorging him, stretching the skin surrounding his shaft until it felt ready to burst with the pressure.

The beat of his heart echoed in the pulse of his cock as he tightened his thighs and buttocks to rock forward and back. Denied the ability to surge hard, he jerked through a tight fist.

But the hands kneading him slowed. The woman working his

flesh stared at his cock, studying him. "You are wondrous." She sighed, then ducked her head. "I'm not supposed to talk to you, but Bethel and I," she said, indicating her helper, "we've been curious. Would you mind if she felt you too?"

His gaze slid to her companion, a fuzzy-haired woman with a soft face and body. "Have you never handled a man's cock?"

"Oh, yes. Often. But not one quite so large."

Amused despite the indignity, Eirik felt a grin tug the corners of his mouth at this fascination they all had with his man parts. Gods, if only he weren't a thrall, he might enjoy spending time as a free man among them. After all, he loved women, loved the act of sex.

When Bethel knelt beside her companion and began to massage him, he could forget the circumstance. Forget the stocks that held him still for their "protection."

"I prefer a mouth to hands," he growled, eyebrow lifted in challenge.

Bethel's amber eyes blinked, but she gave him a sly smile, lifted her chin to the other, who moved in to block the view from the others farther down, working over Hakon's cock. Bethel leaned forward and opened her lips, then gave a little moan as she widened her jaws and sucked him inside her hot mouth.

"Much better," he said softly, wondering if these women could be turned, seduced to his cause. He'd leave no avenue unexplored. "You're very talented."

She gave a muffled giggle and came off his cock, but her hands continued to pump him. "You're all the talk."

"Really?"

She nodded eagerly. "Yes, your arrival. The auction. Pictures are everywhere. We're all excited."

"Why?" Could this help their escape?

"Well, because we rarely see your kind. Usually only Viking pirates standing trial. Off the dock and straight into gaol. It's rather anticlimactic. But everyone's abuzz over the offerings."

"We're not offerings. We're men," he said quietly.

Her eyes softened. "I know." She leaned toward him again, and sank her wet mouth around him.

The woman who blocked the view of what Bethel was doing rubbed her hand against his flanks. "You're hard everywhere."

"And your men aren't?" he asked, trying to hold a conversation while the one on his cock increased the force of her suctioning. She'd pull his seed from his toes with her talented mouth.

The woman stroking his skin wrinkled her nose. "Our men are arrogant. And other than security or the few who are into sports for pay, their asses and bellies are soft." Her hand cupped one buttock. "Not at all like yours."

He gave her a smile, then let his eyelids drift dreamily down. Bethel's tongue stroked his shaft. Her lips pulled harder. His balls were tightening, and in a moment or two he'd spew.

He contemplated erupting inside her mouth, but he didn't want to alarm her, or cause her trouble if she didn't collect his seed. So he cleared his throat. "Bethel, *elskling.*"

Her back-and-forth bobbing slowed, and she gazed up, her eyebrows rising.

"It's time."

She backed away. Her companion lowered the beaker toward the end of his cock. With only her hand to work him now, he concentrated, closing his eyes to feed the source of his passion and hasten his orgasm along.

*Fatin.* Her dark eyes soft and moist as she lay beneath him. Her buttocks quivering while he'd hammered her from behind. Her soft, lilting voice when she'd leaned in to say, "You're mine," a moment before he'd erupted, and his body had broken into a million particles.

Hanging in the stocks, his body slick with sweat, he rubbed his face against his arm to wipe away the moisture beading there, and to hide his sudden weakness of spirit.

Damn her to Hel, anyway.

He hung trembling, while Bethel gently kneaded his balls, and wiped the top of his cock against the glass rim. Ropes of semen slid down the sides of the beaker.

As her companion loosened his bindings, Bethel stood and leaned toward him. "Take heart, Viking," she whispered, sympathy shining in her liquid eyes. "Adem comes for you."

Fatin strode through the sliding doors of the tram and glanced around the station platform.

Guards looked her way, but made no move toward her. So, she wasn't banned after last night's fiasco. They also didn't start at the sight of her face. A large round bruise swelled her left cheek. Not something any amount of cosmetics could hide. So she hadn't bothered. Perhaps they thought one of the Vikings had gotten to her last night.

Making her way to Aliyah's offices in the brothel complex, she didn't turn her head to glance around her. The flagstone pathway led past the exercise field and the pool where Vikings exercised and swam. But from the corners of her eyes, she didn't find Eirik. Just as well. He was a distraction she could ill afford today.

Despite the many aches that twinged with each jolting step, she kept her pace quick.

*Princess* Birget had worked her over last night, taking out her frustrations on Fatin's body. And then once again, she'd been draped over the tall Helio's shoulder and carried out of the ship. They took her to Suffrage House, a flophouse for indigents. One of Adem's haunts.

There, she'd introduced her two new "friends" and acquired a single bed for them all.

Sandwiched between the male's back and the rigid wall, she'd closed her ears to their coupling and drifted into a fitful sleep. She awoke in the morning with them both glaring down.

"There was a message for you, downstairs. From the whore-mistress," the Helio had said.

Birget crossed her arms over her chest. "She says that you're to come early. That you'll get your chance to see your sister while she's getting some sun."

Fatin had jackknifed up, and then groaned as every bruise and tender rib made its presence known.

The Helio male's jaw had tightened, and he'd glanced away.

However, Birget's mouth stretched into a wide, satisfied smile. "So you have a sister inside? If you know what her life is like, how could you send our men to the same fate?"

"To earn her release," Fatin stated, her voice thick. Tired and hurt, she hadn't been able to hide her tears.

The blonde's expression remained set, but she'd glanced at the male.

His gaze when it landed on Fatin again was less militant. "You do know that we could kill you now. That we will find another way inside."

Fatin nodded. Not sure she really cared. At this point, her goal seemed impossible.

"The whore-mistress will keep you dangling. Giving you one job, then another. You will be as much her thrall as your sister. You do know that."

Deep inside, she did. But she had hoped something would come of her efforts, that Aliyah would honor their agreement eventually. Her shoulders fell.

"We have the same goal," the other woman said. "If you work with us, if you help us find a way inside, we'll help you."

"You look too much like them." Fatin shook her head at the idea. "The only way you'd ever get inside is as a thrall."

Birget's gaze held steady, but the corners of her mouth curved.

The male rolled his eyes. "Princess! That will never happen."

"You don't think I'm pretty enough to be in such an exclusive place?"

"You'd be left weaponless."

"True, but they'd have no clue what I can do with just my feet and hands." Her shoulders squared. "I'd have surprise on my side. And I wouldn't be alone. You could pass as a guard."

"Not without a plan. Not without a damn good plan. I won't leave you there long enough to be used."

Birget placed a palm against his cheek. "You're frightened for me. How sweet."

He shook his head, his lips twisting into a snarl. "We're getting ahead of ourselves. She has a meeting."

Birget's head swiveled toward Fatin. "Let the whore-mistress know you have a female."

Fatin stood, hiding a wince. "She'll wonder why I didn't offer you up for sale with the men," she mumbled.

"You're a good liar. Or you wouldn't have been able to trick so many Bearshirts into letting down their guard. You'll think of something."

Fatin had nodded. Playing along. If they allowed her to leave them behind, she could simply disappear.

"Don't think to double-cross us. We aren't without resources.

And Baraq, here, knows this place." Gaze narrowed, she leaned closer. "If you betray us, we will find a way to get to your sister."

"You'd never manage it. She's in the *saray*."

Baraq's jaw tightened.

The blonde frowned, then poked him in the belly.

"It's pricey," Baraq said quietly.

Birget scoffed. "We have a fortune at our disposal. You can buy entry." She glared at Fatin. "You've heard what he calls me. My family owns one of the three mining entities on New Iceland. We have ore to trade for what we want."

That halted Fatin's thoughts of escape. Mines? Instead, she wondered if she could get into their good graces and steal what she needed to buy her sister's freedom.

"I told you we shouldn't trust her," the male muttered.

"Her face betrays her thoughts," Birget said, huffing a breath. "She understands what we bring, but perhaps she needs reminding what is at stake." She clenched her fists and took another step closer.

Fatin groaned. "Just stake me on a grill. I'm already tender enough to eat."

The Helio tsked. "Beat her again and she'll miss her meeting." To Fatin, he said, "We will follow you to the station. We'll meet you when you return. Then we will strike a plan."

She'd agreed. And because she didn't want to leave any opportunity unexplored, she'd do what they asked. Offer the Norse-woman to Aliyah for a steep price. The thought of the woman's eventual humiliation raised Fatin's spirits.

She trudged toward the compound, head down, a hand holding her aching side, when a pair of bare feet stepped into her path.

Not looking up, she silently groaned. "Not now, Viking," she said, even before she lifted her gaze. Only it wasn't Eirik. Her heart skipped a beat at the freckled visage of the redheaded Hagrid. The one she'd dared into a drinking competition before luring him into a dark corner and transporting him.

His jaw looked like granite. His glare cold. His hands were at his sides but slowly curled into fists.

She couldn't outrun him and not pass out from the pain. His face wavered as her eyes filled. Dammit, she wasn't ready for this. She swallowed to wet a suddenly dry mouth. "We're under surveillance here. You don't want to do whatever it is you have in mind."

"'Twould be worth it. To break your scrawny neck, witch."

"And then your brothers would be left one man less. I know you don't intend to be imprisoned here forever. They'll need you."

"And you're worried for them?" he jeered.

"If I say that I am, will you believe me?"

"I wouldn't believe a word that comes from that pretty mouth." His head canted as he eyed her up and down, his gaze focusing on her face. "But it seems someone else has already softened you up a bit."

"Softened me? Yeah, guess you could call it that. So you see? You needn't bother risking your neck over me. I've already been punished." She tried to step around him, but a beefy hand wrapped around her wrist.

A gasp escaped, and she cringed away from the crush of his fingers atop the ring of bruises. Her head spun, and she knew she'd faint given another few moments of his hard grip.

"Hagrid, release her."

*Eirik!* She jerked to keep herself from turning toward him. The urge to seek the solace of his embrace was strong. And strange. The last man she could expect kindness from was him.

And he had a woman willing to risk her neck for him, she reminded herself. Someone a sight prettier than she was.

"Hagrid!"

The redhead growled and dropped her wrist.

She didn't lift it to rub circulation back into her hand, but only because it would hurt too much to raise her hand that high. Footsteps padded toward her. A finger tilted her chin.

Eirik's blue eyes glittered in his hard visage. "Who did this to you?"

She dragged her chin off his finger. "What do you care? Plan to add a few more bruises? Want to know what's not damaged so you can start there?"

Eirik's chest billowed. His muscles tensed.

She darted up a glance and then held at the quiet fury blazing in his eyes.

Before she could duck away, his hand cupped her cheek. "I didn't do this."

"No, but you left plenty of bruises elsewhere," she said, her voice gruff.

Hagrid faded away. The pair of them stood, facing off, both chests rising and falling rapidly. Hers, because her ribs demanded it. His? Fuck, she couldn't read his intent.

"Come."

He walked into a stand of trees, just off the path.

She wasn't going to follow him, but glanced up to find more Vikings gathering at the end of the pathway. Apparently, she would have to do as he asked.

She found him leaning against a tree, legs braced apart. With arms crossed over his bare chest, he looked no less imposing than he had wearing fur head to toe when they'd first met. She dragged her feet toward him, aware of his size, of the depth of the scowl furrowing his brow. When she was close, he dropped his arms and brought his hands up, but seemed unsure where to place them on her body.

"If you're looking for a fresh place to leave a mark, try here," she said, lifting one hand to just below her waist. "And here." She laid the other on a breast, then slowly raised her face. "You look . . . bothered. Is it because someone else got to me first?"

"I want his name," Eirik said, his tone flat.

She snorted. Best not to let him know just yet that Icelanders had landed. If he knew the culprit was his woman, he might act recklessly. "As it's been pointed out to me recently, I don't have any friends."

"You won't tell me?"

"Do you plan to beat it out of me?"

His fingers gently dug into her flesh, and he pulled her closer. Her neck ached trying to hold with his gaze, and she relented, laying her cheek on his chest as he enfolded her.

"I shouldn't care that you're hurt," he said, his voice a deep, soothing rumble.

"I agree," she said, unable to resist the urge to rub her sore cheek against his skin. "You have every reason to want me dead."

"I don't want you dead."

"Because then you can punish me over and over?"

"The thought has crossed my mind."

He said it but without any heat, sounding confused. Which echoed her own state of mind. *Gods, his chest felt like heaven beneath her cheek.* "I shouldn't feel an ounce of guilt over bringing you here."

"You think I deserve my fate?"

"You're a man. One who's accustomed to being served. And I'll bet you never wondered once how your slaves came to you."

"I own no slaves."

"But you contracted for them."

His hands slipped behind her neck, and she stiffened, wondering if he would end her now.

But his fingers slid through her hair, then cupped the back of her head to support it as their gazes locked. "I was entranced when I first saw you. I wanted you from the first moment. I wasn't thinking at all, least of all how you came to be there."

"Because I was something new? A dark bit to play with?"

His jaw clenched. "You were lovely. So small, I didn't know how to go gently with you. I hurt you."

"You surprised me." Fatin shrugged, pretending that fact wasn't something she'd thought about often. "Not many men who buy whores worry over whether they will hurt them, much less whether they will come."

"And you know this how? You were merely posing as a thrall."

Anger trembling through her, she pushed against his chest. "You think being a bounty hunter is a step above a thrall, because maybe I'm not so well used? Think about it, Viking. I lived here." She pushed against his chest again, trying to put distance between them, but his hands gently restrained her.

His eyes glittered angrily. "Tell me."

Fatin shook her head, feeling tears well, which she quickly blinked away. When she spoke, her voice was thick and harsh. "This was my home. For years. With my sister. We were kept together, because neither of us did well without the other, but only I was allowed to buy my freedom. Everything I've done since then has been to earn hers. I'm not sorry I stole you from your home. And I don't give a damn that you're having to fuck an endless stream of women." Her chin jutted out. "Get over it. You live. You'll get a chance at freedom. My sister may be here forever."

"Why is she so special?"

Her lips twisted. "She's an exotic and lives in the *saray*. Only the wealthiest patrons can spend time with her. I can't afford an hour of her time. And right now, I'm missing my chance to see her because you had to be the man and force me here. Well, do whatever makes you happy. I've told you where to plant the next bruise. Just hurry up, please."

His expression remained shuttered. His glance swept her face, sharpening like he was trying to read the truth. At last his hands fell away.

She moved back, turning to hurry away before he changed his mind.

"Go. I won't keep you. But, Fatin . . ."

She glanced warily over her shoulder.

"You could have friends. You just need to learn to trust."

# Eight

Eirik hit the ground with a harsh grunt, teeth rattling from the force of Hakon's angry charge. But before the brawny Viking could pin him, he dug in his heels, strained his thighs, and rolled them both. Then he quickly scrambled away to put some distance between himself and Hakon's beefy fists while he figured out just what was up with his friend.

Knowing Hakon's hatred for Fatin, he surmised Hagrid sought him out to tell him about what had transpired a short while ago— the fact he hadn't taken *their* revenge when a prime opportunity presented itself.

No, Hakon had lulled him into this fight, pretending all was well, so that he could wrest an advantage in this private battle. Although Hakon had pledged to follow him, he withheld unquestioning support, waiting for Eirik to prove himself. He likely thought Eirik had once again sought a safe route, rather than a Viking's more direct and savage path.

Earlier, before Fatin's arrival, the Vikings had been marched to the exercise field, a large area to one side of the compound. An oval track coated in a hardened gel that softened the impact of a runner's stride stood empty. Vikings didn't train for retreat.

Instead, they gravitated toward weight-training equipment—large sand-filled balls, iron bars, and heavy bags suspended on ropes—to pound, kick, and push their way through their frustrations. A few kicked a ball in the center of the track, shoving one another out of the way with great clouts as they tried to steal away the ball.

Lastly, there was a fighting pit, dug into a corner of the field, circular, with a dirt-packed floor, but it remained empty at the start of their workout.

The men were given the freedom to choose their activity. Guards and attendants backed away to the perimeter of the field while the barbarians warred among one another, naked and roaring insults as they played.

They stripped off their skirts, but refused the cotton loincloths the attendants offered. One glance at the garment, and Hakon's face screwed into a grimace. "I'll not wear a baby's diaper."

They laughed at Hakon's disgust, and he gave a sheepish shrug, before heading to a man-sized bag to beat his fists against it.

That had been before Fatin appeared walking at the edge of the field, approaching the whore-mistress's offices.

Hagrid had been closest. Eirik had run from the far side of the field to halt his plans, which had no doubt left a sour taste in every Viking's mouth. While most of the men would be averse to harming a woman, Fatin had earned special compensation.

After Eirik had returned from the woods, Hakon invited Eirik to go a round in the pit. Once there, Eirik realized his mistake. Hakon had a very big bone to pick.

Hakon lurched to his knees, and spat at the ground. "You had her right in your bloody frigging hands! And instead of giving her neck a twist, you let her walk away." His face screwed up into a furious scowl. "Does she have magic dust? Does she sprinkle it on your cock to make you forget what she did to us?"

"I forget nothing!" Eirik fought to keep his voice even, unaccustomed as he was to having to explain himself to anyone save his brother. But he didn't want this argument to escalate. "Think on it, Hakon. We're let out to exercise at the precise time she's passing by? You don't think that's just a little too lucky?"

"Are you a coward?" Hakon tilted his head. "'Watch and listen. Wait.' You're no kin of the Black Wolf. You're a bloody coward."

Heat burned Eirik's cheeks, and his lips drew away from his teeth in a snarl. Hakon was a brutish idiot. "I'm no coward, but this isn't our world. If we want to survive, to escape, we have to know what we're up against. And a target of opportunity, one so fortuitous, doesn't come by happenstance. They're testing us."

Hakon cocked his head, side to side. His neck popped and crackled. Then he narrowed his eyes and raised his fists. "Or perhaps the mistress wants her dead. Why not oblige her? She's the one who holds our papers."

Something Eirik had been thinking too, but wouldn't admit. Not now, when Hakon and the rest of the Vikings were edgy and ready for a fight.

The rim of the pit filled quickly with Northmen come to watch the battle between the two Vikings. Muttered wagers were exchanged, but their gazes remained fixed lest they miss a single blow.

Hakon gave another roar and launched himself at Eirik, but Eirik stepped to the side and lifted his foot to trip the other warrior at the ankles.

Hakon hit the ground and grunted, then rolled, lying back on his elbows to give Eirik another sour scowl. "And you fight like a bloody Valkyrie," he groused. "Why won't you raise your fists like a man?"

"To what purpose?" Eirik shot back, frustration making his body tight, his will pushed to fight if Hakon wouldn't back down. "Do you want to leave us divided into two camps?"

"Not two camps," Hakon said, his tone flat. "There's not a man here who isn't wondering when you lost your balls."

Murmurings rose from the men; a few heads nodded.

Noting the guards edging closer to the fighting pit, Eirik pitched his voice low. "If you want a fight, I'll give it to you. But only to let you lose some steam."

"*Let* me?" Hakon laughed. "You'll let me take a swing? Do you really think you're a better fighter than me? I think all your battles have been fought in a bed. You certainly know enough about that particular battle art."

Eirik shook his head, a grin twitching at the corners of his mouth. Hakon wasn't after blood, but he was trying to make a point. He and his Bearshirts wouldn't wait forever for him to unleash them.

Giving his opponent a nod, he raised his balled fists and crouched into a fighter's stance, and then milled back within range while Hakon stood and dusted off his skin.

When his opponent was ready, Hakon held nothing back, hooking a punch with his left hand that glanced off Eirik's arm, and then landing a right against his ribs.

At the assault, Eirik sucked in air, but kept his fists high, waiting for an opening, thinking through the next few blows, weighing the possibilities. Hakon used his *Berserkir* fury, not his brain, to fuel his fight. Something Eirik wished he'd known when they'd met steel-to-steel in battle back home. Then they wouldn't be having this conversation.

"Take down the proud bastard, Hakon," Hagrid shouted. "He's not one of us."

Abruptly, Eirik stopped worrying about leaving Hakon unharmed. If he didn't win this fight, and decisively, the Bearshirts among them would never follow his lead. And with Hakon's quick temper, that would only lead to disaster for the entire group.

Keeping his ribs covered by one arm, he threw a punch at Hakon's jaw, connecting and jerking the other man's head back. Then he delivered a salvo of short, sharp jabs to his ribs, his chest, gave a dig at his sides before raising an arm to deflect Hakon's next powerful blow.

Hakon had no finesse. Nothing beyond those slow, deadly punches. Eirik couldn't risk being caught by one of those hammer fists.

Eirik waited until Hakon swung again, ducked beneath the blow, and opened his arms and lunged, slamming Hakon to the ground.

Both men growled and roared, pushing, rolling, fists clipping ribs, chins. Until, with one last roll, Eirik pinned Hakon with his body, and held his arms firmly against the ground.

Eirik darted a glance around him, noted the position of the guards behind the ring of shouting Vikings, and leaned toward Hakon. "She has a sister here," he whispered harshly, hoping the shouts from the crowd masked his voice. "In the brothel. A thrall just like us."

"And you believed her?" Hakon said, his voice rising with incredulity. "Did she raise those doe eyes and cry? And what the bloody hell do I care if her own mother is whoring here?"

"Think! She has resources, the freedom to come and go—and a ship. If we can find a way to help her, we can turn her to our cause."

"You'd trust her?" Hakon's lip curled into a sneer.

"Never. But once we're on her ship . . ."

Hakon's gaze narrowed, and then a tight smile stretched across his face. "You're seducing her ship from under her?"

"I'm keeping an eye open to all options." As Hakon's expression eased into amusement, Eirik relaxed his grip.

Hakon grunted. "Would you get off me? There's parts o' me that haven't touched another man—ever. It's embarrassing."

Eirik gave a rough bark of laughter and climbed off Hakon's body. The two men sat side by side, each with a leg drawn up for privacy, and leaned back on their hands.

The men around the pit laughed, then began to fall away.

"A sister, huh?" Hakon said. "You believe her?"

"Someone gave her a beating. Ask Hagrid. He saw her face. She didn't have the strength to lie."

Hakon gave a snort. "Women are born liars. They let you think they're natural blondes. That you're their first. That no one's ever fucked them quite so well."

Eirik grinned, then sharpened his glance. "She invited me to beat her quickly so that she wouldn't miss her appointment."

Hakon's eyebrows rose. "And the embrace?"

Eirik turned to meet the other man's hard gaze. "How does a man seduce a woman? I but offered comfort, something unexpected, to keep her wondering. But enough about her." Eirik dropped his voice. "Something else happened this morning."

Hakon looked away, then leaned closer to hear.

"When we were in the center, one of the women seemed . . . sympathetic to our plight. She said that Adem comes for us. For us to take heart."

"Who is this Adem?" Hakon scoffed. "She only curries your favor because you've a handsome mug. She wants to fuck you. I saw her take you in her mouth." He jerked a hand at his crotch. "I only got a rough tug and pull."

"But what if there is someone working to help us? It's worth investigating."

Hakon's cheeks billowed as he blew out a deep breath. His head tilted toward the sky; then he leveled his steady gaze on Eirik again and held out his hand. "You're a thinker. And we do need someone who can plan an escape."

"I'll be your general, the tactician, but I need your strong arm." Eirik gave him his hand and crushed Hakon's knuckles, wincing as his own were squeezed just as hard.

"I'll still follow you, Wolf. Until you prove weak. And then I'll kill you myself if you get in our way." Hakon gave him a wide-toothed grin.

Eirik nodded and pumped Hakon's fist. "Done. Now, since we've been given privileges, let's not waste the opportunity. You and I are taking a walk."

Hakon lurched to his feet, and then turned to grasp Eirik's hand and pull him up. Then he slung an arm around his shoulder and gave him a crooked grin. "I'm assuming we don't want them to know we'll be reconnoitering for our escape?"

Eirik grunted, shook off the arm, and gave him a shove. "No sense laying it on too thick, Bearshirt." He crossed to the edge of the pit and pulled himself up. Without looking back, he bent to swipe his loin covering from the ground and tied it around his waist.

Hakon did the same.

Then, together, they left the exercise arena, heads bent toward each other as though deep in conversation and oblivious to their surroundings.

"The guards roam in pairs today," Hakon said, still grinning.

Eirik cracked an answering smile. "Let's take a pathway toward the moat. I need to know why they use it as a perimeter. Doesn't seem hardened enough to keep us from simply swimming across it."

They strode at a casual pace, attracting two guards who shadowed their steps from a distance.

The grounds were immaculate with wide expanses of green grass, but even here, wildflowers pushed through the trimmed blades to escape.

"It's almost like a Hel's meadow, back home," Eirik said, glancing around. "But without a cave roof."

"Never had the pleasure, seeing as it's Wolf-held," Hakon said dryly. "But I do like the mead your meadow produces."

The metallic stutter of an engine sounded overhead, and both men cupped hands over their eyes to watch a hovercar skim the tops of the trees. They followed its direction, past the tall main building to the opposite side of the compound.

"So there's the hoverpad," Hakon murmured.

They passed through a grove of gnarled trees bearing purple fruit. Eirik reached up, snagged one, and held it to his nose. The scent was sweet. He turned to glance over his shoulder, and lifted it to show the guards. "Is it safe to eat?"

The guards didn't respond, but also didn't smirk.

He took a bite of juicy fruit and chewed slowly, then handed it to Hakon, who eyed it with distrust.

"You're going to wait to see whether I foam at the mouth, aren't you?"

"Better you than me."

"That's a comforting thought." But Eirik felt no ill effects from the fruit, so they continued along the flagstone walkway.

The path wound through the trees and back onto the grassy lawn, bordering the moat. The water sparkled with glints of sunlight and was clear all the way to the rocky bed. The men veered off the path to approach the banks. Behind him, he heard laughter.

He tossed the half-eaten fruit into the water. Stone and sand stirred at the bottom, blurring the fruit, and then he saw shapes in the muddy water. Long, thick, eel-like bodies darted around the fruit, bit into it, and shivered as they ripped away at the flesh.

The frenzy was over in moments. All that was left was a stony pit lying in the dirt at the bottom of the water.

"Guess we know now," Eirik muttered. "We won't be swimming out of here."

Fatin cooled her heels outside Aliyah's office. Too edgy to relax, she paced in front of the windows. She was half afraid she wouldn't get up again if she sat for very long.

Aliyah was playing with her again. She knew it. Dangling an invitation she could easily grab away, and which she would if the mood struck her.

The door opened and Aliyah's assistant, a bald, sour-faced eunuch named Michael, walked out. Fatin knew him well. His personality matched his expression. "She will see you now."

Fatin brushed past him, striding into the room.

Aliyah sat at a long, tilted table, bent over a thin booklet of papyrus and scribbling away with an old-fashioned ink stylus.

In an instant, Fatin glanced around the room. Aliyah never broke role. If the salons were garish, her own quarters were elegant, timeless. But the amenities suited her classic Persian beauty. A small fountain burbling just outside her window. Pale aqua walls, white marble flooring. Mats woven from the soft, russet reeds that grew along the banks of the Blue Nile River. Even the artwork, small alabaster statues and paintings, reflected the rich, kingly past of Helios, before the captains of industry had co-opted governance of their world, turning an agrarian-based economy into a crass, mercantile one.

Aliyah courted an image. One of gentility and refinement,

which she'd tossed aside the night before in order to prove a point to the Vikings and to Fatin.

With a snap, Aliyah set aside her book and pen and glanced up, her expression set.

Fatin felt her heart sink to her toes. The last time that look had fallen on her, she'd found herself agreeing to organize a raid on New Iceland. "You requested my presence, mistress."

Aliyah steepled her fingers. "Tell me everything you know about the dark-haired one, the one the men call Wolf."

Anxiety grabbed her chest but Fatin held her face impassive. "Is there a problem?"

Without answering, Aliyah raised a brow. "Have you kept anything from me?"

*Just that he's a prince.* "The men elected him their leader."

"Why was that? Do you know?"

"He's large, even for one of them. Perhaps they fear him."

"Hakon is his match in size. Why didn't they turn to him instead?"

"I don't know, except that Eirik isn't rash." Her shoulder lifted and fell. "They were watched while aboard the ship, but there wasn't a lot of communication among them. They were kept drugged for the most part to keep them from harming themselves by beating at their cages."

Aliyah nodded. "I've had a request for his presence in the *saray* for a special event. I have to know if he's suited. His manners seem a step above . . ."

"He's intelligent."

"And skilled as a lover," Aliyah, said, her glance sliding away. "The women were quick to praise his ability." When her gaze swung back, she locked on Fatin's expression.

Fatin's cheeks burned as Aliyah studied her reaction.

"I know that I placed you in a delicate situation last night," she said, her tone unapologetic. "But I needed to know how the men would react when they were still so new to the Garden. You were the focus of their attention." She waved a slender hand. "I had to know that they could restrain themselves from violence. Our clientele likes savagery in their sexual playmates, but they also want to know that at the end of the night they will be safe."

Fatin cleared her throat, wanting to change the direction of the conversation. If Aliyah commented on Eirik's harsh lovemaking, she wasn't sure she could maintain a calm facade. "Was there anything else you wanted?" *What about the audience you promised?*

"You wish to see your sister."

Fatin grew still, trying her best not to let Aliyah see how much she wanted this. "Yes, if it's not an inconvenience, ma'am. And I'm willing to pay."

"You can't afford an hour of her time. But I'll allow you to see her, no payment required." A sly smile grew. "If you'll do one more thing for me."

"Of course," Fatin said, schooling her face into a placid mask to hide her disappointment.

"Be in the men's salon tonight. They will be playing pirates for the women."

Fatin groaned at the thought of anyone convincing the stubborn Vikings to play dress-up for the clientele. "Do you think that's wise? You saw how they acted last night to wearing the loin skirt."

"Like animals, I know." A husky chuckle escaped her twitching lips. "And I think that so long as we can keep them aroused, they will be just as barbaric tonight."

Surprise overwhelmed Fatin's control and her eyebrows shot up. "The take was that good?"

Aliyah laughed. "Each is worth his weight in pure light. Do this for me tonight, and you will be allowed into the *saray* tomorrow when you come back. You won't have to await my pleasure."

Not what she'd wanted, but still better than she had a right to expect of the unpredictable Aliyah.

"I will leave instructions that you're to have the freedom of the chambers. Discover what you can about the dark one they call Wolf."

"You won't be present?" Surprise flashed through her.

"I'll be busy. In the *saray*."

Fatin's stomach lurched. She'd be expected to mingle with the Vikings, but without protection from Eirik or even Aliyah's presence to keep them in check. How odd was it that she looked to Eirik for help? But he'd intervened twice now on her behalf.

Still, she knew this was an invitation she couldn't refuse. She bowed her head. "Thank you for your generosity."

"You will have your own costume. Michael will give it to you, and he will take you to the *medica* before you leave. We can't have you moving around like an old woman or with such an ugly bruise on your face. Tonight, you are free to partake of any male you wish." Aliyah waved her hand, dismissing her.

*Partake of any male you wish* . . . Only the one she wanted wouldn't be there. Fatin managed a tight smile and let herself out the door, her mind racing, glad she hadn't blurted out that she had a Norsewoman for sale. Not just yet. That bit of news would be worth another audience should she need it.

As Michael sidled up beside her, a satchel in one hand, she cursed silently that she still didn't know how she'd sneak Baraq inside. Already, she regretted the fact she wouldn't have someone watching her back that night, even a Helio in love with a Viking.

# Nine

"Why so tense, lover?"

Eirik ignored the sultry voice tickling his ear, but he drew a deep breath and forced his body to relax. If he was tense, the reaction was because he was bored and restless like he'd never been in his entire life. A man accustomed to action, his confinement, even in such luxurious surroundings, was wearing thin.

This night, he lay on his side on a legless couch close to the floor and surveyed a scene straight out of a decadent dream.

Musicians, sitting out of sight behind a filmy screen, played twangy, stringed instruments, accompanied by a skin drum and a musician clicking small metallic discs that clinked together like coins. The rhythm and the song attuned to the throb of his heartbeat and the pulse at his loins, pulling him ever so slowly and reluctantly toward arousal.

The lighting in the salon was low, ore gleaming behind gold

mesh screens to mute its brightness, increasing the intimacy of a stage set for seduction.

Here the decor reflected all the succulent, soft colors of a woman's intimate flesh. Deep pinks, dark rose, and an aroused red, interspersed with flecks of gold, covered the seats and cushions. The walls were a warm buff with a hint of blush—like so many of the women's cheeks this night. Gold and bronze fixtures hinted at the expense of this special salon, without the garishness of the men's salon.

Male and female thralls were hard to separate from their patrons, except for the unusual beauty of every thrall here. Everyone was perfumed, bathed, and costumed.

Across from him, Hakon, dressed in white ruffled shirt and leather trousers, stretched on another low, silk-upholstered couch set on the floor, with a woman lying between his legs and another with her back against his chest, both feeding him by hand. Hakon lifted his chin to Eirik, and then gave a wicked waggle of his eyebrows, making the women giggle.

Eirik snorted, relieved Hakon had heeded his warning to behave this night, and resumed scanning the rest of the room.

Couches were arranged in a large circle, with one cushioned, backless platform in the center covered with swaths of bright gold and red silk.

Satin bolster cushions supported his back as he lazily trailed his fingers over a huge tray of succulent fruit and an assortment of cheeses and breads, large enough it stretched his length and high enough that he couldn't have eaten the artfully arranged manna in a month.

A goblet of wine sat on a low table nearby, but he didn't trust drinking it, instead taking his liquid from the fruit he ate.

A finger trailed down his cheek as he took another bite. "Don't they feed you?"

He grunted, and then turned to give his current companion a thin smile. "My appetite is endless, madam," he said dryly, not bothering to infuse a seductive note. However, the woman stretched behind him didn't appear the least put off as her greedy gaze raked his body time and again and her hands roamed freely.

Her generous mouth stretched into a smile that displayed a scarily white row of perfect teeth. The muted gold lighting in the chamber was kind to the woman, fading the fine lines around her eyes and mouth. She wasn't unattractive, but he wondered if she thought a man would be interested only if she wore all of her riches. Her arms were weighted with thick gold bangles, her neck hidden by a large ruby-colored stone and lengths of white beads with a luminescent glow. Every time she laughed or turned her head, her earrings jangled.

He'd have to strip her of her jewelry before he kissed her or risk getting caught in her golden trap.

Her name was Livia, and she was wife to one of the ruling council members, the head of PG, which explained her wealth.

What she wanted with him was also apparent. Although not too old to be infertile, it wasn't likely that her main purpose was to fill her womb with a Viking's get.

An interesting development that had his head spinning with possibilities. Could a friendship be cultivated with her that might lead to another path for freedom?

Inwardly, he shuddered at her avid stare. She'd been all over him the moment he'd entered the cloistered salon. His plans to ferret out the truth of Fatin's claim of a sister living inside the *saray* were dashed because he hadn't had a chance to approach any of the women living here before the salon had filled with clients.

For the first time that evening he was glad of the costume he wore. Satin pants that laced up his legs. An embroidered white blouse with poufy sleeves that dripped lace over his wrists. He'd groaned when he'd been presented with the pirate's garb, but at least a layer of cloth lay between him and the incessant scratch of Livia's long, tapered nails.

Her hand grazed over his cock again, then cupped it, sliding up and down his length. And, dammit to Hel, that insatiable part of him filled.

Her laugh was a husky growl. "Tell me all the things you will do to please me tonight, Viking."

Keeping the room in his sights, he murmured, "Madam, if I must tell you, then where will be the surprise?"

"I find anticipation sparks a fire." A sharpened nail scratched across his mouth. "And I love to hear you speak. The harshness of your tongue makes me tremble. Your language is so guttural. So crude."

Aiming a half-lidded glance her way, he grunted, moved to laughter for the first time this night. "Do you hope that I will be equally as harsh and crude when I make love to you?"

"A woman can only hope." Her chest rose, nipples scraping his back. "What is your word for darling?"

"*Elskling.*"

Her breath gusted against his ear. "And for whore?"

"*Hóra.*"

He didn't ask which word aroused her more. She bit the lobe of his ear, and he forced a groan, then turned to let her kiss him.

"You can have me any way you want, Norseman," she whispered against his mouth.

So he was to pretend that she was the whore rather the other way around. An act he could perform. He growled and rolled, forcing her onto her back and crawling over her while she giggled like a younger woman.

He nipped at her ear. "Tell me, ma'am, does your husband mind that you play with other men?"

She laughed and gripped his chin to turn his head toward a middle-aged man sandwiched between two young women who were laughingly chewing at the laces on his pants with their teeth.

"Your husband, I take it?"

"We have an understanding that works quite well. If he plays, so do I, but only where I can watch."

The music halted, a lone string warbling into silence.

Eirik lifted his head. A rustling at the doorway leading from the women's quarters sounded a moment before a slender figure stepped through it.

Her dark head was bent, her hands clasped in front. She was dressed in a long, nearly transparent amber skirt that pulled against her perfect curves with each step, revealing long, slim legs and a luscious hint of a cleft. A gold and brown feathered cape draped around her shoulders, which seemed odd given the warm temperature of the room.

He darted a glance around the salon. All gazes were on the woman's entrance, men sitting forward on their sofas, women narrowing their gazes.

And they should be jealous. She was exquisite—pale tan, unblemished skin, thick, silky black hair. A near replica of another winsome beauty who drove him mad. When the woman raised her eyes, however, his breath held. Candlelight caught and reflected against her irises, lending them a golden glow.

When she neared the empty sofa at the center, the brown and black stole around her shoulders opened on its own, seeming to expand, then flap downward, before arching like wings at her back, exposing her bared midriff and the thin strap of gold silk that enclosed her breasts.

His jaw must have dropped, because the woman pinned beneath

him tipped his chin to close his mouth. "My handsome wolf, have you never seen an *avisian*?"

Unable to look away, he shook his head.

"She's a remnant of the feral experiments. A meshing of human and animal DNA." Livia licked his lobe and continued, "She's nearly all human, except for her eyes and those wings. Poor thing. Many ferals can pass as human. Life's kinder when they can, although breeding with them is strictly prohibited."

"*Avisian*? She's part bird?"

Livia turned to stare at the woman sitting quietly in the center of the room, while whispers stirred around her. "She's a Falcon. Her name is Zarah Sahin. 'Sahin' means falcon, her designation for the census as much as a surname. Lovely, isn't she? Zarah is the Garden's greatest prize. The things she can do with those wings..." The woman sighed, and then giggled at his stare. "If you like, I can arrange a *tria*. You can experience it for yourself."

"A *tria*?"

"A threesome, my love. You may have her. I can afford it."

He shook his head. Trying to think. Fatin's sister lived in this *saray*, and the only woman close enough in resemblance—height, skin and hair color, the shape of her lush mouth, was this... half-animal woman. It couldn't be. But his gut told him it was true. Could she be a full sister to Fatin?

Zarah Sahin blinked and glanced his way. Not a flicker of emotion showed on her face as he continued to stare.

"Viking, you're boring me."

Eirik glanced down to see a pout forming on Livia's painted mouth. He stifled a sigh. "I'm sorry, madam. But we haven't such... oddities on my world." He forced his gaze to remain on the woman who slipped her hand inside his shirt and circled a nipple with the pad of her forefinger.

Her thighs clasped his hips, and she rolled her own to grind against his cock. "Tell me about your world. I hear it's numbingly cold." She trailed another finger through the sweat beading his brow. "However do you keep warm?"

"We wear thick fur."

"Even when you sleep?"

"We huddle together. Several to a bed for warmth," he said. Not exactly a lie. Sometimes, they did indeed, but for pleasure, not necessity.

"And if one grows . . . uncomfortable?"

He let his eyelids droop and forced his voice to a husky note. "Our women oblige us in all things."

"Truly?" she said, sounding breathless.

No, but for his purpose now . . . "Yes. And they are happy to do so."

"The reward is so great?"

He pushed her hand between their bodies, down to his cock, and held it tight against himself as his sex stirred and filled. Not due solely to her attraction, but because he remembered just such a night. Wedged between two tall, leggy blondes who sought to warm him in the sweetest way possible. "What do you think? Would they be disappointed?"

Her breath blew between pursed lips.

He bent and sucked her lips, pulling on the lower until she moaned. "There are buttons at the placket of these pants. Unbutton them with your tongue and teeth." Then he rolled to his side and pushed on the top of her head, forcing her down his body—not that she fought him.

Chuckling, she agreeably scooted down. Her mouth kissed him through his shirt, and then she licked him through the silk trousers before going to work on the buttons closing the flap at the front.

While she eagerly opened the buttons, he glanced back at the bird woman. She still sat in the center of the sofa, her gaze unblinking.

"She can be yours . . ."

He jerked toward Aliyah, who perched her perfect ass on the back of his seat and stared down into his face. Nothing in her sedate features gave away her thoughts.

"As you can see, I'm already engaged, mistress."

"Livia won't mind adding a third, will you, dear?"

Livia lifted her rosy face. "I've already offered Zarah, but he didn't seem moved."

"Perhaps he's hesitant because he's never seen an *avisian* before." Aliyah's eyebrow lifted. "Is she your first, Viking?"

He glanced at the pretty bird who sat near enough she had to hear them speaking, but gave no outward response. Was her intellect stunted by her bird DNA? She seemed so calm. So distant from her surroundings.

If he could get near enough to question her quietly . . .

However, if he did accept this *tria* and discovered she was Fatin's sister, how could he prevent having to take her? Although Fatin wasn't his lover, wasn't someone he even particularly liked, he remembered the quiet horror mirrored in her eyes as she'd talked about the sister she wanted to save.

The thought of being just another of the men Zarah must accept in her bed left him uneasy. She was beautiful. Ethereal. And if she were also simple, he'd balk for sure. The act would be like making love to a child.

"He thinks too hard, this one," Livia said, stroking his cock again. "A thrall as lovely as this one shouldn't have to worry about a single thing."

Eirik grimaced at the description. "Lovely" wasn't something he'd ever been called before. And to be spoken of as though he were a dumb, inanimate object insulted his manhood and heritage.

Aliyah laughed. "Beware of challenging him. He will leave you legless with fatigue."

Livia arched a thin, dark brow. "Is that meant as a deterrent?"

Aliyah's laughter trailed off into soft chuckles. "The decision is yours, Livia. Although your husband may be jealous, I'll offer you first taste of Zarah this night."

"I think I'd like to see how these two will play together." Livia gave an exaggerated shiver. "They're both so beautiful and *exotic*."

"Just what I was thinking." Aliyah inclined her head. "It is done." She turned to the pretty Falcon. "Zarah, dear, take them to your quarters."

The Falcon's eyelids fluttered. Her amber gaze lighted on Eirik and stayed.

Intelligence was there. So was an edge of anger, which she quickly blinked away.

Feeling a little less alarmed, he followed the women as they trailed through the salon. Passing Hakon, he gave his second a quick warning glare to behave.

Hakon's eyebrows were raised high, his head turning from the Falcon back to Eirik.

Eirik shook his head and passed him by, thinking hard about how he might influence tonight's play. For certain, he wasn't going to frig with the bird even if she wasn't Fatin's sister.

Not because he wished to spare Fatin pain, he told himself.

That was the least of his concerns. And not because the thought of fucking a half-wild creature put him off. In truth, he was intrigued. No, Eirik resisted the idea because he knew how the creature must feel. Pressured to perform. Helpless to refuse. He'd find a way to spare her.

* * *

Fatin strolled through the Viking's salon, keeping well away from the men. The tenor of the evening wasn't as highly pitched as the previous night. Many of the same women were among those gathered, but they'd already made their choices. Calmer groupings of women surrounded each of the men, awaiting the moment when everything would take a carnal turn.

The Vikings were fed by hand, their pirate's clothing admired and primped with eager hands.

The fresh batch of clients had arrived dressed like pirates' whores, just as she was, low-cut blouses hanging on the tips of their breasts.

The men played at exposing the women with casual touches that shifted the edges of their blouses. Then they bent to plant kisses on ripe, beaded nipples, much to the ladies' delight.

Their full skirts made for another sort of sport as the Vikings flipped them up for a spank or a casual caress, and played at ravishing the women.

Feeling faintly nauseated by the display, Fatin grabbed a bunch of grapes from the buffet and idly popped them into her mouth. Then she eyed the entrances, the guards, and wondered how easily she might overcome one of them and steal his uniform . . .

Only she was in no shape to do the deed herself. Although the *medica* had used heated wands and liniments to ease the bruising enough that it didn't show, she was still stiff and her ribs hurt when she breathed hard.

Still, she'd have something to report when she returned to Baraq and Birget. She'd found a hole in security aboard the tram that they could take advantage of to sneak inside the compound. Perhaps Birget wouldn't need to place herself in a risky situation after all.

Fatin's steps slowed as she realized that she was already looking at Baraq and Birget as accomplices, rather than just another set of keepers. She'd do well to remember that she had her own priorities. If theirs all aligned, well and good. If not, she'd have to strike out on her own again. Just as she had with the pirate Roxana. The partner she'd duped. The one whose stolen ship sat at dock, awaiting her next venture.

Her breaths felt constricted, as much from the web of deception she'd woven tightly around herself as from any bruised ribs.

She sat on the ledge of a window and turned her back to the room, dragging in the cloyingly sweet night air. Roses and gardenias blended into a sickly perfume, one she'd breathed every night she'd lived within the compound.

The succulent sounds of openmouthed kisses and fingers twiddling cunts beneath skirts fed the sickness in her soul. *Zarah, where are you?* She knew the location of the *saray*. How hard would it be to slip into the darkness and find her—just to look and assure herself that Zarah was well?

Surreptitiously, she glanced around the salon, but the guards at the doors were watching the men, not her. With a slow move, she slipped her legs over the ledge of the window and dropped silently to the ground.

She kept to the side of the building, staying beneath the curtain of tall plants hugging the walls. Not until she reached the edge of the building did she dart from foliage to a fountain, crouching low but moving swiftly to keep from being too long on any one screen of the surveillance monitors. She darted from a path to a wooded copse, then followed the edge of it to the next edifice—the walled compound of the exotic's *saray*. Here, she knew the location of footholds in the walls, outcroppings of foundation stones and decorative blocks with sharp edges that she could curl her toes around.

Nerves taut, she kicked off her boots and began to climb. Once she slipped a knee over the top of the wall, she hunkered low and crawled to a point opposite the window into what had been Zarah's room. It wasn't changed much since she'd shared that chamber, other than new silks for the bedcovers.

Catching her breath, she lay on the wall, hugging the rim, and waited.

Familiar sounds of music floated in the air. The same old love songs meant to inspire passion. They grated on her nerves. Low murmurs of conversation were punctuated by soft laughter.

This wasn't the raucous gathering inside the men's quarters. Here, patrons were offered a more genteel experience. One where strokes of feathers or the plying of strong hands in a sensual massage were foreplay. Here a client wouldn't expect to be thrown over a shoulder and carried off to a couch for a quick tumble in view of an entire room of people.

Fatin winced at the memory of what she and Eirik had been forced to do. Not that she truly regretted a single moment of what had transpired. He'd turned something ugly and tawdry into a sensual scene that would haunt her for a long, long time.

The door into the bedroom opened.

Fatin raised her head, and her heart tripped as Zarah appeared inside it, as sedate and beautiful as ever.

Her sister stepped over the threshold and stood aside as Aliyah and a woman in costume entered, and then a tall, brawny man in rumpled pirate's garb followed them inside.

When the man turned, giving her a full view of his face, Fatin's heart stopped for just a moment, and then thundered hard against her chest. *No, no! Not him.*

And although she knew Eirik had no choice, that her sister had none as well, she couldn't stop the welling of resentment that flowed through her and left her shaking.

As odd as that sounded, she'd begun to think of him as hers. No matter that he had likely plowed a deep furrow through the gathering of women the previous night. That didn't touch her. They were patrons. Faceless whores. But this was too close. This made her chest feel brittle. Made her fingers curl into claws. How could she be angry with either of them? She had no right. They had no choice.

Her glance went back to her sister. Zarah looked much the same as she had four years ago. Outwardly, she was healthy, her skin glowed, her hair shown like an inky sky brightened by starlight flickering in the muted lighting.

Her expression, however, was dull, as though her life held little joy.

Fatin had been the one to coax a smile from her. Had prodded and poked to get her angry. Had sung to her and brought her to tears because she possessed their mother's lilting, soprano voice.

Had she been cruel when she'd sought her own freedom? She'd told Zarah that one of them had to be first in order to get work and earn the thrall-price for the other.

Her sister hadn't pleaded to be the one, and Fatin had selfishly taken it as assent for her plan, eager as she'd been to quit the Garden. *Using their pooled funds.*

However, looking at her sister now, she knew the truth. Her sister believed Fatin had abandoned her.

A pain shot through her chest. She had to get closer. Had to find a way to let Zarah know that she hadn't forgotten her promise.

She edged one leg over the side of the wall, then the other, and dropped silently to the ground.

# *Ten*

Eirik closed Zarah's chamber door, then leaned against it, still pondering his problem. For the first time that night, he felt charged with something other than irritation or grudging lust. Here was a problem that required a bit of strategy. Not exactly the sort of engagement he preferred, but a battle nonetheless.

He thought of Dagr and nearly smiled at the thought of his grim, serious brother at the mercy of the women. Would Dagr have ever been duped in the first place, his mind clouded by desire?

Eirik shook his head. Knowing Dagr, his brother wouldn't have accepted the female in his bed at the mining camp. He'd have stayed in the mine, inspecting every cavern, speaking with every worker to assure his comfort before his own.

Perhaps he deserved this fate. Maybe Odin himself had set this task before him to make him a better man, a better leader. He certainly hoped he'd get the chance to prove that fact.

Livia strode toward the large, sumptuous bed, her lithe body swaying, a slight twitch to her firm ass. An unmistakable invitation.

Without waiting to be given leave to do so, she sat on the edge of the wine-colored coverlet and smoothed her hands over the cloth. Her cosmetics-enhanced complexion glowed with the blood surging throughout her body. Her nipples poked at the front of her white cotton blouse. Her gaze swept over Eirik, and she gave him a hungry look, but he withheld a reaction.

Undeterred, her look flitted to the whore-mistress. "Aliyah," she said, stroking the silk, "you must tell me where you shop. This is so soft it's sinful."

Aliyah smiled. "Only the best for my Zarah." She hovered near the Falcon, a hand floating over the edge of one of Zarah's tightly furled wings.

Despite the tension evident in her wings, Zarah's expression remained set in a calm mask, although Eirik thought he detected a slight lifting of her lip.

"Darling," Aliyah said, stroking her feathers, "you can disrobe."

"I'll undress her," Eirik said, straightening from the door. "Are you staying, mistress?"

Aliyah looked tempted, but darted a glance to Livia, whose eyebrow arched. She demurred with a soft laugh. "I have others to attend. It's a busy night. I'll leave you all to play."

Eirik bowed as she passed. Her hand touched his shoulder, sharp fingernails digging into the skin. Leaning close, she said, "Don't disappoint. Play well and your share will be generous."

He gave her a nod, silently cursing the bitch, but kept his face clear of all emotion when he walked to Zarah, whose wide, unblinking eyes locked with his.

Keeping Livia in his line of sight, he angled Zarah so that the

Helio woman could see what he did, but his face would be turned away.

He attacked the knot between Zarah's breasts. "I am new," he murmured quietly, pretending to fumble with the tie.

"I had heard Vikings have joined us," she said, her tone even.

"We were captured on our home world."

"I am sorry," she whispered. "I know what it is to be far from home."

He dropped his voice again while he pretended to nuzzle her neck. "A wily bounty hunter, a former thrall, from here I believe, captured us. You might know her." He pulled back to watch her face.

Her eyes betrayed nothing, not even a gleam of curiosity, but her breaths deepened, lifting her chest against his fingers.

"Don't you want to know her name?" he asked softly, dropping his hand from the knot.

She gave a quick, curt nod.

"Her name is Fatin."

Had he not been standing so near, he never would have detected the lightning-quick catch of her breath. He moved closer and bent to her ear. "She says she has a sister here. Is it you?" He slid his hand beneath her chin to cup it and raise her face.

"Are you here seeking revenge?" she whispered.

Eirik shook his head. "Not against you. You had no part in my capture. I hold no grudge against you."

The first glimmer of deep emotion was there in her golden depths. A welling of tears.

He bent and kissed her mouth. Just a soft, innocent touch. "She swears she works to free you," he said against her lips.

A deep, ragged breath rattled through her chest, and her wings snapped outward, and then closed around them both, heavenly soft feathers and wispy down surrounding them. Their movement soothed over his skin in the softest caress. Her head fell against his chest, and her arms slid around his waist.

Inside the blind she'd provided, he held her close, petting her back, her shoulders, as she fought to even her breathing.

When at last she raised her head, a radiant smile stretched across her face, and in spite of his vow, his sex stirred.

A snapping of a twig sounded from outside the window, and he glanced up. At one side of the casing, out of sight of Livia, he glimpsed Fatin's face. Silvered by moonlight, her skin was pale, her eyes glittering. Only the thinning of her full mouth gave a hint that it wasn't sorrow but anger that filled her eyes.

*Sweet Fatin, what are you doing here?* He gave her a narrowed glare, tilted his head for her to leave, but she shook hers, glaring daggers back at him.

He couldn't tell Zarah that her sister was near. Not and have a hope that he could keep Fatin's presence a secret from Livia as well. He kissed Zarah's forehead. "We still have a game to play," he murmured.

Her hand sought his, and then her wings flared outward and settled gracefully behind her.

Livia's breath sighed. "Gorgeous!" she said, clapping her hands. "I knew you two would be beautiful together. Now, come join me."

Zarah gave him a shy smile, angling her head to gaze from beneath her eyelashes.

He nearly moaned aloud. The invitation was there. But Fatin's presence put a damper on his ardor. How would he counter it and make sure that his cock sought mooring in only Livia's body?

At the bed, he held Zarah's hand while she knelt on the mattress. Then he stood back and slowly folded his arms over his chest. When both women glanced up, he set his features into a mask of displeasure. "Wenches!"

Livia giggled. "Oh, my!"

"Turn me back fer a second," he said, scowling and exaggerating a pirate's brogue, "and both ye wee harlots are lazin' about me bed!"

Zarah's mouth twitched. Her eyes danced with delight.

The sight of that slight smile infused him with happiness because he didn't think she did it much.

Livia giggled again. "We only seek to warm our bodies. We await your pleasure, sir pirate."

"Ah." He shook his head in mock disappointment. "I work hard for me wee pot o' ore. But never let it be said I'm not a generous man. I'll not intrude on yer little tryst."

Zarah's eyebrows shot up, and she stared from him to Livia's delighted face.

Keeping his features stern, he backed up to the windowsill and sat, blocking Fatin's view of the room. "Shouldn't have to tell ye twice."

Livia gave him a wink, then turned to Zarah and finished opening the knot he'd wrestled with.

He let out an exaggerated groan at the sight of her perfect breasts, and then leaned back. "Fatin," he whispered out of the side of his mouth. "What do you think you're doing here?"

"I needed to see her." Fatin's voice was small, but sullen. Her sharp gaze, when he glanced her way, could have flayed a man's skin.

"I'm assuming you snuck past the guards?"

"Of course."

"You'll have to share with me how you managed that," he muttered.

"They aren't watching me that closely." Her fingers touched his arm, hesitantly. "Eirik?"

To cool his anger, he drew in a deep breath. She'd taken a horrible chance with her own safety. "Yes, Fatin?"

"Are you going to fuck her?"

Although surly, her voice held a breathless note. At the telling revelation, he sighed. "I'll do my best to avoid it."

Her fingers cupped his elbow, and then drew away. "Will you pass her a message?"

"What would you have me say?"

"That I love her." She paused, then let out a sigh. "And I *will* come for her."

He gave a short nod. "You'd best disappear before you're caught."

"I thought you liked being watched."

That bitter note made him shift his seat. He leaned closer, bending his head toward hers while he kept the two women stroking each other's skin in sight. "Neither of us is comfortable with this, Fatin. Spare yourself."

Her hand snuck inside his. Small and warm. Fingertips rougher than those of the pampered women on the bed.

His throat tightened and he gave them a squeeze. "Go."

"Be gentle with her," Fatin said, an echo of pleading in her voice. "She's not . . . like me."

When he turned his head, she was gone. What had she meant? *Not like me?* Because one was a bird and one was not? Or because one was an innocent, despite her profession, and Fatin was very far from innocent?

"Sir piiraaate . . ."

The trill of Livia's voice set his teeth on edge, but he pasted on a smile and pushed away from the windowsill. Time enough later to discover the truth about sweet Fatin. Two naked women with lust in their eyes waited to dance.


Fatin climbed the wall again, dropped to the ground, and sped into the woods, her mind filled with images—her sister's lovely, sad face forced into a smile while she played with the nipples of the

Helio whore; Eirik in pirate's garb, compassion gleaming in his eyes—for her, Fatin. But what did it mean? Fatin wasn't very smart reading others' emotions. She'd done her best to sublimate her own for years, to avoid reading pity or lust in another's eyes. She wished now that she hadn't been so studiously oblivious.

Something in his expression after he'd scolded her for being there had been different. Had made her feel warm and protected. Best not to read too much into it or she'd drive herself mad with regrets.

As she approached the men's salon, she heard the stomp of booted feet on the pathway between her and the men's quarters.

Dammit, she couldn't hide in here. If one of the guards looked her way, he might spot her with his night-vision visor. And if she appeared to be hiding, she didn't know how she'd explain herself. *Better to brazen it out.* She took a deep breath and stepped out onto the path.

A thickset guard halted in front of her. His helmeted head angled downward to scan her body. "You shouldn't be out here, bounty hunter."

His angry drawl set her teeth on edge. "I was given freedom of the grounds."

"It's dark," he said, his voice edging toward a growl. "I might have mistaken you for a thrall trying to make a run for it. I might have poked you with my spear."

She forced a laugh, but it was high-pitched, tightened by nerves. "And where would a thrall go?"

His head turned, peering through his visor into the woods beyond her. "You alone?"

The way he said those two words sent cold skating down her spine. "There's no one with me. I wanted fresh air. The salon stinks of sweat and sex."

"Something you should be used to." The deepened rumble held an ugly note.

She shivered and gave him a thin smile. "I'll head back inside. Thanks for your concern."

A hand grabbed her arm, fingers digging deep. "Not so fast."

She stilled, her mind racing as his hand swept up, then slipped across to cup her breast. His thick fingers pinched her hard.

Knowing that running would only fan his arousal, Fatin stood her ground and tried to push away his hand. "You shouldn't risk Aliyah's anger. She doesn't like the staff mingling with the guests."

He cupped her again. "You're not exactly a guest, now, are you? And you wouldn't want the mistress to know you were sneaking around outside."

Her stomach plummeted. "You're paid to patrol, not to molest visitors."

"We'll just have to be quick, then. Into the woods with you. There's no surveillance here." A chuckle sounded. "No one will bother us."

His hand tightened, then slipped to her arm. He pushed her backward. Then he reached for the button on the side of his visor. A glimmer of light shone behind the dark mirrored surface, and then blinked out.

He'd turned off the visor and the feed to the surveillance team. They were truly alone now. A knot grabbed her stomach. She shook off his hand. "The ground's uneven. I'd rather walk under my own steam than have us both trip." She turned to lead the way as his hand slid from her arm.

"I haven't seen your face," she said, keeping her voice lazy and sultry. "I might be more amenable to play if you'd take off that visor."

"My face isn't what's going to fuck you."

She forced herself not to react while sheer terror shuddered through her. "Still, I might want a kiss. Something to get me warmed up. Sliding into a dry hole won't be so pleasant for you." She stopped beside a large tree with a low, horizontal branch. With a wiggle, she sat atop the limb and pulled down the top of her peasant's blouse, baring her breasts.

His helmeted head dipped, his hands reached for her, but she batted them away. "The visor. I'd like a kiss, here." Then she cupped her breast and plucked the nipple, drawing it to a point and releasing it.

He reached up and unstrapped the helmet, sliding it off his head. His face was brutish, his nose askew. His eyes were small and piglike. His smile was a lecherous stretch of thin lips. Two gold teeth sparkled.

In a flash, he dropped the helmet and reached for her again, hands twisting her breasts, his body trapping her thighs against the thick branch beneath her.

Wincing as he managed to find every bruised rib, she snuggled closer, sliding her hands along his sides, up and then down, as he rutted his cock between her legs.

Swallowing bile, she stroked him again and touched the leather of his holster. She quickly tugged the snap and pulled his stun gun free.

When she stuck it in his side, he froze. "Bitch!"

"Fucker!"

His arms closed around her back to hug her hard. Did he think she'd care whether she shared the blast? Better that than to suffer his rape.

She pulled the trigger, then felt the painful jolt arc through her body. Her jaw snapped; her muscles went rigid.

He stiffened like a board, body jerking, but then slid down her body, crumpling at her feet.

Still quivering in the aftermath, she forced her body into action. With a jerky move, she tugged up her blouse, bent and scooped up the helmet, then bolted from the woods, hoping he'd be too afraid of admitting just how he'd been overcome to report the incident and the loss.

Slipping through the door of the salon, she hid the helmet beneath the draping of one of the buffet tables, straightened her stretched bodice again, and walked back into the center of the room. Away from any door where she might be snatched without being noticed.

The salon was nearly empty. The few Vikings who hadn't elected to retire to the private chambers were eagerly bouncing women on their laps or swallowing breasts.

Her lips curled in disgust. Were all men pigs?

"How does a wench as comely as yerself manage to be alone?"

A gasp escaped. She spun to find one of the younger Vikings, one whose name escaped her, standing right behind her.

Dressed in pirate's garb, he touched his cocked eyebrow and executed a short bow.

She jutted her chin. "This wench has more particular tastes."

His arm snaked out and wrapped around her ribs.

"Yii." She cried out, hissing between clenched teeth.

In an instant, he dropped his arm, a frown bisecting his brows. "Not that I blame the man, but I've never harmed a woman. I won't start with you."

Surprised at his even tone, she studied him. Brown-haired with gray eyes. Barely out of his teens. A pang of guilt struck her. What had she been thinking to take one so young? "Thank you," she mumbled, and made to move around him.

But he stepped to the side, blocking her path, gaze narrow and scathing. "Eirik said to watch for you." By his tone, he was anything but happy with the duty. "To make sure you weren't harmed."

"And you'd follow his orders, despite the anger I see in you? Why?"

"Because we've chosen him to be our leader."

She nodded, wishing he'd move away. She didn't need this young man hovering. "How have you managed to be unclaimed by the women here?"

With a quirk of an eyebrow, he gave a thin-lipped smile. "I stayed a long time in the latrine. The woman who requested me finally grew tired of waiting, and is now with Garm."

Fatin relented. Maybe it wouldn't be a bad idea to have him close. "I'm sorry. I don't remember your name."

"I am Kaun. Do you even remember my capture?" His lips twisted. "You stole me from my bed, and you don't remember?"

Her throat grew dry and she shook her head. "No, I'm sorry."

"I'm from the southern continent. Not a Wolfskin or a Bearshirt." His shoulders squared. "I am a *Drake*, a Dragon. You took only me."

"A *Drah-keh*." She drew a deep breath. His capture had been a challenge. She'd very nearly been caught herself. "I remember. I didn't stay long. Security was tight. As soon as I transported to your hamlet, I was chased. I hid in your chamber, but it was dark."

"I thought you were Lina, come to join me in bed," he said angrily.

"Your girl?"

"My wife," he bit out. A tic twitched in his jaw.

Her gaze dropped away from his stone-cold glare. He'd welcomed her, flipping back the covers in the darkness. Because he'd been an easy target of opportunity, she'd taken him in seconds, glad to be away from the remote southern kingdom. "You protect me, even though I ripped you away from your family? I swear I tried to take only single men."

"Three of us captives are wed. We have wives who must be insane with worry."

Coloring beneath his continued hard stare, she said stonily, "I will make this right."

"Woman, don't make promises you have no intentions or abilities to keep." His chest rose around a deep breath. "We can't just stand here. Let's seek a chamber where we can lie abed and pretend we tup."

"Of course."

Together, his hand at her elbow, they sought a chamber, walking past doors, some open, some locked, according to the patrons' preferences, until they found an empty one.

Inside, they turned from each other and stripped away their costumes.

Kaun strode to the bed and slipped beneath the covers. "Join me." He flipped the edge of the bedding and gave her a bitter smile.

Reading the pain in his eyes, she knew she had much to pay for. She'd considered only her own pain, her own misfortune. Never once did she consider the plight of the men whom she'd considered ruthless barbarians.

When she slid between the sheets, she snapped her fingers to dim the light. "They will watch," she whispered, moving closer to his side. "We must do more than sleep."

His curse was soft, but he rolled toward her, edging a thigh over hers, pressing his semierect staff against her hip. "How long must we do this?" he asked, his voice pitched low.

With his sex snuggling against her, she fought the urge to pull away. But they had a game to play. She laid a tentative hand atop his hip. "I don't know. Aliyah will want to know that I engaged in sex with someone or she'll be suspicious. Also, she gave me orders to find out more about the Wolf."

His lips grazed the top of her shoulder.

She feigned a loud moan, which caused his chest to shake against hers, even though his cock was growing more rigid by the second.

Her fingers combed through his hair, and she dug her head into the pillow, feigning ecstasy. "What other orders did Eirik give you?"

"To keep you safe," he said, his voice muffled against her skin. "Unmolested."

She snorted.

He nipped her breast. "I'm not to enjoy the comfort of your woman's channel."

Warm lips on her skin caused a pleasant, sensual stirring inside her. "No fucking?" she asked, her tone wry because that left so many other things on the table to try.

"No fucking."

Her fingers curled around his ears and pulled. "I have to ask my questions."

His teeth clamped around a nipple and bit.

Hard enough to make her gasp.

"Ask away. Loud enough for them to hear. Then dive beneath the covers."

She grunted. "Why don't you?"

"Because I am the one you wronged." He smiled against her breast. "You deserve to lose a little dignity."

When his mouth glided across her chest to nip and suck her skin, she couldn't keep her reaction to his touch a secret. Her nipples bloomed, drawing tight like sun-dried raisins. "'Tis harder to feign the act than to just do it. And we must leave semen on the sheets."

"Then do it. I have a preference for a firm grip with a little twist at the end."

A gust of laughter surprised her.

His teeth flashed white in the darkness.

This one wasn't a rough barbarian, wasn't a womanizing lech. To survive, he'd lie abed with other women and pleasure them, but she could tell from the steadiness of his gaze that he hated this.

Her palm cupped his cheek. "I'm truly sorry," she said softly.

"'Tis good to hear. But I need more than words to soothe the anger boiling inside me, Fatin."

"Close your eyes." Her thumb grazed his jawline. "Pretend another soothes you. It's how I got through many a horrible night here."

"Don't think I won't tell every man here what I press upon you. Each one of them would do so much more to make you squirm."

"You want revenge. I get that. You're entitled."

His chest expanded around a deep breath, his lips thinned, and he scooted up her body, then rolled to his back, arching an eyebrow. "You have questions," he reminded her under his breath.

Fatin came over him, straddling his hips and pulling the covers up to her waist.

With a slow move, he reached for the edge and held them to keep their lower bodies hidden from the watchers.

Rolling her hips, she centered her slit over his cock and rubbed him forward and back, tossing back her hair and sighing loudly.

His mouth stretched into a tight grin as he played along. His gaze didn't veer from her swaying breasts.

She covered them with her palms and squeezed, then bit her lower lip. Her performance was for more than show; she needed the watchers enthralled so that they forgot about the lengthy conversation she'd just had, which they hadn't been able to hear.

When Aliyah asked them about what they'd observed, they'd fight smirks and rush to tell the high points of what Fatin wanted them to hear and see.

She leaned forward and braced her hands on his broad chest, pumping her hips to mimic fucking. Then she cleared her throat. "The one called Wolf, do you know him well?"

"Not as well as you," he said, narrow eyes glittering with mirth.

She banged his cock with the hard bone of her pubis. "Why did you choose him to lead you?"

His shrug was casual, but a hand clamped on her hip to keep her from being rough with him again. "We chose him," he said, his tone biting, "because he wasn't known to us, but seemed strong and calm in the face of everything that had befallen us."

"Do you know his family? What he was within his clan?"

"A mason, I heard. Working on the Wolfskin keep's curtain wall." His hands closed around her waist and he lifted her off his cock. "But why talk about him? You chose me this night."

Knowing he thought they'd shared enough with the watchers, she let him push her down the bed. By flipping her hand, she pulled the sheet over her head.

His laughter was low and husky. "Are you shy? We all saw how well you pleasured Wolf last night."

"Last night's demonstration served a purpose," she gritted out.

His fingers twisted in her hair as he pushed the top of her head lower. He bent his knees and closed them around her shoulders to keep her where he wanted her.

Hidden under the covers, Fatin made a face. Then smiled and cupped his balls in her hands. She gave them a squeeze and slight twist, which made him gasp, then growl. His knees eased their hold.

Now that she'd made her point, she licked her palm and began to massage his cock, working him with a practiced intent.

The sooner he came, the sooner they could stop this farce. She needed to get that helmet away before the staff found it when they replenished the tables.

"We've all noted the way he looks at you. Wolf," he said, his voice coming through, muffled by the sheet.

Fatin slowed the motion of her hand. "What do you mean? If a glance could kill, I'd have been dead several times over."

Through the sheet, he bracketed her face, and brought it directly over his cock.

"Not what we agreed on," she hissed.

"I but pretend, as you told me to."

Amused and annoyed, she bit the tip of his cock, but not deeply. Then she stroked her tongue over the place she'd bitten. What did it matter if she gave him ease? She swallowed the cap and resumed pumping her hand along his thick shaft.

His knees fell farther apart. His hands gripped her tighter. "His gaze follows you wherever you go. His face tightens. But it isn't anger. Hakon thinks he's soft for you."

Her chest filled with pleasure. "Hakon's an idiot."

"I've seen it too. Why else would he ask that you be protected?"

"So that he will have first taste of revenge."

"Perhaps. But think on it, Fatin. You know what he is. You know that a Viking, once his anger or his passion is aroused, will move mountains to achieve his goal. If you are now his goal . . ."

The thought was heady—more attractive to her than it should have been. But a lie. She sank her mouth deeply over his cock and quickened her strokes to finish him.

If she let him continue trying to convince her, she might begin to believe that more than hatred, more than sexual attraction, drew Eirik to her. But she knew the truth.

Fatin Sahin would never have a place in any human man's life.

# Eleven

Sweat beaded on Eirik's upper lip, and he licked it away. Watching Zarah pleasure Livia, his blood heated to a slow, aching boil.

Aside from the wings, watching the woman before him was like watching Fatin loving another woman. Soft dark hair, like sensuous, gliding fingers, slithered and stuck to the thin glaze of sweat on Livia's breasts. Rosy brown nipples beaded into sharp points and scraped across Livia's paler brown. His mouth watered, imagining them scraping his tongue.

A lush mouth opened and closed around a nipple, pulling it with rhythmic tugs he felt all the way to his toes. He couldn't look away. Not when the Falcon fluttered her wings behind her, moving the air to brush against the parts of Livia she'd wet with her tongue.

When she moved lower, nipping and sucking at Livia's taut abdomen, producing shivers and moans from the woman whose legs moved restlessly open and apart, Eirik struggled not to grasp his cock and stroke himself. He could imagine all too well what being pleasured by Zarah would feel like, to feel the slide of the soft down and the stroke of her golden feathers over his body.

However, mindful of his promise to Fatin—one he'd made because he courted her cooperation, he told himself—he fought his arousal, breathing deeply to calm his heart.

Too bad his cock wasn't quite so noble.

His sex stood at attention, tenting his satin pants. And because he was sweating, enclosed in so many sticky layers, he began to quietly disrobe.

Naked and much more comfortable, he thought on the fact that he'd gotten accustomed so quickly to his constant nudity. All the men, it seemed, were equally unabashed, treating their bodies, their arousal, with humor and a steadfast acceptance.

If he were home, he'd not remark on a man striding about with a cockstand—but only when the hour grew late and the children were abed. A joke, a gesture, soft laughter at the sight might occur, but there'd be a similar acceptance of a man's natural needs.

In fact, for him and his brother, their aggressive sexuality was something to be boasted, to be held up for all with pride. Their ability to breed being a necessity for their survival as the ruling family within the *Ulfhednar* clan.

While their family had ruled Thorshavn for several generations, their crown wasn't something assured. Each generation had to prove their continued strength of body and character. Every new day on their harsh planet was a test.

But had he already failed that test? Had his capture proven his unsuitability to succeed? His brother was the king now, but had never seemed disposed to take a wife or sire an heir of his own.

Eirik wasn't eager to assume the position. Brother to the ruler held its own obligations and benefits. He'd played hard, battled to prove his prowess, swived through most of the comely women within his own keep, but never with an eye toward usurping his brother or assuring his own future.

He loved Dagr. Wouldn't wish him harm. His brother had always seemed indomitable, a rugged, forceful man whose blunt ambitions were simply to keep his clan safe and healthy.

Now Eirik's love of pleasure seemed to have fated him to live out his days in its endless pursuit. Not his own pleasure, though. And there lay the rub.

Livia sighed loudly, drawing his attention.

Stretched on the bed, side by side, the two women touched and petted each other. Slender fingers stroking over soft curves, trailing down bellies that shivered with delight.

If Fatin's sister wasn't truly aroused, she was a consummate actress. Her darker nipples dimpled; her nude labia swelled. When Livia rubbed Zarah's clitoris with vigorous back-and-forth strokes, Zarah's wings extended and quivered. With her head thrown back, tiny, broken, birdlike cries leaked between her lips.

Eirik watched, caught by her splendor, and wondered if she pretended in order to please the patron or indulged herself for her own sanity. He couldn't imagine living for years in this environment and not becoming affected by the constant attention. The constant demand to be aroused, to touch, to love.

Fatin's hard outer shell was brittle and thin. What would she have been like if this place had not left its mark on her psyche? He'd worked hard to pierce the armor she'd erected. Unless her surrender was also part of an act, a game she'd learned here.

The women rolled together, thighs pressing against mounds. One wing stretched on the bed, and now both women lay atop it. Livia rubbed her back and ass against the feathers. "It's heaven. You've yet to revel in her, Viking."

Knowing that was his cue to join the party, he strode to the bed and knelt on the edge with one knee. His glance cut from Livia, whose languorous undulations and rosy cheeks proved her excitement, to Zarah, whose face, once again calm, was in stark contrast to the spiked breasts and the slick of feminine arousal that glazed her inner thighs.

Livia reached for his hand, then, cupping the back, guided his palm over the feathered edge of the wing Zarah had drawn up behind her. His fingers riffled the soft and silky feathers, which released a spicy citrus fragrance into the air. A blend of lemons and the white flowers in the garden.

The Falcon's breaths shortened. Her golden eyes blinked lazily, then opened wide to meet his stare.

With a gentle push, Livia guided his hand to her shoulder.

He was surprised to feel a soft, fine down cloaking the skin along the top, then around the back to where the wings jutted from between her shoulder blades. The down was the same warm, pale color as her skin, which explained why he hadn't noticed how far the down extended.

"Lovely, isn't it?" Livia said, catching his gaze and smiling.

"Yes," he said, smoothing his hand upward to cup the Falcon's chin.

Zarah's eyelids dipped. Her gaze slid to the side.

Eirik wondered how she felt, being on display like this. Touched as though she were a beautiful animal rather than a woman.

He wondered if the mix of bloods affected her mind as well, her emotions. She seemed so removed, so emotionally distant. Not something he could ever achieve. Not living here. Every day he spent inside these walls he grew angrier, more frustrated.

He'd not treat her like an object, like a novelty. Not speak of her in the third person as though she wasn't a person at all. Not until he knew her better.

Catching her gaze, he held it. "Zarah, don't you think our generous patron needs our attention?"

Livia's breath left her in a soft, delirious laugh. "Gods, Wolf, I thought you'd never get down to business."

Eirik lay beside Livia, opposite Zarah, whose hand stroked over the patron's nude folds. He moved closer, slid an arm beneath Livia, and pulled her against him, her back to his front, her head resting on his shoulder. Eirik brought his hand under her long, dark hair and pushed it up, baring her nape, then kissed her there, trailing his lips and tongue from her neck to her shoulder. At the same time, he centered her buttocks against his cock and rode the crevice, stoking his own arousal with her warm globes heating his length.

Zarah moved closer, kissed Livia into a low, aching moan, then raised her mouth to his. The veil of calm she wore slipped. Her gaze was dewy; her lips parted around shallow, excited breaths.

How did one disappoint an angel? He gave her a gentle kiss, rubbing his mouth over hers in small circles. Her tongue pushed against his lips, but he resisted, groaning, his cock digging harder between Livia's cheeks.

When Zarah bit his lower lip, his cock jerked, his mouth opened around a deep growl, and he stroked his tongue inside hers, bending toward her, over Livia, to ravage her mouth.

Gods, she tasted like honey. Kissed like a goddess—sweet, pure, silken heat. And because he knew she could make him forget his promise, he lifted Livia's thigh, dipped his hips, and speared into her woman's channel, fucking her while he continued to kiss the sister forbidden to him by his word and Fatin's sad, doe's eyes.

* * *

Fatin slid from the bed, not looking back at the man who lay with his legs splayed, cum sticking to his belly.

His eyelids drifted upward. His hard gaze speared her, then fell away.

Had he just remembered he had a wife? Did he feel shame? His couldn't begin to match her own.

She made her way to a stand beside the door and poured water from an urn into a basin and quietly washed.

*A whore's bath.* She dipped her hands into the water again, then let the water grow still. Moonlight shone on the surface. Her haunted reflection wavered. She'd been here so many times. After so many men.

She splashed the surface to erase her image, then dipped her hand into a pot of scented soap and scrubbed her hands together, sudsing to the elbows to remove the cum, the sweat, the scent of the man she'd just left. She hadn't come all that far in four years, after all.

Shivering, she picked up her costume and slipped out the door, pulling the loose-fitting gown over her head and dropping the corset on the ground as she made her way down the corridor to the salon.

She didn't pass anyone. Didn't see anyone at all in the common room. Acting as though she didn't have a single purpose in mind, she paused to eat a sliver of cheese and popped a grape into her mouth, then dropped the next one and bent to retrieve it, her hand fishing beneath the table for the helmet.

But it wasn't there.

She straightened and glanced around. Had the guard come searching for it? Or had the staff found it? "Damn, damn," she whispered furiously.

All for nothing. She stalked out of the building, heading straight for the tram, hoping the guard she'd knocked out wouldn't be waiting there with friends to punish her. But no gray uniforms lurked.

Waiting on the tram platform for the commuter to arrive, she avoided the bright lights, staying in the shadows as workers milled about, talking softly among themselves as they too killed time until the conveyance arrived to take them home.

A footstep scraped behind her, and she whirled, fists coming up. But it was Baraq, leaning toward her with a finger to his lips for her to keep silent, then drawing back into the shadows.

She faced the tracks again and glanced around. No one had noticed her alarm. No one watched. "What are you doing here?" she whispered harshly.

"Making sure you come back to us, bounty hunter," he said, his warm voice evenly pitched. "Too many places you could disappear, if you skipped our stop. Did you get your audience?"

Fatin shook her head. "No, but Aliyah said I can see my sister tomorrow."

He tsked. "She's playing you—you do know that?"

She wanted to ignore the cynicism in his tone, but shrugged. She already felt stupid enough after her disastrous day—the last thing she wanted was to have her nose rubbed in her many failures.

Strong hands landed on her shoulders, kneading them gently. "Fatin, you're wasting time," he whispered in her ear, "waiting on something you will never have. Aliyah will never release your sister, not so long as she can profit from her and force you to her will."

"I know. But I've lived so long in hope . . ." His grip tightened and she wished it didn't feel so good. She felt suddenly sapped of energy.

"We have to make plans now before anything befalls the men you abducted. This Adem. Can he help us?"

"I think so. But I don't know how quickly he'll be willing to act. He's waited for weeks for me to return as it is."

"How can he help?"

"He has friends inside the facility. And he has access to weapons. He's been studying PG for a while."

"Weapons from illegal trade?"

She nodded. "Yes."

"So unregistered."

"Completely off the grid and all tracking removed."

A tram rumbled down the track. They both stepped to the edge of the platform.

Fatin shot him a sideways glance. "So, Baraq, where's your girlfriend? Is she still in my room? I'm shocked you managed to get her to stay put."

He flashed a smile. "You caught on that she's not very patient? No matter that the sight of her would draw too much attention here, she didn't want to wait until I returned."

Fatin grunted. "What did you do? Tie her to the bed?"

His laughter was husky, deliciously masculine. "Of course. And I had to strip her to make sure she hadn't any clothing if she managed to untie the knots. Any trouble tonight?"

She grimaced. "Maybe."

Baraq's dark eyes flashed. "Tell me."

The train slid to a halt, giving her a welcome pause in the conversation. The doors opened and the other riders stepped inside, heading toward the front of the car. Baraq and Fatin headed to seats in the rear.

Seeking a padded bench, Fatin sat slowly but winced. From head to toe, she was one big ache. And she needed rest.

Baraq tucked a finger under her chin, forcing her gaze to meet his. "What happened?"

She wrinkled her nose. "I got caught alone by one of the guards."

"I noticed you lost an item of clothing," he said, eyeing her gown. "Did he hurt you?"

She gave a quick shake of her head. "The corset was biting into my ribs."

"I thought I'd laced it loosely enough," he said, an edge of humor in his voice.

She smiled thinking of how Birget had itched to be the one to pull the laces tight.

"I didn't remove it for him, if that's what you're thinking. He never got that far."

"I don't like the sound of that. Fatin, did he hurt you?" he repeated, his tone stern.

She cleared her throat. "I dropped him with his stun gun."

Baraq cursed under his breath. "Why did you let him get that close?"

She shrugged, pretending unconcern when her stomach still roiled at the way he'd rutted between her legs. "I had to let him move in. Only way to catch him off guard. I left him on the ground and stole his helmet."

His expression sharpened. "You have a helmet?"

"*Had.* I couldn't very well walk around with it under my arm. I thought I'd hidden it well enough, but when I went back for it . . . it was gone."

"Fatin, dammit to Hades." His body stiffened. "We could have used it. Think he'll report it?"

"I don't know. But I do know I'm not going to be safe on the grounds anymore."

"Which only proves we need to move fast—if we're to have any hope of getting back inside to break the men out."

"And my sister."

He nodded. "And your sister. We have to see this Adem tonight."

Weary, she sat deeper in her seat and leaned her head against the scratched leather.

The tram rattled and turned, and she slid and jerked herself awake.

"Scoot."

She blinked.

Baraq moved in closer and put his arm behind her. "Sleep. Don't you dare tell Birget I offered you comfort."

"Afraid?"

He grunted. "For my balls. She's still got an ax to grind with you."

"And you don't?"

"I'm a little more pragmatic. We need you. And you won't be of any use if you drop dead from exhaustion."

She settled her head against his shoulder and let out a sigh. "I've made a mess."

"That you have, bounty hunter. That you have."

Attendants arrived in the early-morning hours to roust any clients still abed, as well as to turn out Hakon and Eirik from the *saray*. Left to find their own way back, they discovered that the men's salon was also being emptied of patrons who were being dressed and led back to the hoverpad for transport home.

What was unusual was the fact the men weren't snoring away the effects of the aphrodisiac or eager to find their own cots in the barracks. Instead, they sat in a grouping of couches pulled together.

When Eirik and Hakon entered and the doors closed, Hagrid waved them over, a broad smile splitting his face. "Did you sleep on feather beds and drink from gold chalices?" he said loudly, his gaze making a quick dart to the "eye" in the gold fish sitting on a mantel.

Alert in an instant that whatever was on the men's minds shouldn't be relayed to their watchers, Eirik feigned a yawn. "Don't know what the fuss is all about. It's not so different from here, except the women are a sight prettier than you."

He sat beside Hagrid and watched as Kaun slid over to make room for Hakon in the seat nearest the watcher's eye. Then Kaun laughed and punched Hakon's arm and asked for details of what transpired that night in the women's *saray* in an overloud voice.

Hagrid leaned toward Eirik. "I'll never say another word against that bounty hunter," he whispered. "She left us a gift."

"A gift?"

"I watched her tonight. She hid something under one of the tables after she came in from outside. Looked as though she'd either been in a fight or had frigged a guard."

Eirik's body stilled, mind racing, wondering what had happened after Fatin left Zarah's window. But he kept silent, as Hagrid's expression became more animated.

"You'd never believe what she gave us."

"Out with it."

"A helmet. One of the guard's helmets with a visor. Don't know how she stole it, but it's ours now."

What luck! Eirik leaned forward. "Have you had a chance to examine it?"

"Aye, Kaun and Garm took a look. They think the visor has night vision and there's a built-in transmitter-receiver."

Eirik groaned. "Bollocks. They'll track it."

Hagrid's grin stretched even wider. "The tracking, everything, was turned off."

Eirik studied Hagrid's expression, while he mulled over what this meant. "Still not much use without the rest of the uniform."

Hagrid's eyebrows waggled. "There's a wee bit of a bather who's meeting me while the rest of you exercise later today. She's bringing me one from the laundry."

"And you trust her?" Eirik's mind rolled over the possibilities.

"She's in love." Hagrid leaned back and rubbed his cock. "Or loves little Hagrid. What does it matter? We have something now."

"But only one of us can use it."

Hagrid's gaze narrowed. "Only takes one to get out and get to Consortium offices."

Which meant they wanted him to use it. He was the only one who might gain entry due to his rank.

"Think on it," Hagrid said, glancing over his shoulder, then leaning closer. "Bypass Helio enforcers altogether. Once you report to Consortium officials the fact you were taken, no Helio can touch you."

Like a wisp of fire fed with kindling, Eirik's excitement flared. Hope came alive in his chest. "I could then relay word to Dagr and arrange a shipment of ore to purchase your freedom."

Hagrid's gleeful expression slipped. He cupped Eirik's knee and clenched his fingers tight around it. "I don't trust you, Wolf. But we have to believe you won't turn your backs on Icelanders and leave us to rot."

"Get me the uniform. Tonight I'll break out. But I'll need a distraction. Something noisy enough to bring the guards running."

Hagrid grinned again and sat back, stretching his arms along the back of the couch. "I'm thinking the Helios need to see what Vikings are all about."

The men seated all around them began to laugh, throwing back their heads as the sound grew and grew. Eirik sat back, drinking in the moment.

Hope set free sounded wild and uninhibited. His chest expanded. At last, they had a chance to shake free of their shackles. He'd not fail them.

# Twelve

With Baraq at her back this time, Fatin stepped inside the murky *meyhane*, heading directly to the bar.

As she approached, Samson's eyes widened, his gaze going from Baraq to Fatin. He gave her a one-sided smirk. "I see your friend found you."

Fatin stepped onto the ledge beneath the bar, reached for Samson's collar, twisting it tight, and pulled his head close. "No fucking around, Samson," she bit out. "My friend and I aren't playing games. I want to know where to find Adem."

He choked until she eased her hold. Then, red-faced, Samson whispered, "Adem's a busy man. And the last time I spoke with him, he wasn't all that keen to see you again." His lips twisted. "Guess your pussy isn't as attractive as you thought."

She fisted her hand in his collar and slammed his head against the counter.

The bar around them grew quiet. A bouncer stepped out of the shadows, tapping a cudgel against his open palm.

Baraq turned to face him. "It's not your fight. Our business is strictly with Samson. I'll make it yours if you don't back off now."

The thick-necked Helio raised his hands, but didn't step back, continuing to eye Fatin and Samson.

Fatin leaned closer to the barman, whose face was breaking out in a clammy sweat. "Where is he? He won't come looking for you. My promise. He'll want to hear me out."

"Bitch." Samson gritted his teeth. "I hope he hangs you from a meat hook. He's in the cannery. Dockside. You know the one."

She eased her hold just enough to let him breathe. "Doin' good, Samson. Don't stop now."

"He's been there for days," he said, an ugly scowl furrowing his forehead. "Guards all around it. No one in. If you go through the front, you might end up on the menu."

"And that would suit you fine, wouldn't it? Why didn't you say so in the first place? Would have saved you kissing the counter." She let him go and jumped back, just missing the blade he pulled from under the counter and swung toward her face.

Fatin gave a laugh, the ache in her ribs worth the trouble to see the fury turning his skin purple. "You'll have to try harder than that." She tipped her chin at Baraq. "Let's go. I have what I need."

"That whore of a sister you have . . . seen her lately?" Samson shouted after her.

Blood pounding in her ears, Fatin picked up a pot of ore from one of the tables and flung it at the barman, who raised an arm at the last minute to deflect it. The crockery shattered the glass behind his counter.

With his curses following her out the door, she laughed again. After being the one on the receiving end of a bruising one too many

times in the past couple of days, she felt more herself. In charge
again.

"You're feisty for such a little thing," Baraq murmured. "Might
have been wiser not to make such a scene."

"Who's anyone going to tell?" She flung an arm outward. "The
men don't want their wives knowing they're fucking whores. And
Samson and his crew certainly don't want enforcers crawling all
over them."

Baraq shook his head. "Back to Suffrage House?"

"Yeah, your princess might be gnawing through the ropes by
now. Besides, we'll have to wait for night again to pay Adem a visit.
Depending on how tightly buttoned up he is, we might have to slip
through the guards to get a chance to talk to him."

"Wouldn't mind some shut-eye," he murmured.

"Sleep?" She snorted. "Just keep it down. Your princess is a
screamer."

For the first time since he'd awoken in this nightmare, Eirik felt
like his old self. A round of fisticuffs with Hakon and then a
couple of the other Bearshirts had left him relaxed, his body humming with energy and a fiery heat that hadn't a thing to do with the
weather on this godless planet.

Tonight, he'd make a break for freedom or die trying.

The uniform was stuffed beneath the mattress in the chamber
he'd claimed. The helmet and boots hidden in the washstand cabinet. His men had already increased the staff's wariness by their
rowdy behavior on the field and during their evening meal, pulling
all their attention, while he'd kept himself removed from their
antics.

Even Aliyah's usual calm facade was frayed. Tension dug lines into her forehead; her lips stayed in a thin, full line. "Can you do nothing to calm them?" she muttered beneath her breath.

"Mistress, they are Vikings and unused to confinement." He gave her a sideways glance. "You really should have done a little study to confirm our fitness for this sort of life before you had us abducted."

"There are remedies," she muttered.

He forced himself not to glance down at her amulet. He hoped she wouldn't resort to that. And he'd cautioned the men not to get too out of hand before he had a chance to handle that particular problem.

"The women don't seem to mind the ruckus," he drawled.

Aliyah frowned. "The women are hoping all that unspent energy will be directed toward their pleasure."

*Pleasure.* He was thoroughly sick of the word. And wondered if he'd ever be free with his sexuality again. He'd fucked so many women in so few days that their faces were a blur. To be honest, he'd gotten more enjoyment from the solid thuds of Hakon's fists against his belly than pounding between clasping thighs. "Aliyah, these men are warriors."

"I know—it's why they're perfect for our needs." She met his glance with a pointed one of her own. "There are worse fates than being sex-thralls, Wolf. I might have to arrange a demonstration to show them the alternative."

He didn't like the sound of that, or the nasty curve of her thinned lips. Whatever she had planned wouldn't be pleasant. "Have the women made their selections?"

"Do you want to know who will claim you first?"

Impatient with the conversation and the fact she might decide to wait until the women left to approach him again, he blurted, "I had hoped that we might take another turn."

Had he been too quick? Would she suspect?

Her gaze studied his face. The lines smoothed, and a blush stained her cheeks. "It might be possible. I'm anxious. A little play might help ease my tension. The guards can handle this if things get out of hand." Her hand landed on his arm. Her fingers stroked him. "I have thought of little else since last we spent time alone."

"Hakon will be disappointed when he's left out," he murmured, but smiled, drawing her in.

She stroked her tongue over her lower lip. "Hakon wasn't the one who commanded my attention."

Eirik grasped her hand, turning it to kiss the inside of her wrist, inhaling too much of her cloying perfume. "Check the list. See if you can move a name."

She nodded, then turned away with a trill of breathless laughter.

He almost felt regret for playing her. Almost. She was a woman at her core. One who craved a strong master. But she'd denied her nature for a long time. She'd enslaved others to feed another, greedier hunger.

Feeling regret that he would have to wait to make her suffer his full revenge, he looked across the crowd to Hakon and gave him a subtle nod. Once he'd removed her from the room, the rest of the plan they'd sketched out between them while they'd traded blows would be enacted.

He tried not to think about what would happen once he'd escaped the compound's walls or how he would find a Consortium office. One step at a time. The most dangerous part would be slipping through security once the others started the commotion.

Aliyah returned shortly, her cheeks flushed. "It's arranged."

"I've claimed a room. Everything we need is there."

Her lips parted. Her hand slid into the curve of his elbow.

With one last pointed glance to the two guards positioned at the doors, she allowed him to lead her out of the salon and down the hallway to the private chambers.

His heart began a steady, heavy thrumming. He forced himself to keep his pace leisurely as he drew her along down the corridor, toward the room where he'd arranged a surprise for her.

She leaned her head against his upper arm. "Tell me more about your world."

"Why?"

"Because I'm curious."

Eirik arched a brow. "What things do Heliopolites think about us and New Iceland?"

"Only what our history tells us, and what the few who have visited on trade missions have mentioned to the press." She turned to peer into his face. "That you wear fur. That there are dragons in your oceans. That it's so cold tears freeze into icicles. Is that all true?"

"Yes. But there's also a rugged beauty to our world. Mountains so tall they scrape the clouds. Fire that rages in the night sky."

"Fire?" Her dark eyes widened.

"A borealis, really, but we prefer the old stories that it is the light reflected on the shields of the Valkyries."

"Valkyries?" She shook her head. "Your names . . ."

"The *Valkyrja* are female warriors who serve Odin under the command of the goddess Freya."

"Female warriors. Like our Amazons."

He shrugged. Bored with the conversation. "I suppose."

At the door of his chamber, he opened it, then stood aside for her to enter. With her back to him, she removed her broach and stepped out of her gown, then folded it and placed it on the windowsill.

Her movements amused him. "Afraid I'll shred the gown?" he

drawled, bracketing her body between his arms and leaning down to kiss the back of her shoulder.

"Do what you must. But I'm fond of this gown," she said, giving it a pat.

"Shall I help you with your necklace?"

"I can manage."

Eirik drew away and strode toward the bed. He adjusted the lid on the ore pot, twisting it to lessen the amount of light emitted through the grapevine pattern on the lid. With only a faint glow to glaze the oil rubbed into his muscles, he undressed slowly, knowing her gaze clung to his toned frame.

The display was only the beginning of the seduction he planned. He glanced at the large mirror, then back at her. "Do we have company?"

"Always. Think I'd trust you?"

"You don't mind that they will see everything I do?"

"It is only one. My eunuch. And he knows about my proclivities."

He rested both hands on his hips. "And if I am inhibited by the thought of another witnessing our passion?"

Her head tilted to the side and her eyes narrowed. "Why are you so insistent, Viking?"

Eirik cursed silently. He didn't need her growing suspicious. He dropped his voice to a low purr. "The last time you gave me leave to pleasure you, I held back. Partly because we don't know each other that well. Partly because I didn't want to reveal too much about my own preferences to Hakon."

Her breath caught. Her head canted, eyelids dropping midway. "Are your preferences so extreme or strange?"

He remained silent, closing his expression, leaving it up to her imagination exactly what he meant.

Aliyah walked toward him, her nude body swaying. She touched his chest, fingers tracing the indentions beneath his chest, trailing over ribs, the layered muscles protecting his belly, until she reached his cock.

It twitched as she ran a finger down his length. However, he remained as still as a statue, his jaw grinding shut.

"If I send Michael away . . ."

At her statement, he angled his head and let her see the satisfaction building inside him.

She turned to the mirror. "Leave us. Now, Viking, I am yours."

Eirik gave the silk rope a last turn around a slender ankle, then stood back, eyeing his work. Aliyah looked lovelier than ever, at least in his estimation. He'd slowly wrapped her wrists, teasing her breasts with the frayed ends of the ropes now and then until she panted with frustration. He trailed them along her slit until the rope shortened, then talked to her, telling her all the ways he'd ever pleasured a woman when she was bound and in his bed.

Her pussy clasped tightly. Her labia had grown red and thick with the blood heating her sex.

With a slow move, he eased onto the edge of the mattress and held up a wad of soft cloth. Her mouth opened obediently and he filled it, then tied a gag around her head to keep it there.

When her gaze locked with his, he trailed a finger through her nether lips and thrust one inside, and then chuckled at the moisture seeping from her channel. "Give me a moment and I'll return."

Her eyebrows lowered, anger flashing.

He tweaked a nipple. "You're in no position to complain, now, are you?" With a grin, he padded to the door and stepped into the corridor.

Loud laughter and shouts sounded from the salon. He headed to the panel in the wall he now knew hid a closet situated behind the mirror.

He plunged a fist into the thin wall and pulled the panel away, knowing the noisy party would mask the crash and any shouts. Just as he'd suspected, her watcher stood there, his bald head jerking toward Eirik, his hand going for a button beside the mirror.

Eirik grasped his wrist and wrenched him from the room, then dragged him by the arm back into the chamber, where he tossed him on the floor beside the bed.

He tsked and cocked an eyebrow at Aliyah. "And you wanted to be able to trust me?"

The eunuch glanced wildly around the room, spotted the neat pile of Aliyah's clothing, and crawled quickly toward it.

Eirik stepped past him and lifted the amulet from where it nested in the center of her folded silk. Holding it high, he smiled at Michael. "Is this what you're looking for?"

He dropped it on the floor and stomped on it with his bare feet, shattering it. Satisfaction fueled his movements.

Aliyah groaned.

Michael whimpered. "Do you think you can escape, Viking? Where do you think you can go? You'll be recognized on sight."

Eirik picked up Aliyah's gown and shrugged as she screamed behind her gag. "I would have spared it if you had been true to your word." He ripped it in half, then spun the fabric in his hands, making a rope.

Michael tried to dart past him, but Eirik stuck a foot in the center of his back, pushed him flat against the floor, and then quickly tied his hands.

With the other length, he made another rope and tied the man's ankles, looping it through the rope at his wrists to stretch and lift his legs from the floor. "You won't be going anywhere. And I'll be long gone when they find you."

He turned to Aliyah. "I do regret causing you discomfort. Warriors from my world seek to provide women comfort and pleasure. But you understand I must do what I can to escape. It's my duty."

Then he slid the clothes from under the mattress, the boots and helmet from under the washstand, and quickly dressed. When he was ready, he cupped a fist to his chest in quick salute, then climbed over the windowsill and onto the ground below. The darkness swallowed him.

Outside, the sounds of the raucous gathering made him smile. Hakon and the others would keep the guards' attention for some time.

He headed toward the rails, taking pains not to walk too quickly to attract attention. When the station house came within view, he ducked into the shadows of the building.

Passengers were entering the cars. He walked up behind a group of attendants and ignored their surprised stares, hoping that his behavior, his size, wouldn't make them suspicious. He hurried to a seat and slumped into it, making his silhouette against the window smaller. He didn't dare remove the helmet and reveal more of his skin. Despite time spent training beneath their hot sun, he was still pale in comparison to most Helios.

The tram doors closed. The lights within the cars blinked out. He released a sigh and gazed out the window as the car pulled away from the platform. No one rushed forward; the walkways were empty of scurrying guards.

When they crossed the moat, he dared breathe a sigh and began to think that maybe he'd done it. But he still had big hurdles ahead.

Not knowing what lay at the end of the track, he decided to stay close to the group of workers, to follow in their steps. It couldn't be unusual for a guard to take the train, but he knew they usually showered and changed beforehand.

If anyone commented, he'd prepared a little speech. He'd been in a hurry to meet a girl. Wanted to impress her with his uniform. He wished he had a weapon, a knife, a cudgel—anything he might use if he were stopped.

The train slowed, passing through the edge of the Helio capital, the rails rising above the streets, above short one-storied buildings with streets outlined by small blue tracks of lights. Only a few overhead lamps broke the darkness, save for signage above establishments and lights suspended above every intersecting road.

The place was a maze of narrow roads. How in Hel's name would he ever find what he sought?

The tram rumbled to a stop. The doors whooshed open. Not willing to be trapped inside the conveyance for a minute longer, he followed on the heels of a group of women who glanced behind them and tittered to one another.

A reaction he was glad to use. He'd let them think he followed out of interest. When they paused outside an establishment with music and soft conversation floating out the door, he stepped into an alley beside it.

He didn't have to wait long for what he needed. A three-wheeled conveyance braked to a stop in front of the bar. A passenger stepped out from the back door. Eirik rushed from the opposite side, opened the door, and slid into the seat.

The man in the front of the car glanced over his shoulder. "Look, freak, didn't you see my lights? I'm a private car. Get the fuck out."

Eirik leaned forward, snaked an arm around the seat in front of him, and clamped his palm against the man's skinny throat and squeezed. "I haven't time to be polite. I want you to take me to the Consortium offices."

"Where?" the man croaked.

"A Consortium-controlled facility."

Hands scratched at the backs of his.

He relaxed his hold while the man dragged in a lungful of air.

"Not from around here, are you?" the man wheezed, glaring at his image in the rearview mirror.

"You will do as I say. Now drive!"

"And I can drive around and around just to keep that shovel you call a hand off my throat, but it's not gonna change a thing. I can't drive to Consortium headquarters. They're in the estuary. *On an island*. You'll have to take a boat or a hovercar."

Eirik struck his seat with his fist. "How do I find one of those?"

The man's eyebrows furrowed as he strained to see into the mirror in the center of his front window. "You got money to pay?"

Eirik cursed, then shook his head.

The man shook his thick golden hair. "Didn't think so. You one of those poor bastards they just trucked off Iceland?"

Eirik gave a nod, wariness stiffening his back.

But the man gave him a wide grin. Then he reached a hand behind his back, slipping it into the space between himself and the seat, and pulled something out. Something that flicked back and forth. A tail. "I got no love for PG. They fucked my ancestors. Everyone tells me I should just cut this sucker off and try to live out from under the scope, but I am what I am." He shrugged. "And some women dig it."

Eirik stared at the tail, then at the man's split-lipped grin. "What are you?"

"Part lion and man." With those words, he bared his teeth.

Eirik jerked back at the row of long teeth, the corner ones longer than a lynx's fangs. "You are part cat?"

"Never heard of the feral experiments?"

The term sifted through his mind. Eirik nodded. "It was explained to me, but not fully."

"Well, I have a story to tell you. One that'll make your skin crawl. And I got a friend who might help you. Name's Adem."

# Thirteen

The cannery warehouse serving as Adem Pantheras's latest head-quarters was a wooden building sitting on the sandy bank of the Blue Nile. The darkened storefront and covered porch faced away from the river and was supported on tall wooden pylons to prevent the building from being flooded in the rainy times.

Fatin eyed the boardwalk leading past the entry, then glanced across the rutted road to the buildings on the opposite side of the street. All ramshackle bait and boat rental shops. Small, peaked-roof stores with narrow alleyways separating them. Plenty of places for Adem's men to survey the store.

She drew back into the alley she and Baraq had used on their approach from the street running parallel to this one where they'd left Birget and the rest of her crew of Vikings cooling their heels.

"Why can't we just walk through the front door?" Baraq asked, sounding exasperated. "I thought Adem was a friend of yours."

Maybe he should have gotten a good night's sleep rather than

banging his girlfriend through the early-morning hours. "Adem is."
Guilt flashed. "Or was. But we had a difference of opinion."

Baraq leveled a glare on her as he hunkered down beside her.
"About?"

"My taking the assignment to snag the Icelanders. He thought it
was . . . unethical." Baraq's soft snort had her lips curling into a snarl.

"I think I like him already."

She jutted out her chin. "Adem is willing to sacrifice my sister
for the greater good. I'm not."

"Will we have to hold a knife to his throat to conduct this
conversation?"

"Maybe." No maybe about it, but she'd had just as little sleep
and enjoyed prodding Baraq with a little ambiguity. "For sure, we
have to sneak through his guards."

"You're sure there are people watching?"

Light flared as a vehicle turned a corner and barreled toward the
storefront. "Shhh." She crouched lower and peered around the
corner.

A small three-wheeled car pulled to a sharp stop in front of the
cannery. From one breath to the next, figures dressed in black
spilled from doorways and alleys to surround it.

"Guess that answers that question," Baraq muttered.

A man with a wild, full head of tawny hair stepped out into the
light beaming from the entrance. "Got a visitor. Someone Adem
will want to see."

More booted feet approached on the walkway next to Fatin, and
she pulled back, shoving Baraq behind her and sliding down behind
a trash bin as the guard passed.

When next she peered around the corner, the car sat empty. The
driver and his passenger had moved inside, likely under escort. The
rest of the guards had faded into the alleys again.

She tilted back her head, studied the wall they leaned against, and noted a narrow metal ladder that led to the roof. She elbowed Baraq, and then crept quietly to the ladder. Her first step up creaked.

Baraq hissed for quiet.

Aiming a scowl over her shoulder, she faced the ladder again, took a deep breath, and began climbing, doing her best not to swing too far on the bars to keep it from squeaking. At the top, she peeked over the edge of the roof, but found it clear and slipped over.

Turning, she lent a hand to Baraq; then together they climbed the pitched roof, straddling the peak, then sliding down the other side to the gutter. An arm's span divided their rooftop from the flat roof of the cannery.

Baraq glanced down and blanched.

She smirked. "Afraid of heights?"

His deadly glare didn't frighten her. He glanced down again, grimaced, but squared his shoulders. "After you, bounty hunter."

Grinning, Fatin crouched and sprang lithely to the other rooftop. When she turned back, she caught Baraq's tense expression and stifled a laugh. When he landed beside her, she patted his shoulder. "You fly through the heavens and you're afraid of a little leap through the air," she said with mock sympathy.

Baraq gave her an acidic smile. "I'm a man, not a bird."

Fatin felt like punching him in the gut, but grunted instead. "Look for a way into the building. There has to be a hatch or doorway somewhere."

They found a trapdoor and pulled it back to reveal a narrow shaft with a ladder leading down one side.

Taking a deep breath because she didn't like dark, tight spaces, Fatin began the climb down into the cannery. At the bottom of the ladder she found a door. Light gleamed beneath it. She depressed the latch and inched the door open.

A loud bang sounded behind her, then a solid thump. She glanced back to find Baraq seated on the ground. "Shhh! Never would have guessed you're this clumsy."

"I'm not a—"

"I know, not a bird."

"Was going to say not a goat, since you seem to have been offended when I likened you to a bird."

"Just shut up. We aren't there yet."

When she turned back to the doorway, a shadow darkened the crevice. So much for the element of surprise.

Blood thumped against her temples, but she pushed open the door, lifted her chin, and stared up into the face of Adem Pantheras.

Accompanied by men dressed in dark clothing, their faces darkened with soot, Eirik followed the driver through the shop front, past tall shelves filled with tins of fish by the pictures on the labels. He wrinkled his nose at the thought of eating fish that didn't come fresh from Hymir's Sea.

At the back, they passed through a set of automatic doors that whooshed open, then shut behind them. The temperature inside was cold, and smelled strongly of sea creatures' flesh. Long metal tables stood beside conveyor belts. Very like miniature versions of those used in his mines to transport the ore from the caverns to the workers who packed it into transport containers. Here, the tables held buckets clipped to the rear, likely where the unused parts of the fish were tossed.

The smell was overwhelming, but he resisted letting his nose so much as twitch because he knew he was watched. He could sense others lurking in the shadowed corners of the cavernous room.

At the rear of the large room was a corridor feeding to the right and to the left. The armed escorts in the lead headed toward the left, passing closed doorways until they reached the one at the end.

The driver stepped forward and pushed through it, then stood aside to hold it open for the rest of the group to enter.

The room was dark, except for a single greenish light in the center that hung from a wire suspended from the tall raftered ceiling. A door opened to the side and slammed. Footsteps scuffled in.

"We have a surplus of visitors," came a deep voice that held an odd, growling texture. "Strange since this location is supposed to be a secret." The footsteps drew nearer and a tall, broad-shouldered man stepped into the light.

Only like the driver, he wasn't entirely a man. His face was something horrific, yet beautiful, a blend between human and cat.

His eyes were large, nearly round, and a pale reflective green. The skin of his face was cloaked in fine hairs, golden with irregularly shaped spots of brown. His nose was flat and broad at the end, his palate split down the center over a thin human mouth. Shaped throughout his body like a man, he was thickly built and muscular. The hair that swept away from his crown was long and pitch-black. Both hands fisted on his hips as he eyed Eirik, fixing on the helmet. "Remove it."

Eirik unsnapped the chin strap and lifted off the visored helmet, making the room instantly brighter. He shook his head, then raked a hand through his hair, finding it matted with sweat.

A gasp sounded behind the cat-man, but he didn't turn toward it, and instead held that green gaze as he was assessed, judged.

"You're a Norseman," the cat-man said, his tone dead even. "One of the twenty."

Eirik pushed out his chest and nodded. "I am."

The cat's gaze slid to the driver. "You did well, Leo, bringing him here."

"Thanks, Adem, but I'd best hurry back. I tapped out of the system to come here, but if I'm much longer..."

"Don't risk scrutiny. We wouldn't want you tracked back here. You're free to go."

The driver gave Eirik a quick grin, then hurried out of the room.

"It's interesting," Adem drawled. "A Viking strides through my front door, and his captor sneaks down from the roof." With a lightning move, he reached behind him and dragged a figure forward.

When the woman tossed back her messy hair, Eirik stared into Fatin's mutinous eyes. Her hands were restrained behind her back, and another figure, a tall, muscular man, was pushed into the light. This one a Helio by his dark features.

Adem's unblinking stare homed on Eirik. "The question is whether you and the bounty hunter work together or she followed you."

Before Eirik could decide which answer the cat-man was fishing for, Fatin stepped between them.

Her gaze raked Eirik, dropped to the helmet he still held, then quickly fixed on Adem. "I didn't know he'd broken out," she said huskily. "I was trying to get inside here to talk to you about him."

Adem reached out a hand, combed his long, thick fingers through Fatin's hair, and pulled to tilt back her head.

Eirik's body tensed, not liking Adem's roughness or the charged glances the couple exchanged. A hint of vulnerability surfaced in Fatin's pleading gaze as she stared back at the cat-man.

"You came to me," Adem purred, "and yet you know I've lost patience with you, little bird."

Fatin's face tightened, her eyes flicking to the side.

"That's right, you don't like that endearment. And since I no longer find you endearing, I should give you another." He jerked his hand, pulling hard on her hair. "How about 'traitor'?" he asked, his voice deepening to a growl.

Eirik's free hand fisted and he took a step forward, but one of the black-suited men stepped in the way.

Fatin's eyes filled, but she lifted her chin in defiance. "I did not intend to betray."

"And yet you accepted PG's contract to steal breed-worthy specimens for their purposes."

Eirik bristled at being called a specimen, but kept silent, because he was curious now how she would respond. It was apparent from the way the two stood so close, their bodies straining apart, that they shared an intimate past, which he found shocking given the fact the male wasn't fully a man.

"I came to you first for help," Fatin said, her voice ragged.

"And I said I would give it."

Her face screwed up into a tearful grimace. "You took too long. Four years I waited."

"And you think that starting a revolution is something that can be accomplished in the short term?"

"I can't think about your revolution," she replied, her voice thick with tears. "My sister pines inside her prison. I saw her, Adem. She's losing hope."

"Do you believe that I don't think about her? But I can't throw away this chance. We're gaining followers, helpers, inside the compound every day. You should have trusted me."

"I trust no one," she said, her voice filled with emotion, and then her gaze slid to Eirik.

He swept his expression clean of all emotion, refusing the plea in her moist eyes.

Adem's glance cut between them, then narrowed. He released his hold on Fatin's hair and turned to the Helio who'd been captured with Fatin. "Bring him." He walked to a cabinet and brought out a box from which he plucked a device. He tapped a button, then held out the device. On the top of the box, the outline of a hand glowed.

The Helio's hand was forced forward, then held down against the device. Light illuminated the edges of his palm and between his fingers, then blinked out. A beep sounded.

Adem turned over the device and read from a screen. "This gets better. This man's a crew member from the *Proteus* whose current mission is to transport cargo from the surface of New Iceland to off-load onto cargo ships." He gave the Helio a narrowed glance. "You, my friend, are a long way from New Iceland. And you're far more interesting to me than these two at the moment," he said, pointing toward Fatin and Eirik. He turned his head toward one of the black-suited guards. "Put them in my quarters. Men at the door. I don't want them wandering away until I'm through with this one."

"He might harm her," the Helio blurted, aiming a glare at Eirik.

Adem's lips curved. "And I should care?"

Eirik was shoved from behind, forced to lead the men filing out of the room. Behind him he could hear Fatin's fierce mutters as she cursed Adem and men in general.

They were herded to a small room with a single mattress and a desk. As plain and humble as a soldier's barracks. Shoved inside, he turned in time to see Fatin pushed through the door, her hands still behind her back.

As the door slammed shut to close them inside, the corners of his mouth rose.

Fatin aimed a deadly glare his way. "Whatever you're thinking. Just un-think it."

Eirik slouched against the wall. "And what am I thinking?" He doubted she had a clue that anger did amazing things for her appeal. Her spread-legged stance drew his glance to the juncture of her thighs.

"You're thinking that you've just been given permission to have your revenge on me."

Revenge wasn't foremost on his mind. Her squared shoulders and the jut of her chest brought to prominence her budding nipples. "Why do so many people mean you harm?"

"My effervescent personality?" Her face screwed up as she fought the restraints. Her cheeks grew red.

He knew she didn't want to ask him for help. That he was the last person she wanted help from. He sat on the bed with his back against the wall and pulled up a knee to watch as she grew redder.

"Eirik!"

"What, sweet Fatin?"

"Don't call me that."

"It's your name."

"The sweet part. You only ever say it when you're ready to take a piece out of me."

His blood heated. "Oh, I want pieces," he murmured, letting his gaze trail down her body.

Her eyebrows lowered over a scalding glare.

For the first time since he'd climbed out the window at the brothel, tension faded. A smile twitched at his mouth. The bottom of her trousers and her face were coated with dust, her hair scraggly and escaping her braid.

As disheveled as she was, she shouldn't have been attractive to him, but he could smell her too. Her spicy scent was heightened by her struggles, so unique, so completely her.

His body reacted on a primal level, recognizing the rightness of her aroma, triggering his body to mate. More animal than man himself at this moment, he embraced his arousal rather than bother to deny it. His heartbeats strengthened, beating against his chest in a steadily building tattoo. His thighs tightened; his loins heated, blood rushing to fill his cock, which thickened and stretched against his leg.

Fatin gave up struggling and stomped a foot. Her gaze didn't meet his.

But he knew she fought her pride to ask for his help. "Fatin, *elskling*, do you want me to untie you?" he asked, keeping his voice even and cheerful.

She rolled her eyes and blew at a strand of hair that squiggled across her forehead. "I could do this myself, but it'd be faster . . ."

*Liar.* He didn't mind that she lied. And very likely about most things. The habit only made it more of a challenge to discover the truth about her. "Come to me."

She stomped toward him, then turned her back, presenting her hands, which were bound by a rough rope. The fibers were digging into her wrists, which still showed vague traces of bruising. "You shouldn't have fought the ropes. You're hurting yourself."

"Just untie me."

With a lazy caress, he cupped her hips and centered her in front of him. Then, instead of reaching for the knot, he glided his hands around to her waist and opened her trousers.

Her body tensed. "Eirik? What are you doing?"

"What calls to me," he said, smoothing her trousers down her hips.

"My ass calls to you?"

"I can smell your arousal, *elskling*." He leaned toward her and kissed the tops of her buttocks, which were nearly clear of the marks he'd given her when he'd spanked her.

"Just means I need a shower."

"A cold one?" Two fingers rode the divide down her buttocks, glancing by her tiny furled hole, then tucked between her legs to glide into moist, slick heat.

Her pussy contracted, squeezing around his digits. "Won't you be embarrassed when the guards come for you?" she said, her voice tight.

"I've fucked a dozen women in full view of a hundred Helio women and nineteen Vikings. A couple of guards won't cool my ardor." Tipping up her bound hands, he forced her to bend at the waist, admiring the pretty peach-shaped buttocks. Her nude pussy was coated with a thin gloss of her desire.

"Eirik!"

"Yes, sweet Fatin?"

"This hurts."

Humor vanished. He slowly drew her arms down and untied her wrists. With her pants still around her upper thighs, she lifted her arms one at a time and rolled her shoulders to ease the ache.

When she dropped them, she glanced behind her, eyes flashing.

His breath hitched. Blood thrummed.

Her gaze was steady, her face flushed. Her teeth pulled at her bottom lip, as though unsure what course she should take.

Eirik took the decision from her, grasping her hips again and turning her, bringing her closer. "Raise your arms," he said, his voice gruff.

She did so, and he dragged her shirt over her head and tossed it away. "Give me a boot," he said, patting his thigh.

She backed up and placed the toe there, then grabbed his shoulders for balance because he tugged it off and dropped it.

Fatin didn't wait to be told to do it again.

When he shoved her pants down her legs, she bent to the side to assist, pulling them over her small feet, and then straightening in front of him. "If you want to see me humiliated, you can stop right there. The marks on my body are faded. All will know that I was willing, here and now."

Eirik's response was to pull off his own shirt and work his pants off his hips. He couldn't stop now, not even if he wanted to.

Fatin gave him a faint smile and backed away to pull off his boots and trousers. When he was nude, her gaze dropped to his cock, which stood perpendicular from his groin, proof he was every bit as aroused as she was.

Smiling wider, she climbed over his hips, facing him, her knees snuggled beside his thighs, her slit riding the length of his cock. "Seems we've been here before, Viking."

"We have." His voice grew husky. "In another place, another life."

A swallow worked her throat. "Feels like forever since that afternoon."

"I never meant insult when I said I'd see you compensated."

She shook her head and pressed a finger over his mouth. "You didn't think."

Eirik kissed her finger away. "I never did, before. About where the women came from. How they came to that life. Will you tell me now how it happened to you?"

Fatin's eyes, always so expressive whether snapping with challenge or wide with apprehension, were soft now, and filling. "Our mother died," she said, a trembling edge to her voice. "We should have been taken to foster, but because of my sister's appearance, we were told we'd be separated. I couldn't let that happen. Instead, we ran with only the clothes on our backs."

Her hands settled on his shoulders and began to knead. Her gaze grew unfocused as her thoughts turned inward.

"We scavenged—in trash bins—and when we couldn't find

enough food, we stole. Some shop owners and cooks took pity and gave us things to eat and wear. We were both in our teens, old enough by law . . ." Her face dropped.

And he let her hide, because he wasn't sure he could keep his own emotions from scrawling across his face. Her life had been so different from his.

Sure, he hadn't been raised in comfort, but that had been by choice. Wolfskin males weren't coddled. They fought and trained, braved the elements in fur and wool as opposed to modern cold-weather gear because they sought to harden their bodies and their minds.

He waited patiently for her to continue. And at last she lifted her chin, firming it, while tears filled her eyes.

"One day we were caught stealing and taken into court. Because we were indigent—and pretty—we were sold at auction."

"Aliyah?" Involuntarily, his grip tightened.

"Yes, she bought our papers." She let out a ragged breath. "So now you know. I come from nothing, Eirik. I've been a thief and a whore."

He didn't comment on that last bit. "What of your father?"

"Not of this world." Fatin lifted her face, eyes haunted but lovely. "Eirik, Zarah and I are full sisters. Our father was *avisian*. Our mother human."

His heart stopped for a beat, then thundered hard against his chest. Understanding at last some of what drove her. "You're also a Falcon?"

Her smile was sad. She gave a weak shrug. "Luckier than Zarah because I don't have wings. But I carry the same genes. I'm not breed-worthy. Not marriageable." Her head shook. "I will never have any family other than my sister."

Eirik's jaw tightened. The brittle armor she wore around her heart had a purpose. She'd likely suffered slurs all her life, and she truly believed she'd always be alone.

Not knowing what to say, or really how he felt, he gently cupped her chin and pulled her face closer.

When his mouth touched hers, she gave a mournful sob but molded her lips against his, offering him a sweet, soft kiss that tore away another piece of the jagged anger he had harbored against her.

Whatever their future, Eirik had to believe there was a reason they'd come together, a reason he'd been placed in her path—a test offered by the gods. Only a deity with a higher purpose would have thought to mate a Wolf with a Falcon.

# Fourteen

When Eirik threaded his fingers into her hair and pulled, Fatin gave a deep, anguished moan. Sex had never been about anything other than survival. Before the Icelander.

Sure, she'd sometimes found her pleasure with a man, but she'd sought it only because she'd wanted a taste of what was normal between men and women. To dream about a lover who would have a care about her body and her passion. Who might want more from her than just his own physical release.

Being with Eirik was like drinking from a naiad's well. Both beautiful and frightening. Beautiful because of the glimpses of true tenderness he gave her; frightening because she knew this couldn't last.

He cupped her head, holding her still while he deepened the kiss. His tongue swept into her mouth to lap at hers.

Wild, urgent heat filled her. With a flex, she rose on her knees and reached down to guide his cock inside her.

With the tip poised at her entrance, he broke the kiss and clutched her hips, halting her before she could take him inside. "Not so fast," he rasped, turning his head to nuzzle her cheek while he breathed deep, ragged breaths.

Panting already, their mouths so close they shared breaths, she shook with need. "Bastard," she whispered, but without any true anger.

"The sweet things you call me," he murmured, pulling back and staring down at her breasts where the skin flushed pink with arousal.

"Eirik!" she said, reminding him he held her above him.

He gave a short, harsh bark of laughter, then shook his head and looked up into her eyes. "Let me do this right."

Her eyelids drooped. "There's a wrong way?"

He shifted her to his side, laid her on the mattress, then came over her, taking his weight on his elbows. Again, his glance raked down her body.

Uneasy with his perusal, she gave him a frown. "Why are you staring at me?"

"Because you're lovely."

She swatted his shoulder. "Stop it."

His face came up, features tinged red and blurred with passion. "Stop what?"

"Confusing me."

Eirik's features tightened. "When this is done . . . When we've rescued your sister and my men are free, we will take time with each other."

"So that you wreak revenge on me slowly?"

"*Elskling*, I'm not thinking of revenge right now. I might skip that altogether. If you don't betray me again, we can start fresh."

Her lips twisted, and she huffed out a breath. "A new start. What will we do differently? Will *you* capture *me*?"

"Perhaps." His gaze studied her face, then dropped to her shoulders, her chest.

"Are you thinking that you can find the falcon in me if you look hard enough?" she asked, her voice rising.

"You've said there are no outward signs. Zarah's shoulders have a fine down covering them." He kissed her shoulder, slicked his tongue along the crest. "But your skin is as smooth as any human's."

Lord, why couldn't he let go of the fact she wasn't pure human. Now he'd only search for the animal inside her. "Sometimes it's like that. A recessive gene or some such. I don't understand it all. I only know my sister wears her curse for the world to gawk at."

Eirik bit into the tender skin at the base of her neck. "Your sister is beautiful. Like a goddess."

The sensation of that bite, followed by his wicked licks, had her curling her head and shoulder together to hold him there. "You liked her? My sister?"

His head rose, gaze narrowed. "I didn't fuck her. I kept my promise."

She licked her lips, trying to read in his flinty eyes whether his anger was because he'd restrained his desires or because she'd insulted him. "Would you have wanted to, if I hadn't asked?"

"No. I didn't want that between *us*. However, know this: On my world I am allowed concubines and a wife. If I wanted her or any other woman, 'tis my right."

"Wife." Her lips lifted in a snarl. "Have you one of those you've failed to mention?"

His body stiffened and he grunted. "A betrothed. My brother arranged it. I've done my best not to think on it."

Surprised, and not a little amused at his disgruntled expression, she asked, "Haven't you met her?"

He shuddered. "The wedding night will be soon enough to see her. I have no love for her kind."

"But she is Viking, the same as you."

"She's *Valkyrja*." His jaw clenched. "Thinks she's as strong as a man. Battles like one. I prefer a softer frame to bang against." He frowned, then cleared his throat. "Was I too crude?"

"Crude? I'm a whore. Why should I be offended?"

"Stop." Still frowning, he rested on one elbow, his body angled over hers. He stroked her cheek with the back of his hand, then cradled it, his touch tender. "You were forced into that life, the same as I was. I don't hold it against you."

Her eyes closed, shutting out the sight of his earnest expression. He said that now, but if he were home, among his own kind, he'd change his mind. "You don't hold it against me," she whispered, then opened her eyes. "But you could never forget. Tell me, if your future wife were to be in a similar situation, could you forget that she'd been so well used?"

A flush darkened his cheeks. "A wife carries the hope of the future in her womb," he said, his voice even. "It's different. A concubine is a man's companion, the one he chooses as his friend, his lover."

Fatin stared, realizing he didn't even see the insult he'd dealt her. "I thought Helios were despicable. The way the husbands and wives look the other way so they are free to seek their pleasures, but you're far worse."

His jaw tightened. "Perhaps we shouldn't talk."

"Agreed." She swallowed the bitter taste burning at the back of her throat. Then, determined to lighten the mood, because she didn't really want to waste the time they had together fighting, she arched a brow, giving him a challenging look. "You wanted to do this right, didn't you? Do you have some sort of process you step through when you fuck a woman?"

Eirik snorted and moved closer to nudge her hip with his cock. "Nothing so regimented," he drawled, "but I would know that she has found the ultimate pleasure in my arms."

"Why such a high standard?"

A smile twitched. "Because I am always the best."

"My expectations aren't that high. I would be satisfied if you would just remember to ply that cock that dangles between your legs."

"Nothing of mine dangles," he said, his tone deepening.

At the hint of humor curving his mouth, the darker emotions swirling inside her retreated. A new flush heated her cheeks and crept slowly down her neck to her chest. "No, it doesn't dangle. It thumps against my belly like a fist against a drum."

His hand glided down her side, then back up to cup a breast. "Does it seem as large as a fist?"

With a toss of her head, she scoffed. "You're built like a bull. And you well know it."

He leaned over her, covering half her body, crowding ever closer and setting her skin to tingling everywhere he touched.

"Does it cause you alarm, my size? You've felt me inside you—in one particularly tight corner of your body—and I didn't hear a complaint. Only gasps and moans, and perhaps a tiny squeal."

She chuckled. "I never squealed."

"But you did scream." He bent and nuzzled her neck, then her ear. "Would you like to scream again?"

Fatin's groan ended in a breathless laugh. "I'll scream, but only from frustration because you take too long to push that bull's cock of yours inside me."

He tsked and lifted his head, revealing a wicked, boyish grin that set her heart fluttering.

*What would it be like to see that grin each day upon waking?* Fatin lifted her head and cupped the back of his neck to hold him there as she pressed a kiss against that smile. "Make me scream," she whispered. "Prove the first time was no accident."

Eirik growled and pushed her down again and shoved both knees between her legs to force them apart. Then he scooted down her body until his mouth was even with her breasts.

Already tightly beaded, her nipples quivered as her breaths shortened.

He cupped the tender underside of one breast, plumping her flesh. Then he rubbed the roughened pad of his thumb over the areola. "'Tis like velvet. This tip. And a pretty rosy brown when aroused."

"It's a nipple, and it tingles." Her heart raced, secretly thrilled at his words. "Do something and end this agony of waiting."

He bared his teeth, then glanced up before biting gently on the nub.

She bit into her bottom lip to still the moan scratching at her throat.

Torture was clearly on his agenda. He reared back his head, pulling the nipple, then released it. His tongue darted out to lap at the sides and toggle it before giving more lazy swipes around the whole areola.

Watching him, enjoying the wet heat of his flashing tongue, Fatin felt as though a slender thread, stretching from nipple to womb, was tugged with each wicked flick. He was slow, precise, and so thorough she ground her teeth until her jaws ached. "Eirik, please!"

An eyebrow arched. He licked across her chest and latched onto that lucky nipple with his lips, and suckled gently . . . at first . . . then harder and harder until her fingernails dug into his shoulders and raked his skin.

Her belly curled, her pussy pumping against his abdomen, rubbing ineffectually.

Still, he teased and tormented, nibbling, chewing, raking the turgid nub until she writhed wantonly beneath him.

Until this moment, she hadn't known how sensitive her breasts could be. And she wasn't certain that it was his technique so much as the fact he was hard, aroused, and yet he withheld his own release to pleasure her.

Something she'd never experienced before.

But was he driven by pride or by some small affection for her? Part of her wanted badly for it to be the latter. But another shied away, afraid that if she believed he cared about her, she'd be left vulnerable. Her heart couldn't take any more disappointment.

Eirik clamped his fingers on her nipples and pinched the bases of the tips hard.

Her face screwed up with delicious agony. A long, thin whimper broke.

He held them tight for a long moment, then released them. Blood rushed into the tips. They throbbed with a delicious ache.

Scooting down her body, Eirik suctioned at the skin of her belly, making loud, lush sounds as he paused each time, before moving along. At the top of her mound, he rubbed his lips over and over her there, the shadow of bristles on his jaw scraping her sensitive skin, driving her crazy.

Blood pounding, she tried to open her legs, to tempt him lower, but his elbows kept her thighs pinned together. When the tip of his tongue slid into the tight seam of her sex, just at the top, and prodded her hooded clit, she cursed and bit her lip again, her head digging into the pillow as she arched.

He plucked her labia, pulling apart the top and dropping spit into the well. Then his finger scraped the nub, swirling over and over it.

Fatin ached to open her legs and tilt her hips. How easy would it be to fly? But he kept her wings clipped, her legs restricted. She pushed his shoulders, pinched his skin, then sank her hands into his thick black hair and pulled hard.

His laughter was muffled, but so sexy she moaned. He gripped her hands and held them away, and then lifted first one elbow, then the other, letting her spread her thighs.

She panted. The moment the pressure eased, she lifted her knees and let them fall open, but they shook. Never had she felt this way, this desperate for what a man could give her, but she conceded everything at that moment. Her will to fight, to force him to move faster, fled. Her head rolled slowly side to side; her eyelids drifted down.

When his fingers slid inside her, she couldn't hold back the lonely sound that escaped her lips.

"Sweet Fatin," he groaned, kissing her inner thigh, his fingers plunging deep.

Rasping thickness filled her. His fingers twisted, screwing into her, building friction. They curled, raking a spot at the front of her channel. Her breath hitched and she gave another helpless moan.

"Is it there, *elskling*?"

"Mmmm? Why are you talking?"

He pulled away, and she forced her eyes open. When she met his gaze, he inserted his fingers again and found the place, the one that made her toes curl and starved her lungs for air.

"Did I find it?" he said slowly.

Her lips opened, but only a whimper escaped.

"Yes, right there," he murmured. Then he bent and latched his lips around her clitoris again while circling inside her. He sucked, gently at first, but when her hands gripped her own hair and pulled, he suctioned harder, igniting a firestorm inside her.

Her orgasm vibrated from her core, radiating outward, causing her to buck and kick. Too much, too fast.

She was outside her body, falling through darkness, her body shaking so hard, her cries broken. She heard it all, saw it, but she was beyond herself.

When she returned, she was cradled against his chest, a hand soothing her hair, the other pressing her body close to his.

The thickness of his own desire pressed against her belly, pulsing with slow ripples.

Afraid to look up and see his smug smile, she burrowed her face into the corner of his neck. His hot skin pulsed with his heartbeats, dull, insistent throbs that forced hers to echo them.

The sensation was soothing, but also arousing. Although how she could possibly want more when she felt so limp and sated, she didn't know. Fatin held still within his embrace, savoring the sensation of the strong arms surrounding her, hot skin, his unique musk. She wasn't accustomed to lingering in a bed. Didn't quite know how to act.

His cock still required attention, but she didn't want to lose this feeling welling up inside her. Of gratitude and tenderness.

The emotion wasn't real. She knew it. And she'd never have considered it something she'd want. This inner warmth was alien, impossibly rare.

Lips touched her forehead. A low, rumbling growl rattled against her. Tamping down disappointment, she forced a smile and leaned back to look into his face.

His expression was anything but smug. An earnest worry showed in eyes and turned a storm-cloud gray. "Forgive me now?"

She wrinkled her forehead, not understanding.

"For nearly raping you before the assemblage."

"You didn't rape me," she whispered, unable to hold his gaze. "I know what that feels like."

His lips thinned with self-recrimination. "I forced you."

"I reveled in it." The words rushed out before she could stop them.

"I made you cry," he said, his voice harsh.

Fatin drew a deep, jagged breath. "I cried because I don't understand myself."

His thumb traced her lower lip. "I don't understand myself either. Every time I come near you I forget to hate you."

"And you should . . . ?" She quirked an eyebrow.

"Aye, I should. But I can't. Something in you draws me closer."

To bring his lower body closer, she eased a thigh over his hip. She ground her mons against his thick ridge. "You shouldn't matter to me either. Not one bit."

"But I do."

With a nibble on her lower lip, she nodded. "I had a plan. A good one. You're messing it up."

"I can't be sorry about that," he growled, his cock stirring.

Her hand slid down his side and cupped his ass. She dug her nails into his backside and pressed her groin harder against him. "I think I'm recovered now."

His head leaned toward hers. Their lips met in a soft, questing kiss. Her tongue slipped between her lips and touched his mouth.

He opened, inviting her inside. Then he rolled to his back.

Without breaking the sweet kiss, she slid her knees to either side of his hips and rose.

His fingers sought her slit, cupped her folds, massaging them. Then a finger thrust inside, causing her inner muscles to clench and loosing a fresh wash of silky fluid.

With a gasp, she broke away. "Inside me, Eirik. Come inside me . . . *now*."

His smile was tight, desperate. "I think I waited too long. I won't be able to go slow."

"Then don't. Let me do this for you." She glanced down between their bodies and watched as he placed himself at her entrance, then braced her hips with his hands.

She pulsed on his cock, taking him inside with rough, jerking pushes. With each deep thrust, she grunted and dug her fingers into his chest.

When she was seated on his cock, to the root, she tossed back her hair. "Oh, gods, Eirik. *Fuck!*" She rose and slammed back down, rose again and groaned.

His hands helped her, pushing her faster and faster. His face reddened, sweat glazing his face, his chest.

Again and again, she slammed into him. Her channel grew hot again, slick with her lust. Breathless, shuddering, she felt another amazing wave of pleasure rising. "Eirik!"

With a jerk, he flipped them both, causing her to squeak with alarm, but he laid her down, thrust his arms beneath her knees, and raised her ass from the mattress to hammer into her, harder and harder.

Their gazes locked, and she wondered what he saw. She felt wild, feral in a way she'd never claimed before. Unfettered.

He set the rhythm; he controlled the depth. And yet he freed her to soar.

Breath rasping, she flung out her arms and arched her back, opening her lungs and her throat for her sharp, broken cries.

Had she wings, she could not have felt lighter or risen higher. Her legs straightened in his grasp, toes pointing.

She tensed her abdomen to hold her hips high to receive his

quickening, powerful thrusts, and reveled in his strength. The sounds they made, juicy slaps and glides, were their own music, punctuated by the rasps of their breaths, his harsh grunts, her gusting whimpers.

They strained against each other. Her face grew hot. Her head felt ready to explode from the pressure, and then she did, sobbing his name as she came.

At last, he rocked hard and held still inside her.

The first spurt of his essence heated her channel and she squeezed her inner walls around him, wringing his cock, as he gave her slower, jerking strokes and emptied himself inside her body.

Like the pouring of his soul into hers, she thought whimsically. Her own heart didn't feel alone—*for one perfect moment.*

A knock sounded at the door.

Fatin froze. A chill making her skin instantly clammy.

Eirik reached down for the sheet and pulled it over them, then lay over her, bracing himself on his elbows. His gaze locked with hers.

The door swung open, but neither of them looked toward the intruder. "Adem's ready for you," came a grating voice.

How cruel was it to force them apart when they'd finally found a beautiful accord—if only a physical one. "Tell Adem we'll be along," she said, dragging in air to calm her racing heart.

"Not you, bounty hunter. The Viking."

# *Fifteen*

When Fatin smoothed her hands along Eirik's sides, she wanted to wrap her arms around him and hold him against her, but the moment was past. Reality had intruded.

"Get out," Eirik rasped, not looking at the guard. "I'll be there in a moment."

The door clicked shut. Fatin let her hands fall to the mattress, forcing herself not to reach out. She turned her face.

Eirik didn't say a word, but pushed up, letting her thighs slide away. Then he pulled his cock from her body.

The connection broken, Fatin bit her lip.

A wet kiss pressed against her bitten lip. "We aren't through." His voice was rough and brisk.

She wasn't reassured. Another kind of excitement was kindling in his eyes.

Fatin snorted; the moment was lost. "You'll know where to find me," she muttered.

Eirik sighed. "This isn't just about you or me."

"I know. Your friends are being tortured to death. Fucking themselves stupid."

"You think because they're men, it shouldn't feel any less like rape?" His fist clenched the sheets. "They didn't seek that life."

She closed her eyes for a moment, hating how she'd sounded. Why did she always do that? Strike out with hurtful words? "I'm sorry. I shouldn't have said that. I don't know why I did."

"Well, I do. You become a bitch whenever you think someone will hurt you. It's the armor you don against pain."

Did he think he knew her better than she did herself? "Don't you have someplace to go?" she said, her tone snide.

"Look at me." He pinched her chin and forced her to look.

Fatin's breath hitched. Large and fierce, he looked every inch the warrior, even slick with sweat and his cock glistening with their juices. He looked no less than what he was. A Viking prince. Strong and proud.

"I'm not finished with you."

Was this part of his strategy for revenge? To break through every barrier she threw up between them? She was as naked as he was, but she felt . . . less worthy. "I guess we'll see," she said quietly. "Neither of us is in control of what happens now."

"This Adem. He's like you? Feral?"

The last word ground from his mouth. She nodded, feeling sick inside. Did he think they were freaks like most Helios did?

"Then he has a reason to help us?"

Back to business. She tamped down her disappointment. Eirik needed to understand a few things before he spoke with Adem. "Ferals are second-class citizens. We're denied access to the best neighborhoods, the best schools. There are laws to assure a human's equal rights, but we're treated like animals. Some of us like property.

"Adem was a gladiator. Trained in hand-to-hand. Part of the spectacle. He fought the fiercest beasts and ferals in the arena. But he escaped that life. He's part leopard. Perhaps more leopard than man. Stronger than an average man. Perhaps stronger than a Viking." At a sudden thought, she gasped. "Don't provoke a fight. He could shred you with his teeth."

Eirik grunted. "The Helio you were with? What's his story? How do you know him?"

"There's no time to explain. I promise. I'll tell you everything I know . . . after."

Tension tightening his frame again, he climbed off her. She pulled up the sheet, and tucked it under her arms, watching as he dressed in his stolen clothing. When his boots were tugged up his calves, he gave her one last look.

Her breath hitched in her throat. She didn't know what that look meant. Tried not to read too much into it, but the tension in his face, the way his gaze clung to hers—it felt like a promise.

Fatin sat on the edge of the cot to pull on her boots, trying to keep focused on the task, not on the emotions roiling inside her. She was worried about what Adem might do once he discovered the full truth about Eirik's heritage.

Adem might have been her friend once upon a time, but his friendship was something transitory—and something that depended on whether the person he befriended could serve his cause. All those years fighting in the arena had cauterized his heart. Closed it like a wound to deeper emotions. When one battled to the death against men one shared close quarters with, deep emotions other than fury and triumph were a liability.

If Adem saw Eirik as someone to exploit, he wouldn't kill him on the spot. But even then, his agenda would be served first. Something she didn't see Eirik tolerating.

A knock sounded at the door, but it swung open before she could reply. Baraq stood there, his posture so straight, his expression so sour, her heart dove to her toes.

"We're free to go," he said woodenly.

"Really?" She stiffened.

"Finish dressing," he said, eyeing the messy bed, his mouth drawing into a straight line.

A flush heated her cheeks. Why should he look so disapproving? He had no room to judge. She'd been crushed against the wall of the room at Suffrage House while he'd nailed his princess. "What about Eirik? Is he coming too?"

"Adem's keeping him for now."

"Did he say whether he would help him and the others?"

"They were discussing how to free the rest of the Vikings when I was told to leave."

Fatin tugged on the other boot, then planted both feet on the ground and lunged up from the bed. "I need to talk to Adem."

Baraq blocked the door. "Adem says you're lucky to leave with your life. I had to talk him out of killing you. It's only because he knows you'll be in my custody that you can leave."

Fatin pushed at his broad chest, but he didn't budge. "He doesn't know the full story. Doesn't understand what's at stake."

"He knows more than you do."

Fatin eyed him with suspicion. "How'd he get your trust so quickly? You told him how you came to be here rather than sitting in orbit around New Iceland, didn't you? That's a story I'd still love to hear."

He gave her a baleful glance. "Since most of that story begins with you and your thickheaded plan to kidnap Vikings and make them into playthings for the wealthy, we both think we'd do better without your counsel. Let's go."

Fatin planted her fists on her hips. "But I need to see Eirik. To make sure he's going to be all right."

Baraq grabbed her upper arm and pulled her toward him. His face lowered, bronze skin deepening in caste with a flush of red. "You haven't any say in what happens next." He pushed her toward the door. "Go! And hurry before he changes his mind about letting us leave. Birget and the others have been cooling their heels so long I'm surprised they haven't already stormed this place."

They were let out a side door on the opposite end of the building from where they'd entered. The night was still pitch-black. Frustrated and angry, she hurried down the narrow alleyway heading toward the road that ran parallel to the cannery. "How did Adem react when he heard who Eirik was?" she asked over her shoulder.

"As though Zeus himself had handed him a thunderbolt of his very own."

"Damn." Her hands drew into fists. "I needed to warn Eirik. Adem will use him."

"Eirik may be a Viking, may be plainspoken, but he's not stupid or unsophisticated."

"And you know this on long acquaintance of what . . . five minutes?"

"I know Birget. She's cut from the same cloth."

"Yeah, how does that feel? Knowing you were rescuing her lover?"

"They've never been lovers. Never even met. Still haven't."

How could that be? "But she came for him."

"Because she swore to free him. They're betrothed. An arrangement their families made."

*Birget* was his betrothed? Fatin stumbled, but righted herself before she landed on her knees. "And they've never met."

"Not so unusual, even in Helios's upper strata." He waved a hand. "A merging of kingdoms."

They turned a corner. Shadows moved away from the walls to stand in their path. Large shadows.

"Birget?" Baraq called softly.

"Here." Birget stepped around the men blocking their path. "Will this Adem help us?"

"Not us. Eirik escaped and is with him now."

Birget's breath caught. "He belongs with us."

"Adem and his followers are well armed. It would serve no purpose to oppose him. And from what I've seen of him, Eirik won't hide in safety while others risk themselves to free the captives."

"But this is our fight too."

"We're to stay low. You're all too noticeable. He doesn't want enforcers tipped off. We'll wait at the ship. He'll send word when things are about to go down."

"What about me?" Fatin asked.

Both Baraq's and Birget's heads swiveled toward her. Birget's upper lip curled.

"He wants you to stay in lockdown," Baraq said.

"I can't." Panic grabbed her chest. "Tomorrow I'm supposed to see my sister. Aliyah might guess something's wrong if I don't show up."

Birget snorted. "Why would she care whether some ex-whore doesn't show up to see another whore?"

Anger welled inside. Fatin balled her fists and launched herself at Birget. The fist landed with a satisfying thud against the other woman's jaw, but Birget turned with it, grabbed her by the waist, and slammed her chest first into the mud-brick alley wall.

She saw stars for a second, and then shook her head to clear it. Birget twisted Fatin's arm behind her back and leaned in close.

Gritting her teeth to prevent a groan at the extreme angle of the hold, Fatin gave up struggling.

"I don't give a frig for you or your sister," Birget growled. "I care only that my people are set free. You are responsible for this. I have no pity, no mercy inside me. I haven't killed you yet because Baraq says you might still be of some use to us." She gave Fatin's arm another twist.

Pain shot through Fatin's shoulder, but as soon as Birget loosed her hold, Fatin spun, dipped, and grabbed Birget's arm. She pulled and rolled Birget over her back. Before Birget could react, Fatin sat in the center of Birget's chest while the other woman gasped for breath.

Fatin leaned toward her face. "I've taken enough abuse from you." Her breaths huffed, short and choppy. "Your betrothed and the rest of your barbarian friends are all alive and extremely well sated. The worst they've suffered is chafing from overuse of their man parts. You and I have the same goal. To free people we love. Next time you strike me, prepare to draw away a stump."

She stood, stepping over Birget and passing through a line of Vikings who all stood away as she stomped past. Behind her, she heard the clearing of a throat.

"Guess our little bounty hunter has more grit than you imagined, Princess."

A smile tugged at Fatin's mouth, but she kept her head down. Her body might be aching from everything she'd endured the past couple of days, but she wasn't beaten. And she'd be damned if she sat this fight out.

Eirik bent over maps laid on a table. For the past hour, he and the leopard-man had pored over maps of Heliopolis, the PG compound, and now the islands dotting the mouth of the Blue Nile

River. That was, after Adem had thoroughly questioned Eirik about the men who'd been taken, and in particular why there was such interest in Eirik from Baraq and the others who'd accompanied the Helio in search of the Vikings.

For the first time since his capture, Eirik revealed who he was, trusting Fatin's estimation of Adem. He didn't care about the leopard's motives, only that he was capable of helping him.

Adem was indeed eager to help, but only because he hoped to weave the Vikings into his own plan to bring down PG.

"The Consortium has an embassy on an estuary island," Adem said, pointing toward an unremarkable island. "Their security is unlike anything the Helios have. Their technology is far advanced."

Eirik's jaw tightened. "I was under the impression that the Consortium worked in tandem with the Helios. Why fortify themselves against intrusion?"

"The Consortium doesn't trust the Helios. With good cause. They consider them nearsighted and far too short-lived to share in governance over anything other than the human worlds in this galaxy. They've seen how Helios treat their own people. How they've treated you Icelanders. They tolerate Helios only to a point. As long as pure light ore continues to flow from your planet to the rest of the worlds, they leave Helios alone."

Eirik shook his head. "And yet they enforce certain laws. Like a prohibition on murder and abduction of ruling families."

Adem's lip curled. "Only because the supply routes tend to be interrupted during times of war. It's always about money."

"If security is so impossible to breach, how do I contact them? Will we be able to approach their island in the open?"

"All communication is made through encoded transmissions, which are carefully safeguarded by Helios's ruling council."

Eirik raked a hand through his hair. "You're not offering a solution. Just declaring more obstacles."

"I'm telling you how it is so that you will know what I'm about to suggest is your only option."

Eirik didn't like the sound of that or the hard gleam in Adem's pale eyes. "There's a reason you sent Fatin and Baraq away so quickly."

Adem snorted. "I don't want you distracted or playing the martyr to save Fatin."

"Which intimates there's to be a sacrifice." Eirik didn't need to hear more to know that the sacrifice would be his own. He shoved back the maps. "Why don't you just tell me your plan."

"You're not going to like it."

Eirik aimed a steady glare at the leopard. "Will your plan secure the freedom of my men?"

Adem nodded slowly. "That is my hope."

"Will Fatin be safe?"

"If she does as I instructed Baraq she should do, then yes. Again, I didn't want you concerned for her safety. You will have more than enough to contend with."

Eirik studied Adem, noted the proud set of his shoulders, the unbending straightness of his back. His eyes, although eerily inhuman, remained unblinking as Adem waited for his decision. "It seems I have little choice," Eirik murmured. "I can escape to a ship and flee to New Iceland, but that choice is a coward's tactic. I will not leave my men behind. Aliyah is unstable. If she thinks to refute any claims I make from New Iceland, she can easily hide the proof of her crimes by killing them."

Again, Adem nodded his agreement, as though he'd already thought of the same argument.

Eirik continued, thinking through options as he spoke. "Seeking an audience by contacting Consortium officials directly would require my getting inside the compound. And I cannot simply walk in there without being noticed. Even with the uniform. Security will be tighter than ever." Eirik let out a breath. "This plan of yours . . . Will I at least be able to fight like a Viking?"

Adem's split grin stretched across his face. "I can almost guarantee that. Eirik, you will get your chance to show all of Helios why they should fear the wrath of a Viking."

Fatin straightened the silk tunic she wore, then brushed away a speck of dirt from the hem of her trousers. Birget had allowed her to return to her own ship to retrieve clothing and make sure that the crew she'd left behind still maintained the ship's systems. Miriam had rushed to her when she'd crossed the gangway, muttering a list of complaints but not even commenting on Baraq's presence at her elbow.

Miriam should have recognized the Consortium security officer. His dark, striking face and broad build were distinctive. The woman had been aboard the *Proteus* with the rest of her crew when they'd been busy ferrying captives from the surface of New Iceland. And yet, Miriam chattered on about needing to pay the crew again since they were staying so long on Helios, and when would they be returning the ship to Roxana on Karthagos?

She hadn't realized that Fatin's change of plans, to bypass Karthagos altogether and deliver the Vikings directly to Aliyah, hadn't been part of any plan the pirate had been privy to. But then again, Miriam was single-minded and didn't think beyond her own comfort or needs.

Baraq had remained silent while she'd brushed aside Miriam's concerns, wrote a note for Miriam to cash and pay the crew. Then she'd shooed away the woman, changed the launch codes to ensure no one tried to leave port without her permission, and gathered a change of clothing.

With his arms folded over his chest, Baraq eyed the shambles of her cabin.

"What?" Fatin said, flushing. "I don't spend my time aboard cleaning."

"Did I comment?"

"No, but that look said plenty."

Baraq grunted. "I met Roxana. While we searched for you. She's furious with you. She didn't seem the forgiving type. Do you really intend to return her ship?"

Fatin shrugged. "Of course. I'm not a thief. Not by trade. This was necessary."

"How do you intend to repay her for the proceeds from the cargo you hijacked?"

"I'll share whatever's left." And Roxana would likely take the rest of what she owed from Fatin's hide. But that was a problem for another day.

"You'll share proceeds after you've paid for your sister's papers?"

Baraq's raised brow annoyed her. So she wasn't the most trust-worthy partner a pirate could have. She nodded sharply.

"Even though you know it's not likely for Aliyah to honor her promise to sell your sister's papers . . . ?"

Fatin gave him a sour scowl. "Aliyah has one chance to make this right. If she refuses me, I'll find another way. I had hoped Adem would provide that option, but since he's not talking to me . . ." She shrugged and stuffed her clothing into a bag.

"Fatin, you could put your trust in Eirik and Birget," he said softly. "Neither thinks only of a cause or of themselves."

She didn't glance up. Didn't want to see his expression softening.

She needed him to stay angry because anything else would weaken her. "Why would either help me?"

"I don't claim to know Eirik, but he hasn't harmed you."

Fatin shot him a glance and raised an eyebrow. Baraq knew good and well that she'd sported a few bruises the first time they'd met.

"Nothing lasting," he insisted, "and I'm guessing nothing you didn't enjoy. My point is, he's had his chance for revenge, and let it slip through his fingers. And that room back at the cannery wasn't awash in blood. It reeked of sex."

She blushed, but lifted her chin in defiance.

"He doesn't sound like a man bent on revenge. And as conflicted as you are about how you feel about him, my guess is that he's in a similar state. These Vikings are honorable people. You have to trust someone."

"I don't know how."

"Not even your sister?"

"With my secrets. But I've been the one to make the decisions for us both."

Baraq moved away from the door, dropping his arms. "Well, it's time, don't you think? To lay your trust in someone?"

"Maybe," she muttered, wanting the conversation to end because she felt a stab of emotion deep inside her chest that felt like loneliness. "I've just been so focused for so long." She gave herself a mental shake. "We should head back. I need to shower and change."

# Sixteen

Fatin headed directly to the women's *saray*, remembering that Aliyah had promised her she didn't have to seek permission from her office to enter. If she were stopped and questioned about Eirik's escape, her surprise would be more plausible if she proceeded according to their arrangement.

Stepping across the fragrant threshold brought back bittersweet memories. She and her sister, giggling during those first months, when they'd still been in awe of the changes in their circumstances. After months of hunger and fear, they'd felt giddy with the abundance and attention showered upon them.

They'd been bathed, groomed, clothed in silk, and instructed in etiquette, in how to pleasure a man or a woman. Everything had seemed a very funny game, and they'd felt beautiful, like petted princesses. It hadn't been until they'd been put into service that reality struck.

Fatin had drawn an old man for her breaching.

His breath had smelled, his sex had revolted her, and despite the remedies she'd applied, she hadn't been able to keep him erect long enough for him to pierce her maidenhead.

She'd begun to cry, and fight, and only then had he hardened.

He'd hit her face, her breasts, then clamped her thighs against her chest and thrust home.

Afterward, Zarah had come to her, shooing away the attendants to care for her by herself.

Zarah's breaching hadn't been a violent experience, and yet they'd both hugged each other close, crying.

After that, Fatin had burned with the desire for freedom, while Zarah had quietly retreated from the world, withdrawing inside herself.

Fatin shook away the memories and straightened her shoulders. She had a purpose today. To let her sister know that rescue was on the way.

The common room was empty. She tried Zarah's door, but again saw no sign of her sister. Beginning to grow fearful, she didn't relax until she found Zarah in the garden behind the *saray*, sitting on a bench beside a fountain, feeding birds, brilliantly colored crimson sparrows. Prey for falcons.

A disturbing scene, but one only she would recognize for what it was. Zarah no longer felt a sense of self.

Fatin cleared her throat, drawing her sister's attention.

Zarah's expression didn't change; there was no note of curiosity, no expression of joy, but Fatin knew her, saw her blink and turn away her face.

"I'm happy to see you too," Fatin said softly, sitting beside her and taking her hand inside her own.

They sat like that, listening to the birds chirp, letting the sun filtering through the leaves warm their faces.

Her heart felt at peace, and if it was to last for only this moment, it was enough for now.

"You've been away so long," Zarah said, her voice sounding hollow.

Fatin squeezed her hand, fighting to keep her tone even when tears burned the back of her throat. "Did you think I had forgotten you?"

"I wondered if you were safe. You had such plans. And when you didn't come to visit—"

"Aliyah didn't allow me to come back. Today's the first time she's granted me an audience."

Zarah tugged her hand free and clasped hers together in her lap. She breathed deeply, as though calming herself. "You should get on with your life. She will never let you purchase my papers."

"I'm coming to realize that. Already she's raised your price. She had promised an exchange—the Vikings for you—but now she's wanting more."

Zarah raised her eyes, her gaze unblinking. "I am well, sister. Fed and clothed. Pampered. You can leave me without feeling guilt for it. Begin a new life."

Fatin's eyes burned because she knew her sister had resigned herself to living out her life inside this prison. She wanted to argue with her, to make her angry enough to throw off her odd tranquillity, but knew it wouldn't be fair for her to make her feel, and then leave her again. "When you close your eyes to sleep, what do you dream about?"

Zarah closed her eyes and lifted her face to the sunlight. "I dream of the aerie," she whispered.

"Of our father?"

"I see his wings spread as he soars. I hear his call to the others as they swoop toward the sky."

"We left because you would never fly. Your wings are only . . ."

"Vestiges of a bird? It didn't matter. I was one of them. The aerie was high above the ground. There was freedom there. To breathe the wind. To feel it ruffle my feathers. It was enough."

"Our mother worried we'd be trapped. That you or I would stumble and fall over the edge."

"Would that have been so terrible? A moment of pure freedom?"

"You would prefer death?"

"To this life?" Zarah smiled, at last, but it was filled with bitterness.

Fatin scooted closer. "That's why I can't leave you here," she whispered urgently.

"I won't live forever. Neither will you. You risk too much for me."

"But I've found a way . . ."

Zarah's gaze sharpened. "Don't speak of it here. There are eyes and ears everywhere. Forget it."

"Trust me. Not to give up. We are sisters. You're all I have."

Zarah shook her head and a hint of devilish humor entered her expression. "You have the Viking. I saw how he was with you when you spied on us."

"You saw me?"

"Of course."

Fatin felt her cheeks warm beneath her sister's teasing glance. Still, she couldn't resist asking. "What do you mean about how he was with me?"

Zarah's expression softened, her gaze growing tender. "He cares. And he seems to be able to temper your impulsiveness. He makes love like a god. I can well understand why you like him."

"Did you and he . . . ?"

Her sister shook her head. "We pleasured our patron. He was careful to only give me the most circumspect of caresses. Enough not to make Livia wonder."

"I shouldn't be selfish. He really is very good. Although at times he is controlling. And a little violent."

"He's a strong man with a lusty appetite. But with the right woman, he will turn that passion to provide her unending bliss."

"You learned a lot about him. More than I and I've known him a few weeks now."

"I have little else to do but study people. They think I'm simple, that I am a sensual animal. People talk and act without filters around me. I know by watching him that he's honorable. That he has you in his sight."

Fatin sighed. "He wants revenge. I was the one responsible for his capture."

"He told me this."

"That he wants revenge?" Zarah laughed, the sound so beautiful, Fatin's heart ached. She gave a rueful smile. "Am I too quick to assume the worst?"

"You haven't changed. So surly and sweet. I love you, Fatin."

"As I love you. Please don't give up. Be ready. I will find a way. And it won't be much longer."

In the distance, the sound of a door crashing broke the peaceful stillness.

Fatin jerked and started to rise.

Three guards barreled into the garden. One flashed gold teeth, and Fatin's stomach plummeted.

"You!" he said, pointing the end of a long stun-spear.

Aware of her sister clutching her hand, she straightened the rest of the way and lifted her chin. "I have the mistress's permission to be here."

"Permission is rescinded. By her order."

Fatin fought the urge to fly at the man and scratch his smirk from his face. She forced herself to remain calm and turned to Zarah. "I'll speak to her. Remember what I said." She dropped her hand and headed toward the guard, wondering why it had been necessary to send so many.

A tremor of fear shivered through her, but she kept her head high, preceding the guards out of the building and walking toward the main office.

"Not that way."

She glanced back, saw his sneer a moment before he jabbed his spear. Too late to dodge away, the guard's spear tapped her buttocks, delivering a searing charge.

"Bastard!"

"Bitch. I'm taking you to induction."

"What?" Just the word sent a chill through her. Induction. The first stop when a new, fractious slave entered the compound. It was a place where a slave learned to fear punishment and lost her will to resist. Not a place she or her sister had needed to experience, but she'd heard enough to know what happened there. "There's some mistake. I'm a free woman."

"No mistake. I have orders. Now move that ass or I'll give you another jab. And if you happen to fall, I won't be so quick about letting you get back up again."

His intent clear by his leering smile, she swallowed hard, her heart beating against her chest.

The men fell in around her, behind her and at her sides, as they escorted her to a dimly lit cell in the basement of the induction center.

When the door slammed shut behind her, she stood, shock and despair holding her still. There had to be some mistake. Aliyah hadn't the right to do this to her, not unless she'd discovered something of her plans.

The door opened behind her. She glanced back to see Aliyah step inside, then gesture to the guard to leave them. Aliyah's expression was hard and emotionless as marble.

"Aliyah, why are you doing this?"

Aliyah stepped close, raised her hand, and slapped Fatin hard across the face. Then she grimaced, glared at her palm as Fatin cupped her hand to her own stinging cheek.

It was almost funny, that look. "Not as satisfying as you hoped?" Fatin quipped, unable to halt her tongue.

Aliyah aimed a withering glare. "Shut up."

"Why am I here? You haven't the right to hold me."

"I do since you've conspired to steal my property."

Fatin held her breath. Gods, was she talking about the helmet or Eirik? "Conspired? What are you talking about?" she asked, schooling her face into a confused mask, which wasn't hard since she wasn't sure which crime she was being accused of.

"Don't play coy," Aliyah snapped. "You know damn well Wolf has escaped."

Fatin blinked. "Really? How could I know that? I've spoken to no one since my arrival other than my sister—whom you granted me an audience to see."

Aliyah stepped closer, her face studying Fatin's with an avid, scary intensity. "At this moment, every enforcer, every off-duty PG guard is searching for him. He won't stay free for long. Save yourself, Fatin. Tell me where to find him."

Fatin pretended an angry affront. "I don't know where to find him. Why on earth would you think I would? I captured him for you. I gladly accepted payment and left him here to rot. Why would I help him now?"

Aliyah's lips thinned into an ugly snarl. "Michael suggested it. Said he thought that there was something between you two."

"Nothing other than loathing on his part."

"What about yours?"

Fatin blew out a deep breath. "He's handsome, but I didn't appreciate being mauled by him. There's no love there." All true, which she hoped Aliyah would read in her eyes.

Aliyah jerked away and paced the length of the cell. "This isn't good. Those who pay to play like to think that our thralls are happy here. That they are well treated, spoiled. And I do my best to see that this is true. I can't let them think the men are so unhappy they'd rather risk death than stay in my care. They'd become sympathetic toward the men. Already they sigh and moon, but they can't begin to think the men are more than what they are—barely leashed barbarians, better off here than out in the world." She halted beside Fatin, fury in her red face. Her eyes narrowed to slits. "Prove your loyalty to me."

"How, mistress? I've done everything you've asked of me."

"Find him. You did it once before. You can get close to him."

"If I get near him, he's likely to snap my neck."

"Then make sure you capture him first. Prove you're mine, Fatin."

Fatin nodded, feeling dazed. If she didn't bring Eirik in, she'd be back at square one with Aliyah. Persona non grata. Unable to see her sister or even discuss the price for her freedom. "If I catch him?"

"I will free your sister."

Fatin didn't bother hiding her disbelief. "You've waved that promise beneath my nose before. Why should I believe you now?"

"Are you calling me a liar? Can I help that she becomes more valuable, more prized, every day?"

Fatin remained still, sensing Aliyah didn't expect an answer. When Aliyah raised her hand again, she didn't flinch away.

This time, the whore-mistress cupped the cheek she'd slapped, caressing it. "I am not a liar. And I'm not your enemy."

Bile rose to the back of her throat, but Fatin said through tight lips, "I know that, mistress."

Aliyah kissed her cheek, then drew back. Her dark stare glittered with a maniacal excitement. "I promised you current market value. Now I promise that I will settle for what you have paid now. Bring me the Viking. *Then* you may leave with your sister."

Eirik tossed his head, sweat spraying in an arc from his wet hair. His muscles burned. His heart thrilled to each gleaming arc of the steel blade he swung.

He met the jarring thrust, planted a foot behind him, and shoved hard to push Adem back, then raised his borrowed sword again, slicing from the side, knowing Adem would meet it. Another step forward, and he had the leopard jammed against the wall.

Adem's cat's mouth stretched into a smile. "Well done!"

Panting with exertion, Eirik offered him a grunt and stepped back, resting the sword point on the floor and leaning on the hilt. "I'm winded," he said in disgust. "You've not broken a sweat."

"But then, I never sweat," the other man said, pale eyes gleaming. "However, I do believe you're ready."

A commotion at the door had both men turning at the sound.

Two of Adem's men entered, carrying inside a squirming bundle wrapped in a blanket, which they deposited on the floor at Adem's feet.

Adem laughed and bent to pull away the wrapping with a tug that sent the figure in the center rolling across the floor.

Eirik didn't know why, but he wasn't all that surprised to find Fatin, spitting and cursing as she shoved up on her arms.

"Why am I not surprised?" Adem said, echoing Eirik's thought.

"Why is everything such a bloody production with you?" she said, shaking back her hair, which was loose and tangled around her head.

Eirik grinned at her appearance. Dressed in pretty, wine-colored silk, she looked like a feminine bundle of fluff. Far from the hard-edged bounty hunter—more the lithe bit of femininity he'd first met in the mining camp. Except for the fire sparking in her eyes.

"And you!" she said, wagging her finger at Eirik. "You've caused me nothing but trouble. I should have known it the first time I set eyes on you."

Eirik shot out a hand to wrap around that pointing finger and pulled it, forcing her to rise and come closer. "What's happened, Fatin?" he asked, grinning. "Did you miss me?"

Her eyes bulged, and she shook off his hold. "What's happened?" she asked, her voice rising. "The whole city is looking for you. Ali-yah set her guards on me, sure I had something to do with your escape. Why? I have no idea. If you show your face in daylight, the bounty's so fucking high there's not a Heliopolite living who won't give chase."

"Not unexpected," Adem said dryly, flashing him a glance, before narrowing his gaze on Fatin again.

Fatin straightened her shoulders, and her expression calmed, worry casting a shadow across her face as she turned to face Adem. "She's holding my sister ransom—for him."

Adem shrugged. "Since you've always known the price would be too steep, why are you so enraged?"

"Because . . ." Fatin blew out a deep breath, then closed her eyes for a moment. When she opened them again, she stared into Adem's eyes, imploring. "I have to get him off planet now," she whispered. "Before it's too late. You can't use him, Adem. He has to leave now.

If he's ever caught, I fear what she'll do to him. She'll want to make an example for the others."

Eirik stepped beside her, cupping her shoulder to force her to turn his way. "You'd trade your sister's freedom for mine?"

Fatin stiffened beneath his grasp, but turned her head. She didn't quite meet his gaze. "My sister wouldn't want her freedom, not in exchange for yours," she said, her voice raw. "I know this now."

"She's tricking you, Viking," Adem bit out. "She'll lead you from here and straight into a trap."

Fatin waved a hand at Adem. "Shut up." She held Eirik's gaze as she angled her body toward him. "I promise I am not trying to trap you. Come with me. To my ship. I'll get you off planet. You have the wealth of a kingdom to seek the release of your men. But you will never be able to do it, never be able to tell your story to a single person who cares that you've been wronged if you're recaptured."

Eirik lifted his sword and held it out to Adem. "Fatin, I want to trust you. But I'd be a foolish man if I listened only to my heart."

"Your heart?" Her face screwed up, confusion mixing with anger. "Dammit, Viking. You have to flee Helios. It's your only hope."

More men rushed into the room. "Adem, enforcers! They're all around us."

"Bitch," Adem said, taking a step toward Fatin.

She shook her head, her face draining of color. "I promise I didn't bring them."

"Then she had you followed."

"I took precautions." Her gaze swung back to Eirik. "I swear I had nothing to do with this."

Eirik squeezed her shoulder. "It doesn't matter, Fatin. It's done."

"What are you talking about? We can still get away."

Eirik aimed a glare at Adem. "Can you and your men get out of here?"

"Underground, yes. Through a tunnel, although it's likely half-filled with water this time of year."

"Then use it." Eirik grabbed Fatin's arm and pushed her toward Adem. "Take her too."

Adem bared his teeth in a snarl. "She's responsible. Why not leave her here to greet them?"

"She didn't betray me. Not this time."

Fatin pulled on his arm. "Eirik! What are you doing? Aren't you coming?"

He gave her a crooked smile. "A plan's afoot. This doesn't change a thing. I'll be all right."

Her eyes widened. "You didn't see Aliyah. She'll punish you. Make you pay for humiliating her."

"We haven't time for this, Viking," Adem shouted.

Eirik gripped Fatin's waist and pulled her against him.

Her hands shoved against his chest. "Eirik, please. Don't do this. I swear there are worse things than selling your body. Adem, tell him!"

Eirik shook her. "He's already warned me what I likely face. I'm prepared."

"Fatin," Adem said, urgency in his voice now. "He knows what he's about."

Her eyes filled, but her lips snarled. "I don't understand. I can help you."

Eirik bent toward her, locking glances. "We finish this. As Vikings. And Vikings don't retreat." He cupped her head and tilted it back. "Do what you must to get through this, Fatin. I will also."

She shook her head, the corners of her mouth turning downward. "Eirik . . ."

"I do know you care. To set aside your plans for me . . ."

"You believe me? You believe I would have helped you?"

Eirik didn't answer her. It didn't matter. Fatin's body shook inside his embrace. She was afraid. For him. It was enough.

He kissed her, mashing his lips against hers, circling as he stroked his tongue into her mouth, tasted her for what might be the last time.

When he set her down, she swayed, which made his lips twitch. He raised his gaze to Adem, who arched a brow. "You see now?"

"I do." Adem returned the sword, then gripped his forearm. "You do know you may not have a chance to warn them once you're back inside."

"My men aren't letting themselves get fat. If they have a chance to act, they will. You have only to tell them the Wolf sanctions this. Every man will be eager to join the battle."

"Good luck," Adem said, then dropped his arm. "Fatin, come with me."

He still had to grasp her arm and pull her behind him, but she didn't fight. Her steps were slowed because she gazed behind her at Eirik, as though unwilling to miss a single moment.

And he knew just how she felt.

Alone now, he stood in the center of the room as the door crashed open and uniformed PG guards flooded inside, bodies crouching, weapons raised as they sighted on him, then searched every corner.

Eirik stood, his sword raised, the calm in the center of the storm that was about to erupt.

# *Seventeen*

Aboard the *Daedalus*, Birget eyed the mishmash of fur-covered and black-uniformed men crowded into the ship's hold. Her army. Or Adem's, depending on whose history would be written.

Adem had arrived at her ship at short time ago, striding up the gangway bold as he pleased, demanding entrance. She'd been caught off guard, her attention snagged by his strange appearance, too distracted to hear everything he'd said.

Baraq let him aboard, then sent out her Vikings to provide covert cover, should the ferals Adem brought with him require it. They'd run aboard, under the cover of darkness, in pairs, darting inside. Baraq had only just returned after ensuring Adem and his men hadn't been followed. Now both contingents stood by as Adem related what had happened and why he'd abandoned the cannery.

One fact caught her attention. "Eirik remained behind?" she asked, eyeing the leopard-man and trying hard not to stare.

Adem's nod was curt. "It was his own choice. He sacrificed his freedom to ensure we would escape."

She grunted, impressed. "As he should. Against how many?"

"I don't know. But my lookouts said the cannery was swarming with PG security."

"Not enforcers?" Baraq asked.

At Adem's nod, she turned to Fatin, who sat tied to a chair. "Why would that be so?"

Fatin's expression didn't hold her usual sullen scowl. She was white-faced, her lips trembling. She looked frightened for the first time, as well she should. Birget wasn't convinced she didn't have something to do with the raid on the warehouse. Neither was Adem.

"If Aliyah discovered where Eirik was before the enforcers," Fatin said, her voice small, "she would want to bring him in herself to save face. And to maintain custody."

"What will happen to him now?"

Fatin's eyes filled with tears. "She will want to make an example, as a warning to the other thralls, especially those who followed him. Likely, she'll send him to the lists. He'll fight or die in the arena."

Birget noted the other woman's stilted speech, her dull eyes. "Adem thinks you led them to his headquarters."

Fatin raised her head. "Not knowingly. I was careful. I changed trams. I skirted the sector, by foot, before making my way there. I don't know how such a large force could have followed me undetected."

Birget met Adem's gaze. His face was taut, his expression without any pity. "I would know if she tells the truth. If she's responsible, we have no further use for her."

Adem nodded. "Clear the bay."

Birget waved her own men out of the hold. Adem's men followed. When it was just Adem, Baraq, and herself standing over Fatin, Baraq cut her free.

"Strip," Adem said. "We need your clothes."

Fatin's face drained of what little color she had left, but she lifted her chin. She stood and slowly peeled away her trousers and the pretty silk shirt that had suffered through the escape, and which was now drenched with tunnel water and ripped. When she stood nude, she squared her shoulders and met Birget's steady gaze, accusation in her dark eyes.

Birget didn't wince. Couldn't show a moment's remorse. Not even when Baraq aimed a glare her way, telling her silently to stop this.

Despite the pallor beneath her burnished skin, pride burned in Fatin's posture. Birget felt a moment's regret that she couldn't trust the Helio, that Fatin had made so many deplorable decisions. She had strength in her small frame, and courage.

And she was achingly lovely. Slender and small-framed, warm bronze skin, dark oval nipples with perfectly beaded tips. Even her sex was pretty—neat and nude. A man would favor her looks. Seek to taste her exotic flavors.

Birget dragged away her gaze, feeling ashamed for the other woman's vulnerability.

Adem picked up the clothing and pulled it through his hands, crushing it. When he was finished he shook his head. "Fatin, come here."

She stepped woodenly toward him, and he cupped her head, his fingers combing through her thick, dark hair, pulling at her ears to peer inside, opening her mouth, then smoothing his hands down her body to her toes.

When still he found nothing, he came to his feet. "Spread your legs."

Fatin's face screwed up into a terrible, anguished frown, which made Birget feel uneasy, squeamish for the indelicacy of the search.

"Princess," Baraq whispered harshly, "is this necessary?"

Birget firmed her resolve and raised her hand to cut him off.

"I swear there's nothing for you to find," Fatin said hoarsely, her gaze pleading with Adem.

A tic pulsed at Adem's square jaw. "I don't want to do this. Truly. But they found us. If you weren't followed, how did they track you? How can we be assured they won't follow you here?"

Fatin stomped her feet apart and gazed toward the far wall as Adem thrust his fingers inside her. "This isn't any different than when I stood for inspection in the *saray*," she said, bitterness strengthening her voice. "Except then, the men were only curious about how tight my cunt was, how well I'd squeeze around them."

"I mean you no harm, little one. But we have to know."

When he was done, he moved back and wiped his fingers on his thighs. He turned to Birget. "She's clear."

Fatin snorted, but her mouth gave away her emotions. One corner trembled.

"If it wasn't her, then we have a bigger problem," Baraq muttered.

Birget gave a sharp nod, then turned a steady eye on Adem. "One of yours betrayed you. Are any unaccounted for?"

"All my men are here. However, it's possible that the driver who delivered Eirik to the warehouse might have been tracked through his vehicle's onboard computer. That would explain it."

Fatin scoffed. "And you suspected that before you searched me?"

His head swiveled toward her. His features were set, hard. "Like I said, we had to know." Adem held out her clothes.

Fatin pulled the soiled and wrinkled tunic over her head, then slid on the trousers. When she was clothed again, she tossed back her hair.

Birget suppressed a smile at the deadly glare she gave to the leopard-man.

Birget could hardly keep from staring at him herself. Baraq had told her about him, after he'd been released, and she'd seen many strange sights since she'd landed on this world, but the leopard was the most fascinating.

He wore only trousers and boots. His torso was shaped like a man's, but she wondered if the fine spotted down that covered those manly bulges also cloaked the masculine parts that were hidden by his clothing.

"Shall I take off my trousers to indulge your curiosity?" Adem murmured.

Birget's gaze rose to meet his hard, unblinking stare. Heat crept across her cheeks. "I am sorry. I don't mean to be impolite, but we haven't anyone like you on our world."

"I shouldn't exist," Adem growled. "I'm fourth generation. My ancestors were born in a dish inside PG's laboratories. The same place your Viking's sperm will be mixed with Helio eggs to breed their next batch of atrocity. But while it will be human mated with human, they will treat the results the same. They will warehouse the children, test them, train them, and then one day unleash them on your world."

"Lord Dagr, Eirik's brother, suspected that was the purpose. I thought he was insane. For anyone to scheme with that sort of patience . . ."

"Patience? The creatures they will create, are creating now, won't be allowed to grow according to nature. They have learned to quicken maturity. Your planet doesn't have twenty-five years to prepare. Accelerated harvesting is their latest product.

"Already Helios who've lost children can have them cloned and replaced within months. That same technology will be turned to grow an army."

"Dagr had heard this, but even my father didn't believe it was possible." She shot a glance at Baraq. "Were you ever going to mention this to me?"

Baraq's shoulders stiffened, and he stared straight ahead.

Birget walked closer, anger building inside her. "Baraq? *Helio!* Did you know?"

His jaw tensed. "I knew of the experiments, but I've been a ship's security officer for some time. Those matters aren't my concern."

"Why didn't you say something?"

"I didn't believe they could do it yet. And I wanted to spare you the added worry."

Anger boiled over. He'd wanted to spare her? Like some woman in need of gentle coddling. Had he learned nothing about her? "What? I am in command. Everything is my worry. You disappoint me. I thought I had your respect."

"You do, Princess."

She waved her hand, cutting him off again. "Join the others," she said, her voice tight.

Baraq clicked his heels and turned, striding away. She didn't watch, instead tamping down useless, confusing emotions to stare at Fatin.

In the other woman's gaze, she saw compassion, which maddened her. She didn't need the bounty hunter's pity.

"Adem," she said, grinding her teeth, "tell me why we shouldn't kill her."

Adem's smile was thin, barely a curl at one corner of his mouth. Bitter. "Because I would have to tell her sister I stood by while she was murdered."

"Why do you care?"

Adem grunted. "I shouldn't. She's more bird than human. I should eat her up and spit out the feathers."

Fatin snorted. "You still want her. How priceless. You had the means to save us from the Garden, and you let us go."

Adem's hands curled into fists. "I wanted you both safe, fed, clothed," he growled. "I had nothing."

Birget cocked her head, her gaze swinging from one to the other. "You know each other well?"

Fatin glanced away in disgust. "We were children on the streets, in the slum sector."

"Where the half-breeds lived," Adem added.

"Our mothers had abandoned us or died. We roamed in packs. Like wild animals, until the enforcers had us rounded up. Without families, we should have been fostered out."

"Enslaved to human families, you mean," Adem bit out. "To bring out to show their friends their new pets."

Fatin curled her lip. "When I was arrested for stealing, with my sister, we were auctioned to the Garden. But *this one*," she said, waving a hand at Adem, "had long before found a way to make some money. He could have paid the man I robbed, and had us set free, but he let us go."

"I wanted you both safe."

"And like a man, you thought nothing of the fact we'd have to spread our legs for anyone willing to pay." Fatin shivered with rage. "It's just sex to you. Not important. Our pride meant nothing to you."

Adem's jaw clamped shut.

Birget shook her head. "That is it? This happened years ago, and still you hold a grudge?"

Adem raised his chin. "When she earned her thrall-price, she came to me."

Fatin raked a hand through her wild hair. "He was angry that I had left my sister alone. We fought, but the fight turned . . ."

Birget nodded. "You became lovers . . ."

"Not for long. He loves her. But now he's crossed a line he can't erase. We both have."

Adem glanced away. "I liked you better when you were just a street thief, Fatin. You weren't always such a selfish bitch. I thought I held that girl."

She bared her teeth in a feral grin. "You just wanted a taste of everything I'd learned inside those walls. Well, I don't play those games anymore."

"You do with the Viking."

Birget's gaze homed on Fatin. "What is he saying?"

"Her and the one called Wolf," Adem said, lifting his chin. "They cannot share a room without scratching away their clothes to mate."

Birget felt her face freeze. Eirik was the one they spoke of. Her future husband had slept with this dirty urchin.

No matter that she'd taken her own lover; at least she hadn't taken an animal to bed! "Again, tell me why *I* should not kill her?"

Adem fisted his hands on his hips, then dropped his head between his shoulders. His black hair fanned forward. When his face tilted up, his steady gaze fell on Fatin. "You should not kill her because she's not responsible for his recapture. Because she may still be of use. And because the longer she lives, the more she will suffer for her sins against you."

Birget's small smile matched the one creeping across Adem's mouth. "Yes, reason enough right there." She dropped her glance to Fatin. "I will give you to Baraq. Somehow, I do not think he will disappoint me again. Should you betray us, *he* will kill you."

Once again, Eirik stood in the mouth of Hel. Another dingy cell in the bowels of the arena. Only this time, in addition to a barred door, he was chained, hands and feet in manacles, strong metal links running through loops in the walls and on the floor.

More than simply restrained, because he had escaped once. His captor was taking no chances. And she'd left him naked, hoping to humiliate him, but he didn't care. It was sweltering. Even the loin skirt would have felt too heavy.

As before, he was being bathed by two wide-eyed girls who appeared too frightened to do more than dab at his skin before they left. Then Bethel arrived, her cheeks blushing this time to perform the obligatory milking.

"No words of hope this time, little one?" he teased, trying to lighten her grim expression.

Bethel's eyes gleamed with unshed tears. "Do you know what will happen?"

"Aliyah's men said nothing. But I was warned by your friend what fate would befall me."

She glanced away, then firmed her chin. "They watch. I cannot give you what you prefer."

"Hands?"

"I'll be quick."

He nodded and braced apart his legs. Her small warm hands wrapped firmly around his shaft and began the rhythmic tug and pull.

He cleared his throat. "Have you seen the others? Are they well?"

"Privileges of the ground have been rescinded," she whispered, not pausing as she built his arousal. "They are restricted to their quarters. But yes, all are well. This morning, Hakon said to tell you that something was afoot. That their furs and breastplates had been returned to them."

"They will be presented for the spectacle."

"To watch, no doubt."

"Should you have a chance for a private word, tell Hakon command is his."

Bethel's lips quirked. "He's already taken it. Said to tell you that."

Eirik smiled.

Then she worked him in silence, and he let his mind roam. To Fatin as she'd appeared in Adem's headquarters, her hair wild around her shoulders, her eyes wide with fear—for him.

He hoped she hadn't discovered a streak of sacrifice inside herself. Not yet. She would come through the trials ahead, stronger than before.

He wished he would be there to witness it. No matter that an accident of birth made them incompatible in some fundamental ways, he couldn't imagine a universe without her in it.

"There is a chance you could win," Bethel said, although her tone was riddled with doubt.

"A chance?"

"A normal man would have none, but you are stronger, larger. Surely you will be a match."

"I am a Viking, Bethel. And a Wolfskin on top of that. I do not intend to die. But if I do, I will not cower from my fate. I will meet it with my sword raised. My brother, my people, would expect no less."

Her manipulations quickened, her fist drumming on his cock until he bent his head to watch as she brought a beaker beneath him and caught the pearly ropes jetting from his balls.

The door crashed open. The guard with the golden teeth ducked through it, then stood at attention as Aliyah swept inside.

Bethel struggled to her feet. "Mistress, I am finished here."

"Leave us." Aliyah was dressed in a long silk gown, this one a dark midnight blue. The back of it was pulled over her head like a cowl to hide her face. She tossed it back, and strode forward, slapping a short whip against her leg.

Eirik schooled his face into a mask, unwilling to show her even an ounce of emotion.

Aliyah's face was set into harsh lines that deepened the delicate brackets around her mouth. "I would have kept you in the *saray*. An exotic. A man like no other. Already the list of women and men who would have sought a single night alone with you was long."

"You should have known, mistress, that I could not be contained. I am a Viking. Not a sex-thrall."

"So you all keep saying," she said, circling behind him, "and yet the nineteen remain in my tender care. Why could you not have done the same?"

Eirik kept his face forward, refusing to follow her as she continued to circle like a lynx around its prey. "I don't know what manner of men you have kept before us, but we are not the same breed. Our pride is in our fists and our valor, not in our prowess in bed."

"I thought we were coming to an understanding, you and I," she said, whispering in his ear. "But you used the favor I bestowed and betrayed me. I'll not tolerate that. I'll not lose face. You will be punished and your Vikings will see their own fate in your blood should they decide to follow in your path."

Bethel gasped as she hovered at the door.

Aliyah stepped beside him, and turned toward the attendant, her eyes narrowing. "Get out," she said through thin lips. "Wait with the guard down the corridor."

As soon as they were alone, Aliyah's gaze swung to Eirik. And in that moment, she ceased to be beautiful. Her face reddened, her lips pulled away from her teeth, and she flew at him, arm rising.

The first lash of her whip struck his neck and face. Eirik licked at the blood on his lip and spat it at her feet.

Aliyah screamed, teeth bared. The whip landed again and again, as she circled frantically around his body, some strikes glancing, some searing his flesh, but she was out of control, striking like a madwoman.

His body jerked against the lash, but he held back his cries, molded his face into a bitter mask, eyes scalding as he glared.

At last, her arm dropped, trembling. She panted with exertion. The whip fell from her limp hand to the dirt covering the floor. Her gaze glittered with angry tears. Then she blinked, her expression settling into a calm mask. She reached back to touch her hair, then gave a low, animal cry when she discovered that hair had fallen from the clasp. She turned away, spun her long hair into a loop, and pinned it again, then slowly faced him. Her gaze swept his frame and blanched.

A gurgling moan slid from inside her. She hurried to the door, reaching blindly, and knocked.

When it opened, the guard stuck his head inside, grinned at Eirik, then held it open as Aliyah swept through it again, her cowl over her head.

After the door closed, Eirik swayed against his bonds and laid his face against the tender inside of his forearm to wipe away the blood smearing his cheeks. His skin was on fire from the sweat seeping into a dozen bloody wounds. But they were clotting; already the blood was slowing as his heartbeats calmed.

Weary, he sagged, drawing in his elbows to relieve the pull against his shoulder sockets, and rested. The bitch Aliyah couldn't be trusted not to unleash her rage on the others. She was insane. He had no choice but to find a way to win.

# Eighteen

Fatin kept her eyes lowered as she passed the guards positioned outside the door of the lockup. So long as she didn't make eye contact, she might slip past without having to make "payment," or so Adem had advised her. And he should know, given how long he'd lived inside these walls. So far, so good.

She'd curled up her lip and snarled when he'd handed her the silver slave's cuff and loin skirt. He'd paid her way into the bowels of the arena, but she'd have to pose as a thrall, come to bathe and service a gladiator.

"Not fair a dead man should have something that pretty," one of the guards said to his comrade, as though she weren't standing right there.

The one he spoke to had just unlocked the metal door at the entrance of the last tunnel, but his gaze was on her bare chest. The air was cool and her nipples had dimpled, the tips drawing tight.

His slight grin said he thought he might have something to do with it.

She tossed back her hair and fought not to mouth off, or her pose as a downtrodden thrall would have a very short life indeed. "Please, sir, I have my orders. I'm to tend to the Viking."

"Pretty little thing like you might need a little stretch first to fit the giant," he said, his finger toggling one nipple.

Bile burned the back of her throat, and she hoped he didn't try to move any closer, because his body odor would have her losing her last meal all over his sandals.

Instead of moving in, he dropped the finger to lift the cloth concealing the contents of the basket she carried on one hip. "No bandages?"

"Does he need them?"

"The other one, Miss High-and-Mighty herself, left with a whip coiled around her arm. Softened him up a bit for the spectacle. Blood always draws the ferals out. Makes 'em mean."

Fatin placed a hand against her mouth.

"Looks green, that one," his friend warned. "Let her go before we have to live with the stink."

The one beside the door stepped aside, but she still had to squeeze between him and the doorframe to get past. Her breasts scraped over the coarse cotton of his grimy shirt.

"You'll be needing this," he said, holding up a key.

When she reached for it, he pulled it away, forcing her to press harder against him to pluck the key dangling off his forefinger.

She didn't bother trying to hide her anger.

He chuckled. "This one's got some fire in her," he said to his companion. To Fatin, he whispered, "I'll be waiting for you when you come back."

She hurried down the dark passageway, lit only by a torch in a sconce every thirty paces. An artifice those who ran the events insisted on—keeping the arena and the games as close to tradition as they could.

The corridor was a rough-cut tunnel through solid stone. This deep beneath the river, which ran beside the arena, water seeped through the stone strata, dripping here and there and feeding the slimy molds and lichens that clung to the rock walls.

The air was cool, brushing against her breasts, whipping up her skirt, but she couldn't care. Not after hearing that Aliyah had been there first and that she might have harmed Eirik.

Fatin passed the first barred dugout cells, but hurried along after quick glances inside at the occupants. All monstrously large, scarred, and with heavily corded muscles. Her heart beat at a heavy, dull throb. Which of these would Eirik fight?

She nearly passed up the next cell. The figure hanging from chains in the shadows didn't move, barely breathed, it seemed. She stepped closer to the bars and squinted into the darkness, then gasped when she recognized him.

Her hands shook as she unlocked his cell door. She closed it behind her, then locked it again to ensure the guard didn't try to follow her inside. Then she hurried toward Eirik and set the basket beside his feet.

"Eirik," she whispered. She didn't know where to touch him. So many bloody stripes and angry welts covered his skin. "Eirik," she said again, then cupped the unmarked side of his face. She stretched toward him, kissed his cheek and mouth. "Wake up, Viking. *Eirik.*"

He stirred, his knees straightening to raise him, his arms moving forward, wrapping around her in a crushing embrace. His growl, an animalistic, pain-filled rumble, alarmed her every bit as much as the embrace squeezing the breath out of her.

"Eirik, it's me, Fatin."

His head shook; his eyes opened to squint.

"Let me go. I have an ore pot with me. I can't help you if I can't see how badly you're hurt."

"'Tis only scratches," he said, his words sounding slightly slurred. His head canted. "Fatin?"

"Yes, Eirik." She was so relieved she leaned closer and wrapped her arms around him, hugging him hard.

Air hissed between his teeth.

Instantly, she let him go. "Sorry. Let me tend your wounds. Adem packed the basket with things he thought you'd need. I have cloths and ointment. But you have to let me go."

"Right." His hold eased but his arms didn't drop away entirely. His face bent toward her, his gaze taking in the sight of their chests mashed together. He blinked. "You're naked. Why are you naked?"

"I'll tell you while I clean you up."

"You're dressed like a thrall," he said, his tone surly.

"It's a disguise. Adem paid so that I could sneak inside and see you."

"'S not safe for you, dressed like that. Guards are bastards."

"Did they do this to you?"

"Bitch. Aliyah." His beard-roughened cheek scraped against hers as he bent closer. "Getting blood on you."

Fatin gave a faint smile. "I don't mind. Might keep the bastards' hands off me when I leave."

"Thor's bollocks," he gritted out. "Not a man, Fatin. Not a man when I can't protect you. Can't keep you safe."

"Eirik." She sighed and held him, her back straining because so much of his weight sagged against her.

"Just tired."

Fatin stroked his hair, figuring it was safe to touch him there. They swayed together, torsos suspended on the chains. Skin to skin, she was right where she wanted to be. She pressed a kiss against his cheek. "Were you hurt by the men who captured you at the cannery?"

His mouth touched her shoulder. "No, but they beat me. Kicked me after they blasted me with their spears."

"I can't undo your chains."

"They mean to keep me hanging. Can't sit or sleep."

Raising her head, she eyed the chains, noting the hooks in the ceiling. "I think I can loosen them enough that you can reach the floor, but you'll have to stand."

His shoulders slumped.

Fatin unwrapped herself from around him, but he still hugged her with his thighs and arms. "You have to move away. Didn't know you Vikings could be such babies."

A low growl rattled through him, and she nearly smiled, only that would have hurt too much.

Eirik gripped her forearms and pushed himself erect, then quickly dropped his hands, bracing them on his knees as he rose. He swayed, but he was standing.

"I need your help to reach the ceiling," she said, locking her gaze with his. His expression was less blurred, sharpening by the moment. When he nodded, she sighed her relief.

"You need to lift me. Or to let me climb on you. Whichever you think you can manage."

His brows drew together in a fierce scowl as he concentrated. Then he braced apart his legs even farther and cupped his hands in front of him.

Fatin gripped his shoulders, stepped onto his outer thigh, then into his hands, and reached for the chain above him. It was a matter of threading the loops through the hook, but they were rough metal and kept snagging. When she was through, she tapped him to let him know to let her down.

When she was on the ground she gave him a hug. "I'm amazed you did that without shaking."

"You weigh nothing," he said gruffly.

"But you're hurt and exhausted."

"My blood needed a little stir, is all," he said, with an all-too-familiar heat warming the sound.

Her gaze fell away. Warmth bloomed on her cheeks. "You should try it now. Make sure you have enough slack."

Eirik pulled the chains in front of him and knelt on the ground, then sat, his back against the wall behind him. His breath left him in a deep sigh. "I'm grateful for that."

Fatin knelt on the ground next to him and gently tucked her fingers under her chin to raise his face into the dim light. "This gash is going to leave a very sexy scar," she said, doing her best to hide her revulsion for the deep, bloody score that ran from the edge of the cheekbone down to his jaw.

Then her gaze swept the front of his nude body. He hadn't been as fortunate elsewhere. Dark bruising, shaped like the toes of boots, marked his belly and sides. "They kicked you."

"Yes. She wanted my face and balls spared. She hopes to still have use of them if I survive." His lips curved into a grimace.

*If I survive* . . . Fatin's stomach clenched. Her breaths shortened. She turned aside and fought to calm herself.

"Don't tell me you will miss me, bounty hunter," he said softly.

Fatin's mouth trembled, and she sniffed. But then she raised her chin and pinned him with a glare. "You will not die. You're just looking for sympathy. I have none for the likes of you."

"So long as we are of an accord, *elskling*." He laid his head back against the stone wall behind him and closed his eyes. "You have something in that basket to ease my tiny scratches?"

"Adem sent a healing wand and salves. It'll be painful, but you'll feel better when I'm done."

"I'll just rest while you work. If you don't mind . . ."

She preferred not having his knowing gaze trained on her. She flipped back the cover on the basket, and pulled the unguents and wand from inside. "Drink this," she said, sliding a jar of wine mixed with a healing potion into his hands.

He drank it, his throat working urgently. "I was thirstier than I thought," he said, wiping his forearm across his mouth and handing her back the jar. Then he turned away, resting his head again on the wall.

After she opened the pot of ore to brighten the room, Fatin worked quickly. Although not trained, she'd had recent experience to guide her. She worked the salve into the cuts, massaged more into the bruises, and then turned on the wand and passed it slowly over every injury.

The cuts closed, the wand mending the tears like a zipper and erasing the discolored bruising as she rubbed it over his skin. When she was done, she sat back on her heels. "I'm finished. How do you feel?"

He cracked open an eyelid. "I must have one of those to bring home with me." He ran a hand over his ribs and winced.

"It's not completely helpful with knitting bones. Those will take time."

He smiled, his expression clearing of fatigue and pain. "My thanks. And now that I can think, what are you doing here, Fatin?"

Rather than answer directly, because she didn't know who might be listening outside the cell, she opened the lid covering the basin in the basket and soaked a cloth in the grass-scented water. She began to stroke his flesh, cleansing him. "I wish I could have warmed it first."

His eyelids dragged downward. "It's refreshing. Don't stop."

The cloth was no protection from the heat of his skin or the curves and hollows of his muscles. She caressed him shoulder to belly, easing under his arms to wash him.

His heavy-lidded gaze never left her face, and she wished she hadn't been so quick to light the room. She'd have liked to hide her blushes. "I would wash your hair, but I have only enough water to bathe your body. You'll have to stand for me to finish."

A small smile tipped one corner of his mouth, but he pushed easily from the floor and stepped forward, giving her room to rub his back and shoulders.

When she knelt behind him, his feet moved apart. "Don't miss a spot, sweet Fatin."

She liked that he called her that now, a reminder of their short, shared history, and that he still held a grudge—although she thought that maybe his anger with her was lessening. That maybe he did care a little bit. That phrase was beginning to feel like an endearment.

Drawing closer to more interesting territory, she dropped the cloth and used her hands to cup water and soothe it over his buttocks. They were hard and rounded, proof of his power. These and his thighs were what he used to power his cock inside a woman. As she stroked, his muscles rippled beneath her questing hands.

Her own skin tightened, warmed. Her nipples bloomed.

She bent forward, smoothed her hands around his front, and fondled his cock while she pressed kisses against his perfect, masculine backside.

"Fatin . . ." His breath hissed between his teeth.

"Do I hurt you?" she asked slyly.

"You are here to serve me?"

"In all things, Viking," she said, smiling. "What service do you require?"

His hand caught hers, closing around her fingers, and he dragged her around his body.

She ducked beneath the chains and knelt in front of him. His eyes glittered. His hands cupped her face, a thumb gliding across her mouth.

She licked his thumb, then sucked it into her mouth, telling him silently what she wanted to do, and moaning when his hands sank into her hair and he guided her forward.

Letting go of her, he gripped his shaft, rubbed a thumb over the tip, gliding it in the shiny fluid glazing the broad head.

She stuck out her tongue and took it, painting her mouth with his pre-ejaculate, then biting her mouth as she tasted him.

His hand glided along his shaft; then he cocked an eyebrow and gently slapped her cheek with his cock. First one cheek, then the other.

Each time, she angled her head to capture him, but he drew away, chuckling softly.

Her mouth eased into a smile and she looked up, locking with his gaze, then opened her mouth like the bird she was, and waited.

The plush, round tip circled her mouth. Her tongue stroked it, laving it with wet caresses.

"I think I like you best like this," he whispered. At her questioning gaze, he added, "On your knees. Adoring me."

She snorted. "Adoring you?" But somehow the word felt right. She did adore his rich, musky scent, the lush feel of his satiny head, the heat in the gaze that raked her face and homed in on her mouth . . . Yes, she adored him.

She licked her lips, then opened again, challenging him to stop playing and let her have him. But she didn't leave it to his whim. She cupped his balls, her fingers closing around the hard orbs to tug and massage.

A low growl rumbled through him. His cock slapped her cheek again, but then he clutched her jaw, his thumb curving over her bottom teeth. He opened her wider and pushed himself inside.

She'd have opened around him, and eagerly so, but he was telling her he was in charge. The man wearing the chains and manacles would master her. Which suited her fine. She closed her eyes and let him fuck her mouth.

His strokes were long, slow, stretching her lips as she rolled her tongue along his shaft, lapping in drugging waves as he thrust.

Gods, how she loved the feel and smell of him. Satin heat, thick, choking girth, stuffing her completely. His musky, steamy scent was more powerful than any aphrodisiac.

Fingers digging into his ass, she rose higher, centering herself, opening her jaws and her throat, inviting him to come deeper and deeper despite the ache building in her jaw.

His breath hissed between his teeth; his hips moved with more purpose. His thrusts not so measured and lazy now. Urgency tightened his abdomen and thighs.

Moaning, she ran her hands over him, feeling the flex of his muscle, reveling in the powerful thrust and pull while her pussy grew wet, her inner muscles clenching in sympathetic need. She suctioned hard, trying to coax his seed into her mouth.

Hands cupped her cheeks. "*Elskling*, enough!"

She shook her head, dragging her mouth on his cock, and sucked harder around him.

"Enough," he said, softer this time, but dug his thumbs into the corners of her jaw to halt her.

Reluctantly, Fatin backed off him, chest heaving. She wiped the back of her hand across her mouth before lifting her gaze.

His fingers combed back the hair sticking to her sweaty face. "'Tis magic."

Feeling dazed and deprived, she said, "What? The wand?"

"Your mouth."

Fatin stared, eyes filling. "I would have gifted you with so much more."

"I find myself greedy for your kiss."

She smiled then, feeling powerful, womanly, in a way she never had before. "Eirik?"

"Yes, sweet Fatin."

The way he said it, sweet warmth in his low purr, raised gooseflesh on her breasts and arms. "I need you inside me. Now." And she did. She trembled with need.

Eirik knelt, twining his hands in the chains.

She straddled him, leaning on the bunched muscles of his broad shoulders, gliding her sweat-slick breasts against his face, sighing as he rooted at one, then the other, sucking and biting, until she was gliding down again.

Then, poised on the tip of his cock, she faced him as she had now on two memorable occasions. In his darkened eyes, she could tell he was thinking about those times as well. "I can't be sorry," she said, her voice ragged with emotion. "Not about any of it."

He rubbed his cheek against hers. "Nor I," he whispered in her ear. "I'm glad it was you."

Her breath caught on a soft sob. "Tomorrow . . ."

He gave a sharp shake of his head. "We'll have more than this. We must." Then his lips captured hers in a wild kiss.

And she surrendered, sinking her fingers into his warm hair, her body slid against his, lifting, then circling to find him, then gliding down to swallow his thickness in her creamy depths.

His sigh entered her mouth, and tears pricked her eyes that she could give him this pleasure. Sex before Eirik had been a means to survive, but was now a joy. Because of him.

Her thighs trembled, her body convulsed, but she forced herself to continue to glide up and down, churning on his cock, squeezing around him to increase the friction, quickening at the catch of his breath.

At the end, his head fell back. Raw, broken groans tumbled out of his mouth.

She watched, stunned by the beauty of the moment, then peppered his jaw and cheeks with kisses as she rocked gently, extending his pleasure.

Sweat coating their skin, they hung together, her hands caressing his shoulders and back, his body shuddering against hers.

"I've never known such joy, Eirik. I want you to know that."

"Stop." He kissed her mouth. "It's not the end."

"Tomorrow . . ."

His hands clamped on either side of her face. His forehead touched hers. "Tomorrow comes. As does the next day and the next. Thor's blessing rests with my clan, my people. His heart is mine. Tomorrow . . ." He closed his eyes, briefly. When they opened again, blue ice cut through her torment. "Tomorrow, Helios will know that a Viking's heart is pure and savage."

She clutched at his wrists, anguish twisting her mouth. "I'm afraid."

"And I can't make you believe. You will have to see."

Footsteps scraped outside the cell door. She glanced over her shoulder, uncaring that she was naked and still impaled on Eirik's cock.

The guard from the corridor banged against the bars. His leering gaze raked her, then landed on Eirik. "Time's up. Prime bit like that wasted on the likes of you." He shook his head and strode down the corridor.

Fatin rested her cheek against Eirik's shoulder, wanting to hold on to the moment.

A kiss grazed her temple. "Perhaps you shouldn't be there."

She leaned back. "And miss your triumph?"

His smile was broad, but something softer, something deeper, rested in his blue eyes. "When we escape, I want you with me."

She shook her head, fighting tears again. "You say that, and you're wearing chains."

"I won't be stopped."

She kissed him hard. "I'll hold you to that promise."

"Go now," he whispered, the sound raw and thick.

She pushed upward. His cock slid from inside her. Already she missed the connection.

Stepping away, she picked up her skirt and tied it with a knot at her hip, then pushed back her hair.

"I hate that he'll see your breasts."

She glanced down at the tight, hard tips. "It's not anything he hasn't seen a hundred times. Women coming from the gladiators, semen streaking down their thighs."

"Use the cloth. Don't give him any more to stare at."

She washed silently, shyly. Keeping her back turned as she brushed the cloth between her legs. "I wish I didn't have such a spotted past."

"I don't hold it against you. I'm not exactly pure either."

"But for a man it's different."

"When we marry, for our family's future, we make different choices. But when we take a woman to bear our hearts, we can't think. We can only trust in the gods, and the tests they place in front of us. The heavier the burden, the more dangerous the path— the greater will be our reward."

She dropped the cloth into her basket. "I want to believe that."

"You will..."

"Tomorrow," she said, her lips curving. She covered the basket and set it on her hip. Then she stepped toward him and kissed his forehead and his eyes as they slid shut, then his mouth. "Take this with you, Viking. Into the ring. I love you."

His eyes opened. His gaze bored into hers.

She gave him a one-sided smile. "Yeah, it's possible. Even for a whore and a bounty hunter. I have a heart. And it's yours."

# Nineteen

Birget sat in a seat high up the stadium, her butt resting on the edge as she leaned forward, tense beyond a simple adrenaline rush.

Not because she was dressed as a woman in a long, flowing robe, and garnering glances from those seated around her, but because her betrothed, the man she'd come to rescue, was on today's program, and there wasn't a thing she could do to change that.

She'd have her first glimpse of the man she'd been promised to, and perhaps her last.

Although she knew he was a powerful, virile warrior, someone who'd bested her own most highly regarded fighters, something in the dread in Adem's face when he'd brought her the program and told her about the event scheduled for that day told her that this was no ordinary battle.

Already they'd waited through the lesser events, battles between popular gladiators. Bloody, maiming fights that had worked the crowd into a frenzy. And even though she was accustomed to battle, had slid on her own feet and belly in blood and entrails a time or two, the sight of the blood seeping into the sandy arena floor made her stomach lurch.

The dark stains, the aftermath of the last fight between two evenly matched men, repulsed her for the abject waste of life.

These gladiators fought for purses. To entertain. Not to defend their homes or their livelihoods.

What manner of people were these Helios that they did not understand a battle should be a last resort? Something to be avoided, if possible. Something you entered with reverence for your gods and your ancestors.

Baraq and Adem sat on either side of her, their glances scanning the crowd and the guards standing just inside the panels ringing the arena floor. They freed her to worry and stare into large, dark openings to the sides of the arena floor through which the fighters would march.

Some of the openings were barred, and behind one barred gate figures crowded, hands wrapped around iron. Some were blond. She leaned closer, squinting to see into the shadows. Were those the rest of the Vikings? If so, why had they been brought here?

A hand slid over her thigh to cup her knee. Baraq leaned close. "Don't you have faith in your future husband? He's a Viking. I thought you believed all Vikings were superior to Helio fighters."

Birget bit into her nail and peeled off a sliver, then grimaced, realizing just now that she'd bitten all her nails to the quick. She covered his hand and pushed it off her knee. "Somehow, I don't think that they intend this to be a fair fight."

Adem grunted to the other side of her. "Your Wolf is listed as the main attraction during the spectacle. His opponent is unnamed, a surprise to please the crowd. That can't be good."

Without looking away from the arena floor, she said, "You know a lot about what happens here."

"I fought here, before my escape."

"And you're not worried about being recognized?"

"No one's looking at the crowd."

Those in the front rows, lower to the arena floor, stood and began shouting. Feet thudded on stone steps, a thunderous pounding she felt all the way through her body. "What's happening?"

"I suspect they are bringing him out."

Guards dressed in odd costumes—knee-length pleated skirts, gold breastplates, and tall fringe-capped helmets—strode from one of the openings. They led a man, his wrists in manacles and stretched to either side of his brawny body. He wore only a short, thin loin skirt, but immense pride cloaked his broad shoulders. He could only be Eirik.

Birget's breath caught. The backs of her eyes burned with the pride that swelled inside her chest. He was a handsome man, despite the many healing marks on his body. His pale torso was crisscrossed with shiny pink lash marks. But if he felt pain, he didn't show it. The hard cut of his jaw, the steel blue gaze he aimed around the arena, as though to challenge every man there, made her heart soar.

Her father hadn't been wrong about him. *Daughter, he is cut from the same cloth as his brother.*

And, indeed, he was every bit Dagr's match in height and breadth.

Inside, the knots tightening around her stomach eased a fraction. Eirik would do their people proud. She'd bear witness. And should he die, she had no doubt that Freya herself would swoop down to lift him from the dirt.

"What do you think of him?" Baraq asked.

"He is a Viking," she said, sitting back and schooling her face into an impassive mask.

Silently, she offered up a prayer to Freya. To treat him gently should she meet him soon. To Thor, the Wolves' god who'd blessed Dagr's sword, to watch over another son of Thorshavn, to lend him strength and courage, although she had no doubts the proud man striding toward the raised dais at the front of the stands had pride aplenty for twenty men.

Baraq bent toward her. "Are you sure you want to stay for this?"

She didn't spare him a glance. "Someone must tell the tale."

"If you'd rather, I'll bring you news."

She shook her head. "You don't understand. Our heroes are honored by the stories we tell of their exploits. I must be the one to tell his brother."

Baraq nodded, then eased back in his seat.

Two unarmed fighters approached to remove the chains and manacles. Eirik fisted his hands and flexed his arms, muscles bulging.

The crowd grew silent and all gazes turned to a figure rising from a thronelike seat. "Viking, will you give us the good fight this day?" he asked, his voice booming.

Eirik's expression remained stoic, but his sharp gaze cut the man with bitter blue heat. Slowly, he turned his back. A direct insult if the gasps around her were any indication that he'd defied custom.

She grinned, liking him more and more.

"Viking!" the man angrily called after him. "We have rules by which you must abide."

From behind, she saw Eirik lift his arms and fold them over his chest.

"Die, then! And when your body's ripped to shreds, we'll not worry about a burial. Your parts will feed Sobki."

Adem cursed.

"What's Sobki?"

"A beast." Adem's eyes closed. When he glanced her way, his gaze didn't quite meet hers. "Your warrior won't live past the hour. Say your prayers now."

Fatin never made it out of the arena the day before. At the end of the first shaftlike corridor, she'd been met by guards from the Garden who'd locked her in an empty cell to pass the night, sleeping on the stone floor.

The sound of marching feet drew her toward the bars. The guards returned, this time with Aliyah, who wore a wide, feline grin.

Aliyah tsked. "He made more of an impression than I'd thought. How is it I didn't know you were so aroused by rough play?"

Fatin fought not to hide her naked breasts from the guards, and in particular one gold-toothed one whose nasty smile widened as she recognized him.

Aliyah stepped close to the bars and smiled into her face. "Since you crave the company of Vikings, I say you should join them."

"Join them?"

"I have them on an outing. A day's entertainment. They stand in a gate to watch the fight." She lifted her chin to the gold-toothed guard. "Put her inside with them."

"Yes, mistress. My pleasure." He unlocked her cell and stood aside as she stepped into the corridor.

"When they see their precious leader torn to shreds, who do you think they will blame for his death?" Aliyah's glance trailed down Fatin's body. "But dressed as you are, will they rape you before they kill you?"

Fatin felt a cold shiver trace down her spine. "Why are you doing this?"

"You played a game with me, Fatin. I thought you were loyal, and yet you stole like a thief. To give him a helmet? And aid his escape? Do you think I did not know? That Otis didn't come immediately to tell me what had happened? Otis is a fool, but I don't pressure him about how he attends to his duties."

"He tried to rape me."

Aliyah's brows arched high. "How does one rape a whore?"

The guard grabbed her upper arm and dragged her down another corridor, toward a darkened tunnel where the shouts from the arena above echoed inside.

When they arrived at a stairwell, he shoved her. "Climb. I'll follow."

Every step upward she was aware of him behind her, lifting her skirt, stroking her ass, touching her pussy. Making her so uncomfortable, so sick at heart, she fought to keep her breaths even and deny him proof he intimidated her.

At the top of the steps, he unlocked a door. "Inside." The gate was more of a recess, a room opening onto the arena floor. It was mostly shadowed, except at the opening. The Vikings, all dressed in fur, were pressed against the bars, their bodies rigid, their gazes fixed forward.

"Get on with you."

At the sound of the guard's voice, all turned to see her pushed to the floor. She came up on her hands, her gaze falling away from their angry glares.

The guard laughed and slammed closed the door, leaving her alone with the men.

The young one, Kaun, stepped forward. "Our leader can no longer command us. His protection is withdrawn."

Fatin kept her head bent, her body beginning to tremble. "I would watch with you," she said, her voice hoarse.

Kaun turned away. The others did as well.

She was left to pick herself up from the dirt and approach them. There was no space for her to slip between them. She pressed against Hakon's side. "Please," she whispered.

Without turning, Hakon reached behind him and dragged her forward to stand in front of him, forcing her to face the arena and remain bracketed between his arms.

His mouth stirred the hair beside her ear. "Should he die today, you will meet the same fate. By my hands."

"If he dies today, I won't fight you. I'll deserve it."

Then, with his large body pressed against her back, Fatin stared into the arena, at the man who strode bravely to the center of the hard-packed floor.

Her gaze swept his tall, muscular frame greedily. With his back to them as he faced the game's emperor, he moved easily, as though the bruising and the lashes were more fully healed than she knew they were.

When he faced away from the dais, she gasped. The Vikings around her chuckled.

"He shouldn't have done that," she whispered harshly. "The emperor of the games has the choice of his opponents."

"Think it matters? He's a Viking," Hakon boasted. "There's not a puny Helio who can stand against any one of us."

"There are men as large and well trained as all of you among the Helios, but it's not the men I worry about."

Then she heard the angry emperor shout. The word "Sobki" struck her like a fist to the belly. She bent, giving a low, wounded moan, her forehead bumping against the iron bar.

Around her, the Vikings grew still. When she glanced up, it was to find Kaun staring. "What do you know?"

"That your Wolf will fight no man."

\* \* \*

Eirik scanned the seats of the arena, wondering if Fatin was there. He hoped she wasn't. His gaze searched the gates, finding a barred opening, and his heart lifted at the sight of his men. They stood tall, dressed in their fur and breastplates despite the heat.

But pushed to the front, between Hakon's arms, was a much smaller, nearly nude figure that sent his heart racing.

His gaze locked with Hakon's, then dropped to the woman, giving him a silent warning. Hakon nodded, but whether he understood she was to remain unharmed, whatever the outcome, he wasn't sure. It would be best if he won, he surmised.

Perhaps he shouldn't have provoked the man wearing the blood-colored robes.

Two men, solidly built, wearing slave's cuffs and pleated leather skirts, gladiators, he guessed, strode toward him, carrying armor and a sword.

He kept his arms folded over his chest while they stripped away his loin skirt and replaced it with a leather one, lined with metal appliqués.

"To protect your groin from his snap," one of them said quietly.

"His snap?"

The brawny Helio's dark eyes locked with his. "You drew the beast for this event. Keep well away from his jaws. The top of his head and back have bony plates which will deflect your sword. However, if you can manage it, his chest is his only weakness. Try to anger him enough he comes at you on two legs."

Looking above his head, Eirik gave a subtle nod, although he didn't truly understand the nature of this beast he would face.

"You will have only a sword and a dagger to do battle. Run if you must rather than be caught within range of his bite." The gladiator turned to the other attendant, who handed him the sword. He held out both hands, the blade laying across them.

Eirik lifted it, and turned, slicing the air with the blade. "It is well-balanced." He felt the edge.

"I honed it myself."

"My thanks. But why would you help me?"

The man gave him a grim smile. "If you slay the beast, then none of the fighters here will ever have to face him again."

"He can't be replaced?"

"Perhaps with another horror, but he's the only one of his kind. The most disgusting of the ferals. Bred to be savage, but too unmanageable to serve a military purpose. But you'll see. May Ares watch over you."

Eirik strapped the sheath holding the dagger to his right thigh as the two fighters left. The soldiers marched to a door at the side of the arena and filed out as well.

Eirik closed out the sounds of the pounding of thousands of feet against the stands. Closed his mind to the faces peering at him through the bars. He bent his knees and crouched, his sword raised. His gaze scanned the openings, knowing he wouldn't hear the beast's approach above the din. He turned in a slow circle, his body hardening, his heartbeat thudding loudly inside his head.

Always thus at the beginning of a battle, a stillness settled inside his mind while his body readied itself. The "wakening," his brother called it. The moment when the gods reached down to touch them. It infused them with their strength.

Perhaps it was only adrenaline released to sear his blood. And although neither he nor his brother believed in talismans or prayer, they both had felt the touch of the gods before. When battles should have been lost, when hope ebbed, a spike of power, of greatness, slid inside their bodies at their moment of need.

If ever there was a moment, it was now.

The crowd's roar was deafening, but their heads turned as one, alerting him to which opening the beast appeared in.

More frightening in appearance than any ice dragon from his home world, this ugly, horrid creature moved with little grace. The length of two Vikings stretched head to toe, its long, green-brown, eel-like body wagged left to right, supported by thick, muscular arms and legs, its long, powerful tail whipping side-to-side. Its front paws were shaped like a human's hands, but with sharp, curved claws that grappled with the dirt, flinging it behind it as it approached.

Most frightening was the head of the beast. A long, broad snout, nostrils flaring at the top, had short spikes across the bridge. Muddy yellow eyes with vertical pupils stared unblinking, having no solid lid to lower. When it neared, its attention locking on Eirik, it opened its jaws and gave a hollow hissing roar that raised the hairs on Eirik's arms.

"The chest," he whispered to himself. "How in Hel's cold arms am I supposed to get that close?"

The creature lowered its head, nostrils scenting, and made a wide circle around Eirik.

Eirik turned slowly with it, his gaze never straying from those cold, dead eyes. The head jerked slightly to the left and Eirik had only a second to react as the tail whipped toward him. He leapt over it, rolling, then came quickly to his feet again.

The monster was faster than his appearance would leave a man to believe. A good thing to know. Although Eirik didn't have a clue how that helped him.

Running seemed a mistake.

He watched the mouth open again as the creature wagged its head, and tried not to fixate on the hundred gleaming teeth. The upper jaw lifted; the lower remained still.

The creature pulled back, then lunged forward, snapping its huge jaws, but Eirik placed his fists atop its head and cartwheeled over the beast's back, narrowly missing the swing of its tail as it lashed around to face him again.

The pounding of feet in the stands was so loud he felt the reverberation bang inside his chest.

Eirik's chest heaved like a billow. The longer he dodged the beast's attacks, the more his energy would be sapped. He tossed his sword from one hand to the other, drawing the stare of the beast. He lunged forward, slicing toward its snout, then jumped back just in time to avoid a bite.

The claws would maim. The teeth would sever a limb. His only chance was as the fighter had said, to go for the chest.

He darted in again twice, slashing, but never doing more than delivering a nick to draw blood and enrage the creature.

But he studied its movements, the ways it betrayed its direction and intent. When he lunged toward it again, instead of dodging back, he tossed the sword away and dove beneath the beast's belly, freeing his dagger as he rolled and stabbing upward at its unprotected torso.

The creature roared and backed onto its hind legs, its body supported on its tail. It walked forward like a man, stalking Eirik, but now the dagger was useless because those forearms swung, claws extended to swipe at Eirik.

A glancing blow opened three long gashes on his shoulder as he rolled and rose. His sword glinted in the sunlight, and his glance betrayed him to the beast. The beast edged toward it, its large body cutting off that avenue.

And, knowing that he was giving up his last weapon, his only protection, Eirik gripped the dagger's blade between his thumb and fingers and snapped it again toward the beast's tough yellow belly.

The blade sunk only a finger's length deep. The creature raised its head and bellowed. Then lowered its face, nostrils huffing steamy gusts as it ran for Eirik.

Eirik's only hope was the sword. Sacrificing the same wounded shoulder, he hunched it, ran forward, and barreled into the beast, knocking it off its tail where it flailed, nearly unseating Eirik as he lunged for the sword.

When his hand wrapped around the pommel, he had only a moment before he felt the weight of the creature stomping on his thigh. Giving a loud cry, he turned, stuck the pommel into the dirt, and angled the blade toward the beast's chest as it fell over him.

Jaws poised above his face, only the length of steel sliding between ribs stalled the fall. Just long enough for Eirik to scoot backward and out from beneath the creature.

The beast's gaze met his. It shook its snout, blood flying from its mouth and nose. It shuddered and slumped, the blade sliding through the bony plates at its back.

Eirik crawled back a few more feet, then rested on his hands, his whole body shaking with exertion.

Fighters flooded the arena floor, racing toward him. They lifted him gently upward, and, straddling two sets of broad shoulders, he was carried in a slow circle around the arena while the Helios shouted and cheered.

When he passed the barred entrance where the Vikings watched, he saw their fists pumping air, teeth gleaming between smiling lips—and Fatin's pale face awash in tears.

# *Twenty*

W hile the crowd was still on its feet, cheering for the Viking
who'd killed the beast, Adem grabbed Birget's arm. "We go
now," he shouted.

"What?"

One look into his face, jaw taut with excitement, she did no
more than spare a glance behind her at Baraq to make sure he followed, then let Adem pull her behind him.

At the top of the stands, he led them to a hatch that already had
its lock cut. He opened it and pushed her toward the hole. "Down
the ladder, as fast as you can go."

She climbed onto the rungs and gazed down. The bottom was
shrouded in darkness, but she didn't hesitate. They'd come to Adem
for help. Now they had to put their trust in him.

Placing her hands on either side of the rungs, she slipped her
feet off the steps and glided down . . . down . . . until her toes touched
earth, and she fell backward against the narrowed walls.

She scrambled out of the way as first Adem, then Baraq, followed.

"There are ventilation shafts, leading off this," Adem said, his tone abrupt. "Follow me. We've got to get to the guards' post before the men are led back to the compound."

On their bellies, they entered a maze of metal boxes, crawling on their knees, hunched over, until they reached a grating that overlooked a dimly lit corridor.

Adem pushed the grate with his feet, loosening it, and then lifted it aside. He dropped to the floor, then waited while first she, then Baraq, joined him.

"Stay behind me. We have friends inside." He moved with such speed running down the tunnel-like corridor that she was soon breathless.

When he halted, he raised his hand to stop them, then ducked around a corner. She slid closer to peer around it, saw him talking with a uniformed guard who passed him a package, and then returned. He broke open the seal and passed them three bundles. "Get dressed. We're joining the contingent guarding the Vikings." At the bottom of the bag, he pulled out a jar. "Birget, cover your arms and face with this."

She unscrewed the top and applied the stain to her skin, coating her hands all the way up to her forearms, then rubbed tint onto her face and neck.

"Don't forget the ears or the back of your neck."

When she finished, she dressed in a dark gray uniform, boots, and a helmet.

"The visors are for show," he whispered. "No comm. No special vision. We'll fall in at the back of the formation and take out three guards. One at a time."

Adem stood shirtless and pulled the last items from the bag, square packages strapped along a band, which he tied around his waist.

At her glance, he smiled. "Fireworks, Princess." His chin pointed to weapons in the bottom of the bag. "Stunners. Charged and set to full. Use only if necessary, and at the last moment."

Birget strapped a holster to her thigh. "Are you going to tell us your plan?"

"Once we're inside the compound, all you need to do is watch for my signal, then get the Vikings running for the gates."

Birget shot Baraq a glance.

He shrugged. "Got a better plan?"

Irritated, she muttered, "Would have been nice to be forewarned that there was one."

"The fewer in the know, the better," Adem said. "Ready?" He turned her and tucked her hair beneath her helmet. "Baraq, make sure you keep behind her."

When he turned again and began to run, Birget couldn't help smiling. It might not be her plan, but at last something was going to happen. She'd still get her chance to earn her own place in the Icelandic annals.

While the Vikings were herded back into the cargo car of the tram, Fatin found herself seated opposite Aliyah in one of the passenger coaches. Guards had prevented anyone entering. They were alone other than a pair of her personal protectors.

Fatin sat, her back straight, her chin raised as high as she could manage, given that she was nearly nude, her skin smudged with sweat and grime, while Aliyah looked as cool and reserved as ever. And completely in control.

"Whatever shall I do with you now?"

Fatin didn't venture an answer, guessing none was required. She was at the whore-mistress's mercy.

Aliyah draped an arm across the back of her seat and toyed with a lock of her hair. "The question I would like to have answered is why did you help him? Did he seduce you into forgetting your sister?"

"He did not. But I don't believe you ever intended to keep your promise regarding Zarah."

Aliyah's lips curved into a sinister smile. "Now that we no longer have to keep that particular fairy tale alive, we should get down to business. You know that you broke the law?"

Fatin kept her expression blank save for a blink of her eye to sweep away a sudden welling of tears.

Aliyah slid her arm off the back of the seat and leaned toward Fatin. "You know that right this moment, I hold your fate in my hands. I have friends in high places, clientele eager for me to continue providing them my entertainments. They will not question how you came back into my service . . . should I decide to offer you again as a sex-thrall. And no matter how you might rail that you own your papers, they will not listen."

Fatin swallowed, her stomach clenching so hard she feared she might vomit. Her fingers bit into the padded arms of her seat, and she waited. She knew Aliyah enjoyed being dramatic. She was being truthful, yes, but was also doing her best to put the fear of the gods in her. Aliyah wanted something.

Aliyah placed two lacquered nails beneath Fatin's chin and turned her face side to side. "You begin to age. These lines," she said, tracing the brackets around Fatin's mouth, "they make you seem old. Too hard for the *saray*. I have other places I can send you."

She was talking about the brothel on the southern edge of the compound. The one with the door opening in the outer wall where anyone could enter and find a quick fuck at a low price.

To be consigned there was to live in a true hell. Especially for someone like Fatin. Her heart stilled for a moment, horror raising goose bumps on her arms and bared breasts.

"Now you understand that you haven't any choices, Fatin. No matter what I want, where I would send you, you will always be mine to command. There is not a place on any Consortium world where you can flee my control. And should you escape to the frontier, remember that I hold your sister, and that as much as I adore her, I will make her suffer for your sins. I am a businesswoman. I cannot show mercy."

Fatin read the truth of her intent in Aliyah's hard, cold gaze. "What do you wish from me, mistress?" she whispered.

"Why, more Vikings, of course."

"Even knowing that they are difficult to manage."

"Even as we speak, I have engineers designing another facility to contain them. One where sensors will track their every move, where the implants will provide the painful reminders, according to an AI-based security module, without a human's intervention. Humans are so gullible, so easily tricked. They will be enslaved. Without hope of escape, ever again."

Fatin's fingers dug harder into the cushion.

Aliyah's gaze narrowed. "You want to ask me something else, don't you, Fatin? Do you want to know what I have planned for your lover?"

She saw no point denying that Eirik and her shared a bond. She gave a nod, then held her breath.

"It seems you weren't forthcoming about his origins, my dear. My friend Livia brought news to me that won't be shared with the media, and that has been blocked thus far from Consortium channels. Wolf, your Eirik, is of noble birth. It's too bad that his brother was mistaken about his being among the men transported to our facility for our genetics regeneration program."

"Mistaken?" Fatin's horror grew. The cool calculation in the whore-mistress's black eyes was fatalistic.

She shrugged a shoulder. "He was never here. Will never be heard from again."

"What will you do with him?" she asked, her throat closing because she wanted badly to scream and rail.

"What I must to ensure the future of Helios."

To still the panic clawing its way up her throat, Fatin swallowed and froze, careful to hold the whore-mistress's gaze. "You will hold me responsible for his disappearance," she said, hopeful that Aliyah would let her make the sacrifice. "Disclaim his arrival? I could return him. With apologies."

Aliyah tsked. "But he would know. As I said, he never made it here. Never existed in my facility."

"And the men who know him?"

"Will never be freed to tell the tale."

"Even should they earn their thrall-price?"

"When I have what I need from them, and have that fresh batch of Vikings you will provide, they will be forgotten too."

"As though they too never existed," Fatin whispered, understanding now. Aliyah's mind was set on murder.

Aliyah smiled. "You really should know better than to bite the hand that feeds you, sweet Fatin."

"What happens now? To me?"

"After a proper punishment, a thrall's punishment, you'll be prepared—bathed and dressed—then transported to your ship, along with a couple of my own guards to ensure your good behavior. Then you will be free to leave."

"My sister?"

"Will continue to enjoy good health in my care."

The tram pulled into the compound's station. Fatin remained

frozen in her seat until Aliyah and her guards left. They never looked back, knowing that she was well aware there was no escape. Not from her punishment, not from her fate.

Then, moving like an old woman, she followed in their wake.

She'd failed on an epic scale. Eirik's life was forfeit. Soon the rest of the twenty she'd captured would be dead as well. And she saw no escape for any of them. No way to end the misery she had caused and would visit on the next group of Vikings.

Her only hope was the destruction of her ship before she made New Iceland again—her and everyone on board sacrificed to thwart Aliyah's ambitions. But someone would replace her.

Could she get word to the kingdoms? Warn them of what to expect? That the Consortium was blind to Helios's scheme to enrich its own population? Would the Consortium even care should the Icelanders inform them?

They might care if the precious ore that fueled the planets was cut off.

Fatin raised her head and moved with renewed purpose. She might have failed Eirik in every way possible, might have spelled the death of every Icelander within PG's purview, but she could still put a halt to Aliyah's cruelty.

She'd do it for Eirik—to fulfill his hopes. She'd do it to cleanse her own soul. The punishment she would endure would be a start, a scouring of her flesh for her many sins. Not the ones Aliyah held against her.



With a prod from Gold-Tooth, Eirik entered the empty chamber situated inside PG's main facility. As soon as he stepped through the sliding door, it closed, locks engaged. Inside, there was running water, a urinal. He made use of both, wiping blood and grime from his wounds while he tried not to think too hard about what was to come.

The door slid open. Bethel stepped inside, a white tray in her hand, her face so pale and strained that his own body reacted to her tension.

Her eyes rolled to the side, and he knew she was indicating the watcher's eye in the far corner of the room. He gave her a nod and a small smile.

"Twice in two days? And no stocks or manacles?"

"Will you give me trouble?"

"No, Bethel. You've shown me kindness."

She lifted her chin toward the cot. "If you take a seat . . . I don't want you standing, not with those great gouges bleeding. I'd like to see to them first."

"Before you take my seed?"

Her lips firmed into a thin line. "I do what I must, Viking."

"And I understand and forgive you."

Her eyes closed. "Don't."

"Don't what?"

"Don't be kind."

"Why, Bethel? Why does kindness upset you?" When her tear-filled gaze rose to meet his, he read his fate. "I see. Why bother with my wounds?"

"Aliyah doesn't wish to look upon them."

"How upsetting for her to see my blood."

"She's . . . upset about many things . . . Eirik."

The last word she whispered, and he at last understood. More than his attempted escape, his existence in this facility had been discovered, and had to be a huge problem for Aliyah.

His thoughts whirling now, unimpeded, the only resolution he could see was his own death. His existence would never be admitted.

Which spelled doom for the men who were equally aware that a noble had been among those taken.

"Do the others know?" he said softly.

Her gaze flicked to his, her lips pursed. "Hold still, Viking," she said loudly as she pushed ointment into the long, deep scratches the beast had left. She leaned closer. "Adem comes. He may be able to save the others."

"Do the men know?"

"What good would it do for them to know? He may arrive too late or be caught. Then what?"

Eirik grabbed her hand. "What of the bounty hunter?"

Bethel pushed his hand away and continued sliding ointment into his wounds. "She's in deep trouble too. Aliyah has kept her close."

"To punish her?"

"She's to be whipped," Bethel said, the stiffness of her shoulders indicating she had little sympathy for Fatin. "On the exercise field in full view of all the thralls and staff. An example to any others who break the rules."

"Will I be there?"

Her nod was sharp. "As soon as your wounds are treated."

"Why not use the wand?"

"She doesn't want you healed. But she doesn't want blood dripping behind you. Her words." When she'd finished, she knelt between his legs. "Would you prefer doing this yourself?"

"Why should I cooperate?" he growled.

"You want to know what happens, don't you? As long as you resist, we'll sit here."

Eirik grasped his cock. "Look away."

Her lopsided smile held more than a hint of grim humor. "Why shy now?"

"I'm not shy. But the last woman who touched me is the last one I ever want."

She shook her head, mild disgust in her expression. "Are you talking about Fatin?"

"Yes." He tugged his cock, then circled the base with his fingers and squeezed, urging blood to the tip. When heat began to stir, he turned his gaze from his own large hand and thought of Fatin.

He'd never been a man to daydream. Never fantasized to fill the well of his desire. But Fatin was never far from his thoughts. Since they'd met, he'd felt a connection that didn't fade with distance or sour with his deep discontent.

Her soft, husky voice came to him again. *Take this with you, Viking. Into the ring. I love you.*

He had no doubt, deep inside, that she'd spoken the truth. His own heart had known from the start that she was his mate.

How else had she gotten past his warrior's cynicism and encouraged him to let down his guard? He'd wanted to trust the passion and the innocence in her eyes.

And he knew now that despite what she'd been, what she'd done, she was a true innocent at heart. And a valiant soul steadfast in her loyalty to her sister.

A quality he valued above purity of body. Above the taint of her blood, which he was coming to believe infused her with a bird's free but lonely spirit.

As he gave up his essence one last time, he held to the memory of the naked beauty of that declaration. Thinking only of her.

Fatin, the procurer. Fatin, the bounty hunter. Fatin, his love.

# Twenty-one

Stripped of even the loin skirt, Fatin faced the pole Aliyah had ordered erected at the end of the exercise field near the moat. Her hands were bound with rough hemp, the ends folded into her palms for her to clench.

She'd been led past the row of Vikings who'd been brought to watch her punishment. Kaun's gaze had fallen away as his jaw clenched tight. Hakon had met her gaze and lifted his chin, a signal that she should do the same. She'd almost smiled. She'd even noted a hint of regret in Hagrid's hard glance.

As much as the men might have wished her harm at one time, she sensed they understood a little better that she was one of them. As much a victim and enthralled to Aliyah's greed for power.

Conspicuous in his absence was Eirik, a fact that made her fiercely glad. She didn't want him to witness this. Didn't want him to see her weak or afraid.

His fate weighed on her shoulders. Caused her belly to cramp with nausea. Her pride had led her to this and sealed both their fates.

She'd take the lashing and pray that her blood spilled in the dirt, that her offering to Zeus would be enough to appease the all-powerful god. Perhaps he would take pity and intervene to save her warrior.

She closed her eyes and leaned her face against the rough tree bark, wishing it was done. But apparently Aliyah wanted her to suffer the anticipation.

A soft, slender hand stroked her naked back, causing her to jerk. She hadn't heard the whore-mistress's approach.

Fingers twisted into her hair, pulling back her head. Aliyah leaned close and rubbed her cheek against Fatin's. "Don't you want to see your lover one last time?" she purred.

Fatin shook her head. "Why be cruel? Why not just get on with it? I'm sure you have better things to do. Stacks of coins to count."

Aliyah tsked. "I loved you and your sister. Thought of you as daughters. But you couldn't be content in my care."

"You'd sell your own daughters to old men bent on rape?"

"It's only sex, Fatin," she said, her lips curling with disgust. "Like breathing. Necessary. Why couldn't you be content growing wealthy? You were a street urchin. I raised you up. Fed you the best foods, dressed you in silks. You were pampered beyond your station. And yet, you were never satisfied."

Fatin knew she wasted breath trying to explain, but she leveled a steady gaze on the woman. "I was never free. I'm a Falcon, maybe not in form, but at heart. I can't soar inside a prison."

"And yet your sister sits inside the *saray*, quite content. No ambitions to soar when she wears the wings. I think you're flawed. Too proud to ever find happiness."

Fatin's shoulders slumped. Her sight shimmered with tears. "Aliyah, please spare him and his men."

"What would you give me in return?" she said silkily. "You know that everything is a transaction. What can you possibly offer me that would entice me to risk my own death?"

"There has to be a way to place the blame on me. Only on me. Free Eirik to return home. You can do the right thing. Do you really think that you can keep this contained, that no one will ever know what you did?"

"I have friends who will protect me, but for them to help me I must erase the proof."

There was no reason, no bargain that would sway her. Aliyah would take twenty lives to preserve her own.

Fatin leaned against the pole again. "Why do you wait? Let's get this over with."

Aliyah's hand tightened in her hair. "You lover comes . . . Look, Fatin. See him one last time."

Her forehead pressed against the hard wood, Fatin turned her face to see Eirik stride toward the field. His hands were manacled in front of him. He wore only the loin skirt and his silver thrall's cuff, but his head was held high, his expression ruthless and fierce.

She raised her head and straightened her shoulders, meeting his gaze. If this was his last glimpse of her, she didn't want him to see her afraid. She gave him a blazing smile.

When he took his place with Hakon in front of the line of his brothers, only then did she turn away.

"Michael!"

Aliyah's uncharacteristically shrill shout made her jump, but she quickly quelled her nerves, breathing deeply as the eunuch approached carrying a long leather whip.

"Ten lashes. Your lovely back . . ." Aliyah sighed, stroking her skin again, then walked away.

Fatin gritted her teeth and clenched tight to the rope that bound her. The first sharp lash stole her breath. The next caused her to hiss between her teeth, tears to prick her eyes, but she blinked them away. Pain seared her back from hip to shoulder.

After the next and the next lashes, she bit her lip, felt blood dribble down her chin, but still she held back her cries.

However, the burning stripes that followed took their toll on her pride and strength. She groaned and embraced the pole, leaning against it to keep her knees from buckling. Warm blood splattered her cheek, and she faced forward. The ooze of more blood trickling down her back, over her buttocks, was the least of what held her attention. She'd lost count and cringed again and again, in unending agony.

Another stroke of the whip, and she sobbed. Her knees gave way. The rough bark scraped her chest and knees as she buckled.

"Fatin!"

She heard Eirik's cry, but couldn't manage a response. Her eyelids drifted down and darkness enfolded her in gentle arms.

Eirik watched Fatin's knees give way and her body sag and slide slowly down the pillar she'd been tied to. His fists were curled at his sides, veins bulging in his arms.

Hakon held his wrist, pulling hard to hold him back. "You can't interfere. 'Tis only a whipping. She'll survive. If you rush to help her, you'll be cut down."

"I'm already a dead man," he clipped. "As are you all. They

know who I am." His gaze slid sideways to meet Hakon's widening eyes.

Hakon stiffened and glanced over his shoulder at the men behind them. "We're not long for this realm, then."

"As soon as this is done, I'm to be killed. You may have a day or so longer to live, but they can't allow anyone who has knowledge of who I am, outside of Aliyah and PG, to live. There is no longer time to plan."

Hakon gave a stiff nod. "We must make our move, even though it will mean our deaths. I understand. 'Tis better to die in battle than like cattle led to slaughter. We'll sleep with Valkyries tonight."

"Why did you stop?" Aliyah shouted, pulling their attention forward again. Although Fatin was clearly unconscious, Aliyah quivered with rage. "How many?"

"Eight, mistress," her eunuch replied.

Aliyah raised a hand and snapped her fingers.

An attendant rushed forward, carrying a ewer. She dashed the contents over Fatin, who sputtered, then moaned.

"Get her up!"

The attendant put her shoulder beneath Fatin's arm and lifted her. "Hold the pole, bounty hunter. It will soon be over."

Eirik glanced around at the other watchers, at the attendants who wore shocked, pale faces or expressions of deep revulsion to the savagery of Aliyah's punishment. "We move now, Hakon. Before we quit this field."

"Now?" The corners of his mouth quirked up; then he took a slight step backward. He murmured quietly to the men behind him.

Eirik heard the rumble move down the line, turned to see nods, subtle tightening of jaws, hardening glances. His men would follow his lead.

He returned his attention to Fatin, willed her silently to hold on.

Her slender body shuddered visibly; even from a distance he could tell she didn't have much strength left inside her.

The bitch Aliyah had misjudged them all. A whipping wouldn't intimidate them. Bloodletting, especially of a woman, would only fire their blood and their lust for reprisal.

When the last lash fell, he raised his bound hands, bent, and launched himself toward the nearest guard, Gold-Tooth. Roaring, he pushed him back, barreling into the guard, forcing him back another step, then another, until the guard's feet met the edge of the moat.

Gold-Tooth teetered there for a moment, his arms flailing, his eyes so wide the whites framed his black pupils. Then he fell over the edge into the water.

Eirik paused only a moment to savor his satisfaction as the sand at the bottom of the moat shivered, then the dark creatures exploded upward to devour him.

Birget's long strides matched Baraq's as they carried the last of the packets of soft, claylike explosives to the cargo lift in the basement of the PG headquarters. Adem had shown them the schematic and the place the charges should be set. Already they'd pushed the sticky clay into hidden corners throughout the building. This last one was the largest, and set to go off beneath the center of the laboratory.

As soon as they were through, they were to head to the men's quarters as quickly as possible. When the first explosion went off at the arrival center near the hoverpad, the hope was that most of the guards would scramble to react to the threat, leaving the barracks mostly unguarded.

The rescuers would herd the captives to the tram. Vehicles

waited at the first station past the compound to carry them to the dock for departure aboard the *Daedalus*.

Baraq pushed the button on the timer. The readout remained blank.

"Do it again," Birget whispered. "Hurry; we need to get out of here," she said, checking the time on the wrist clock that Adem had latched to her arm.

"It's not starting," he said, a worried frown creasing his brow. "You go. I'll be right behind you." Already he was pulling the timer wand from the bundle, shaking it, slapping it against his palm. "That did it," he said. Raising his head, he whispered, "Go! Let Adem know we have everything else in place."

"Don't make me come back for you," she whispered harshly. She didn't like leaving him. But he was right. There were so many parts of the plan she wasn't aware of, and Adem needed to be kept apprised. He'd decided against communicators inside the compound in the event security monitored all frequencies.

They'd scheduled every task. How he'd known how long it would take to move from one target to the next, she didn't know, hadn't asked, but the number of maps he'd acquired indicated he'd been planning this for a very long time.

"Why now?" she'd asked him. "Why did you wait so long?"

"We have friends inside, but they needed incentive, something to help them remain steady. Your Viking and Fatin provided them that. They will help now to save them. He's a noble. At the end of the day, they can honestly say they acted to save him rather than be coconspirators to his murder."

And after his battle in the arena, the whole of Helios would be talking about the brave warrior. Once word leaked that he was a prince, PG and all those involved in the scheme to capture and enslave the Vikings would come under scrutiny.

Once held out in the light, their conspiracy would be condemned.

Today's sabotage might even be seen as an expedient necessity—heading off PG's attempt at mass murder.

Birget ran to the lift, waited impatiently for it to arrive, her gaze sweeping to the corridor, willing Baraq to hurry.

The door opened. She cursed Baraq for his stubbornness. Did they even need to destroy the facility? Wouldn't the point be made when the most public of the buildings crumbled beneath the blasts?

On the first floor, she held her breath as the doors slid open. She walked sedately through the foyer, not drawing any undue attention. Once outside, she loped toward the exercise field. To Adem, who had a bag stashed inside the fighting pit, one filled with weapons. But as soon as she stepped onto the field, she knew something was wrong.

Tall, nearly naked men fought with fists, sticks, heavy punching bags, whatever they had managed to find, to keep the guards' stun-spears from touching them. A quick glance and she found Eirik, his shoulders down, hands bound, barreling toward a pole where Fatin, covered in angry, bloody stripes, sat hunched at the base of a pole.

"Birget!" Adem raced toward her, unspooling twine from around a long bag, and then dumping the contents in front of her. "Spears, swords."

She didn't need his instruction; she gathered an armful of weapons and headed toward the men.

"*Vikingar!*" she shouted. She recognized the largest fighter, a distant cousin, Hakon, and she dumped her load and tossed him a sword, which he caught around the haft midair; then he spun on his heel, laughing as he knocked a spear away from a guard and slashed deep into his side.

Not waiting to see the outcome, she picked up more of the weapons, ducked between fighters, and slapped swords and daggers against their backs, their arms.

Without missing a beat, the fighters turned. Birget threw off her own helmet, grabbed up a sword, and ran for Eirik, who was lifting Fatin to reach the knot binding her to the pole.

"Duck!" she shouted.

When he did, she sliced through the rope. He raised his hands and another slice severed his bonds.

His gaze slammed into hers, then raked over her, his eyebrows furrowed.

"No time now, but take the sword," she said, and unlatched her holster to pull out her stun gun. "We are getting out of here now."

"Birget!" She heard Adem's shout, turned to see him running away from the buildings, waving his arms. Workers in white lab coats rushed after him, covering their heads.

She glanced around the field, down the walkways, but there was no sign of Baraq.

"Now, now, now!" Adem shouted. "Everybody on the ground."

Birget slammed into Eirik, taking him and Fatin down as explosions rocked the air.

Deafening blasts, one after another, caused the earth to shudder beneath them. Debris hailed from the sky. Bits of concrete. Papers fluttering slowly down. She stayed huddled, pressed against Eirik's back.

When she glanced up again, the sky was filled with smoke, and ash fell like dirty snowflakes. *Where is Baraq?*

Eirik pushed her off them. "Who are you?"

Birget gave him a grimace. "Your betrothed."

His expression clouded with confusion. "How are you here?" He glanced around. "There are more of you?"

"Yes, but we haven't much time to make our escape."

"You came for us?"

"Dagr sent me."

His expression cleared. "Is he here?"

Birget pushed to her knees, then lunged to her feet. "Long story. It will have to wait until we're aboard the ship. I have to go. One called Adem will lead you out."

Eirik knelt beside Fatin. "You're not coming?"

"I have to find one of my men."

He nodded, shifted to lift the woman into his arms. The way he held her close to his chest told her in an instant how he felt about the woman he cuddled against him.

She didn't have time to consider what it meant. She ran back toward the main building. The path was filled with a stream of people, heads bent against the ashy fall. Soot-covered, dark gray, all. She pushed past them. The front doors were in sight when a massive explosion ripped through the building, a hot flash of light bursting through the doors, shattering the glass.

Falling to her knees, she covered her head, shards slashed at her, but she struggled up.

An arm slipped beneath hers, wrapped tightly around her waist. "Come. We have to move."

It was Adem.

"But Baraq . . ." she said, choking on the ash. "He is still inside."

Adem shook his head. "It's too late. The building's coming down. Save the rest. We must get them to the tram."

Birget shook off his arm and staggered forward. Adem whipped her around. His fist flew toward her head.

She tried to deflect it, but she was too slow. Pain exploded and she sank downward.

*  *  *

Eirik lowered Fatin onto an upholstered seat. The Vikings had pushed through the crowd on the tram platform, forcing back the workers.

There were others there, Adem's men, wearing black, their faces covered in masks, directing the workers to the back of the platform as the twenty entered the cars, followed by their rescuers. Before the doors closed the black suits commandeered the train.

Eirik watched as the train pulled away from the platform, then knelt beside Fatin. He cradled her cheek with his palm. "Fatin, *elskling . . .*"

Her head rocked on the padded bench; then she slowly opened her eyes. "Eirik?" she asked, her voice husky.

"You're injured. We're making our escape. Rest. I'll watch over you."

"Escape?" Her weary glance fluttered over the crowded car. Tall Vikings crowded the space. Some seminude, others dressed in black or PG gray uniforms. "Adem did it," she whispered.

"He did." He gave her a rocky grin. "We aren't safe yet."

She swallowed, reached out an arm to grip the back of the seat, and tried to raise herself. She winced and gave a moan.

"Don't," he said, and gently pushed her down.

Fatin's dark, liquid gaze lifted. "Did you see her?"

"Who?"

"Your wife," she said quietly. "She's here."

"Not my wife yet, but yes, she found me."

Her gaze swept her body. She reached a hand to one of the bloody stripes that wrapped around her shoulder.

"Don't touch it."

She glanced around again, dazed, then stared down at herself. Hunching, she crossed an arm over her breasts, trying to hide her nudity.

He turned, nudged one of the black-garbed men. He didn't have to ask. The man peeled off his shirt and handed it to him.

Then, as gently as he could manage, he pulled it over Fatin's head.

She winced as the cloth glided over her back, but she gave him a faint smile. "Thanks." Her eyes widened. "My sister?"

He glanced around the crowded compartment. A door leading from another car opened. Adem strode through, his broad shoulders making a path. But behind him, Eirik caught a glimpse of golden, brown-flecked feathers. A smile tugged at his lips. He tucked a finger under Fatin's chin and turned her head.

Her eyes widened, and she stood shakily, her hand clutching his as Zarah stepped past Adem. Zarah's serene expression clouded, and she carefully grasped Fatin's arms. "Sit, sister."

"I can't believe it," Fatin said, a tear rolling down one cheek. Her head fell against Zarah's shoulder. And despite her wounds, despite the dirt smudging her face, her radiant smile made her beautiful.

Eirik raised his glance to Adem and reached out his arm.

Adem clutched his forearm. "If all goes as planned, you'll all be aboard the Vikings' ship within the hour."

Eirik nodded.

"I saw you fight in the arena." Adem tipped his square chin and grinned. "Impressive."

Eirik shook his head. "So much has happened. It seems another day. Another lifetime ago."

"Do you suppose you will have room in your castle for a few refugees?"

"We will make room. My brother and I will welcome you."

"I'll not stay long. I still have much to do here. But it's best I remain off planet for a time."

Both men turned to watch the two women who still clung together, shedding happy tears.

Eirik noted that Adem's face tightened as he stared at Zarah. "How long had it been since you last saw her?"

"Since we were teenagers."

"She's lovely."

Adem's gaze snapped.

Smirking, Eirik raised his hands in mock surrender. "I have no interest in that Falcon."

Adem gave a sharp nod. The tension in his jaw eased.

"Adem!" One of the black-garbed warriors shouted from the front of the car. "We approach the station."

Adem grinned. "Get ready. There's no telling whether enforcers have already been alerted to our escape. Guard the women." He thrust his way through the crowd to the doors.

The tram rumbled to a halt. The doors opened.

Eirik bent and swept Fatin into his arms. "Zarah, keep close to me." He glanced around, caught Hakon's gaze. "Watch our backs."

Then they plunged through the doors, following the black-garbed ferals. The platform was filled with commuters, but appeared free of any law enforcement.

He hurried through the station house and out onto the street. Vans, half a dozen of them, pulled up to the curb, wheels squealing on cobblestone.

They boarded, but in the distance a discordant sound, a high-pitched wail, blared.

Adem ran down the walkway. "Into the vehicles," he shouted. "Hurry!"

Eirik climbed inside, set Fatin on a seat, handed Zarah inside, then stepped onto the rail on the outside of the vehicle and clutched the window frame. He banged on the roof. "Go! Go!"

They careened out of the parking lot, heading down narrow streets, warning horns blowing, which had people drawing close to stoops and ducking into alleys to clear their way.

Eirik glanced behind him. The other vehicles, some plain, some branded with products, bumped along at high speed. He himself clung to the side of a bread van. His heart beat fast; his spirit soared.

They made a sharp turn. He rocked against the van, but held tight. Ahead, he saw the slips he'd viewed on the maps, the tall prows of spaceships above the peaked roofs. They were nearly there.

They turned again. Then wheels skidded, squealing to a halt. The way was blocked by a line of dark vehicles pulled nose to tail to close the widening road.

Behind the vehicles, nozzles of weapons were aimed directly at them. His stomach dropped, and he nearly howled with rage.

A door slammed behind him. "Viking!" Adem shouted.

Eirik glanced back. Adem raised a hand to point to the roofs of the buildings all around them.

Figures rose, standing, peppering the rooftops, all holding weapons, stocks snug against strong shoulders, muzzles pointed toward the enforcers.

Adem stepped onto the rail in front of Eirik. "Hold on!" He raised his hand. A shrill whistle sounded.

The men hiding behind the dark vehicles raised their heads, then dove over their vehicles. An explosion raised one sturdy car, slamming it down on its side. But there was a space.

Adem beat on the driver's windshield. "Drive, drive!"

The driver accelerated fast. Adem and Eirik molded against the side of their vehicle, but the driver took the brunt of the hit on his side, metal scraping, and then they were through the breach.

He glanced behind. The other vehicles followed despite the sharp reports of weapons and explosions sounding behind them.

They hurtled toward the end of the dock. To one particular slip. The gangway was already extended. Men in leather trousers and light wool vests stood at the sides, with weapons in their hands, signaling them to enter.

"Vikings!" he shouted, grinning at Adem.

The vehicle rolled to a stop. Both men jumped to the ground.

Adem reached inside for Zarah, then tossed her over his shoulder and loped up the gangway.

Eirik caught Fatin's arm and did the same. At least her back would be spared. When Fatin folded over him, she gave a little laugh, and he smiled at the sound.

Up the gangway, he set her at the top. To one of the men inside, he said, "Find her a *medica*!"

Then he ran back down the gangway, toward the line of vehicles emptying quickly. Behind him engines roared to life. Warning horns blared.

The last vehicle was empty, but the Norsewoman with the unnaturally dark skin, his betrothed, stood there, staring behind them. In the distance, the flashes and sharp reports of stunners were fading, growing quieter.

She turned, smudges of dirt on her tanned cheek. Her gaze was haunted.

"We haven't much time," he said softly. "You must come now."

"I can't leave him."

Did she speak of a lover? He well understood her horror. "If we wait, everyone risks capture. He will know to hide. One is much easier to hide than all of us together. And if he lives, he will find his way back to you. I promise you. If he lives, we will retrieve him. Come now." He grasped her forearm and pulled her gently behind him.

Her footsteps dragged, but she didn't fight him.

"Eirik!" Hakon shouted from the top of the gangway, waving them forward.

He pushed the woman in front of him. "Run!"

She gave a sob, but loped up the narrow metal plank. Once inside, Hakon locked the hatch. "Hold on!"

The ship rattled, and shimmied, then rocked as it rose free of its moorings.

They hovered for a moment, then suddenly the ship jolted upward. Eirik fell against the hull, pulling the woman closer to shield her from harm as the ship shot toward the sky.

"I am Eirik," he shouted in her ear.

"And I am Birget."

# *Twenty-two*

Fatin was numb. Inside and out.

Not from the cold, although she'd never felt the like before. Endless drifts of snowfall that froze her booted feet. Wind so cold it bit patches of exposed skin.

Not from the enormity of the castle looming above her. Dark gray stone set against a mountain. Crenellated edges scraping clouds. Dark and forbidden. Disapproving of weakness.

She hung back as the others rushed forward.

Two days she'd spent in delirium, tended by her sister while the *medica* aboard the *Daedalus* closed the wounds striping her back. "You'll barely have a scar," her sister had assured her when it was done, but she couldn't be happy about it.

Nothing could lift the dark cloud that chilled her to the bone.

Now that he was free, Eirik had abandoned her. He'd visited her only twice during her treatment, and when she'd been led from the dispensary, she'd seen why.

He stayed close to Birget, who seemed impossibly fragile. Baraq had been lost in the explosions that destroyed the PG headquarters. Her grief had left the princess a hollow shell of her former vibrant self, but Eirik's presence, his ready arm, bolstered her.

Fatin had watched them the few times she'd crept to the captain's deck as they sat side by side, their heads bent close.

The few times his gaze had strayed to find her, his expression had been closed, remote.

So much for his promises that they weren't finished.

"Sister," Zarah said, falling back to take her arm. Zarah was bundled with blankets, just as Fatin was, to ward off the freezing cold. "We mustn't stand too long out here. Night falls. And the temperature will drop as fast as a stone."

Fatin offered her a small smile, grateful for at least this much. Her sister was free. At last. "Where is Adem?" she teased, knowing she would draw a blush. Adem had hovered near Zarah throughout the long flight.

"Eirik wanted him to be among the first to greet his brother, Dagr. I think he wants to make sure he shares the heroes' welcome."

"Maybe he fears his own Wolfskins' reactions to so many freakish creatures entering their demesne," Fatin muttered.

A frown dug a line between Zarah's finely arched brows. "You're hurting. And I understand why. Hakon told me about you and Eirik. It's not well-done of him to abandon you like this."

"I'm only getting what I deserve," Fatin said flatly, fiercely tamping down any emotion, afraid she'd tear up and her eyes would freeze. "Let's go inside."

They climbed the steep steps and entered the plain rock-walled foyer. To one side, doors were opened onto a hall with bright walls and the scents of beeswax and roasted meat wafting through them.

Zarah groaned. "Something to eat besides reconstituted gruel. Come. Are you not starving?"

Fatin let her sister pull her inside. Vikings filled the center of the hall close to a raised dais with a long table that stretched its length.

Above so many tall men, she could still find Eirik. Another man of similar build released Eirik from an embrace, then stood back, his hands clapped on Eirik's shoulders. A broad smile cut across an otherwise harshly sculpted face.

His brother, no doubt. The resemblance was impossible to escape.

Fatin tugged at Zarah's arm. "Maybe we should find a place at the back. Lord Dagr might not be happy to realize I'm here."

Only fading into the back was impossible. A woman approached them. She was near middle age with soft features and figure and long brown hair. "'Tis warm in here. Let me take the blankets."

Fatin nearly groaned, but Zarah answered the Viking woman's smile with a shy one of her own and let the blanket slide away, baring her wings.

The woman's eyes widened. Those nearest them turned at her gasp, then stared, captured by a sight Fatin knew they'd never beheld before.

The brown-haired woman's face softened; her hands reached out, tentatively, toward Zarah's wings. "Are you a goddess?"

Zarah's soft laughter echoed around the suddenly quiet hall.

"Tora!" Eirik called out. "She's a woman. Though blessed with a falcon's blood."

Blessed? Fatin met his gaze across the room, gratitude brimming in her eyes.

The moment stretched, and then Eirik turned again to his brother, severing the connection.

Fatin felt as though a door had closed, leaving her once again in the cold. The crowd of Vikings swelled around the king and his brother, then opened again. Birget stood within the shelter of Eirik's arm, her head resting on his shoulder.

Fatin couldn't help the sudden searing hatred that swept through her.

A soft touch stroked over her arm. She glanced blindly down to find Zarah's fingers smoothing over her arm in comfort. "He's home, Fatin. Surrounded by his own. Reminded of his place. His duties. Let go."

Fatin shook her head and pulled away. She wrapped the blanket tighter around her and fled through the door to the foyer, then shoved at the huge doors leading to the frozen bailey outside.

She blinked hard, her eyes stinging, then plunged down ice-covered steps. At the bottom one, she slid, her feet flying from under her. She landed hard, breath leaving in a hard gust, her head slamming against the edge of a stone step.

Dizzy, she scrambled to her knees, tears at last falling down her cheeks. As predicted, they froze on her cheeks, but she didn't care; she raced back the way they'd come, passing through the tall iron gate without seeing a single soul.

Eirik paused as a soft, icy hand lay against his arm. Dagr's gaze dropped to the woman sidling up beside him, his expression bemused.

Bending toward the slender Falcon, Eirik noted fear in her expression and flakes of snow melting on her dark hair. "What is it, Zarah? What is wrong?"

"My sister. She's gone. She rushed out of the hall, but by the time I retrieved my blanket from Tora, I couldn't find her."

Eirik glanced around the hall. "She's outside?"

"Yes, milord. Outside, and it's so cold she'll not last long."

"Surely the bounty hunter is back inside," Dagr growled. "She managed to trick twenty Vikings into giving up their freedom; she won't be so stupid she freezes to death."

Zarah shook her head. "She was upset. She isn't thinking." Her gaze fell.

"Upset by what?"

"She saw you with her," Zarah said, lifting her chin toward Birget.

Birget's expression tightened. "I told you she loves you. How perfect. Our revenge is complete. She pays now for every crime she committed."

Eirik pushed her away. "Birget, I know you're in pain. And why. Fatin is now in our care, our custody. Wolfskins protect their women."

Birget's gaze cut. "Is that it? Is she yours, Eirik? Because I do not think I can share chambers with her as your concubine."

Eirik raked a hand through his hair, his face turning red. "Not now. Your father will be here soon. Let Tora show you to my rooms. Brother?"

Dagr gave him a curt nod, then signaled to his second, Frakki. With men trailing behind them, they grabbed their furs from pegs outside the hall and hurried into the snow.

Eirik had almost forgotten how to breathe in the cold, through pursed lips rather than freezing his sinuses. The cold was a bitter tease. Everything had changed.

He'd returned to find that all of New Iceland was preparing for a siege. That Dagr had fought a battle on Hymir's Sea against

Consortium soldiers and won. But that the victory was only the beginning of the war.

"This woman," Dagr said, his blue gaze flashing. "You care for her?"

Eirik firmed his jaw. This was getting complicated. He'd hoped to ease his brother into accepting Fatin in the keep, but Birget was an impediment. He had made a promise. One he didn't want to keep, but how could he slip the noose? He hadn't found the answer yet.

"I know that you will need Sigmund at your side, Dagr. But I cannot give her up."

"She's the one who captured you. How did you come to care for her?"

"Always we have lived by a rigid code. We punish those who cause us harm. Protect our children, our women. I will admit that when I first awoke, caged like a beast, my heart burned for vengeance. But she's . . ."

"Become a part of you?"

Eirik blinked, surprised at Dagr's statement.

Dagr sighed and slung an arm around Eirik's shoulder. "We have much to talk about. But it will have to wait. Your woman will be dead if we don't find her soon."

They found her huddled on her knees just outside the gate on the path leading down to the sea. Her blankets were pulled around her head. Her shivers were visible.

Eirik heaved a sigh of relief. Shivers were a good thing. He bent and slipped his arms beneath her, trapping her inside the blanket.

She heaved once, arching her back to escape. He freed a hand and smacked her backside. "Stop fighting, foolish Fatin."

"Another name I don't like," came the muffled, sullen comment.

Eirik grinned and met his brother's gaze.

Dagr's own face broke into a wide grin. "I cannot wait for her to meet Honora."

Fatin watched Tora, bemused as the Viking woman fussed around the chamber she'd been brought to for a warm bath. She'd taken Fatin's clothing, returned with a pile of things she thought "might do for a little slip of a bird," then scrubbed the skin from her back with a vigorous wash.

When she'd moved to wash her breasts, Fatin had folded her arms over her chest and held out her hand for the wool cloth. "I'll manage that on my own, Tora."

Tora had clucked her disapproval, but Fatin could have sworn she saw a twinkle in the other woman's eyes.

Tora was the only Viking who'd treated her with civility. The others had shown her cold, hard faces, and turned their backs when Eirik dropped her to her feet inside the hall.

She'd suffered their censure, dropping her gaze in shame, accepting the shunning as her due. The hall seemed even more crowded than before, but Tora had swooped in, giving Eirik and Dagr a glare. How the woman had dared give either big Viking a setdown, Fatin didn't know, but she was impressed.

Since then, she'd seen only Tora. When she'd asked after her sister, she was told that Zarah had been invited to join the *jarl*'s table along with Adem. Zarah at least was being welcomed. That fact soothed a small measure of Fatin's hurt and disappointment in Eirik.

"Come on, girl. I'll not let you drown yourself in that tub. 'Tis time to come out and get dressed."

"It's not like I'm going anywhere."

"Oh, but you are."

Fatin raised her head.

Tora's gaze met hers, her eyes softening with regret. "We've a guest. Birget's father, King Sigmund, arrived just as you were found. You're to appear before him."

Fatin grew still. Eirik had shown restraint, after a fashion, but how would Sigmund, who'd had the most men stolen from inside his kingdom, react to her presence? Would he insist on exacting punishment, full measure, for her crimes? Would he want her death?

After that, Fatin allowed Tora to push and prod her while she'd dried her hair and dressed her, then escorted her, walking like an automaton to the hall.

Everyone was seated at gleaming tables. All heads turned her way when she entered.

She faltered, hoping she didn't look ridiculous dressed as she was in a thin, sleeveless gown of crisp linen, their version of a slave's garb. When the gold cuff imprinted with a wolf's head had been wrapped around her wrist, she knew it was true.

When she was being dressed, Tora had dragged her in front of a fire and made her turn. "White, he wants you in, but 'tis too thin. They will see all your parts. What is he thinking?"

"What does it matter?" Fatin muttered.

Tora blinked, her gaze narrowing on Fatin. "You're right. You'll go as you are."

Now Fatin walked the length of the hall, down the aisle between the long rows of tables.

Male gazes raked her head to toe, seeing through the gown, no doubt, but she held her head high. She'd been among the exotics, a treasure many had paid fortunes to acquire.

When she stood directly in front of the table, she avoided Eirik's hard face, his brother's, then met the gaze of the elder who must be Birget's father.

King Sigmund pushed up from the table, towering over her. Even before he spoke, she felt very, very small.

"You caused us no end of troubles, girl," he said in a booming voice.

She swallowed hard. "For that I am deeply sorry."

His head canted, eyes narrowing. "You say the words, and yet I detect no true regret. Have you learned nothing about Vikings?"

Fatin fought to keep from trembling, so dark and forbidding was his gaze. But her sudden timidity angered her. She squared her shoulders and lifted her chin. "I've learned many things. That Vikings are a proud people. That they are fierce, incredible fighters, and that they put the welfare of those in their care above themselves."

"That's self-serving."

She shrugged. "I was being hopeful," she muttered.

His mouth thinned. "Some among my men demand your death."

She gave a nod. Nothing she hadn't expected. Although she hoped that the fact he was talking to her meant he'd demand another punishment.

"You did this, stole away our men to serve a terrible plot. To make warriors who would have the strength and will to take our world from us."

She tossed back her hair. "I didn't care about the politics. Or about what they paid me."

"Not quite true. You needed the gold and ore you earned for their capture. You cared only about your sister . . . and your own pride."

"She's all I have."

"And yet, having met your sweet sister, I doubt that she would have approved of how you planned to free her. Did you once consider how she would feel if you'd succeeded? That her freedom cost so many their freedom, and could have given the Helios a powerful weapon against us?"

Fatin didn't dare look at Zarah. Knowing her sweet sister, Zarah would have lived with the guilt all her days. And she'd never considered that. "I didn't think," she said softly. "Not beyond my pride and my desperation."

"I have asked Lord Dagr for the right to you."

Fatin's head jerked upward, not understanding.

"Your life, your freedom, are forfeit, and mine to decide. And since my daughter led the men from this world in that final battle, I am placing your fate in her hands. She's earned it."

Fatin swayed. Birget had many reasons to hate her, foremost being the loss of her lover. She didn't dare beg for her life, and couldn't seek help from Eirik, who was her betrothed.

With the ground shifting beneath her, she gave a nod.

"I am not asking your consent, girl. 'Tis done. We are a hard people. But with reason. Ours is a harsh, cruel world. Games such as those you played cannot go unpunished." He gave a sigh and settled back into his seat.

Fatin glanced to Birget, whose hollow eyes burned.

Birget signaled to men who stood to the side of the long table. "Remove her from the hall. After the wedding, she'll be transported to Odinland. I never want to see her again."

This time, she did glance at Eirik. His face was pale, his jaw taut. He and his brother shared a glance, then returned her stare. If there was a message for her, she couldn't read it. Her eyes were too filled with tears. Without even a good-bye, she was led away.

Dagr, 'tis cruel," Eirik whispered furiously.
         "We haven't any recourse. Would you take us to war with Sigmund when we will need his backing to face what's coming?"

"Did you know he would do this?"

"I had hoped he'd leave her disposition to me. Birget's bitter. Hurt. Her father knows something happened to her, but no one's apprised him to the fact she gave herself to a Helio. And I'll not tell him. Already he looks askance at my choice of wife."

Eirik had met Honora only briefly. Since Sigmund's arrival, Dagr's wife, a former Consortium officer, had been kept from the hall.

"Give it time, Eirik. Tempers will cool."

Only Eirik feared for Fatin. She was willful, prideful. Qualities the Bearshirts would seek to grind into the dirt.

The doors to the hall burst open. *Ulfhednar* warriors rushed inside. Dagr and Eirik shot to their feet.

"What goes?" Dagr said, his voice ringing in the stillness.

"The Outlander, Cyrus Tahir, transported into the bailey. With others. He says that you will want to see them, milord. Now."

Dagr strode down the steps, Eirik on his heels. Sigmund and Birget shared glances, then followed as well.

"Is it another ship?" Sigmund asked. "Are they attacking?"

Dagr shook his head. Before they made the middle of the hall, Cyrus rushed inside. Behind him, men carried a litter with a body on it. "Make way!"

The men deposited the litter on the ground. Dagr gave the man lying in a swath of blankets a glance, then began to smile.

Birget gave a gasp, then pushed past the men and fell on her knees beside the dark-haired, dark-skinned man. A Helio, by the look of him.

"Baraq!" She bent and laid kisses on his forehead, his cheeks.

Eirik sucked in a deep breath, recognizing him.

Although his face was battered, his skin grayish, Baraq offered her a smile. "Did you miss me, Princess?"

"Bastard!" she spat, the gruffness of her voice at odds with the tears in her eyes. "I thought you dead. Blown to bits in that explosion."

"Daughter, what is this?"

Eirik spared a glance at Birget's father. His bushy brows were pulled into a fierce glare.

Birget glanced up at her father, her expression faltering. "'Tis love, Father. My love."

"Birget, no." The Helio rose to his elbows, grimacing against pain. "Hush."

Birget's gaze dropped, and she smoothed a hand over his short, dark hair. "I thought you dead," she said, her voice breaking, "and my heart shattered. I am a *Berserkir*, yes. But at heart, I am a woman. I left part of myself behind when we left Helios."

She raised shimmering eyes to her father. "I cannot honor your promise, Father. He lives. Whatever punishment you wish to give me, if you wish to disown me, cast me out, I cannot hurt any more than I have these past days. He lives. I will wed only him."

Baraq snorted. "Do I not have a say?"

Birget gave him a scathing glare. "I gave you my maidenhead. Now that my father knows that, you have no choice but to offer for me."

"Who is this man?" her father bellowed.

"His name is Baraq Ata," Birget said proudly. "And he is a Consortium officer. Same as Lord Dagr's woman. From the same ship that held the captives during the first leg of their journey."

Her father's face reddened. "He's no Norseman. Not a noble. And you laid with him?"

Her chin firmed and tilted high. "He's everything I want."

"If I may interject," Eirik said softly.

Sigmund shook his head, as though clearing it, then looked up dazedly to meet Eirik's glance. "Yes, Eirik?"

"We Icelanders have been insulated. Forced by the Consortium to live a hard life as we've toiled away to provide the galaxy the one thing they crave. Now we've seen other worlds. We have ships. Don't we also need people who've walked on those other worlds, to help us navigate this new dawn?"

"But she is my daughter. Raised to rule a kingdom." Sigmund waved a hand at Baraq. "He's an *Utlending*, one of those who would have kept the yoke of slavery on our necks forever."

"And I know this man's honorable and a fearless fighter. Something any Norse father would want for his daughter."

Sigmund turned to Dagr. "You endorse this?"

Dagr's expression remained neutral. "I had hoped for a marriage between our clans to cement a friendship, but I think that the trial we've endured serves that purpose. I know Baraq to be everything Eirik says." Dagr's lips curled. "I fought him, and he was nearly my match. I would be proud to call him friend, and I would honor him as I do you should you accept him as your son."

Birget laid a hand on her father's sleeve, all anger washed from her expression. "Father, you've never doubted my loyalty, and I've never asked for a thing but to serve you and our people. But would you really rather I was a Wolfskin?"

Dagr grunted.

Eirik snorted, then thinned his lips to hide a smile.

Sigmund's bushy brows lowered. "I never wanted to give you away. You are my greatest prize."

"Even above my sister?"

"Ilse is a honeybee, forever lighting from one flower to the next. You are steadfast, loyal to a fault." He sighed. "And if you have given your heart to this man, I know that it cannot be returned. If I gutted him here and now, you'd never forgive me. Would you, now?"

Her lips curved into a sly smile. "Are you hoping I'll say yes?"

She leaned against him, resting her head against his arm. "He's wounded and likely freezing to death."

"There's still hope?" He sighed again. "Go. Take him to our rooms. I will think on this." Only the glint in Sigmund's eyes as his gaze followed his daughter said he'd already decided.

"You'll keep her now," Dagr said.

Sigmund's smile split his face. "Much to your relief, I'm sure. Think you I didn't hear what a brat she was?"

Dagr shrugged. "She didn't want to be left behind. I admired her tenacity."

"She didn't want all the glory to go to the Wolves."

Dagr bowed his head. "Frakki will be sure to weave her story into our saga."

Sigmund nodded, his fierce features easing.

Dagr extended an arm toward the *jarl*'s table. "Let's be seated. We still have to deal with the issue of the bounty hunter."

Sigmund pulled up, his gaze seeking Eirik. "Tell me you aren't also ensnared by a Helio."

Eirik coughed. "She's not entirely Helio. You've met her sister."

Sigmund's eyebrows raised. "Zarah is full-blooded sister to the other?"

"She is."

Sigmund looked from Eirik to Dagr. "She carries a Falcon's blood? Does this not tell you how inappropriate such a mating would be?"

Sigmund's shock rankled with Eirik. "I have not said I would mate with her."

"But you wish it."

He did. But he'd not admit it here. "Fatin has much to learn about us. She must learn trust."

"But what of offspring? They'd not be human."

This was one area where Eirik had no doubts. "They'd be *more* than human. Since your daughter is crying off our wedding, don't you think I should be compensated?"

"I heard you had no great love for the match. That you feared she'd be too manly."

"I hadn't seen what a beauty your Birget is. My heart was not convinced."

Sigmund grunted, then turned toward the dais. "I will be a full partner in this battle."

Dagr and Eirik shared glances. Dagr winked. "As is your right, Sigmund. I can think of no other I would have fighting at my side."

Eirik ascended the steps, although he wanted nothing more than to seek out Fatin. But first things first. He and Dagr needed Sigmund's agreement, an alliance. The wily bastard wasn't above holding Fatin over their heads to get exactly what he wanted.

He'd gladly sleep with bears to win his falcon.

# Twenty-three

Tora bustled into the small chamber where Fatin waited, bright spots of color on her cheeks. "Up, girl. No time for dawdling."

Fatin slid up the wall she sat against and wiped her sweaty palms down the sides of her shift. "Is the transport ready?"

"There will be no journey for you today," she said, her voice clipped.

"What's happening?"

"It's not for me to say. And you'd best not keep him waiting. He's not a patient man."

Fatin's heart tripped faster. She wasn't making a journey. And yet she was being summoned to Sigmund? He'd said he had the right to her. Did that mean he would expect her service in his bed? If it were possible, another piece of her heart broke.

Tora held the door for her and gave her a harried look. She waved her arm toward the hallway. "You look as though you're walking to a gallows. And yet, I know you've done this before."

Was she prodding her for being a whore? Tora had been all kindness to this point. Fatin's breaths shortened, and she feared she might cry. Where in Hades was her backbone?

Her feet slapped on polished stone as she was led past the hall and up a flight of rough-hewn steps. At the first landing, they turned down a hallway. Tall wooden doors with wolves' heads carved into the center lined the hall. Toward the end, Tora pushed open a door and stood to the side, waiting for her to enter.

Fatin hung back, her shoulders hunching.

"Fatin," Tora chided, then gave her a soft smile. "Go in, love. All will be well."

So perhaps he wouldn't beat her. But she was far from reassured. She closed her eyes, giving a quick prayer for strength, then swept past Tora and into the room.

The door clicked shut behind her.

Inside, a brazier blazed with lumps of pure light. Warmth surrounded her. She stepped deeper into the room, heart in her throat, seeking Sigmund. She saw a huge bed with draping surrounding it, pulled back at one corner. Beyond it, a hearth fire burned.

"Come inside," came a soft, masculine voice.

Was her mind playing tricks? She came around the bed to find a figure bent over the hearth, stirring embers of a wood fire. "I like the smell of wood smoke," Eirik said, glancing over his shoulder to catch her gaze.

She shook her head. "I don't understand. Did Sigmund give you the use of me tonight?" Not that she cared. To spend one more night in his arms was her most fervent wish. She took a deep breath to quell the tremors beginning to shiver through her.

"The use of you? Did Tora not explain?"

"I don't understand," she repeated, her voice breaking.

"Come, sit beside me," he said, lowering onto a sturdy sofa in front of the fire. He patted the seat beside him.

He wore trousers, but no shirt. His feet were bare. Pink stripes gleamed against his lightly tanned skin.

Fatin sat on the edge of the cushion, her gaze clinging to him. His expression was shuttered. Impossible to read. But he reached for her hand and tugged her closer until she slid over his lap.

She sat stiffly, perched on his knee. A thousand questions whirling in her mind. Foremost being: Did he regret that she'd been given to Sigmund? Would he miss her? Had he forgotten that he'd said they weren't finished?

Was that it? Was tonight to be an ending? Firelight shimmered as tears filled her eyes.

His fingers tipped up her chin and forced her to look at him. "I would know what you want."

Again, she shook her head. "What I want?" she asked, her voice raw even to her own ears.

"Your heart's desire, sweet Fatin." His blue eyes narrowed as he studied her face.

*You are my heart's desire.* But she didn't dare say it aloud, not with him acting this way—watching her so closely but not giving a hint of his mood. Her heart couldn't bear being mocked.

A hand cupped the back of her head, fingers digging into her scalp to tilt her head. His head bent, his mouth hovering just above her parted lips. "I need an answer," he said, his voice tightening.

Held so close, she couldn't hide the shiver that rippled down her spine. Her breath hitched, and her mouth trembled. "I desire you, milord."

He grunted. "Milord? You've called me Viking, spitting it like a curse. Are you afraid of me now?"

She gave a subtle shake of her head. "It's a term of respect."

"Are you saying you respect me now?"

There was the mockery she'd dreaded. Soft, but sly. She rolled her eyes. "Just tell me what you want. I'll give it, and we'll be done."

He was so still for so long, her neck began to ache. Then his fingers pulled her hair. "I want your mouth on me," he said, his voice hoarse. "Service me." Then he released her.

She slid off his lap to kneel between his legs, then reached to loose the tie at his waist. She opened his pants and slid her hand inside, stroking over his hard, lower abdomen, releasing the warm, musky scent of him.

Her nipples peaked, scraping at the linen, and she wished she'd paused to strip first, but she wrapped her fingers around his shaft and drew him out of the opening of his pants.

Without glancing up, because she didn't want to see his face light with triumph, she bent toward him, closing her eyes as she licked around the satin cap.

She'd give him this. Be the best he'd ever had. And hope that one day he'd feel regret for letting her go. She'd spend a lifetime regretting her mistakes.

A sob caught her unaware, and her eyes opened to see whether he'd noticed. His head lay against the back of the sofa, his heavy-lidded gaze trained on her.

She let go of him and turned her face away, breathing hard.

"Why did you stop?" he asked, his voice a soft growl.

"I can't do this."

"I know that you know how," he said, his tone neutral.

"I just can't." She dropped her head, resting her forehead against his knee. Zarah was right. He was back among his own people— safe, and no doubt rethinking everything that had passed between them. Remembering what she'd done. "I'm sorry. For so many things." Her voice was thick. Her heart heavy and aching in her chest. "I can't take anything back. Wouldn't if I could, because then I'd be denying my sister's freedom, but I . . ." She raised her face, let him see the tears filling her eyes. "I need your forgiveness, Eirik. I need to know you don't hate me."

"I don't hate you, Fatin." A fingertip traced the track of her tear, then spread it slowly across her lower lip. "Remove your shift."

She gave a ragged sob and shook her head. "I can't whore for you."

"Can you make love to me?"

He said it so softly, so tenderly, that she blinked, tears falling freely now. "Will you take even the last piece of my heart?"

"If you will give it to me," he whispered.

"I love you," she blurted.

"So you've said."

Her whole body quivered. Her heart thudded against her chest. He needed proof. But did he want it because he cared or because he wanted to take the last of her pride before she entered a lifetime of servitude as an act of final revenge?

Knowing she risked a crushing letdown, she pushed up and slowly drew the shift over her head. When she stood nude before him, she covered her mons with a hand and bent her head.

"Fatin," he said softly.

She shook her head, trembling. "I can't. Please, please, just let me go."

"What if I can't, *elskling*?" He eased off the sofa, and stood in front of her. His hands bracketed her cheeks and raised her face.

She shut her eyes, crying, sobs shaking her now. "Don't be kind. I can't bear it."

Arms enfolded her, wrapping tightly around her.

Fatin stiffened, for only a moment; then she lifted her arms and leaned against him, digging her fingers into his skin to hold him. "I love you. I'll always love you." She kissed his chest, lifted her face to glide her mouth across his jaw.

He cursed and lowered his head, his mouth covering hers, his tongue sweeping inside to mate with hers.

It was a perfect, poignant moment, and over far too quickly, because he broke the kiss. "Sigmund has ceded you to me."

Her eyes creaked open. "I belong to you?" she said, hiccupping.

One corner of his mouth quirked up. "Because his daughter cried off our wedding."

Fatin cleared the lump from her throat. "And you've known this how long?"

"Just a little while ago," he said casually. "We've formed an alliance."

"You knew this before Tora brought me here?" she asked, her voice rising.

"I asked her to bring you so I could tell you."

"And you let me think . . ." She pulled from his embrace and slapped him.

His eyebrows shot up. "Not the reaction I expected," he said, rubbing his cheek. His eyes narrowed.

But she wasn't afraid of him, even if he was a big, hulking Viking. Anger flooded her body, making her hot, searing away her sadness and fear. Her head felt ready to explode. "You knew I thought I was being brought to Sigmund," she said, her voice rising. "That I thought I'd be servicing him like a whore."

His grin widened. "Surprise?"

"Auugh!" She launched herself at him, fists flying. He fell back on the sofa, laughing, and a haze of red blinded her. Fury lent her strength and she pushed him harder, climbed over him, straddling his waist as she reached up to pull his long black hair.

"Bastard! You let me think the worst. Let me think you didn't care."

"I had to know what you felt."

"You wanted me to crawl and beg—and fuck! You made me cry!"

One hand caught her wrists and stretched them high, flattening her chest against his. "Don't you feel better now? Tora always says a woman needs to cry to rid herself of stress."

She wriggled and bucked, her face growing hotter and hotter. But her sex glided over his cock, which was hard and *right there*. Fatin bared her teeth, but backed onto him, forcing her pussy down his length, consuming him with a single hard shove.

When she was seated, she gave him a glare.

"Should I concede this battle?" he murmured, giving her shoulders a hard caress.

She wriggled again, but this time only to force the ridge of his glans to rub her against that inner spot. Gods, how his body pleased her. Her breath left in a long, slow ebb.

"Feeling better?" he asked, rubbing her bottom.

"I take it back," she growled.

"Which part?" he asked with crooked grin.

"I hate you."

Eirik settled deeper on the sofa and pumped his hips, digging his cock inside her, gliding deeper and deeper. "Liar." He let go of her hands, grasped her hips, and held her firm against him as he slid sideways until he lay on the cushion, a foot on the floor for balance with her above him. "Make love to me, Fatin. You have a chance now to prove to me why I should keep you."

He said it with such casual humor, she felt like screaming. "I don't have to prove a damn thing to you." But she pressed her knees close around his hips and began to rock. "I'm doing this for me."

She cupped her breasts, fingers splayed, her nipples peeking between them. She gave herself a squeeze and slid forward and back, lifting her chin, before continuing, "I could get this same pleasure riding any cock."

His lips thinned, but then eased again as he sighed. Fingers traced a healing stripe on her back. "I was insane with worry for you," he said, his voice thick. "Ready to kill every Helio bastard in Aliyah's employ for what they did to you."

"And yet you ignored me," she bit out. "Abandoned me, once we were safe."

"Because Birget wanted you gutted. She'd just lost Baraq, or so she thought. He's alive, by the way."

Her eyes bulged. "And no one thought to mention it to me?"

He shrugged. "A lot was happening. Matters of state."

"Much more important than relieving the worries of one little who—"

He pinched a nipple between her fingers. "Stop. I ignored you so that she wouldn't know how important you are to me. I didn't want to rub salt into her wounds and make her angrier."

"You were protecting me?" she asked, eyeing him with suspicion.

"If I say yes, will you let me fuck you?"

She knew she shouldn't let him off so easily, but she'd nearly stroked herself into a state of frenzy. Tension coiled deep in her core. Fatin rocked again, dragging her pussy along his thick shaft. "Eirik?"

"Yes, love?" he murmured, sounding distracted. His gaze lowered to watch her sexy glides.

"I'm very, very wet."

A low growl vibrated his chest, and he jerked upward, almost unsettling her, but his hands clutched her buttocks and he stood with her still locked to his body and strode to the bed.

He dumped her on the mattress, his cock sliding free, but then he flipped her.

Coming up on all fours, she tossed back her hair and aimed a mock-glare over her shoulder. "Not without lube."

"I want something else hot and wet surrounding me, *elskling*."

Fatin grinned and faced forward, bracing as he entered her again. Then, as he began to thrust, she dropped to her elbows, closing her eyes to savor his strength, the way he stroked so hard against her. "Will I be your thrall?" she asked, not looking back.

"Would that please you?"

She bit her lip, considering. "I'd rather be a concubine, I think. Then I wouldn't have to wear this thrall's cuff."

His thrusts halted, and he came over her back, his hands landing on either side of her. "What do I wear on my arm?"

She glanced to the side, seeing a gold cuff around his upper arm, like the one she wore dangling on her wrist. "Didn't see that before. Did you grow accustomed to wearing one?"

Eirik bit her earlobe. "I should beat you. It's a symbol of the *Ulf-hednar* rulers. It marks you. Concubines and wives wear them."

"Really?" She glanced back, wanting to see his expression.

His face was closed again, his icy gaze boring into hers. However, this time she wasn't worried that it was because he didn't care.

"Eirik, which will I be?"

His gaze broke with hers. But not before she saw a hint of deep emotion glittering there. "I would prefer to make you my wife." His lips twisted in a parody of a smile. "But if your heart's desire is to serve as my thrall . . ."

Fatin laughed. The sound surprised her. She faced forward and laughed again.

Eirik chuckled behind her and resumed thrusting. "Perhaps I won't let you come until you answer."

Fatin tilted her hips higher to let him slide deeper, then groaned. "Maybe I want you to take your time."

"You are never a patient lover."

"True. So wife—?" She gasped when he gave her a sharper thrust. "Are you sure? What of heirs?"

"Dagr will sire the heirs," he said, his voice tight. "But I would have Falcons, feathered sons and daughters."

"They may look just like you."

"Then I will live with my disappointment."

"Eirik, stop." She reached back and shoved at his hips. Halting him. When he pulled free, she rolled beneath him, facing him.

When he hovered over her, his face hard, stark longing in his eyes, only then did she believe. Her Viking loved her.

She traced the hard blade of his cheek, the length of his stubborn nose. "Wife. I want more than anything to call you husband."

He came down, his cock seeking entrance, plunging deep in a single glide. When they were close, arms wrapped tightly around each other, he spoke. "This will not be an easy life. Skuldelev will not be a peaceful place. Not for a long time."

Fatin smiled, cupping his face, and lifted her head to kiss him. When she drew back, she said, "I have not had an easy life, so I think I am ready for whatever hardships lie ahead. So long as I have you."

"My sweet, sweet Falcon," he whispered.

"But no concubines."

Eirik stifled a laugh at her fierce, proud glare. "No one but you, my love." Then he stroked them both toward fulfillment, powering stronger and harder inside her honeyed walls.

As he moved, glorying in her sighs, he mused over how far he'd come. He'd lived a lifetime in Hel's cold embrace. Fought a beast and escaped the fires of Muspellheim. But not until he'd tamed a Falcon did he feel as though he'd conquered all.

When her thighs clamped around his hips, and her body writhed like a wild thing beneath him, he let go, rising higher, lifted on the wings of her love.

# About the Author

DELILAH DEVLIN is an award-winning author of erotic romance with a rapidly expanding reputation for writing deliciously edgy stories with complex characters. Whether creating dark, erotically charged paranormal and futuristic worlds or richly descriptive Westerns that ring with authenticity, Delilah Devlin "pens in uncharted territory that will leave readers breathless and hungering for more" (*ParaNormal Romance*). Ms. Devlin has published more than seventy erotic romances in multiple subgenres and lengths. To learn more about Delilah, visit www.DelilahDevlin.com.